FOREST

BOOKS BY FREDERIC MARTIN

The Vox Oculis Trilogy

Not Alone

The Innocence of Westbury

Forest

FOREST

A VOX OCULIS NOVEL: BOOK THREE

FREDERIC MARTIN

NthSense Books

Published by NthSense Books
Richmond, Vermont
www.nthsensebooks.com

NthSense, NthSense Books, and the NthSense Books logo are trademarks of NthSense, LLC.

Title page images used under license from Shutterstock.com.

ISBN: 978-1-7340240-8-1 (hardcover)
ISBN: 978-1-7340240-4-3 (paperback)
ISBN: 978-1-7340240-5-0 (ebook)

For my father
Paul Almy Martin
The archetype
of the American-style
Renaissance man

AUTHOR'S NOTE

Let me start with an apology. The end of *The Innocence of Westbury* was a cliff-hanger. I know, I know, what a lousy trick to play on you but, unfortunately, that's just the way these stories go sometimes. For what it's worth, I had no idea how book two was going to end either, so it was as much a surprise and annoyance to me as it was, perhaps, to you. Because of that, I felt compelled to add the epilogue just to tamp down my own indignation, not to mention a potential revolt from my readers. Don't worry, *Forest* does not end in a cliff-hanger. After all, this is the third and final book of a trilogy. And a trilogy can't be more than three books (can it?)...

Enough apologies about TIOW, let's talk about the book you are now about to begin. To prepare you for *Forest*, I need to give you a heads-up and that is this: The prologue, "Nox Mortis," takes us back five years to the night of the event that was the unfortunate beginning of Blue's difficult saga. In this flashback, I think you will find welcome relief from some of the nagging questions that were raised in the first two books. However, (you knew a "however" was coming) I guarantee that you are going to stumble across some puzzling new ones as well. At least you can read on with the satisfaction that you will know more about Blue's history than Will as he struggles to make sense of the avalanche of events that crashed down on him at the end of book two.

The first chapter, "Breakfast," jumps back to the present timeline which has progressed to Tuesday morning four days after the Westbury school shooting. In this chapter, we review all the threads that were spun in books one and two. Chief Summer Hannah and Detective Rodney James do their best to weave them together into a vivid fabric that provides a sturdy background for the rest of the book.

The next chapter, "Bus Stop," also takes place on that same Tuesday morning, but just *before* the scene at Flo's Diner from the epilogue of TIOW. Just want to keep you on your toes. You might want to reread the epilogue in TIOW first as "Bus Stop" fills in Blue's activities from the time she flees Westbury on Sunday morning to the moment she takes her first sip of coffee in Flo's diner two days later. I think you'll be impressed, as I was, at Blue's gutsy resourcefulness and determination.

As this book covers a lot of territory (literally!) I have included a map of eastern New York and western Vermont to help orient you with the key physical locations where most of the action and important scenes take place.

I hope that gets you off to a good start on *Forest,* and since I hate long-winded introductions, without further blah-de-blah, I present to you the third and final book of the "Vox Oculis" trilogy, *Forest.* I hope you enjoy reading it as much as I enjoyed writing it.

-fm

PROLOGUE

NOX MORTIS

Five years before the Westbury school shooting
Thursday, November 9th, 2006
Adirondack Mountains, New York

The last glimmer of habitation had vanished long ago but the hulking black SUV continued to claw its way higher and higher into the mountains like a beetle scuttling up a grass-covered mound. Its headlights bored twin tunnels in the thick darkness of the Adirondack night, spotlighting the dense border of trees hugging the shoulders of the twisting gravel road. The car and its occupants had just crossed a critical point in the atmosphere where the thinning air abruptly transformed the persistent, continuous drizzle from a damp, chilling spray into a billowing dust of snow

The SUV's driver was an aging, overweight man. His sagging belly pressed against the steering wheel like a steadying hand while his right hand, slung casually over the wheel, piloted the heavy vehicle along a trajectory that tempted catastrophe at every turn and yet always managed to avoid it at the very last second. His left hand, blissfully ignorant of the reckless behavior of the right hand, calmly flicked a cigarette toward the slightly open window. A bright spark of ash leapt out the window and streaked alongside the car, vanishing behind them, swallowed by the night.

The passenger noted the path of the ember from the corner of his eye but didn't dare turn his head. A movement of his head might invite conversation from the driver, and that was an activity he wanted to avoid as much as possible. The passenger was much younger than the driver, maybe high school age, maybe college age. He sat with the posture of someone who didn't want to be there, but had to be, and didn't dare show it one way or the other. His back was straight, his eyes gazed ahead, occasionally glancing to the right, but rarely to the left unless he had to answer a question. Most of the four hours of driving time he hadn't moved an inch.

The boy's mind had been moving, though—engrossed in a desperate search for some creative scheme that would allow him to escape from this trip. It was pointless, of course. The single-minded ferocity of the driver assured him of that. The driver would never forgive or forget any attempt by the boy to get out of this trip and would go out of his way to make the boy's life a living hell for a long time if he tried. The hell that was in front of him, and was the entire purpose of this trip, was a known quantity and once it was over, it was over and he could put it behind him like he had all the other times. At least that was what he was hoping. The driver had put a question mark on that hope. He said there was a new chore for the boy this trip. Not that the boy wouldn't know what to do or how to do it, just something he had never been required to do because, up until now, the driver had always done it. Tonight, however, he had been instructed to be ready. Some sort of test. A grisly graduation.

"Here it is," grunted the driver as a single forlorn mailbox, once brightly decorated, but now dented and peeling, materialized in the beam of the headlights. The boy gazed at the mailbox and then turned to look out his window into the dark woods. Through the tightly packed black tangle of trees, he could just make out the glow of softly lit windows. The lights looked distant, like a dream.

The driver mashed out his cigarette and stuffed it into the over-full ashtray on the dash as he swung the car into the driveway, although what met the passenger's eyes couldn't really be called a driveway. It was more like a narrow grassy path with only the thinnest of parallel dirt tracks to indicate where someone might be able to navigate a car, but with no promise of success. This questionable route didn't seem to deter the driver's right hand as it guided the SUV as best it could down the path. The boy wanted to shake his head but didn't. He just hoped the SUV's all-wheel-drive wouldn't let them down, and as if to pause and consider this, the SUV came to a stop. The driver turned and looked at the boy. The boy turned to the driver, knowing this was a conversation he couldn't avoid.

"You know the drill," said the driver. "Don't fuck it up. I tell you to do something, you do it quick and without question. You call me 'Dad' and I break your nose. From here on in, you're Alvin, and I am . . ."

"Dave," answered the boy. One of his dad's weird quirks—an obsession with code names. This one based on a 60's cartoon show about talking chipmunks.

His dad nodded and then as if the nod had acted like a trigger, his dad was seized by a violent spasm that caused his body to convulse with a sudden severe rasping cough. He reached for his pocket and pulled out a handkerchief, putting it to his mouth while the seizure continued, rocking his body in a series of suppressed explosions that the boy knew would last for several seconds. The thought occurred to the boy that it wasn't too late for his dad to die on him then and there. He was visited by a brief euphoria of a fatherless future that was quashed as his dad's seizure came to an abrupt end after a final prolonged throat-clearing hack followed by a couple of little coughs—unfortunately, none life-threatening. The boy knew that episode was over. For now.

As if nothing had happened, his dad calmly turned and reached into a tool bag that was wedged behind the passenger seat.

He pulled out one black Colt .38 revolver and a Smith & Wesson M&P 9mm. He handed the Smith & Wesson and an ammo clip to the boy. The dad kept the .38. The boy watched his father flip out the cylinder, spin it, flip it back, and click it back into position. It was a blur of practiced motion that was hard not to admire even though the boy considered the gun ancient and awkward, a relic, a design that was far from state-of-the-art. But like the obsession with cartoon code names, the .38 was one of his dad's quirks. "Semi-automatics are too damn complicated. They can misfire. This baby is simple. Pull the trigger and bam, it just works. Never misfires, it's simple, and it's cheap," he would say. They were also heavy and made a bulge so big, there was no concealing them. "Don't want to," his dad would say, "makes negotiations move quicker." His dad slid the gun into a worn leather chest holster.

The boy turned to his weapon. Much better feel, and much lighter, even with its silencer and target laser. He shook his head. Whatever, Dad, he thought. He slapped the clip in, made sure it was fully latched, pulled back the slide, and checked that the round was secure in its chamber. He turned on the laser then slid the gun into his much sleeker Cordura chest holster and zipped up his jacket halfway. He turned to his father, knowing his every move had been critically observed.

His father gave a slight nod of approval, the best the boy could expect, and said, "Follow my lead. We'll be done and out of here in five minutes." He paused and then added another, "Don't fuck it up."

The boy nodded, and took a slow deep breath, concealing it as much as possible from his dad. And then he began his internal ritual. This isn't you, it's the lizard taking over now, he chanted to himself. Get to that altered state that lets you endure these trips. Let the lizard go through the motions. The real you will go somewhere else while the lizard does the dirty work. When it's done and you're back in the car and safely away, you can reclaim your body and store the lizard back in his glass cupboard in the back of your mind. Forget what the lizard did. Don't want to think about it. Don't need to.

His dad put the car in gear, and they crawled carefully down the track, dried stalks of dead weeds scraping the bottom the entire way. The drive was even longer than it appeared, as it refused to take a straight course to the lights in the trees and instead snaked down a slope, over a creek, and then finally back up to a clearing. In the clearing was an old, but well-kept farmhouse with one ground floor and a very squat, half-high second floor. A barn was attached to the house by a narrow extension on the right side. As the headlights swept along the building, the boy could see a long, modern-looking greenhouse attached to the side of the barn. It looked oddly out of place.

As they came to a stop, they saw a man walking swiftly out of a small orchard adjacent to the barn, taking a course that would put him between the car and the house. In the doorway of the house, they saw a woman with a little girl standing beside her. A hand signal from the man caused the woman and girl to retreat quickly inside.

His father got out first, as they'd agreed, and the boy got out a moment later. "He'll get spooked if we both jump out. Just ease out one at a time," he had told him. His dad hobbled slowly toward the man. The hobble was real and his father liked to use it to his advantage to relax his victims.

"Mr. Stanton, sorry to bother you so late," said his dad.

Mr. Stanton slowed to a stop a few yards away. He clearly was not completely at ease. Who would be with two strange men showing up after dark in this god-forsaken place, thought the boy.

"What can I do for you Mr. . . . ?"

"Seville. David Seville is the name. Again, I'm sorry to visit you so late, but a friend suggested it should be after dark. You see," he pointed at his legs, "I suffer from quite a bit of leg pain and my friend suggested you might be able to help."

The boy was aware of his dad's strategy. There was a strain of cannabis called NY Thai that had gained a reputation for its pain-relieving properties. It was hard to get because you had to know somebody, and that somebody had to know somebody else, and on and on until you reached the end of the somebodies and arrived where they were now. Whoever had hired his dad knew the entire chain of somebodies, and apparently had a grudge with the guy at the end. A pretty bad grudge. The boy's mind registered all this and was uncomfortable with it, knowing what the outcome was going to be, but he was in his altered state. He was just watching. The lizard was in control now.

"This is Alvin. He's my live-in assistant. He's a great help."

The man, Stanton, turned to look at the boy and as their eyes met, a surge of apprehension drilled right through the protective shell of the lizard and made the boy squirm. His father had warned him of this. "Look him in the eye and keep your mind blank," he had instructed him. "Think of something benign, like what you had for lunch." The boy thought of the rich, moist ham sandwich he had eaten for lunch at the rest stop. It had been the best part of the trip so far.

Stanton turned back to the dad and gave him the same intense examination, but the father looked as if he were practiced in this type of scrutiny. Stanton didn't show any sign of alarm, but clearly wasn't satisfied, yet. "I see your legs are good enough to let you drive," he said.

This man was no idiot, thought the boy.

"They are, barely," replied the dad. "Alvin, here, is on my case about it all the time," he turned and smiled at his son. "He insists he should do the driving, but I insist that I am not that decrepit."

Stanton continued his intense stare for a moment and then turned his gaze to the driveway and then toward the road. He was looking for our backup, thought the boy. We might be law. Or mob. One of those was right. But Stanton would see no backup. There was a long pause before he finally spoke, "I might have something that could help but I'd like to ask you to stay where you are."

"Absolutely," said the dad. "I am most grateful for anything you could provide. And I am, of course, more than grateful. I do have cash."

The boy had a hard time not showing the astonishment he felt at the performance his dad was putting on. It was impressive—impressive because it was so out-of-character for the abusive asshole that the boy was overly accustomed to.

Stanton took one more glance at the boy and then said, "I'll just be a moment." He turned and walked casually toward the house without looking back. As Stanton mounted the steps, his dad raised his right hand to his nose. The boy's signal.

The lizard's reflexes were quick, as his father knew they would be. In three long strides he was at the door, his shoulder slamming hard into it, pushing it open. Stanton had turned to push it shut, his hand already on the lock, but he was knocked down to the floor by the unexpected impact. The lizard saw that the situation was entirely in his hands now and he did his job, putting a single bullet into Stanton's gut.

His father hobbled up behind him and they both entered, quickly taking in the situation. Stanton was gasping on the floor, his wife standing petrified in the kitchen just adjacent to the door. The wife was trapped. The little girl was nowhere to be seen.

"Babineau . . . sent you!" the man croaked. The boy could tell the lizard had hit something vital. Stanton wasn't going to last long, but he had enough fire in him to gasp, "You . . . got what . . . you came for. Now leave!"

The father looked at Stanton as if he was a talking bag of sand, then turned to the trembling mother. "Where are the girls?" he asked.

"NO!" cried Stanton. His father was watching the wife and saw her glance fearfully toward a steep stairway across from the doorway.

"Please!" said the wife. But in reply, his dad stepped over to the stove, picked up a skillet that was there, and struck the wife senseless. She slumped to the floor. The lizard watched without emotion, but the boy's mind turned away in shock. He had seen the beauty of the face, framed in long dark hair, beauty made even more striking by her fear for her children. And now she was a crumpled pile on the floor.

Stanton groaned, but apparently did not have enough life left to muster any other protest.

The father looked at the boy. "Your job," he said nodding at the stairs. "No way I'm getting up those fucking farmhouse stairs." He held out the .38 with one hand while indicating with the other that they were to swap guns. The lizard took the .38 and handed the Smith & Wesson to his dad.

The lizard started up the ridiculously steep and narrow stairs, but the boy's mind was having trouble staying disengaged. This was the test. Get it over with and life will go on normally and he could graduate high school and finally leave his fucking father with a reasonable assurance that his father would let him go. Fuck it up, and he was sure his father was capable of making the rest of his life one long unending nightmare, if he let him live at all. The lizard, of course, didn't hesitate and headed straight for the stairs.

He reached the top, where it was dark, and found a light switch and flicked it on. The light illuminated a hallway with a low ceiling that ended at what looked like another steep stairway—more like a ladder—at the other end, a stair that must have descended into a pantry or a mudroom between the house and the barn. The hallway had a door on the left and a door on the right. He looked through the door on the right first. It was an empty bedroom. A kid's bedroom. He didn't even have to step inside to see that no one was there—it was so tiny that there was no place to hide. He turned to the other room. Another bedroom. This one wasn't empty.

The lizard raised its lethal hand, but the boy's mind reached out and stayed it. He considered what he was looking at, not as a bag of sand or a rodent as he had been trained, but for what she was. A girl, maybe eight years old. A creature without sin, with eyes that penetrated his physical vision and burrowed into the part of him that was trained to turn away but couldn't. She almost shimmered with innocence, unstained by the actions of her father, unlike him. His job was to extinguish that shimmer. End it. Spare her the living hell she would endure living on without parents she loved. His hell, of course, wouldn't end. He was doomed to carry on with a parent he loathed.

He pulled the trigger once. The bullet slammed into the mattress and shattered the wood of the wall behind it but didn't touch the girl. The girl squeaked in fright, not knowing what, exactly, had happened. The boy put his hand over her mouth and whispered, "Shhh. I won't hurt you. You need to be very quiet now. Is your sister in the house?" The girl shook her head. "In the barn?" She shook her head again. "Outside?" She nodded. The boy thought for a moment, and then looked steadily into her wide eyes. "Go find your sister and hide. Don't be seen, understand?" She nodded. "I am going to shoot again, but don't make a sound, okay?" She nodded and covered her ears. He put another round into the bed. She jumped but was quiet. As frightened as she seemed, she was also remarkably calm, he thought. He lifted his hand off her mouth slowly, and she didn't move. He held his finger up to his lips to signal silence and then gestured for her to go. She nodded, got up, and vanished. He did a double-take. She had literally vanished in complete silence. He looked quickly down the end of the hall and just caught the top of her head as it disappeared down the stair at the barn end of the hall. A shout from below brought him back to his senses and he quickly went to the other bedroom and put two rounds into the empty bed.

He stopped at the top of the stairs and took a breath. Time to disengage. He let the lizard reassert itself and take over as he descended calmly, his father glaring from the bottom of the stairs.

"What are you doing? Bring the bodies down here!" his father said.

"Get them yourself, fucker," said the lizard in a completely flat and toneless voice.

The father stared at him, then chuckled. "All right. We'll leave them there. Doesn't really matter."

That was the test, thought the boy. You've taught me to be heartless, but you've also taught me to deceive. And I passed the test. Consider yourself deceived, fucker, he thought.

The boy looked around. His dad had been busy. The mother was still unconscious or dead where she lay, but the skillet had been placed next to the motionless man. His dad gestured for the revolver and after the lizard handed it to him, his dad took it and carefully aimed it at the side of the man's head. The sudden blast made a mess of Stanton's head and even the lizard jumped at the shockingly bloody spectacle. His father pulled out a cloth and carefully wiped down the gun and placed it near the man's splayed hand. Like they'd planned. His dad had put a bullet from the .38 through the man's head, wiped his own prints off the skillet and gun, put them near the hands of the man, and then artfully distributed everything in a still life of a murder-suicide—the kids presumably dead from the same gun. Presumably.

There was one last step to the father's plan, but it didn't become clear until he pointed to a glass kerosene lantern that sat next to the stove. "Knock that lamp over. Make it look like it was knocked over accidentally and make sure it breaks on the floor."

The lizard did as he was told. He carefully reached over and tipped the lamp until it fell on its side and rolled off the counter and smashed, sending shards of glass and splatters of kerosene across the kitchen floor and onto the inert victims on the floor.

"Time to go," said the father, looking at his watch. "Took us more than five minutes, though." He looked at his son and reached out a hand. The hand was holding a silver jacketed lighter. "You do the honors, Alvin. Big night for you."

The lizard took one more look at the scene and then squatted down. His finger flipped the lighter open and flicked the wheel that sent a spark to the lighter's wick which popped to life with a teardrop of flame dancing on its tip. The lizard paused just a moment before touching the fateful yellow tongue to the shining kerosene. A smokey orange flame leapt up and eagerly spread across the floor and onto Stanton's clothing. One tongue of flame reached the cabinet and started crawling up a dishtowel that had been splashed with kerosene. After that, it was breathtaking how quickly the fire intensified, and it soon became unbearable to stay inside.

They stepped outside and stood in the dooryard next to the car and watched. It didn't take long. The house was old and its frame loaded with so much highly seasoned heavy timber that the locals would see it smoldering for days afterward. As soon as it was well underway and clearly unstoppable, and before any neighbor could spot it and raise an alarm, they got in the car and left.

As the dad turned the car around and eased it cautiously down the winding track, the boy looked back at the house and the barn and the greenhouse. The entire scene was lit with an intense orange glow. The attached barn was already starting to catch, and he wondered what would happen when the fire reached the greenhouse. The flames were bright enough to illuminate the area around the house. He saw that there was more than just the orchard. There was a field with neatly planted rows of what looked like berry bushes. He had a ridiculous notion that he might see the two girls standing there, waving to him from the bushes. But there were no girls to be seen. Instead, he was overcome with a strange sensation—the same sensation he'd had when the man was boring through him with those eyes—eyes that seemed to have the ability to stare into his soul.

NOVEMBER, 2011

1

BREAKFAST

Four days after the Westbury school shooting
7 am, Tuesday, November 22, 2011
Westbury, Vermont

NYPD Detective Rodney James took a last look at the tidy lines of text marching down the pages of the report sitting in front of him. The text attempted to bring some order to the chaotic images, rendered in high-resolution color, that were sprinkled throughout the pages. It failed.

He closed the manila folder over the report, shut his eyes, and leaned back, tapping his chin thoughtfully. The images were harsh and lingered in his vision the way a camera flash lingers in your vision, preventing you from seeing the things around you clearly until it gradually fades away. This flash contained charred human remains lying among a tangle of burned beams, random blackened household goods—all covered in a thick layer of ash. It was so abstract it was hard to imagine the victims, Samuel and Elizabeth Stanton, ever having existed as living, breathing human beings. They had, though—the only blessing being that they were probably both dead before the flames consumed them. Dead from sudden trauma. Samuel Stanton, an apparent suicide from a single shot to the head. A revolver, a Colt .38, recovered from a location adjacent to Stanton's right hand. Elizabeth Stanton, probably deceased prior to immolation. Evidence of blunt trauma to the head. Shape and size of skull fracture indicates impact caused by a heavy object with a rounded surface with a 6-12" radius and hard edges—consistent with a weapon the approximate shape of a fry-pan. According to the proposed scenario in the report, the entire event happened in an instant. A fry-pan to the head in a moment of rage, the swift dispatch of a bullet to the head, a fire started by a kerosene lantern knocked off a counter. No prolonged death by fire. Much different from the fate of their daughters.

Heather Stanton, dressed only in bedclothes, and Blue Stanton, fully dressed in winter jacket, hat and gloves, had been found unconscious and lying next to each other just inside the exterior door of a greenhouse that was attached to a barn. The barn was fully engulfed in flames when they were found. It was a neighbor a mile down the road who spotted the glow of the fire and came to investigate. By the time he arrived, the flames had started to deform the rigid polycarbonate walls of the greenhouse, twisting them into ghostly curves that curled toward the two girls as if intent on snatching them up and pulling them into the fire. If he hadn't spotted Blue's booted feet sticking out of the greenhouse and pulled the girls clear, the entire saga of Blue Stanton—aka Belle Amélie DuBois, aka Blue DuBois—would have ended right there.

Tragically, it did end for Heather Stanton. Lightly clothed, she had suffered extensive second and third-degree burns and had been evacuated by helicopter to a burn center in Syracuse and then airlifted to Shriners in Boston where she died two days later. Even Blue Stanton, protected as she was by her winter clothes, suffered first and second-degree burns. However, the life-threatening injury for her was smoke inhalation. She wasn't breathing at all when they found her and despite reviving her as they rushed her by ambu-lance to Lake Placid Medical Center Emergency Room, it wasn't enough. She died from respiratory failure at 2 am the next morning. At least according to the death certificate and report of the attending physician, dated November 10th, 2006. Five years ago.

Now that he knew better—that Blue was alive—nothing was certain, except one thing. The physician report from Lake Placid, along with the physician involved, was going to go under critical reexamination. There had to be some serious intervention and cooperation going on somewhere for a false death certificate to be fabricated for Blue. And even more people had to be complicit in getting her absorbed quietly into the foster system. It all pointed to an effort to continue witness protection for Blue, the sole survivor, and yet WITSEC[1] denied any involvement. They presumed Blue's death certificate was authentic and had closed her file. Were they lying? If so, why would they? And if they weren't lying, who else could possibly pull this off?

A tapping sound made Rodney turn and realize that someone had been standing next to him, perhaps for quite some time. He looked up into the deadpan face of Westbury Diner's red-haired waitress and owner.

"So you *are* alive. Just wanted to make sure. For a minute it looked like you had a sudden case of rigor mortis." Mona grabbed his coffee cup from the table and glanced at the tepid pool sloshing inside. "This isn't good for anything except drowning flies and certainly won't work on rigor mortis. I'm bringing a fresh cup." The tinkle of the diner doorbell caused Mona to turn and then add, "Two cups, then. Maybe three if you need my help." She winked at Rodney, "I'm available whenever you two run into a dead end."

Rodney smiled and said, "You know, I have half a mind to deputize you, Mona. Pay isn't very good, though."

Chief Hannah slipped into the booth opposite Rodney. "'Morning, Mona. Just coffee right now, I'm not very hungry yet."

"You won't get any hungrier based on the pictures I saw in Rodney's folder there," Mona said over her shoulder as she headed to the kitchen.

"Pretty grim, then?" asked Chief Hannah.

"Yeah, pretty hard to get the images out of your head, but part of the job, you know?"

"Boy, don't I," she said, shaking her head.

"We don't need to look at them now," said Rodney. "It wouldn't do much good anyway—it's difficult to conclude anything from just the photos. What I'm more interested in is a second look at the autopsies for Samuel and Elizabeth Stanton, which I am afraid weren't as thorough as they should have been."

"Not thorough?" asked Chief Hannah.

Rodney nodded. "I think they may have missed a second wound to Samuel, one that could not have been self-inflicted. I think the wound to the head happened later."

"Adding to the case that he was murdered and that it wasn't suicide."

"Exactly. I think it was staged. I believe he was shot or stabbed or knocked out prior to the shot to the head and then the gun arranged next to his hand. They weren't looking for a second wound so they may have missed it. And there is this . . ." He turned to his folder and flipped through a few pages. He pulled out a picture and placed it in front of Chief Hannah. "Don't worry, this one isn't grizzly," he said.

The picture had captured a crumpled piece of white cloth lying on the ground, embedded in a slushy puddle of mud. Flecks of what looked like blood were visible on a corner of the cloth. Rodney tapped the photo. "This is the hard evidence that changed everything."

"This is the DNA hit?" she asked.

"That's right. This is a handkerchief with blood and mucus from Justin Farrell, aka El Segador. It was found outside the Stanton house on the ground the day after the fire. The DNA search at the time didn't turn up anything."

"Because Farrell wasn't in the CODIS[2] database at the time?" asked Chief Hannah.

"That's right. And, in fact, he still isn't, and neither is El Segador."

Chief Hannah's eyebrows rose in surprise. Her wide expression allowed Rodney to notice for the first time that her eyes were a dark, luminous green. It caused him to hesitate for just a moment before he continued, "We tried something that is a little unconventional—not illegal—but unconventional. When we didn't get a hit from CODIS, we did a genealogy DNA search through a commercial service and found his family tree. We got a high probability match that the DNA was from Justin Farrell. It's not strictly admissible in court, but it gave us a lot of leads to follow. We decided to try a DNA sample from an unsolved murder that we were certain involved El Segador and compared it to the DNA from Farrell. It was a total match."

"So you have hard evidence that El Segador is Justin Farrell and that his handkerchief was found at the site of the Stantons' deaths."

"You got it." Rodney smiled. "Now, if we were to do a comparison with Bronco's DNA . . . ."

"It would be additional confirmation that Bronco actually is William Farrell—the son of El Segador and potential accomplice," Chief Hannah finished his sentence.

Rodney settled back in his chair. "Exactly. Do you have any problem with us doing that search?"

Chief Hannah twiddled her spoon in her cup. "I'm willing, but the State Police are holding all the evidence. I haven't talked to them about the Bronco-William Farrell theory yet and I'm not sure how they'll take to a DNA test."

Rodney felt his head jerk back slightly. "Did you just say theory? You do have credible evidence that Bronco is William Farrell, right? I mean, how else would you have made the connection?"

More spoon twiddling. Chief Hannah was staring at the table when she replied. "Umm, it's complicated," she said.

Rodney suddenly felt uneasy—an unraveling kind of unease—

a feeling that his case was in danger of falling apart. "Summer, I *need* William Farrell. He is our key to finishing this case and nailing Babineau. We need to turn him into an informant and for that, I need the leverage of your warrant for Bronco for drug trafficking, kidnapping, and assault with a deadly weapon. A hard evidence-based Bronco-William Farrell link allows us to arrest him and plea bargain with him for incriminating evidence against Babineau. Without it, we're kind of screwed. We don't have any other plausible means of arresting and detaining him and even if we did, not much chance of bargaining with him."

Chief Hannah looked up at him. "Like I said, it's complicated, but it's not a wild-ass guess—I have a credible source—but just like your genealogy link, it probably isn't admissible. And before you ask . . ."

Rodney's mouth clamped shut over his un-uttered question.

". . . I would prefer that you don't press me about what that source is. You're just going to have to trust me." Her green eyes were glowing with their own message.

He got it. Some things are by the book, some things are not. Sometimes that's okay if it comes from someone you trust. He looked hard at her for any sign that he shouldn't trust her. "Okay," he said, with only a moment of hesitation. "For now, anyway. We can probably apply enough pressure from my office to convince your State Police to release some of Bronco's blood samples. If we can get that, I'm pretty sure a match and your warrant will be enough for us to convince a particular judge to issue a court order to detain William Farrell."

Rodney saw the intensity in Chief Hannah's expression relax, but only a bit. It reminded him of what additional pressure she was under from the school shooting and the missing girl. "We can at least take that load off of you. We're partners in this now and NYPD can take over tracking Bronco down."

"Thanks for that," she sighed. She picked up her coffee cup and held it against her cheek, closing her eyes.

Watching her, Rodney recognized a kind of exhaustion that he had witnessed before—an exhaustion he'd observed in colleagues that had investigated one too many affronts to humanity in too short of a time. "Hey, I wish I could do more. I'm sorry if I get a little hyper-focused on my own cases sometimes. It makes me oblivious to what else is happening. A school shooting is a cop's worst nightmare and a missing kid on top of that?" He shook his head. "If there is anything I can do to help you with finding Blue, or anything else, please let me know."

She opened her eyes and looked at him, "Thanks, but I'm not sure where else you could help. The state's pretty much taken over the shooting investigation and the school security issue isn't going to really blow up until January when school is back in session and that's pretty much a local issue that only our local Police Chief can handle." She lifted one hand and pointed a finger at herself. She smiled grimly. "What would help, though, is for you to answer this irritating question that's been driving me crazy: How in hell did Blue die and then miraculously come back to life?"

This time it was Rodney's turn to twiddle his spoon. "Boy, don't I wish I could tell you. Right now all we have is a five-year-old crime scene investigation and coroner's reports and that's about all. Dead is dead in a bureaucracy. There are no records kept on the activities of the dead. Believe me, I want to find out as much as you do."

He stopped twiddling and pushed his cup aside. He spread his hands palm down in front of him. "But I can at least give you what I do know, starting with where Blue and Heather were found." He reached into the case folder and pulled out a picture. "This is the greenhouse attached to the barn. As you can see, there isn't much left of the barn, but the greenhouse was made of rigid polycarbonate panels, which didn't burn. They only twisted from the heat. These circles," he tapped on the picture where two white circles had been drawn, "are the approximate location where the neighbor said she found the girls unconscious. Heather was dressed only in nightclothes while Blue was fully dressed for outdoors—hat, gloves, jacket, boots. Now, the fire started well after sunset for certain, and probably around Heather's bedtime. That would explain the bedclothes," said Rodney. "Blue was older. Our theory was that she had a chore to do outside before bed which would explain the outdoor clothing."

"But why were they just inside the door? Were they trapped inside?" asked Chief Hannah.

"We don't think so. Blue was partly in the doorway and ..."

A plate slapped down in front of Rodney. It held a breakfast sandwich and sliced apple. It was followed by a plate that slid down in front of Chief Hannah. Her plate contained scrambled eggs, toast, and cottage cheese with pineapple.

"The younger girl was unconscious inside the greenhouse and the older girl was trying to get her out," said Mona. "The older girl passed out from smoke before she could drag her out."

"And that is what we concluded, also. Like I said, Mona, I should deputize you. The important question, though, is that I don't remember ordering any breakfast."

"It's what you want though, right? And you, Summer?"

Chief Hannah smiled as Mona headed back to the kitchen.

Rodney shook his head and then took a bite of breakfast sandwich. "Well, I have to admit, she does have super waitressing powers." They both ate for a while until Rodney wiped his mouth with a napkin and said, "Here's the thing. Mona isn't far off, but she doesn't know about one detail: Blue had a contusion on her head."

Chief Hannah rubbed her chin. "You think Blue passed out from smoke and fell and hit her head?"

"Right."

"What about Heather?"

"None in her report, but Heather had severe burns on her face and scalp which might have obscured any obvious contusion."

Chief Hannah pushed her plate away and looked down.

"Sorry, I didn't mean to upset you with that."

"I'm okay. Like you said, it's part of the job." Chief Hannah sat quietly for a moment and then looked up, latching onto Rodney's eyes. She spoke with a voice of quiet urgency, "Just promise me this: don't ever share those details with Blue." She nodded her head toward Rodney's folder, "Or show her any of those pictures. Ever. There is no reason she needs to see those."

A long-dormant pocket of empathy twisted uncomfortably in Rodney's chest. It was a warning flag. *Don't get too personally involved in these cases or you won't last long.* That was his mentor Harris's sage advice from a long time back. He looked at Chief Hannah and could see that there was no avoiding personal involvement. It was too late for her. And maybe for him.

He spoke solemnly, "I promise." She nodded slightly and then looked down at the table again.

He hesitated a moment but decided that it was best to get all the unpleasant parts out at once. "There is another detail that you should know, and I promise not to tell Blue. Stanton was growing dope. The greenhouse was full of it."

"Jesus." Chief Hannah looked at him shaking her head. "I guess I shouldn't be surprised. Kind of rounds out the whole drug-crime motivation."

They both sat in awkward silence until he cleared his throat and continued. "Hey, on the brighter side, Blue did survive, and we can be thankful for that. I am looking forward to meeting her someday, not just because she has the answer to a lot of these questions, but to meet the kid who is tough enough to survive all this." He paused. "So, no sign of her yet?"

She shook her head. "No, nothing. We are doing all the standard stuff, entering her in the NCIC[3] database, reporting to NCMEC[4]. It's about all we can do. And then wait. And hope." She turned and looked out the window. "A kid like her, if she doesn't want to be found, she'll find ways not to be found. That's what worries me the most."

"What do you mean?"

She turned back to him with raised eyebrow. "Have you ever run away?"

Rodney smiled. "Well, to my grandmother's once, if you can call that running away. She only lived a block away." His smile faded as he looked at her. "But I'm guessing that it's not all that funny, what you're thinking."

"That's right. Not that funny." Her voice had a steely edge to it that got his attention. "When you're serious about running away at that age, you run into two very big challenges very quickly and it isn't long before those are the only things you think about all day, every day: where am I going to sleep and where can I get some food. At night you either find a shelter or sleep in the bushes or join a homeless encampment somewhere. For food, you either get a free meal at a shelter or shoplift it or cadge some money and buy it. For Blue, the shelter is unlikely because they are going to ask too many questions. A homeless encampment is possible, but that could attract attention, too, so bushes are the most likely. In the winter. And as for food, she apparently has enough money to last her a while but it's going to run out at some point or get stolen and that's going to be the crux for her. She may try shoplifting to eat but there's too great a chance of her getting caught. That means begging for handouts or finding some way of earning money. And that is what has me worried."

Detective James pursed his lips. "I get it," he said after a moment of uncomfortable dead air. "Not many options for finding money at that age. You don't have to tell me what they are. For a girl . . ."

"Yes, for a girl." She looked back down at her coffee. "All we can do is pray that she drifts into the good part of humanity instead of the bad part."

"The patrons versus the predators."

"Right. The shelters versus the street."

Rodney didn't want to share what her words had brought to his mind—how kids he had seen who were on their own at a young age had gotten sucked in by the predators and trapped in the drug dens and worse. He looked at Chief Hannah's furrowed brow. "Hey, she's already demonstrated that she's a pretty resourceful young woman, and tough."

"She is tough, but she is still so young," said Chief Hannah shaking her head. She looked back at Rodney, "And how is she supposed to protect herself from people who mean to take advantage of her or cause her harm?"

"Well, recognizing a bad situation is the first step to avoiding it and she seems to have a sharp perception of bad situations. Leaving a bad situation was not a bad strategy. A lot of people don't have the courage to leave a bad situation."

"What are you saying?" said Chief Hannah with a flash of irritation. "Are you telling me she showed *good* judgment by running away?"

"No, no! That's not what I meant. I wasn't talking about judgment, I was just saying she is perceptive and courageous. She made a courageous decision about the threat from Babineau, but she didn't realize she might be running away from one problem just to be confronted with new problems that may be as bad or worse. Of course she would have been better off if she had stayed."

Rodney became aware that Chief Hannah's intensity was causing him to sweat, but what he had said seemed to have mollified her. Her look had turned from hostile to intense pondering.

"Part of the problem," she said after a moment, "is that I still don't get this revenge motive of Babineau's. Why is he a threat to her now? Is he really so bent on revenge, or 'balancing the accounts' like you said, that he would try and track her down even after she disappeared? Isn't Bronco Babineau's real threat?"

Rodney scratched his chin thoughtfully. "It's complicated but let me try and lay it out the way I see it. First off, the mob-type accounting is real. I really do think Babineau is a threat to Blue because of that. I just don't know how far he would take it. The fact that he already sent Purcell is extremely troubling, but my guess is that he won't spend a lot of effort looking for her. It is more likely that he will just wait for her to reappear on her own. As for what he would do if or when she does, I don't know. Maybe there is a mob statute of limitations, maybe he would 'pardon' her, but I'm not so sure. I think he means her real harm. It doesn't make sense, I know. Like you said—the real threat to Babineau is William Farrell, but I get this gut feel that something more sinister is motivating him. One thing is for sure, Babineau probably guesses that we're after Farrell and that we'll try to turn him against him. He also knows that Farrell would have to have pretty strong motivation to turn on him—like I said, mob accounting is fairly brutal and unforgiving." He paused. "That brings the accidental and natural deaths of Justin and his son Ethan into question. It makes me wonder if Babineau was involved in those deaths. It makes me wonder if he knows the William Farrell-Bronco connection. If he does, we can't let Babineau get to Farrell first or he might make Farrell disappear, and then we're sunk." He looked at Chief Hannah, "Which brings me to the question I have to ask: how did you make the Farrell-Bronco connection? I know, I know," he held up his hand to stifle what looked like the beginning of a reprimand from Chief Hannah, "I don't expect you to tell me the specifics, but you can at least tell me if there is any chance that Babineau could make a Farrell-Bronco connection from the same source that you did?"

Chief Hannah eased back in her seat and turned away with a look of concentration. She started tapping her fingers on the table and remained that way for what seemed like minutes. When she finally stopped tapping, what followed caught Rodney completely off guard.

"The answer is no, absolutely not. But there is something from my source that I *can* tell you, and again, I'm asking you not to press me on how I know this." Chief Hannah looked over her shoulder, and seeing that Mona wasn't within earshot, she leaned over and said quietly, "Ethan and Justin Farrell's deaths were not accidental or natural. But it wasn't Babineau!" She made the last remark probably because of the look of surprise Rodney felt take over his face. She continued, "I think—no, I *know*—that you should move forward with the assumption that Justin killed his younger son, Ethan, and Bronco murdered his father because of that." She paused, acting hesitant to go on. She looked again over her shoulder, and seeing no one, apparently made her decision and added, "Blue knows this. And Bronco knows that Blue knows."

Rodney opened his mouth. Then shut it again. He opened it again, looking for something to say, and then gave up completely. He was rescued when Mona came hustling out of the kitchen and sliding into the booth next to Chief Hannah, pushing her along the seat with her hips and then leaning in urgently.

"Sorry to butt in, but I just learned something you two should know."

Chief Hannah's face now joined Rodney's in surprise.

"What is it, Mona?" asked Chief Hannah.

"I just learned that it's pretty likely that Blue took the Megabus to Rensselaer. A homeless girl just told me."

"A homeless girl?" asked Rodney.

"Yeah." Mona looked at Rodney. "I get a lot of street kids in here. They cadge a few bucks and come in here for a cheap breakfast and to get warm. I give them a good deal. At least to the good ones. This girl—the one that wears the knit hat with the earflaps—you know the one, Chief—she's a good one—she was here when you first came in. She left in a hurry when she saw you, Chief, but she came round to the back door and told me she recognized Blue from the paper and saw her get on the Megabus—the one that goes to the train stations in Rutland and Rensselaer. A lot of college kids use it, especially around holiday time. You know, from the Albany train station she could take either the Adirondack or the Ethan-Allen Express. Both go south to NYC. I think the Adirondack goes north to Plattsburgh."

Rodney and Chief Hannah sat in silence, each in their own personal daze, trying to process the mass of new information that seemed to drop on them like a cloudburst. Rodney was the first to speak. He looked at Chief Hannah. "You can use this to get help from the FBI. They are bound by law to follow up on any lead for a missing underage kid. I mean anything, including rumors from a homeless girl. And it might be enough to get the New York State Police involved in the search. But if this information is out on the street, that isn't good."

He turned to Mona. "Can you do me a favor, and keep this to yourself? And maybe ask that street girl to keep it to herself?"

Mona shook her head and said, "Well, I can keep a secret, but I don't know about Hope—that's the name of the girl. I'll ask her next time I see her, but it may already be too late."

Chief Hannah pulled out her wallet. She slapped a twenty on the table and slid it over to Mona and said, "Next time Hope comes in, it's on me. Give her a Deluxe. This is the first lead I can get my teeth into."

Mona snapped up the twenty and said, "This will buy her a Farmer Special. And a pair of mittens." She looked at Rodney and said, "I think you should pick up this good lady's tab." She stood, grabbed the plates, and then paused, looking from Rodney to Summer, and added, "And maybe take her out to dinner." She winked, but Rodney wasn't exactly sure who she was winking at.

He just shook his head. "Well, that's a bit of good news, but you really threw me a curve ball there. If what you're saying is true, and I trust it is, even though it is a real stretch for me . . . if it's true, then tracking down Bronco is more important than ever. It means we have even more leverage on him, but at the same time," he looked at Chief Hannah in dead seriousness, "if any of this leaks out on the street, that sort of information can spread quickly to the wrong people. We'd better find both Bronco and Blue. And soon."

2

BUS STOP

Earlier that same morning
Malone, New York

"Eeeeeeeeeeeek!"

The sudden high-pitched squeal jolted Blue out of her fitful sleep with such ferocity that her body reflexively sat bolt upright and rammed her head straight into something flat and hard. The impact was enough to send a burst of stars whirling across her vision. What she saw behind the stars was a very confusing scene. She was looking out into a room from inside a ground-level cabinet. Sitting on the floor opposite her was an Hispanic woman wearing a housekeeper's uniform and she was crossing herself madly while chattering in a rapid staccato.

"*¡Dios mío! Virgen María, sálvame de este pequeño diablo. ¡Nina, ven rápido! ¡Tenemos un roedor gigante!*"

Blue propped herself half-upright, her head still spinning from the impact with the top of the cabinet, her just-woken brain still foggy and trying to figure out what the hell was going on. She looked down and saw that she was lying on stacks of white linens, and then it all came back to her, and she closed her eyes and flopped down on the linen. Outside the cupboard, she could hear the machine-gun pace of a second Hispanic voice joining the first. She groaned. She'd been caught. The jig was up. She was sure they'd call the police and that would be the end of her run. But right now, she just wished they'd stop chattering and go away so she could go back to sleep. Her head was throbbing, and her brain was so rattled and exhausted that all it wanted to do was switch off for a while.

And like a wish come true, the chatter was stopped abruptly by a firm query from a new voice. It was a calm and confident voice that continued in gentle, halting Spanish. When Blue ventured a peek, she saw a young woman speaking quietly to the two Hispanic housekeepers. The first housekeeper got off the floor, grumbling and mumbling in Spanish, and then both housekeepers left the room.

The young woman had jet-black hair styled in tight cornrows that were adorned with little white seashells at the forehead and temples. The cornrows continued down to form long braids that ended in bright multi-color hair-ties. Her expression was hard to read. It seemed to be trying to assert an air of authority, but it was being undermined by an undercurrent of amusement.

"Aha! So that's where you went. I wondered if you might show up somewhere."

Blue's foggy brain finally recognized the young woman. She was the motel desk clerk that was there when her bus arrived at midnight last night.

Blue closed her eyes and rubbed her face with her hands. "Are you going to call the police?"

"Mmmm, now why would I do that?" said the woman. "Did you murder someone?"

Blue ventured a look again. The woman had sat down, cross-legged like she was settling in for a long chat. Her face had a soft smile. "No crime in falling asleep, is there?"

"Depends on where, doesn't it?" said Blue closing her eyes again. "I'm in a motel. Rooms aren't free."

"As far as I'm concerned, you were just helping fold the laundry and fell asleep."

Blue wondered why this woman was being so nice to her. "What about the two housekeepers?"

The woman's gentle smile turned to a gentle laugh. "Oh my God, girl. Those two aren't going to say a thing. They're undocumented. You think you frightened them? Immigration agents, that's what they're terrified of. No way they would call the police. You did scare the crap out of Lolita, though. She fell right on her ass when she opened that cupboard door!" This time, the woman's laugh was unrestrained, yet relaxed.

Blue couldn't help but feel better at this good turn of fortune. She studied the woman for a moment. Maybe early twenties and she was dressed like a college student. For a moment, her foggy brain made her think she was back in Westbury.

"We'd better get you out of here, though," said the young woman. "My shift is over. I was just heading out when I heard Lolita. Lucky for you. I don't think the morning desk clerk is quite as sympathetic to girls like you and me. In fact, he's a raving male chauvinist. C'mon." The woman stood up and gestured for Blue to get out. Blue extricated herself from the linen cupboard and then pulled out her backpack and duffle.

"Girl, how did you get back here without me hearing you? Did you do all that when I hit the bathroom last night?"

Blue nodded.

The woman shook her head, "You must have some mad skills getting in here without making a sound. I mean, this supply room is right behind the front desk. I wasn't more than ten feet from you all night!" She paused and then looked at Blue. "Now if it were *me*, I would have crashed in a housekeeping closet on the second floor. You don't have to be as careful about noise. I'm not saying *I* ever did anything like that." She winked.

Blue stared at the woman curiously.

The woman smiled and said, "Hey, been there, sister. Trust me. You did a good job fooling me last night with that fake phone call crap, though." She changed to a falsetto voice, "Bob, my bus is here, why aren't you here to pick me up!" She laughed. "And then you go outside like you were waiting to get picked up by 'Bob' and instead you just were waiting for me to go to the loo. Nice one. My name's Sylvie, by the way."

Blue smiled but didn't reply. She realized she hadn't fully thought out how to introduce herself and she was way too tired to work it out right now. Thankfully, Sylvie didn't press her.

They reached the lobby of the motel where a very neatly dressed young man with tightly trimmed hair stood behind the check-in desk. He was checking out a frumpy man who was dressed in a disheveled mess of clothing. The two men turned in unison to stare at the two girls as they walked by. Sylvie waved and said, "Hi, Frank. I'm checking out. Have a good shift!"

Frank replied with a stern stare.

"See what I mean," whispered Sylvie. "Don't worry, though. He looks stiff but is pretty harmless. Just stick with me until we get outside, and it'll all be good." Sylvie grabbed her things by the desk and then they both put on their jackets and stepped out the lobby doors. It was still early, the sky just starting to look like day. Blue breathed in the crisp air, thankful for the frosty blast as it cleared the morning grogginess from her head. The first thought that popped into her newly refreshed mind was that she had miracu-lously made it through two nights on the road without serious mishap, thanks to a couple of lucky encounters with kind people, like Sylvie, but now she wasn't sure what was next.

"You going to be okay?" asked Sylvie.

"I'll be fine," said Blue, not feeling exactly fine.

Sylvie stood in front of her and looked her up and down. Blue felt a little self-conscious, wondering just how much a mess she was after two days on the road. Sylvie shook her head and said, "Uh-huh, right. Well, look, you aren't asking for it, but here's some advice. I would start by walking down this road here to the right about half a mile where you'll find the best diner in the entire universe. Go in there and get yourself some breakfast. You need some meat on those skinny bones of yours." While she was talking she had been rummaging in her purse. She pulled out a scrap of paper and a pencil. "Now I don't know where you're headed, but if you get stuck in town tonight with no place to go, you call me. Okay? Only if you get stuck. You got money?"

Blue took the scrap of paper and nodded. "I'll be fine."

Sylvie studied Blue for a moment, her face no longer smiling. With a stern voice, she said, "Look at me." Blue looked into Sylvie's eyes. They were a deep brown. There was no *chiss* from them even though it looked like Sylvie was thinking hard. "It doesn't look like you're using. You've got some beautiful eyes there. You should keep them that way."

Blue must have looked puzzled because Sylvie suddenly put her hand on Blue's shoulder and squeezed it. "Look," she said, "there are some rough characters in town that would see those pretty eyes and want to reel you in. You know what I mean? You steer clear of them, okay? I know, more unasked for advice." She nodded at the scrap of paper and said, "You've got my number. You use it if you need it. You've got a phone, right?"

Blue nodded. "Look, I'll be fine. Really. And thanks. Thanks a lot. I owe you one."

Sylvie smiled and gave Blue's shoulder a final squeeze before letting her go. "You don't owe me a thing. I'm just payin' it forward. Remember that. Someday you'll pay it forward, too. Now, I got to go. I've got classes in about an hour. No rest for the weary. Now shoo!" Sylvie's bright smile had returned, and she laughed once more, turned, and headed down the street, her dark braids bouncing as she walked causing the bright shells to dance in the morning light. Blue watched Sylvie go, fighting a strange urge to run after her. Sylvie turned and waved one last time just before she disappeared behind a building. Blue waved back and then Sylvie was gone.

She closed her eyes and tilted her head back, taking in a long breath, and then she let it out slowly. She opened her eyes and watched her misty breath float up and swirl into a feathery circle surrounding a faint white star—the last vestige of night. It seemed to her that her breath and the star vanished together at that moment in the brightening sky.

She looked wearily down at her old duffle. It had been feeling heavier and heavier the further she got into this little adventure of hers and it took her a couple of tries to get the strap up and slung on her aching shoulder. She tried to ignore the ache and think about the meal ahead, her suddenly growling gut driving her on.

As she trudged along, she wondered: how long was this string of luck going to last? It had started two days ago when she just managed to catch the morning bus from Westbury to Rensselaer, NY. The driver had already closed the door when she came running up and banged on it. The driver had looked at her and rolled his eyes, frowning. As she got on, he said, "You're lucky I'm your driver today. The regular driver? He would have just driven off without you."

A few hours later she had gotten off and walked into the Amtrak station in Rensselaer which she had expected to be grimy and cold but found surprisingly warm and spacious and modern. There, she had plenty of time to create a Gmail account, get her emails off to her friends and Chief Hannah, and then delete the account. Then there was the long wait until the departure time for the train she had chosen. To kill time she had walked around the station. As she passed a newsstand, she spotted that damned photo on the front page of a tabloid, displayed prominently for everyone in the station to see—her flying form emerging from the corner of Westbury High—a startled policeman with an assault rifle aimed right at her—a headline screaming, "Safe Sanctuary No More!"

It hadn't occurred to her that the picture would be everywhere.

It was then that she realized that if anyone recognized her, this disappearing act would be over before it started. She had crammed her wool hat firmer down on her head—she didn't dare take it off—and when no one was looking, she had stuffed her long hair up into the hat. She was pretty sure that would let her pass for a boy, but only if she kept her cap on. And her jacket. Her damned hips and boobs were starting to assert themselves a little too much to be overlooked without it.

The jacket caused her to sweat like a roast pig inside the warm station, which caused her to grab her bags and head for the door which caused her to pass by a notice board where something caught her eye. It was a flyer for a salon. A beauty salon. It had a little map on it and showed that it wasn't even five blocks away from the station. Open all weekend. "Treat yourself to a makeover! You deserve it!" it shouted in big pink bold letters. She had paused for only a moment before plunging out the door and hurrying as quickly as she could down this new twist in her journey.

When she got to the salon she was shocked by how busy it was for a Sunday, but a chair was open and one of the girls took her under her wing. "I need to look completely different," she had told the girl. The girl replied, "How much time have you got and how much money?" Several hours and $250 later, she had been transformed into a platinum blonde with a stacked bob haircut, "Truffle Tease" lipstick, gold eyeliner, blush, and mascara. When she looked in the mirror, she wasn't sure whether to laugh, cry, scream, or faint. She couldn't recognize her own face. In the end, she had started giggling. Giggling! Everybody in the salon stopped to look at her and then they all started clapping and cheering. And then she started crying, for whatever reason. The girl had to spend another ten minutes repairing the damage.

Fortunately, the makeover survived the long night she spent in the train station. She had parked herself on a bench where she read and dozed and read and dozed until finally, early the next morning she caught a train to Plattsburgh. From Plattsburgh, she took a bus to Malone which was apparently the slowest bus on the planet and didn't arrive until midnight. The bus stop was the motel where she had played her little ruse on Sylvie in order to sneak into the supply room behind the check-in desk (it was nice of the motel chain to post the floor plan of all their motels online—another bit of luck).

And now, here she was walking through the cold upstate New York air in a town she knew little about and that knew little about her. And that was exactly the plan. That, along with her new look, and she felt like she had completed a clean getaway. She glanced in the window of a store as she passed just to experience the bizarre out-of-body sensation of seeing a completely different girl looking back at her. The girl she did see looking back was a couple of grades less fresh than the one she saw yesterday. She sniffed her underarms—not terrible, as long as she didn't get too close to people—good enough to get through breakfast anyway. She'd need to find someplace to freshen up after that. Where that would be, she wasn't exactly sure. The makeover and bus and train tickets had taken a significant chunk of her cash, so there weren't a lot of options. A motel room would tap her out real quick. A shelter was risky—they'd ask too many questions. And it was way too cold to just crash in a bush somewhere. Sylvie's offer was sounding pretty good right now, but she only felt like she could do that after she exhausted every other possibility. Even then she would have to find someplace to hang until tonight. Maybe a public library. A shopping mall. Something.

She sighed. All she wanted right now was to put down this goddamn duffle bag and have a good breakfast at the best diner in the universe. She was just too tired and hungry to think any further than that.

And as if the universe was timing everything right, the smell of bacon and coffee drifting through the air stopped her dead in her tracks. She realized she hadn't been paying attention to how far she had walked and when she looked toward the smell, a blazing pink neon sign in the window of a shiny metal-sheathed building greeted her gaze. The glowing sign proclaimed, "Flo's Diner." Her stomach did a little victory dance as she pushed through the door and the delicious aroma that only a breakfast diner can produce wafted over her.

Blue heaved her backpack and duffle bag onto a red leatherette bench in a small booth below the front window of the diner and let out a moan of pleasure as her shoulders rebounded in relief. She slid her exhausted body into the booth next to the duffle bag and fought the urge to keel over and fall asleep on top of it. The brief period of alertness that the fresh air had brought her started to drown in the warmth of the diner and the depth of her fatigue. How long had it been since she last had a decent full night's sleep? She had to ponder this question for far longer than she should have to come to the realization it had been last Thursday night. The night before Black Friday. And now it was Tuesday morning. Jesus. Four days. Now she really wanted to slump down on her duffle. Not yet, she said to herself. You have to get through this day and figure out where you're going to stay tonight.

There was a newspaper on the empty table next to her and she reached over and grabbed it. She looked at the front page and read, "The Malone Telegram. Tuesday, Nov 22, 2011." Today. Well, the paper was as good as any place to start.

A coffee cup and saucer plunked down on the table with the crisp clatter of ceramic on Formica. A menu slid down next to it. Blue looked up to see a middle-aged woman standing in front of her, coffee pot in hand. The woman was sporting bright red lipstick and her light brown hair was pulled back into a tidy bun. The pocketed apron she wore was adorned with "Flo's Diner" in pink embroidery across the front and her name tag had three capital letters on it: "FLO." Blue's eyes met the waitresses for just a moment, but in that moment, Blue was overwhelmed with an unexpected wave of nostalgia. Of homesickness. It was so profound, she had an irrational impulse to grab her bags, bolt for the door, and get a bus back to Westbury, but that thought was interrupted.

"Coffee, honey?" asked the waitress. She had started pouring even as she was asking the question. As she poured, a *chiss* floated into Blue's brain, "IT LOOKS LIKE YOU NEED IT WHETHER YOU DRINK IT OR NOT." Blue wasn't normally a coffee drinker, but the rich aroma that wafted up to her nose and drifted deliciously into her olfactory organs convinced her exhausted body and brain that maybe this was exactly the right time to start.

THE NOZZLE from the gas pump clicked off abruptly and a little puff of gasoline odor burped from the fill pipe, bringing Chainy's attention away from the window of Flo's diner and back to what he was doing. He didn't really need the gas, but the gas station was a good vantage point, and filling up was good cover for watching the girl as she entered the diner and conveniently sat near the front window.

He had spotted her earlier walking down the street—she was probably right off the bus—and she had instantly caught his eye. She fit the mental checklist he had for a girl that might fill a spot that was voided when Neurotic Nina decided life with her overbearing, but rich, parents wasn't so bad after all and lightyears better than the wretched stench of Chainy's crash pad and its occupants (her words, not his). She had started acting real weird the last few weeks, to the point that he was ready to make an anonymous call to her parents anyway. But fortunately, she left on her own. Thanks, Nina. You won't be missed much except by a couple of regulars that were kind of into your weirdness, he thought to himself. For him and his two remaining girls, though, it was a relief for her to be out of there.

But kind of a problem, too. She was weird but she was productive. She brought in enough extra cash for him to stay pretty comfortable. He was going to miss that and yet it wasn't like he needed to go out of his way to do something about it right away. He was still pretty flush. And he still had Becky and Nora. Better to wait and see if this new girl popped up on her own. If she was the right kind of girl, she would stay clear of the shelters and wind up hanging on the street and if she did, she would soon be looking for a crash pad out of the cold weather. And if she looked, after getting a tip here or a tip there as she gained street cred, more than likely she would show up at his door.

The chain bracelets adorning his wrists rattled in a reassuring way as he hung the gas nozzle back on the pump. He took one last glance at the girl. She was now sipping coffee with her hands wrapped tightly around the cup—just like a street girl might whenever she'd cadged enough money to sit inside a café to defrost.

He turned away and headed for the gas station office and as he did, he started whistling his happy tune. He felt the pleasant heft of his tight, neat roll of cash as he pulled it from his pocket and plucked out a twenty to give to the attendant. He could afford to wait, he thought, and if she never showed up at his door, there would be another. There always was. In the meantime, though, he was going to bask in the relatively drama-free scene at his pad—the bulk of the drama having exited along with Neurotic Nina.

3

WILL'S BATTLE

Later that same morning
Westbury, Vermont

Will was slumped across the kitchen table, his head lying on his left arm, his brain exhausted, reeling from the merry-go-round of thoughts that had been flashing by in a continuous stream, each one carrying its own special package of guilt or disbelief or sadness or, worst, stomach-wrenching horror. Occasionally one swept by with hope—hope that Blue would come back. He tried to hold on to that one longer than the rest.

His right hand turned an empty water glass round and round in the same spot, making a glass-against-Formica wobble-wobble noise as it turned. It was oddly soothing and seemed to calm the merry-go-round a little.

"I need a beer," he mumbled.

Will's mom, sitting across from him, cracked a small, wan smile and shook her head. "No, dear, that won't help."

"It's a sedative, right?" he said. "I want to self-medicate." He loved to turn his mom's psycho-babble back on her.

"I've got a better idea." She took a book that had been sitting in front of her and slid it across the table to him along with a pencil. Once the book was in front of him, he realized that it wasn't a regular book, it was a small, bound, hardcover notebook. He opened it to a perfectly blank, perfectly white first page.

Will groaned. "I see a snowball fight in a snowstorm. I'm clearly deranged."

"Very funny," she said. "This isn't a test. It's a journal. For you. Your own private journal. You can put whatever you want in it."

"Like, nothing?" He peered up at her eyes. He knew he was being an ass, but he was tired. And angry. And frustrated. His mom must know it. He had given up hiding anything about how he felt. She probably didn't even need *veraque*[1] to know how he felt.

"How did you sleep last night?" she asked.

Will couldn't help rolling his eyes. She knew he hadn't slept.

"Like, you don't know?" he said, sarcastically.

"Will, you have experienced more trauma this year than any normal human being can be expected to handle. Your brain is trying to process it, but understand that no one is born with the tools to process this easily or to make sense of it. All I'm trying to do is give you some tools that will help."

"And a blank notebook is supposed to help?" His hand wandered over to the pencil and picked it up. He twirled it absent-mindedly between his fingers while his head lolled listlessly on the table. "I still think a beer would be better." He knew he should feel bad about being an ass, but some important control in his brain was missing, and he didn't care.

His mom pressed on. "The idea is to get some of this out of your head by recording it in something you trust. Once it is there, you can let go of it for a while—give your brain a rest—free your mind a little."

"Free my mind. Free my mind. Are we in the Matrix?" You're being an ass, Woods, he thought to himself. And she was right, of course. His mind *was* clogged, completely spinning with the second-guessing, frustrations, guilt, and, most of all, anger. He couldn't name specifically why he was angry, and it was frustrating him, and maybe the frustration was the reason he was angry. An endless spiral of anger feeding on frustration. He glanced again at his mom and a sudden pang of sadness slammed his angry spiral to a stop. She was on the verge of tears and it was because of him. And now instead of anger, guilt pushed its way in. He looked up at her from the table.

"I'm sorry, Mom. I'm sorry. I'm just so tired."

"Um . . . no, I'm the one who should be sorry, honey," she said. "Perhaps I shouldn't be the one trying to help you. I'm too close. It might be much better if you saw someone else."

Another wrenching sensation seized Will's gut as his guilt morphed into panic. It happened so fast, he almost felt sick. "No! Mom!" His words blurted out reflexively, "I need you! You're the best! Please! You're the only one Blue trusted and you're the only one I trust." And even just saying Blue's name was enough to kick an extra spiral of guilt mixed with anger into his constantly shifting whirlwind of emotions. "God, if we just knew that she was all right, somewhere safe . . . the least she could do is send us a fucking email!" He banged his fist on the table. He banged it again, softer. It evolved into a rhythmic thump. Thump, thump, thump . . .

If his mother was shocked at his behavior, she was managing to hide it from him. When she spoke, it was with a steady voice. "Write that down," she said softly.

"*Write what down?*" he thought. He didn't really vox it, but he knew she could hear. More of a *chiss* than a vox. Thump, thump, thump . . .

"*Write it to Blue,*" she voxed.

He stopped thumping. He looked at her. He looked at his hand. Miraculously, he hadn't destroyed the pencil. He yanked the journal toward him and wrote furiously.

Dear Blue,
You suck! You should be sending us updates! Do you realize what
you're doing to us back here? God dammit, you asshole!
P.S. I hope you're okay.
Love,
Will

He felt better.

He looked at his mom and voxed her for the first time for real. "Okay, Mom, nice one. How did you do that?"

She shrugged. "I didn't. You did. Pencil and paper are pretty useful, although I was thinking of giving you a stone and some ochre—a little more Cro-Magnon, perhaps more your style, but alas, all I had was pencil and paper."

He felt his cheek twitch as it tried to smile. He fought it but the corner of his mouth curled up anyway. The skin on his face felt taut, like it hadn't been stretched that way in a while. The sensation sparked a brief moment of lightness, like breaking the surface of a lake for a breath of air.

"Like I said, Mom, you're the best."

His mom let out a big sigh. "Okay, I'll stay on the job. But I still want you to see someone in addition to me, okay?"

"Should I keep writing?"

"Does it help?"

"Yeah, it does." He sighed, doubly exhausted from the whiplash of emotions his brain had just put him through. He stared at the journal and what he had written. "It does, but it feels weird. I mean I just wrote a note to Blue, but she'll never see it. Isn't that kind of schizo?"

"Oh, my, no. It's completely human and healthy. Why do you think religions exist? People talk to God or Jesus or Allah or any of a dozen saints all the time. It's comforting because you're sharing your troubles with a very good listener—one who never interrupts."

"Yeah, but Blue is a real person. She's not a god."

"But you are sharing your troubles."

He looked at the notebook. "Do you think she might ever read this?"

"Only if you show it to her. It's your brain's private workbook. It's *your* private workbook. You don't have to share it with anyone. Think of a journal as a way of working out your thoughts on paper, outside your brain, before you share them with anyone."

"So, I don't have to show anyone what I just wrote?" He looked sidelong at her. "*Not even my therapist?*"

"*Not even your therapist. Or your mother.*"

He tapped the pencil on the journal and then started to write another note to Blue. He stopped.

"Mom, I don't know whether to tell Blue the whole Bronco-is-Bill-Farrell-is-the-son-of-El-Segador-is-your-family's-murderer thing. I know she can't read this, but I still feel like I shouldn't be writing it down. I mean, what if she does come back? Do we tell her then? At all? Ever?" He felt his face suddenly flushed and hot with the mention of Bronco. Another thing that was keeping him awake. Another thing that was aching to get out. He almost wanted to scream but his voice came out strangled instead. "I can't believe Bronco helped murder her family! I can't believe that she actually *was* avenging her family when she tried to take him down! I can't believe he didn't recognize her! And I really, really can't believe that I didn't help her! All of this shit wouldn't have happened . . ." his fist slammed down on the table again, *thump!* "if I had just" *thump!* "fucking," *thump!* "gone with her," *thump!* "that night!" *thump-crack!*"

The pencil finally gave out and he stared at the broken stub that he held in his clenched fist. He threw it across the kitchen.

His mother sat calmly while he sat breathing hard. He was starting to feel like those Christmas snowballs that you shake and the snowflakes swirl around frantically before gradually settling to the bottom of the ball. As his brain settled down again he noticed that his mom had pushed a fresh pencil across the table.

"Write it down. Write to her," she said. "I think you already know my response to what you said, and probably Blue's response. Maybe write that down, too."

"I know, I know," he said, rubbing his face with his hands. "Don't blame yourself, 20-20 hindsight, blah blah blah. Still, I want to kill that guy. And I mean I really want to kill that guy."

His mom reached over and tapped his journal in response. He stopped rubbing his face, picked up the pencil, and started writing.

It did feel good. It felt like he was doing something with the stuff in his head which was better than the stuff doing something to him. He quickly got so engrossed in writing that he almost didn't notice that his mother had pushed a note over to him. It read "Talk to your friends, Wu and Anna, too. They need to share as much as you do. They are hurting, too. There is power in sharing." He looked up, but his mom was gone, and sitting in front of him was a fresh cup of hot tea. He sniffed and recognized the scent of lemon balm. He sipped it and continued writing until he could no longer hold his head up and laid it on his folded arms for just a moment, just to rest, just for a minute . . .

4

RADIO SILENCE

The next day, November 23rd

"This is some effed-up stuff, dude." Wu handed the journal to Anna who gingerly took it from him and glanced warily at the page.

"Yeah, well, I was feeling pretty effed up at the time," said Will. He was only showing them one page from his journal, one with a whacked-out drawing. "Maybe I am still. And don't you feel that way, just a little?"

Will tried to gauge Anna's reaction to the drawing. He had drawn three severed heads in a birdcage—caricatures of Babineau, Bronco, and Purcell—with gore pouring out their necks. Flames and smoke surrounded the birdcage and lightning bolts and exclamation points surrounded the entire scene.

"I think this is a little more extreme than my feelings on the matter," she said flatly. "Arrested and put in jail? Yes, but decapitation and burning and lightning bolts? That might be a bit over the top. Maybe a slap in the face."

"Or a fist to the face," said Wu. "Repeatedly," he added.

"Non-stop," added Will.

"For a month," said Wu, smirking.

"Times a hundred," said Will, smirking back.

"Boys!" Anna looked at them sternly. She handed the journal back to Will. "You said you slept for how long?"

Will looked at the journal and shook his head. "Mom said I'd been asleep an hour when she woke me up and shuffled me to my bedroom. I fell right back to sleep and I didn't get up until about nine this morning."

"Good! You look about a thousand times better today. I was really worried about you," said Anna.

"Me too," said Wu, "especially with all the shit that's on Face . . . ow!" Wu rubbed his shoulder and turned toward Anna whose hand was in a fist.

"Facebook?" asked Will.

Wu turned warily toward Anna. She gave him a dirty look and then turned to Will, "Well now that *that* is out in the open, you may as well hear it from me." She looked sternly back at Wu. "A bunch of the usual characters are claiming that you were Jordy's accomplice because you started that fight with Mike and Pike, BUT . . ." She put a hand on Will's knee and locked eyes with him and her *chiss* came through, "*Nobody is buying it!*"

"Don't do that! I'm here, too," said Wu. "What did you just tell him?"

"She told me nobody's buying it," said Will. Just hearing those names—Mike, Pike—brought a flash of memory—Mike looking down at the blood in his hand, Pike staring dumbly at Mike. The second flash of gunfire. The tinkle of the shell. He felt himself sway a little and he glanced at Anna. Her hand was still on his knee, steadying him. He had felt the sincerity behind Anna's *chiss* and a wave of affection for her pushed the memory away. It was like an echo from the night that Blue had rescued him, and that thought in itself was like a balm to his soul. He took a breath and then looked at Wu. "Don't worry, I've already seen it. It's like last summer all over again. Lots of nice posts and emails and then the occasional torpedo with crap like this in it. Mom suggested I get a new email address, but I can't. I mean, what if Blue tries to contact me? Us? I have no way of telling her a new email address."

"She could still text or call," said Anna.

"I don't think she would—it would be too easy to trace. The phone companies have records of what tower a phone is using." He looked at Wu and then Anna with a look of chagrin. "I only know that because Blue told me."

Anna nodded. "I don't think people realize how wicked smart she is. That's what worries me the most. I think she could disappear forever if she wanted to."

"Not forever," said Will. At least he was hoping not. "She's smart, but I think it would be impossible to stay missing for long— especially if there are some stubborn people like us looking for her. What worries me is why she isn't contacting us. If she felt safe sending us a message on Gmail, why doesn't she do it again?"

"I'm sure she's still freaked out by the DFC thing," said Wu. "Maybe she's worried that they will seize our emails or something. They could, you know. Blue, Sam, and Nate are all still fostered. I mean, Pa Bill manages the email account, but a court could make him hand over our emails."

"What? Seriously?" This, apparently, was news to Anna. Will had known it a long time.

"Yeah, Ma Beth and Pa Bill can appeal, but they can't override the DFC. The only way they could do that is through adoption," said Will.

"Yeah and that's not likely to happen," said Wu, "especially after all the crap that's gone down. And look, fourteen kids have come through our house so far—all fostered, none adopted. The DFC could pull all of us from here if they wanted."

"Gosh. That's terrible. I had no idea. You guys seem like just . . ." she paused as if she wasn't sure the next words were right, ". . . such a together, tight-knit family."

"Well, we think we are," said Wu, "except our all-powerful overlord may not see it that way. I mean, face it, we all started out as misfits in the first place and haven't had exactly a stellar track record. Blue sneaking into Will's house? Meh, that's kid stuff compared to some of what's gone on." He looked at Will and grinned. "Remember when Sean threw a flowerpot through Walter's garage window?"

"Because Walter was swearing at him for walking through his flower bed?" Will laughed at that. "Yeah, that was epic! And then when Sassy sprinkled cat litter on Billy Walker's creemee and said it was licorice?"

Wu and Will started giggling, actually giggling.

"Well, boys, I don't find either of those particularly funny," said Anna with a disapproving frown, "but at least you guys are laughing for the first time in about . . ."

Wu and Will stopped laughing and were still smiling, but as they both finished counting in their head at the same time, they became more sober.

"Six days," said Wu first.

"Almost a week," said Will.

They were all quiet for a while until Anna finally said, "And three days since we've heard anything from Blue."

"If there was just some way we could contact her," said Will.

Wu held up his phone. "We might as well keep leaving messages. Maybe she'll turn her phone on just long enough to listen to them."

"Um, I think there's a problem there," said Anna, her face filled with guilt. "Her voice-message box is full. I confess—I've been kinda calling her non-stop."

"Yeah, me, too," said Will.

"Oh. Hmm. Well, I guess that's out," said Wu. "We can still send emails to her regular account. Pa Bill is keeping that open, as well as her phone. She can't cancel those, only he can. She might check her email online from a browser. I think that would be safe, right Will?"

"Yeah, I think that's true, as long as her location tracking is turned off. And I'm sure she has that off," said Will. "Like I said, she's the one that showed me all that security stuff."

"Maybe she has been reading her email. I mean how would we know? There's no way to tell, is there?" asked Anna.

"Not with our email service. Not unless she replies," said Wu.

"I think she'd reply," said Will. "She's tight as a drum on a lot of stuff, but I don't think she'd do that to us. We're still her friends."

"*MORE THAN FRIENDS.*"

Will glanced at Anna. "Yeah, well . . ." He turned away blushing.

"Maybe it's something else." Wu had been looking out the window thoughtfully, apparently ignorant of Will and Anna's *chiss* exchange. "Maybe she can't get internet where she is. Maybe she can't log on or maybe her connection isn't private."

"Yeah, any of those things," said Will. A long stretch of silence followed. Will tried to come up with some other brilliant observation to fill the space but in the end, all he could say was, "I guess we just wait until she finds a way to get hold of us safely." He had forced those words to sound rational and wise even while his heart was wondering if she even *wanted* to get hold of them.

I SHOULD BE USED to this now. That's the thought that kept repeating itself as Blue studied the features of the room she found herself in. Once a girl's room, long unused, now only a spare room used for storage. Not even a bed, just a thin camping mattress under a sleeping bag on the floor. Not unlike the other strange new rooms she'd found herself in each year as she moved from foster family to foster family. But it was different this time. This was the first time she felt like she was away from *home*.

Flo had offered to let her stay overnight in her estranged daughter's ex-bedroom. Blue felt like she shouldn't touch anything which was an awkward feeling, but at least she wasn't in a train station or a motel linen cupboard. And tomorrow she would have an apartment. Flo's beau owned an old house that had been converted to apartments and he had just finished a tiny studio apartment. She had a job. She had an apartment. It was surreal. It didn't seem possible.

There was a knock on her door and Flo peeked in.

"All right if I come in?" she asked.

"Uh, yeah, of course."

Flo stepped in. "Sorry for the mess. If you need to move anything, go ahead." She looked around and sighed. "I don't know what to do with half this stuff, so I just let it sit there. My daughter and me, well . . ." she looked at Blue. "Let's just say we aren't on the same wavelength and leave it at that." She looked at her watch. "It's late. You need to be up by five-thirty. We have to head over at six. Don't worry about breakfast, we can grab a bite there. Chet will have plenty of scrambled eggs and coffee ready." She looked at Blue. "In other words, I suggest you get to sleep pronto."

"Don't worry, I will," said Blue, and she meant it. She could tell that a complete collapse from the fatigue that had built up over the last few days was imminent. Her last shreds of energy were just enough to keep her awake so she could do one last thing before she gave in completely. "Um, do you have wifi?"

Flo pointed to a scrap of paper in the corner of a bulletin board festooned with the random collections of a decade or more of adolescent and teenage memorabilia. The scrap was the only item that seemed to have a purpose in the real world. It had a wifi network name and password on it.

"Don't get sucked into the web. You're going to be a busy girl tomorrow."

"Don't worry. I'm dead tired, I just haven't checked my email in days and . . . well . . ."

Flo waved her hand. "I don't need to know . . . that's your business. You do what you have to do. But then get to sleep! Okay?"

"Okay," she said, and then, "Flo?"

"Yes, honey?"

"Thanks. Thanks for everything. I was, well . . . I was—"

Flo waved her hand again, interrupting her. "Like I said, I don't need to know. And you're welcome." Flo's gaze hung on Blue for a moment. "CHRIST, THERE'S PROBABLY SOMEONE JUST LIKE ME WONDERING WHERE YOU ARE AND HOPING TO GOD YOU'RE SAFE." A melancholy feeling accompanied this *chiss* as it flowed into Blue's mind. Then Flo shook her head, smiled, and said, "Sleep well, Sam."

After Flo closed the door, Blue reached into her backpack and pulled out her laptop. She stared at it wondering if she had enough energy left to confront what was in her inbox. How many bridges had she burned? How many agencies had she pissed off? And what about Will and Wu and Anna and Sam and Rose and Nate? And Ma Beth and Pa Bill? She at least owed Ma Beth a note to say she was safe.

She opened the laptop wearily and told herself she'd just send an email to Ma Beth, and everyone else would have to wait until tomorrow night. She connected to the wifi and brought up the browser version of her email. She had already deleted the lame email app. She was sure it was pretty insecure. Her fingers instinctively typed in her password, and she hit return and closed her eyes for a moment, giving them a rest before she opened them to the expected barrage of emails. But when she opened her eyes her mouth spit out a hoarse, "What the fuck?"

Your password attempts have been exceeded. Your account has been locked. You can try again tomorrow or contact customer service.

Her fatigued brain took a moment to process what she was seeing. She hadn't tried to log in for days. And she never got her password wrong.

Someone else had tried to log into her account.

Someone else was trying to read her email.

Who the hell would try to do that? Who even knew her email address other than her friends? She closed her laptop, flopped down on the sleeping bag, and rubbed her eyes with the heels of her hands. God, I am too tired to deal with this right now, she thought. But her brain slowly worked the problem on its own and popped up with the answer she didn't want to hear: Her friends weren't likely to try, which meant her email address must have leaked somehow. Police wouldn't be so brute force but some kids at school might. There was another possibility and right now it seemed like the most likely one because it was the worst possible one.

Babineau.

5

BABINEAU'S NET

J im Purcell had spotted a few nicer old homes on the route his GPS was guiding him down as he drove through the northern suburb of New York, but they were crammed together and interspersed with tacky raised ranches and split-levels. He had yet to spot a classic well-crafted older house with a roomy yard and decent landscaping. It seemed that real estate so close to the city was too precious to waste on relaxed living space.

It was a little disappointing, but it wasn't like he had time to think about it much. He had at least three more contacts in three towns to visit today before he returned to his plain, cramped, 50's era apartment in the city. As it was, he had little hope of getting back before midnight and probably little hope of finding any architectural inspiration in any of the other towns.

He checked the GPS. Only three more blocks to this next contact. He rehearsed the three points of the message he was to deliver from Babineau to each of these contacts: 1) Delinquent. 2) Blue DuBois—a fifteen-year-old girl. (Yes, the one in the school shooting photo.) 3) Track only. 4) $10k. That was the message. No more, no less.

This was how Babineau had explained the meaning of the

message:

"Jim, I'm going to tell you this because I want you more involved in the business. Delinquent means delinquent account, as I explained to you before. The girl is an oversight from an earlier job, something that needs to be fixed. An account that needs to be balanced. 'Track only' means I want to know where she is, nothing more. I have another plan for what to do with her when she is found. And $10k? You know what that means. Now, each of these people knows how to contact me so those four points are all they need to know. And sending you? Well, sending you is a message in itself. It shows how serious I am. It shows them that I trust you and that you are not to be messed with. Now ask me a question."

And that's how Jim Purcell knew he had just leveled up in Babineau's inner circle. Not because of the explanation, which he didn't really need, but the invitation to ask him a question about it. So he had asked, "These contacts are all in New York. Don't you want to cast a wider net?"

Babineau's reply was reasoned but not entirely convincing. "This net covers most of the northeast and I don't think it has to be wider than that. In fact, I don't think it has to be much wider than New York and Vermont and I will tell you why." Babineau looked at Jim and asked, "Where would you gravitate if you ran away from home? Would it be someplace unfamiliar or someplace near home?"

Jim thought for a moment. There were advantages to both, but at fifteen years old, he probably would have stayed in familiar territory. "Someplace familiar," he said.

"Good answer," said Babineau. "I learned something from the internet. Most runaways are girls and a lot of them wind up on the street whoring for money or food or shelter or drugs. And more importantly, most are within fifty miles of home, and most wind up going home after a few months. It's pretty likely that our little delinquent is still in Vermont or in upstate New York close to where she grew up and if she is on the street, a $10k reward is a powerful incentive to someone out there to let us know about it. Now, ask me another question."

Jim was hesitant to ask what was really on his mind—Babineau might find it impertinent—but he seemed to be in an exceptionally accommodating mood, so Jim decided to go ahead and see what happened. "Boss, I know you have a big old-school network, but the internet is a thousand times bigger, and there is lots of technology you can use to track people down. It seems to me we should get an IT guy working on it."

Babineau broke into a giant smile. "Jim, I knew I was right to trust you. In fact, when you get back from this chore, I'm going to introduce you to Ari Kumar, internet-wizard. He's got a lot of tools he's going to put to use on this project. I know I was a little slow to the internet game, but he's helping us catch up fast. In a lot of ways, DuBois did me a favor, killing my old business. Dope was old school and losing that business forced us to reinvent with opioids and at the same time get savvy with the dark net and VPN. Are you surprised at me using those terms? Dark net? VPN?" He laughed, "Well, me too. Anyway, Ari is opening my eyes and he's already got us into some new business. And he's set up some kind of code that can watch for any traffic that might give us a clue to where our little waif is hiding. I'm betting that when he does find something, it'll be in New York or Vermont. If we already have the ground game going, we can just use his information to zero in on it. So that's why I'm sending you out now."

So here he was, on a tour of the burgs and boroughs of New York, passing the word to Babineau's network to set the net to capture a fifteen-year-old girl. A week ago he would have considered this ludicrous, but after his personal encounter with her, and now that he knew of Babineau's genetic trait, nocte venatori, Jim was starting to understand Babineau's obsession with tracking her down. What he didn't quite understand, and what he could tell Babineau was withholding, was exactly what he intended to do with her, or to her, once he had her.

6

BRONCO SETTLES IN

B ronco stood in the cavernous camp living room, enveloped in the glow of a well-fueled fireplace and infused with the warmth of two shots of spiced rum. In front of him on the floor lay four foam-lined customized equipment cases, all open, displaying their Machiavellian hardware neatly and efficiently. "Arsenal on the half-shell," his miserable POS father would've said. The brightly colored woven rag rug provided a stark contrast to the utter darkness of the black cases and their contents. The silky ebony barrels and handgrips were nestled neatly in their respective depressions, waiting to be picked up and caressed before being deployed in their dubious mission, which, in stark contrast to their grim appearance, was to be non-lethal.

Bronco grunted as he assessed each item in turn. The first case contained a pair of handheld stun guns, a charger, two extra batteries, and a belt holster. These were for close-contact immobilization and intimidation. Next case, a pair of compact taser pistols with built-in flashlights and targeting lasers, two extra taser cartridges, extra batteries, and two soft holsters. These were the latest in compact models, small enough to wear concealed, not like the monster tasers law enforcement used. Nice. Then there was the case with a weird new invention—it looked like an oversized flashlight only it sported a laser and short barrel six-shot pepper-ball gun. He plucked it out of its case and regarded it with a generous amount of skepticism. There was always someone trying to come up with the next great thing. The million-dollar idea. Ninety percent of the time it was just a way to part you with your money and fill your trashcan with useless junk. He took another sip of rum as he flicked on the targeting laser and pointed the flashlight-like device at his reflection which was hovering in the large picture window like a ghost in the snowy landscape outside. The laser projected a steady red beam which continued straight and true out through the window, but part of it reflected back and created a bright red dot on the chest of his reflection.

"Pop, pop," he said, pressing the fire button. His mind imagined a couple of pepper balls shooting out the end of the thing, striking the red dot, and exploding in puffs around the figure in the reflection. Hmm, this might not be that bad, he thought. Point it like a flashlight and hit the trigger. Pepper-balls were pretty damn effective as he knew from personal experience. Maybe this thing was for real after all.

He put it back in its case and reached for the next case. This was more like it, he thought. A pepper-ball gun that looked like a proper rifle. He put down his glass and held the gun in firing position with both hands. Nice feel, good balance, and if the range was decent, he could see it being a nice non-lethal sniping weapon. He examined it—laser targeting, good sites, ten shot magazine. He put it back in its case and took another sip of rum. Maybe practice on some gray squirrels tomorrow, he thought.

There was one more item Babineau had sent along: A hypodermic kit with several bottles of anesthetic and sedatives. Useless for capturing, but perhaps useful for questioning. More evidence that perhaps Babineau was telling the truth—this would just be a "detain, threaten, and release" deal. Someone that needed to be reminded of an obligation—reminded that they couldn't run from it. So, capture the guy, let Babineau do what he wanted with him, sedate him, and drop him off somewhere he would have a nice nap and wake up with a new sense of purpose. No fuss, no muss.

Bronco drained his glass. He was looking forward to playing with this stuff—something new to do and God knew, he needed things to do to kill time. Ice-fishing was still interesting, but he wasn't going to be one of those crazy fuckers that sat in their shanty all winter.

He poured himself another rum and then went over and pulled out one of the taser pistols. It was surprisingly light. He stuck it inside his belt and walked around. Barely noticeable. He could see wearing one of these things all the time instead of his Glock. Maybe both. Why not? Be prepared for anything.

He stepped over to the big easy chair in front of the fireplace and settled into it. He fucking hated Babineau with all his heart, especially since Babineau had him by the balls, but the way things were looking, maybe this wasn't the worst thing Babineau could have asked him to do. And if it truly evened the books, it would be worth it. A lot would depend on just how difficult this guy was to capture and how long he had to sit around killing time before he showed up.

There was one thing bugging him about this whole thing, though. Babineau had said the name "Stanton." It had to be a coincidence because it couldn't possibly be the same Stanton. That Stanton was dead years ago. Could be a relative, though. Part of a family feud? Babineau vs. Stanton? These fucking mob family feuds seemed to go on forever. Wouldn't it be a kick in the ass, though, if Stanton was part of his dad's deal with Babineau and that he had offed his dad before he could finish it? Whatever. As long as this job evened things up with Babineau, he didn't care.

He drained the last of his drink and sank into the chair and tried to not care, but it wasn't working. Instead, an involuntary shiver went up his spine. He shook it off. "Well, Mr. Stanton," he said out loud, "whoever you are, whatever you are, you are a lucky bastard if all you get is a pepper-ball in the face. Maybe a pepper-ball and a taser, or the other way around." Either way, you are going to be one surprised son-of-a bitch, he thought. No doubt about that.

He closed his eyes and settled back into the soft upholstery. As drowsiness overtook him, an image started dancing around in his almost-dream-state mind—a gorilla-sized Stanton screaming and coughing and pawing at his eyes as Bronco sent pepper-ball after pepper-ball popping around him. And when the gun ran out of pepper balls, he tazed him. But Stanton, now a real gorilla, just shook it off and started coming after him. Bronco ran but for some reason, his feet couldn't get any traction. He reached for another weapon but all he found was a banana so he threw it at the gorilla. And then there was no more.

The fire gradually burned lower and lower until there was nothing left but embers, leaving the room in darkness except for the red glint from the weaponry and the glow from Bronco's twitching, snoring face.

7

JOURNAL

_ _ _ _ _ _ _ _ _ _ _ _ _ _ _ _ _

Nov 24
~~Dear Blue~~ Hey,

*Mom said writing to you in a journal was a good idea, even
though you ~~might not~~ won't ever read this. At first I thought it
would be weird, but actually it's okay. Wonder why that is.
Anyway, today is Thanksgiving and we're having our usual
turkey dinner. It smells great in the house and seems to make
things feel more normal but at the same time it feels weird. I
mean it's like it looks and smells normal, but it's like I'm seeing
everything ~~abnormal~~ at a distance or through a movie camera
instead of through my real eyes. Does that make sense? It's only
been a week since the shooting and ~~five~~ four days since you left.
Every minute I'm not doing something normal, I think about it.
The shooting, I mean. It's like I can't relax, so I just try to go back
to something normal so I don't think about it. But I kind of have
to because there are memorial services this weekend and I have to*

make a decision and I'm kind of weirded out about it. I mean, do I go to Jordy's service or not? Right now I feel like I was his only friend and that I should go, but I feel guilty about it at the same time, like it was partly my fault. But someone should go, right? It's not like he wasn't a victim, too, right? I don't know. I'll let you know what happens after. Don't worry about me, though. I'm pretty much okay most of the time and the times I'm not, I talk to Anna or Wu or Mom. I do worry about you, though. We all do. I just hope you're safe and someplace where you can have a decent Thanksgiving meal. I just wish you were here. I wish none of this happened. I wish, I wish, I wish.

-Will

Will closed his journal and set it on his nightstand, careful not to jostle the curled-up sleeping form snuggled up against him. Rosie had climbed in with him every night since Blue had left, each night with the same questions—"Willy, when is she coming home? When will everything be normal again? Can I sleep here tonight?" He had no answers to any of those questions except for the last one: "Of course."

As for the second question—normal? What was normal anymore? Maybe this was normal. Maybe this was what growing up was all about—dealing with non-stop disaster. If this was grown-up normal, he was ready to crawl back into his ten-year-old self and go and snuggle up to his mom for comfort. But he couldn't. He was almost sixteen. His sister was ten.

I guess I'm the comforter now, he thought. With a sigh, he turned off his light and hunkered down carefully under his sheets, doing his best not to disturb Rosie. He turned to look at her one last time before he made his own feeble attempt at sleep. A wisp of hair slanted gently across her relaxed face and her chest rose and fell steadily. As he watched, he felt an ember of peace and security glow inside of him. Maybe it's not so bad being the comforter after all, he thought. And as he turned away and pulled the covers carefully around his shoulders, an unexpectedly deep sleep surrounded him and held him until morning.

8

JOURNAL

Nov 24
Hey Will,

It feels weird writing in my sketchbook, but I just feel like writing and I don't have anything else to write in. Yeah, and it's even weirder that I'm writing to you knowing you'll never see this. I don't know. Maybe it's not weird because it feels right. It would feel righter if I could write to you for real, but since someone tried to hack my email it's just too risky. I know, I know, I Gmailed Ma Beth, so why not Gmail you or Anna or Wu? Well, I couldn't NOT let Ma Beth know I'm okay. I mean, then I'd really feel like shit, leaving her like that, so I took the risk. But I just can't bring myself to risk anything else. You probably think I'm ultra-paranoid, but if you heard the chiss that I heard from Babineau's goon Saturday night and later you tried to log in to your email and found yourself locked out because someone tried to hack in, I think you would get it.

But I still have to tell you somehow that I'm okay even if it's just writing to a virtual you. So hey, I'm okay. I'm more than okay, I actually have a job and an apartment! Can you believe it? And the job is pretty good. The people are really nice. And since you'll never read this, I can tell you all about it and not worry about giving away where I am.

It went like this—I was looking at the want ads in a local newspaper while I was having breakfast at a diner—Flo's Diner. (Hah! dead giveaway right there. I just Googled it and there are only five Flo's Diners in the U.S. (Yeah, I'm still in the U.S.— Another dead giveaway!) The owner, Flo, saw me looking at the want ads and offered me a waitressing job on the spot! She asked where I lived, and I told her nowhere yet and she said her boyfriend had an open apartment in a building he owns—so here I am in the world's tiniest apartment. But it's mine. And it's warm. And it beats the hell out of sleeping in the train station (yeah, I slept in a train station).

There you have it. I just wrote to my imaginary boyfriend. Hah! I just called you a boyfriend. I'd like to see your reaction if I told that to your face. God, maybe I should do this more often—write to nobody—it's kind of fun. Kind of a relief. Is this the same thing as talking to myself? Only insane people talk to themselves, right? Well, I already know I'm insane, so why not chat up a storm? One thing is for sure and that is that it's late and I'm exhausted. I can barely keep my eyes open. So now I am going to curl up in this sleeping bag Flo loaned me and go to sleep. Yeah, I have to borrow everything right now. I'm a bum. So sue me.

Hey, Happy Thanksgiving. Say hey to Wu and Anna, too, when
you see them. Give them a hug, too.
And Nate and Sam.
And little Rosie.

-B

Shit. She grabbed the first soft thing that came to her hand and swiped it across her sketchbook before the wetness that had dripped off her face could ruin the paper. She wiped her eyes, too, and then looked at what she had wiped them with—a four-day-old-dirty t-shirt. She sniffed it and crinkled her nose. God, she knew she should wash everything tonight, but she was Too. Wiped. Out. She'd just have to pick out the best of what she had for tomorrow. It would have to do.

She turned back to her sketchbook and tried to reread what she had written, but she couldn't focus on the words. All she saw were blurry scribbles and as she watched even those faded as her eyes sagged closed. She tried half-heartedly to snap them open again, but a mysterious force was pulling them down and she was powerless to stop it. She was only vaguely aware of the sensation of her body collapsing into the soft, warm sleeping bag that sat nestled in the center of an actual mattress—the first real bed she'd slept in for days. But she was just aware enough to appreciate the feeling of every muscle and every joint sighing in relief as she surrendered to a complete and welcome oblivion.

Aside from the gentle rise and fall of her chest, she lay motionless, the scattered contents of her duffle bag surrounding her like a hastily prepared nest. It was a familiar nest. It was the same nest that had been constantly dismantled and rebuilt over the years in a never-ending cycle of uprooting and displacement—a cycle that seemed to be the only constant in her life.

9

WPD BLUES

Monday, November 28th

Westbury Police Chief Summer Hannah contemplated the ripples radiating across the surface of her coffee. They were reflecting off the sides of her mug, generating a complex pattern of wavelets. A thin cloud of steam that wafted up from the hot liquid contributed to the illusion that she was looking at a miniature mountain lake with the morning fog rising off the warm water. Each time this imaginary scene started to diminish, it was renewed by the rumbling of a truck passing by outside the station as it set off a fresh set of ripples and steam.

She gave her head a little shake. It's just a cup of coffee, Summer, she thought to herself. She picked up the mug, took a sip, and closed her eyes as the hot liquid slid down her throat and spread warmth into her core. She opened her eyes again and faced reality. "Well, Ed. I guess our Thanksgiving respite is done. It's time to tackle the new week."

Officer Ed Simmons was sitting on his usual stool behind the tall front reception desk, a clipboard in his hand. He sighed and said, "Yep, afraid so. Unfortunately, this list looks just like it did before Thanksgiving, only a few days riper." He looked down at the list and continued, ticking off the items one by one, "Let's see. An angry town demanding answers followed by an out-of-state detective chasing a ghost followed by a search for a needle in a haystack followed by a request for school security followed by an obstinate State Police followed by a press conference with the mayor and governor. Yep, just another ordinary day here in Westbury." He plopped the clipboard down and looked at Chief Hannah. "Ugh. This must be what it's like to be a big city cop. What first, boss?"

Chief Hannah took another sip of coffee. What she really wanted first was for someone to magically appear and take over everything so she could put her full-time efforts into the search for a runaway girl—a beautiful young girl with a life ripe with potential ahead of her, a life and potential that was in danger of going off the rails and down a dark road—or even ending completely. Another young life cut short. As if there hadn't been enough lives cut short already. Christ, what was more important than preventing that? All this other crap was just politics. Unfortunately, there was no magical person, she was it, she knew it, and the best she could do was to get everything else out of the way as quickly as possible.

"Well, Ed, why don't you go and talk to the high school principal about setting up security at the school and I'll go talk to the mayor about the press conference. First, I'm going to badger the Feds about our missing minor requests and make sure they're on it. I'm also going to check in with Detective James to see if he has made any progress on Bronco."

Ed shook his head, "That effing Bronco. It's like he's always one step ahead. If even Rod can't find him, you gotta wonder what he's up to. I don't like it at all. He's the one we should be focusing on. Rod can just keep tabs on Babineau and his buddy Purcell."

"It's Detective James, not 'Rod'," said Chief Hannah, annoyed that she was annoyed because that is just what Ed wanted. "And I think they're all bad and there is more to it than we know. I mean, what are the chances of all these coincidences? I don't think they are coincidences. I sometimes feel like we're in the middle of some-body else's deadly game and we don't know what the rules are."

"So, *Detective James* told you that Bronco, aka William Farrell, just up and disappeared?" asked Ed.

"Yeah. Early in the fall apparently, right after he split from here. And he did it thoroughly, not leaving any breadcrumbs behind. At least not any Detective James has found yet. He said he's not at the end of his list, but he'd expected to find him by now."

Ed picked his buzzing phone off the desk and looked at the screen, "On another note, some good news. It looks like Amtrak responded to us. They said the security cam footage from the Rens-selaer station is getting archived and they'll send a link to it later today. Looks like they dug into their to-do list, too."

Chief Hannah felt her heart leap a little. She checked her phone and saw the same message. "It's funny—I shouldn't be looking forward to searching through hours of security cam record-ings, but the thought of catching a glimpse of Blue at that station excites me more than anything has in a week."

"I know what you mean," said Ed. "I just hope that girl, Hope, was right."

10

MESSAGE IN A BOTTLE

- - - - - - - - - - - - - - - -

Nov 29
Hey Blue,

I wish you could see how everyone is walking on air around here. Your Gmail message to Ma Beth made everyone so happy. Wu told me Ma Beth couldn't stop crying and smiling. Everyone is relieved. I can't believe you have a job and an apartment. I don't know how you're getting away with it, but I guess I shouldn't be surprised. You must have been lying your ass off!

So I said everyone is relieved but in fact, we're still all really worried about you. That whole thing about Babineau and the creepy guy watching you kind of shook everyone. Why would Babineau send someone after you? Is there something you know that threatens him? Detective James tried to explain something about "mob accounting" but it doesn't make sense to me. And then there's the other bombshell you don't know about—that Bronco turns out to be the son of "El Segador," the assassin sent to kill your family. And WTF? Why did you never mention that "Stanton" used to be your last name? And did you know that they actually made out a death certificate for "Blue Stanton"?

It's driving me crazy that I can't sit down and talk to you about this stuff. For all I know, you already know all this and probably even more. It's always hard to tell with you. Nothing would surprise me at this point.

BTW, Detective James is the NYPD guy who came up to interview you. I really think you'd like him. I think if you had met him you wouldn't have run away. He is really motivated to put Babineau and Bronco in jail and figure out exactly what happened the night your family died. He was one of the detectives on the case at the time and it was left open as a cold case. It was your picture in the paper that got it rolling again. So I guess in a way it was Jordy that got it going again. Maybe it was me that got it going again. I could've stopped Jordy and didn't. Fuck, this karma stuff is shit. I get going in circles about it and it drives me crazy.

It helps to talk to Mom and Anna and Wu, but then when I'm by myself, the karma cyclone starts spinning in my brain again. Writing here helps, but only so much. It really really sucks that you're not here. I just hope that you'll find a way to communicate with us. Please.

-Will

He dropped his pencil and rubbed his face with both hands hoping to wipe the frustration from his brain. Eleven days so far. Eleven days since the shooting, nine since Blue disappeared, five since Thanksgiving, and each day had been a different flavor of vanilla-normal mixed with chunks of fucked-up. He'd start to think he felt fine but then something would happen and suddenly he'd be reliving the shooting or racking his brain on how he could've prevented it or getting outraged at Blue for running away or getting angry at the police for not doing enough. So he would talk to his mom or write or distract himself by hanging out with Wu and playing video games or poker. But it wasn't enough to fill the whole day. And then there were the nights to deal with. Some nights he slept, and some nights were dark alleys of bizarre paranoia dreams where he'd wake up sweating.

He sighed and looked at the pile of books sitting next to his journal. His mom had put them there. "Get away from the internet and get sucked into a good novel. It's good medicine." He looked through the stack and thought, yeah, Mom, but some novels are just garbage. He spied an author he recognized and looked at the title: *The Good Shepherd*, a book he'd never read. Title seemed lame but it had a picture of a WWII destroyer on the cover, so it was worth a try.

He grabbed it and flopped onto his bed and within a few pages found himself drawn into the story of a person from a long time ago that was faced with the daunting task of protecting thousands of lives from an invisible menace that he had no power over and only very limited ability to detect.

Something he could totally relate to.

11

PACING THE CAGE

Tuesday, December 6th, 2011

B ronco closed the book he'd been reading and set it on the table next to his coffee. It was a bright morning made brighter by the sparkling light reflecting off the inch or so of fresh snow outside the big picture window. He took a sip of coffee and then held the warm mug against his cheek, staring at the cover of the book he'd just finished, *Worth Dying For*. It was a good book but not exactly worth dying for. Still, it was a bit of a letdown finishing it. It was the last book in the series and now he was going to have to find a new distraction. He shook his head in wonder at himself. He'd read more books these past couple of weeks than he had in his entire life.

The books had kept him from going nuts. The other stuff—ice fishing, messing with his weapons, watching streaming videos—all that could only fill a fraction of his time. And there hadn't been a peep from Babineau since he originally laid out Bronco's "mission." He was starting to wonder if maybe he should just take a chance and bail on Babineau. But to do that he'd have to bail on his gold, and he couldn't bring himself to give up on that yet. Maybe I should work a little harder on retrieving it before the ice is out, he thought.

He reached for his computer to see what kind of equipment and skills it would take to dive under the ice in a lake in the winter. What the hell, it might turn out to be an interesting new skill to learn, he thought, but when he flipped up the screen there was a new text waiting for him. A text was a rare thing for him because there were only two people that knew how to text him. One was Babineau. The other was his one trusted friend in NYC. The text was from his friend and what it said sent a chill through him: "NYPD is looking for you. Watch your ass."

12

TANTALIZING PEEK

Dec 7th
Hey Blue,

Something pretty cool happened today. Chief Hannah invited me over to the station. She had some security cam footage from the Rensselaer train station, and we saw you! It was surreal to actually see you for the first time in almost three weeks! And weird— it was like it wasn't the real you—just a movie of you—like the shadow you. We saw you walking around and then lying on a bench for a while and reading and then you left. And that was it. Out the door and nothing after that. Poof! Just like from here. You disappeared twice on us now. Chief Hannah is working on the theory that you stayed in the Albany area since they didn't see you come back into the station for any of the outbound trains after. Not that it makes much difference. Albany's a pretty frigging big haystack to hide a needle in. Still, it's better than searching the whole country. Nate thinks you're in Florida— claims you could have gotten a bus anywhere from Albany. He's

probably right about that last part, but not the Florida part. I've
got a feeling you're a lot closer than anyone thinks. I'd like to hope
so, anyway. Gotta go—I get to see a new shrink today. Mom
insists on it. I don't know, I feel fine most of the time now and am
sleeping pretty well. Except when I don't. Anyway, hope you're
safe. Hope you'll write somehow.

Will stared at what he wrote. His journal was supposed to be
where he got everything out of his head, where he could be honest
and know that no one would judge what he was writing or thinking. So why couldn't he write down the complete truth? He wasn't
fine most of the time so why did he write that he was?

And then it hit him. He was doing exactly what Blue had done.
He was just playing at "fine"—not only to everyone else, but to
himself. He grabbed his pen and scribbled down a final note:

Okay I get it now. I get you now. I'm NOT fucking fine. I'm
trying to be, and I'm doing better, but I still feel messed up for at
least a part of every day. Writing to you feels like the sanest thing
I do even though it seems insane. I just hope you're fine for real,
too. I hope Mom helped you. And I really hope you have someone
to talk to now.

Hope is good,
Miss you,
Will

13

NETFLIX

Dec 19th
Hey Will,

Today is one of my days off and I spent the whole day in bed. I guess that's partly because my bed is the only furniture in the room and partly because it's fucking arctic outside and my room just won't warm up and partly because—well mostly because I am fucking depressed. When I'm at work it's fine, the people there are great and I like a lot of the regulars, even the jerky ones, just because they're interesting and their chiss is epic. I've ditched my glasses for the most part because I like hearing the inner dialog going on at the diner. But today, there's nothing to do and nowhere to go. I can't go out because it's so fucking cold (have I mentioned how fucking cold it is?) and depressing because of all the Christmas decorations that are up making me homesick for the stupid elves they put on the lampposts in Westbury. Go throw a snowball at one for me. The wifi here sucks and ten other people are trying to use it at the same time. Flo's beau, Alan, says he'll fix it but not likely until after Christmas. I can't get through a movie without it hanging every five minutes. Flo invited me to their house for Christmas morning, and I'll go, but it won't be the same. Don't worry about me, though, depression isn't the worst thing I've dealt with. I'll get through it. If nothing else, I've got work all the way through Christmas and it's busier than ever, especially with the retirees tomorrow for "Senior Tuesday." Hah, of course you're not worrying 'cuz you're not reading this. Well, thanks for listening anyway.

Love, Blue

Blue closed the new spiral-bound journal she had purchased that afternoon at the little bookstore in town and slid the green tortoise-shell pen into the rings of the binding, clipping it to the top two rings. Together the pen and journal rested silently in front of her as she sat cross-legged on her comforter. Her little desk lamp was the only light on in her room. Its narrow beam illuminated her lap and journal, turning them into a bright little universe that hovered in the shadows adjacent to her window. Outside her window an iridescent flock of snowflakes danced quietly under the white glow of the streetlamp across the street, forming their own little universe.

A familiar tightness in her throat caused a little wateriness to squeeze out of her eyes. She brushed it away with one hand while her other hand slid down to her lap where it wound up resting on her journal. It felt unexpectedly solid under her hand, stabilizing her in a way she wasn't expecting.

Yeah, I'll get through this, she thought to herself. Between the bookstore, the art store, Flo's, and Netflix, she would make it through. She grabbed her laptop and doused her lamp, plunging the room into total darkness except for the rectangular glow of the laptop screen as it hiccupped its way through another choppy movie stream. She shivered and pulled the comforter around her, and without thinking, scooped up the journal and hugged it to her chest. Then she let her mind give in to the distraction of a two-dimensional actor on a flat screen who was dealing with a fictional disaster in a fictional world with a fictional ending where everything comes out just fictionally fine and dandy.

14

TINY HOLIDAY LIGHTS

It was dark in the office. Other than a few blinking holiday trinkets sitting on some of the other desks in the room, the only light was the lamp on his desk, illuminating the area around him like a little oasis. Outside the two windows on the far wall of the office he could see a few snowflakes flitting through the air the way they did in the walled canyons of the city—not straight down but in a flight pattern that defied physics, like many things that were defied by the city.

Rodney wasn't surprised by the judge's decision denying his warrant for William Farrell, but he had been irrationally hopeful. He had gone in pretty much empty-handed other than the hearsay from Chief Hannah—that Blue had shared information leading to the identification of Bronco. He had hoped to go in with a genealogy match based on Bronco's blood sample, but he had been unexpectedly stone-walled by the Vermont State Police. Apparently, someone, somewhere, had created some bad blood between the NYPD and the evidence room at Vermont State Police as they seemed to be deliberately creating a bureaucratic barrier around themselves. He shook his head in frustration.

He should go back to his apartment and at least think about the holiday spirit, not that he had anyone to share it with except his mom, who he would spend Christmas day with. There was the office party in a couple of days and that was something, at least. But his close friends had all moved into a different phase of life— married, kids, out of the city— and were all wrapped up in their own private family Christmas/Hanukkah/Kwanza gestalt lately. It was this time of year that made it way too apparent that he needed to get a life.

He looked at the phone on his desk—old-fashioned and hard-wired—and then looked up a number on his cell phone, leaned over to the desk phone, picked up the receiver, and punched the number into the keypad. He plunked his feet on the desk and leaned back into the shadow, his legs extending into the pool of light. He listened to the purr of the line as it rang a phone on the other end. There was a click and then, "Westbury PD, Chief Hannah speaking."

Rodney smiled, "Hi, Summer. I was hoping you'd still be there."

"You mean there are other places to be?"

He laughed.

15

CHRISTMAS

- - - - - - - - - - - - - - - -

Hey Blue,

Merry Christmas. I hope you are with good people today. Everyone is hoping for a message from you but I'm guessing we won't get one. No worries, just hope you're okay. It's kind of depressing here anyway. Since the memorial services for Mike and Peter and Alice and the awkwardness of the service for Jordy over Thanksgiving, everyone has been in kind of a weird mood. That and everyone is stir crazy because of school being closed for another month and the weather being pretty awful. Nate claims that you're probably soaking up the sun in Florida. Ah, Nate.

I should tell you about Jordy's service. It was pretty weird. No one seemed to know what to say and so no one said anything except the priest who hoped that Jordy would find forgiveness in heaven. Whatever that means. A lot of people are hoping he is burning in hell.

I did have another nightmare about the shooting, but I scrunched a pillow up next to me and pretended it was you and I went right back to sleep. Funny that I can write things like that in my journal but probably would never tell you to your face. Or anyone. I'd be too embarrassed. Maybe I'll need to burn this thing before anyone gets a chance to read it. Still don't understand why it feels good to write it down.

Anyway, Merry Christmas again. Stay warm. Still no news about Babineau, Purcell, or Bronco.

Love, Will

16

CHRISTMAS

- - - - - - - - - - - - - - - -

Dear Ma Beth, Pa Bill, Will, Rosie, Wu, Sam, Nate, Anna, Mr. and Mrs. Woods,

Merry Christmas, I hope . . .

Fuck. I can't do this.

17

A NEW YEAR

Jan 9th, 2012!
Hey Will,

I know it's been a while, but I just couldn't bring myself to write through the holidays. It was too depressing. I just read and drew and watched Netflix the whole time. I'm glad that's over. Things are quiet here and at Flo's now. I'm actually getting to know some of the regulars and on Saturday morning Sylvie popped in for breakfast. I don't think I told you about Sylvie. She was the desk clerk at the motel who found me sleeping in the linen cabinet and didn't bust me. This was back in November just after I got off the bus here in Malone. Yeah, I can say it in my journal, Malone, N.Y. Just writing it makes me nervous that someone will find me, but that's ridiculous. I've already mentioned Flo's diner to you, and it wouldn't take long to track me down with that. That's why I don't write to anyone for real. I would probably screw up and give myself away.

Anyway, Sylvie seems like a pretty amazing person, and she invited me to eat dinner Monday morning at her apartment. Yeah, I said dinner. Yeah, I said in the morning. Sylvie works the night shift at the motel, goes to classes in the morning, and goes to sleep around noon. Has breakfast at 11 pm and doesn't bother with 'lunch.' A lot different than my relatively normal 7 am to 2 pm shift. I am making a lot of money though. (Not wages! Flo pays me less than minimum wage, which is crap, but the tips are amazing). I also get a lot of food from the diner, so I don't spend much on food. Chet doesn't like wasting it and there's always a few leftovers that either go to me or the other waitresses. And since my rent is pretty cheap it looks like I'll be able to save up cash pretty quick. The other waitresses are pretty nice but it's usually just me and Flo in the mornings. I guess the real money in tips is at night, so the older waitresses get the later shifts. Other than that, it's pretty boring—just me and my books and drawing and computer.

Sylvie says she's going to talk me into taking a class or two at the community college, but I doubt I can fake my way into that. She said I could audit some courses—just sit and listen—as long as the professor was okay with it. It's kinda cool thinking about sitting in a college class with a real professor so maybe I'll do it. Everything will probably be way over my head, but hey, why not try it for free?

I guess I should tell you that I've also been looking into Babineau. I won't write down how I feel about that fucker because my notebook might spontaneously combust. I can't even think about the fact that he is free to walk the earth without wanting to explode myself. My favorite song right now is Bruce Cockburn "If I Had a Rocket Launcher." I try not to play it too much because then I get in an angry spiral for about an hour before I cool off. I swear, though, if I ever get the opportunity . . . and this is where you would try to calm me down and use logic and reason to explain why I should let the cops take care of it. And I would probably stomp off. Well, you're not here and you can't hear me, and so I am free to indulge in my fantasy without anyone spoiling it. So there. If I had a rocket launcher . . . some son-of-a-bitch would die! And burn and boil in hell.

Okay, I walked away and I'm cooled off now. If I ever feel comfortable Gmailing again, I'll let you and everyone else know how much I miss them. Life here isn't terrible and it's getting less lonely, but it's not the same. It's late, I've got an early shift tomorrow.

G'night.

She closed the journal and flopped onto her back letting her breath out in a huff. She had lied to her journal. She had lied to virtual Will. She had lied to herself: she wasn't cooled off, but she wasn't cross-eyed with rage anymore either. Instead, her brain was in a hot zone, wrestling with a memory—a memory of that night—a memory of a face bathed in a fiery orange glow, staring out the back window of a car retreating down their driveway.

This memory, along with a number of other flashes of memory about that night, had come back to her spontaneously and sporadically, sometimes when she was half asleep, sometimes when she was fixing dinner, sometimes when she was walking to work. It was as if that closed-off area of her brain had started shedding its secrets, like bits of scab coming off a nasty scrape as the skin healed underneath. The thing about it was, they didn't seem to be yanking that panic chain like her old nemesis had—her dreaded night visitor, her nightmare replay of that night. The panic had been replaced by something much less acute, something tolerable, a mental state that was a blend of melancholy, sadness, and anger.

She wasn't sure exactly how or why this was happening. Maybe it was triggered by her running away, or living in an entirely new place, or meeting new people, or maybe it was because her sessions with Dr. Woods had started a healing process that had taken off on its own. Or maybe it was just that she had so much more time to sit around and think. It didn't matter. All she knew was that her nightmare had lost its grip on her and for the first time, she had been able to relive it while staying calm and rational and it was slowly piecing itself together into a more complete picture of what happened that night.

The reappearance of that face in the car window was what was bugging her. If Babineau was behind her family's murder and the face in the window was one of the accomplices, then she shouldn't be feeling what she was feeling now—the sense that the person was someone she knew. She was so young at the time that she had no context for understanding the *chiss* she heard from that face then, and now time had diminished the recollection. But what remained disturbed her. It was like when you hear a voice and it sounds like someone familiar, so it brings them to mind, but you know it couldn't possibly be that person. What her mind couldn't grasp was that the person in the car sounded like—their *chiss* felt like—it was from someone who it couldn't possibly have come from: Bronco. It couldn't possibly have been Bronco, not only because it would be an insanely improbable coincidence, but because the *chiss* emanating from this face, this memory, faint as it was after the passage of so much time, was undeniably laden with remorse.

18

WACKY WHS

– – – – – – – – – – – – – – –

Jan 18th
Hey Blue,

So school reopened today and it was pretty effing weird. For starters, you have to walk through a metal detector to get inside. Yeah, that's right, a metal detector. And there's a security officer to check your backpack. We had to stand forever in the cold to get in. First period class was basically a joke because they couldn't get everyone in on time. Chief Hannah stood outside with us and pretty much kept everyone from rioting. She apologized and said things would smooth out, but this was the best they could do in the short amount of time after the school board decided it had to be done. There is apparently one raging right-wing school board member that was a butt-hole about it and wouldn't give it up until it passed. The crazy bastard even wanted to arm the teachers! Chief Hannah didn't tell us this, but the story got around. I kind of feel sorry for her because it wasn't her fault, and I don't think she wanted to see it come to this.

Anyway, the rest of the school day actually went pretty much as normal except that the lockers in front of the cafeteria (mine) moved. So now my locker is in the hall by the gym and lunch is in the gym now, too. The old cafeteria is walled off for construction. Rumor has it that they are going to turn it into an expanded library. They are going to have an assembly Friday to talk about the shooting and the new security rules. Fortunately, they didn't pass a proposal to put security cameras inside. I think there would have been a revolt if they had.

Wu is psyched because basketball started up again. They spotted us four games in division 2 to let us catch up. I've decided not to play the rest of JV this year to have more time to let my arm flexibility get better.

But there is also some bad news. Bronco still hasn't been found. Detective James said that he didn't have any leads on where he might have gone yet. Apparently he expected to find him pretty quickly because of Chief Hannah's discovery that he is really William Farrell and William Farrell had lived for a long time in NYC. Well, apparently William Farrell up and disappeared shortly after our little encounter with "Bronco." One theory is that he got out of the country. Apparently he had a good chunk of money from an inheritance and that money was all cashed out last fall. That means he could be anywhere, but Detective James is still pretty confident that they'll find him.

You, on the other hand, are proving to be hard to find. The FBI (yeah, FBI!) couldn't even figure out where you went after the train station. What's got everyone scratching their heads is that with your picture splattered all over the news during that week everyone figured you'd have been spotted by now. Which makes me wonder what you did to camouflage yourself. God, I hope it wasn't too drastic. Did you go Goth? Punk? I'm trying to imagine a flock-of-seagulls haircut on you. Gah! Or lipstick?

Well, anyway, half of me hopes you get found and half of me is hoping you stump everyone. No, forget that. All of me wishes you were here and all of me wishes that Babineau, Bronco, and Purcell all have heart attacks and die. Okay. On to really weird day number two at RWWHS.

-W

19

BECKY

B lue closed her eyes as she tied her apron around her back.
With her eyes plunged into darkness, she was no longer
distracted by the sights and *chiss* that floated non-stop in the
crowded little building and could thus immerse herself for a
moment in the motley, yet comforting, mixture of sounds and
smells that were packed inside the silver-shelled diner. It was a
sharp contrast to the quiet hermitage of her tiny apartment or the
long cold walk through her neighborhood and then out onto Route
11 and the busy early morning traffic. Here, the air was warm and
full—saturated with the scents of fried potatoes, coffee, waffles,
syrup, a touch of sudsy steam from the dishwasher, and a hint of
smoke from the hot griddle—all accompanied by hisses, clinks,
sizzles, and the murmur of distant morning conversations. The
background music from the ceiling speakers completed the
comfortable atmosphere.

Flo used to insist on playing 80's top 100 in the morning until
the staff revolted and hid her CDs. An armistice ensued and now
there was a rotation. This morning it was Chet's choice and he had
selected some classical music which raised the eyebrows of
everyone—including the customers—until everyone realized the

transformation that came over the diner. It felt calmer, more sophisticated. Everyone seemed to be more courteous than usual. The music also provided a new source of amusement for the staff after Flo waved them over to the kitchen plate-pass window and pointed to Chet, who was humming and swaying and swinging his spatula like an orchestra conductor, unaware that he was being observed.

"Table two food's up and there's a solo at the window table."

Flo's reprimanding voice knocked Blue out of her momentary reverie. She shook her head and opened her eyes, turning to Flo.

"Sorry!" she said as she stepped toward the pass window for the waiting plates for table two. She grabbed them and headed for the dining room with Flo shaking her head behind her. As she wound her way to table two, she glanced toward the front of the diner. Sitting in the booth under the front window was a girl, maybe late teens, maybe early twenties. Blue's immediate thought was that she was looking at herself in a few years. This startling insight rattled her for a moment. She studied the girl closer. Dark hair, silver nose-stud, well-worn jeans adorned with patches artfully embroidered around the edges, a dark heavy knit sweater, a blue turtleneck with a butterfly tat peeking out the top, a tiny bit of mascara around the eyes, but no lipstick. The girl looked lost in thought, looking out the window, chin in hand, her head bobbing up and down as she chewed her gum.

Blue dropped the plates off at table two and then wound her way over to the girl's booth and as she did, the girl turned. She looked Blue up and down.

"Looks like Flo resorted to robbing the cradle," the girl said, resuming her gum-chewing with a *chiss*, "Woo, CHECK OUT THAT BLEACH JOB!"

This double-barreled frank observation caused Blue to pause her stride just a little. She felt her brow crease but managed to ask, politely, "Can I get you some coffee?"

"Yeah, but don't waste the green pot on me. The swill works just fine." The girl laughed, "Don't look so surprised! I used to work here."

Blue's brow went from creased to raised. "You're Becky," she said.

"Bingo boingo!" said Becky as she reached over and checked the sugar bowl and the cream pot. "And when you get the coffee you can bring some more cream. I need lots of cream." She looked back at Blue. "And you can take my—"

"Waffles," interrupted Blue. "Belgian waffles with real maple syrup and lots of butter." She wrote it down on her pad and smiled in satisfaction at the look of surprise on Becky's face. She didn't wait for Becky to respond, she just turned and headed for the kitchen, clearing a dirty table as she went, without looking back.

"I see you've met Becky," said Flo as Blue entered the kitchen with her load of dishes. "She's a piece of work, God bless her." She said this as she unloaded some dishes from the dishwasher. "There is a good kid buried inside her, though. Just doesn't come out right away."

Blue put the dishes from the cleared table in the dirty dish tub and as she rinsed her hands, she turned her head to Flo.

"Why did you let her go?" she asked.

Flo had grabbed a couple of plates of food from the kitchen and was ready to head out to the dining room, but she stopped just short of the door.

"I couldn't afford her," she said in a tone that was tinged with past disappointment, and then in a calmer voice, she continued. "You probably think I'm pretty flush, owning a restaurant and all, but let me tell you. This is a gritty business. I'm barely getting by. When push comes to shove, you can't always put likes over needs. I like Becky, but I can't afford 'like.' I need 'reliable.'" She nodded at Blue. "You are reliable. Becky wasn't."

Flo moved toward the dining room door and then stopped again. She looked at Blue and said, "Sometimes I get lucky—I get 'reliable' and 'likable' in the same package." She winked as she turned and disappeared through the doorway, meals in hand.

Chet, the cook, stepped over to Blue as she was drying her hands. He was chuckling. "Flo seems hard but she's a softy. You know she has a daughter?"

Blue nodded and the nod turned to a shake as she thought about the night she spent in Flo's daughter's old room.

"Yeah, they didn't get along so good. Her daughter, Sofie, ran off to stay with her deadbeat dad in Ohio. Flo takes it pretty hard. I think she tries to make up for it by mothering you guys."

Blue gave him a puzzled look. "Us guys?"

"Yeah, you and Becky. She likes you." Chet smiled. "She likes you, but she'll let you go in a heartbeat if you mess up. Don't worry, though, it would take a lot to mess up. Becky messed up pretty bad, but she's pretty messed up."

"Messed up?"

Chet shook his head. "Aww, I shouldn't really be getting into it. I'll just tell you that she showed up the same way you did—off the bus, on the move, maybe running from something." He paused and shook his head again, "Eh, I've said enough." He turned away to the kitchen and said over his shoulder as he went, "These waffles will be up in a second."

Blue grabbed the green pot and headed back out to the dining room. Flo was just turning away from Becky's table and shaking her head with a grim look on her face. Becky was staring fiercely after her, chewing hard on her gum. Blue walked up and poured the coffee, the rich Sumatran aroma wafting into her nose.

Becky was staring after the retreating Flo but turned suddenly as the aroma reached her. She didn't say anything. She just dragged the sugar bowl over and started spooning sugar into the coffee. She followed the sugar with a generous dose of cream.

"I told you not to waste the good stuff on me," she said, and then she gulped down half the cup and held it out for a refill. "Man, I needed that."

Blue refilled her cup and Becky started spooning in more sugar. It was mesmerizing. Who could handle that much caffeine and sugar? Blue felt her teeth buzzing just imagining the rush that Becky must be getting.

Becky looked Blue up and down again, her *chiss* whispering, "SHE COULD REPLACE NINA, MAYBE." "You know, you could be making a lot more money than you are here. It takes some guts, but no special skills."

Blue had turned to go to the next table, but she hesitated. "What are you talking about?"

Becky smirked and shook her head. "Never mind. Just look me up if you start to get tired of Flo's bossiness."

"Look you up?"

"Yeah, I'm around." Becky's right leg started bouncing up and down rapidly and she looked intently toward the kitchen. "Chet just put my waffles up. I'm starving."

The realization of what Becky might be suggesting hit her like a brick. She felt a flush rising in her face, and she turned quickly away and made her way back to the kitchen where Flo was standing in the doorway, with a look and posture that was the perfect model of a disapproving mother. "Did Becky order waffles? God, the last thing she needs is more sugar in her system." She turned and looked hard at Blue and said, "I'd stay away from her." Then she abruptly brushed past and into the dining room.

Blue looked over at Chet who glanced at her and shrugged. He pointed at the plate-pass window indicating that the waffles were up. Blue grabbed them and took them out to Becky.

"Oh God, I miss Chet's waffles," said Becky, but Blue had already turned and walked away. That was the last thing that was said between them. Becky left a spotless plate and empty sugar bowl and disappeared without waiting for the check, but she left a twenty on the table. The bill was only $8.50. Blue studied the twenty before picking it up. It looked like an ordinary twenty but this one had an aura about it, like touching it might put a curse on her. A call from Chet in the kitchen meant another order was up. She paused just one more second and then snatched up the twenty, pinching it inside the check so her fingers wouldn't touch it. She dropped them both on the register as she passed by, ignoring the concerned look on Flo's face.

20

CAMARO

One month later, Feb 14th
Schroon Lake, New York

Detective Rodney James cursed for at least the tenth time as he extracted himself from the awkwardly angled black hulk that was once a sleek Camaro. He paused to examine the tear in his trousers, noticing a splotch of blood that must have come from a cut, though he couldn't feel it. His skin was anesthetized by the frigid wind piercing his ill-considered city garb. The notion that he might die foaming at the mouth from tetanus hovered in the back of his mind, but his bigger concern was navigating back through the junkyard without killing himself outright, impaling himself on any of the countless shards of broken metal littered across his path back to the yard entrance.

When he had made the decision to follow up on Chief Hannah's suggestion, he wondered if either of them knew it was going to involve him picking through jagged metal in the freezing cold in an upstate New York junkyard with numb fingers and bleeding shins. It had all started when he called her with the bad news that his boss had called off the surveillance of Babineau and

Purcell due to his lack of hard evidence thanks to the stubborn Vermont State Police dragging their feet on the blood sample.

"You know," she had said, "you might be better off finding the car itself. It was registered in New York. You might be able to get a DNA sample from it."

"I thought about that," he had said, "but as you know when I dug into Farrell's DMV record, the car was totaled last summer, and he never registered a replacement. That's one of the main reasons he's been hard to track down."

"But the car still exists," she had said with a bit of incredulity like he was overlooking something that should be obvious.

He had replied patiently, "Um, not likely. Junk cars don't hang around long, at least not in New York. They go straight to the shredder these days. If he was as smart as you've told me, he would have made sure it did. A lot of potential evidence winds up in the shredder before we can get our hands on it."

"Mmmm. Maybe in the city," she had said. "Us poor mountain folk don't have shredders. We have junkyards."

He had to give it to her. She was right about that. When he dug a little deeper and called the Essex County sheriff that had written the accident report, he found that the sheriff had a deal with a junkyard in Schroon Lake to haul off car wrecks. A call to the junkyard confirmed that the car still existed. That Camaro was apparently a plum for the junk dealer and what hadn't been parted out now sat before him, covered with a layer of mid-winter hard-crusted snow.

"Find anything?" This came from the yard manager who was hanging out a dozen yards away at a gap in the chain-link fence that marked the entrance. The guy was almost as obstinate as the Vermont State Police, initially refusing to let him in the yard, and then, when threatened with obstruction, unlocked the yard, and said, "Knock yourself out." Rodney found it very odd and irritating behavior for a man that makes his living selling parts extracted from the mass of wreckage in the yard.

"A lot of snow and broken glass," he replied. He decided the guy didn't deserve a more detailed answer which would have included, "A lot of your dirty fingerprints smearing anything that might have been useful." The guy also didn't deserve to know that yes, indeed, he may have found the motherlode: a used gauze dressing stuck against one of the floorboards. It had somehow survived being submerged without having lost all the blood it had absorbed— more than enough for a DNA comparison. It was almost certainly a dressing Bronco had used for his gunshot wound. If it panned out, and he was pretty certain it would, that alone would make this trip and his shredded pants worthwhile.

He turned around and took a few pictures of the car and as he did he played out the accident in his head. The crush points in the front right and back left corners showed how the car must have tumbled end-over-end before dropping into the lake. Either of those impacts could've been the reason the windshield had popped, assuring that the heavy car would sink rapidly yet allow an escape route for the driver. It also would have been an easy pathway for much of the contents of the car to spill out.

There was nothing left in the car now except for trash and this gauze pad. What hadn't fallen into the lake was certainly gleaned from the interior and long gone, sold by the junkyard man. As for what might have fallen in the lake, he shook his head. There was no way he could justify dredging for anything else that might be evidence, at least not at this point. And not at this time of year. Not from what he saw when he drove past the site of the accident before he came to the junkyard. There was a section of gleaming new guardrail right at the tightest point of that wicked curve at Eagle Lake, but instead of sparkling water beyond, there was a sheet of solid ice peppered with fishing shanties. He could call some divers in to look, but it would be a tough sell coercing them to dive under the ice in January. As he passed by, he had half a notion to stop and ask the ice fisherman if they had pulled up anything interesting other than fish.

Of course, that would have been foolish and impulsive, but perhaps not as impulsive as his side trip to the Stanton homestead. That is, the former Stanton homestead. He didn't know what he had expected to accomplish there—some divine inspiration that would give him some insight and guidance in this crazy case, perhaps—the long shot that Blue DuBois wound up there when she ran away, though that had been checked into already.

When he got to the homestead, the site itself was completely devoid of any trace of the old buildings and in their place was—no surprise—new high-end construction that was apropos for the area, at least that's what it looked like from the road. He didn't examine it closely as he recalled the treacherous driveway and considered the complete inadequacy of his sedan in the snow and the remoteness of the location. He just observed from afar, peeking through the bare trees with binoculars.

Perhaps that's what he took away most from the visit—an appreciation for the utter remoteness and isolation that the Stantons' had chosen for their new life and new identity in witness protection. And it was ideal for Samuel Stanton (aka André DuBois) and his continued pursuit of marijuana cultivation, a pursuit Rodney had recently gained a new appreciation for.

"You're just biased because you're a cop," his best friend, Hector, had told him. "You just aren't willing to bend your mind a little and think that maybe, just maybe, this shouldn't be an illegal drug." What could he say? He wasn't keen on chasing marijuana convictions, it was a waste of his time, but the law was the law except, perhaps, in Hector's case. How could he help but overlook the fact that his best friend since kindergarten was a stoner? How many times could he have booked him for possession? More times than he was willing to think about. And now he had let Hector talk him into giving it a try.

"You got to try it, man. I'm tired of you cranking about your arthritis all the time." So he did try it and it helped. And apparently, that was DuBois' specialty—a strain of pot for pain relief. He learned that not through Hector but through retired Detective Harris, his mentor.

"André was an honorable guy," Harris had told him. "He was mainly interested in developing strains for alleviating chronic pain. He just didn't have a good grasp of how heartless and brutal bureaucracies and cartels can be when it comes to illicit drugs, and he got crushed between them."

And this was the result. DuBois' presence was erased from the earth right down to the last board and nail. Except for one daughter.

A sudden gust of wind bit into his face and sent a bitter chill down his back bringing him back to the present. He stepped away from the snow-covered wreck and picked his way back to the gate.

"Thanks," he said to the yard manager. For being an unhelpful ass, he thought to himself. He brushed past the manager and as his thoughts turned away from the car and to his trip home, he became aware that he was shivering. He cursed under his breath and made a beeline to his car, every inch of his skin now craving to be rescued from the cold with a blast from the car's heater.

As he sat steaming in the idling car with the heater on as high as it would go, he scrolled through the pictures he had just taken. A black American sports car with aluminum wheels and New York plates (gruffly confirmed by the yard man) and enough left of the car that he was confident Chief Hannah's farmer witness could confirm it was the same as the one stored in his barn last summer. With that and a positive match on the blood sample, he hoped he would have a compelling enough argument for a judge, allowing him to get a warrant for William Farrell on the suspicion that he was wanted in Vermont under the name of Bronco, aka Bob Kelly.

More importantly, he hoped it would be enough to convince Chief Daniels to reactivate surveillance on Babineau and Purcell. It would be a hard sell—dedicating resources to monitoring the movements of two people was not cheap or easy. He was hesitant himself to push hard for it—it was a long shot that they would be able to track them to either Bronco or Blue. But thinking about Blue out there on her own and vulnerable, it was worth the long shot. After all, what other leads did they have? Nothing.

"It would make everyone's life easier if you just showed up on your own, Blue," he said out loud to the empty car interior. On the other hand, he couldn't help but admire her gutsiness. Well, all we can do is what we can do until then, he said to himself. He put the car in gear and headed back to the city, looking forward to getting in a nice hot shower.

21

SETTLED IN

- - - - - - - - - - - - - - -

Feb 15
Dear Will,

I can't believe it's been a month since I wrote to you in my jour-
nal. I did send another email to Ma Beth. FWIW used Hotmail
this time. Call me paranoid. Sorry I didn't send anything to the
rest of you. Well, I'm not really sorry. It just kind of would not
have been helpful for me. It makes me sad, and I feel like things
are moving on. I'm pretty settled here, and I think I could stay
here quite a while. Sylvie has turned into a pretty good friend. I
also have a pretty good customer friend named Jeremy. He's
retired and in his seventies but a really sweet guy that comes in
every Tuesday for breakfast and he loves to tell me about the old
days.

You'd be amused to know that I've turned a little nerdy—I'm
playing Realms of Zokar (!) Sam would be thrilled. I saw his
avatar online which made me kind of giddy and sad at the same

*time. Maybe I'll do a quest with him when I get better. My avatar
is called Snow Princess—yeah a little girly but also no chance
anyone would guess it's me.*

*And in other news . . . believe it or not, I audited a sociology class
at the community college for a couple of weeks and it was very
interesting and actually not that hard to understand. I stopped
going just because they were getting into some workshop stuff
and I didn't want to get involved with that.*

*The thing is, everything here is drama-free. I'm not putting
anyone in danger and bad stuff doesn't seem to be happening to
me. Why would I give that up? It's what I've always wanted. I
have an apartment, I have enough to eat, I have enough money,
and I live alone. I don't have the DFC hanging over my head or
police or Bronco's ghost or Babineau's goons. What more do I
need?*

-B

Yeah. What more do I need? She read over her note again and
ticked off her life list: I have a job, have an apartment, have enough
money, and left my troubles behind. Everything she had yearned
for. Reinventing herself like this was the first time in her life she felt
in control. So why wasn't it enough to quell the annoying question
echoing in her head, "Why do I feel so numb?"

22

OVERLORDS

- - - - - - - - - - - - - - - -

Feb 28
Dear Blue,

Wow. My last journal entry was in January. I can't believe it. I guess high school kind of engaged again and I went on automatic. Back to the school routine. I can't believe how normal everything is here. It's like the shooting never happened. Even the security stuff has kind of become normal. It's scary how fast that happened. It makes you wonder. I mean there are still counselors around and at assemblies they stepped up the "see something, say something" message, but other than that, all the normal social garbage is back. Nobody asks about you anymore. It's just like you said the night before you left—after a couple of months everything will be back to its dysfunctional self. Everyone will have forgotten about you and then it's over. But it isn't over. Not for anyone that matters. Everyone that matters wants you back. Wu, Nate, Sam, Rosie, Ma Beth, Pa Bill, Anna, me. We miss you!! We'll never get back to anything normal until you're here. Every day seems like there is something missing. I wish there was a way to let you know. Especially let you know about something that's developing with the DFC. Wu said Ma Beth and Pa Bill have been talking to them and meeting them in Burlington. I think something big is happening with the whole custody thing. Not sure what it is, but it sounds like it would take the DFC out of the picture, in a good way that is. Sam and Nate and Wu seem pretty excited about it. That means the whole DFC overlord thing might go away, which means that problem would be out of the way. If only there was a way to let you know. . .

Will

23

KUMAR

The next day
New York City

"You see, it is all very much here in the header. And please, could you not smoke in here."

Babineau's eyebrows rose ominously at Kumar's audacity, a warning sign for anyone who knew him, but apparently completely lost on Kumar, who just kept rattling on.

"You see, of all the people she would be emailing, the woman she calls 'Ma Beth'—a very curious name, by the way, I have never heard of anyone being called that—anyway this woman's password is very typical of people that are not technically sophisticated. It was a simple matter of looking at some of the easy combinations of birthdates and anniversaries and children's names that people use —it only took two or three days—and I was able to determine her password and log into her email without her ever knowing it and there it was. And please do not do that, you could start a fire."

Babineau's eyebrows rose for the second time. He had tapped his cigar out using the trashcan next to Kumar's desk. "There what was?" asked Babineau, a tinge of annoyance in his voice.

"I just told you," said Kumar, acting annoyed himself, "the header. The IP address of the originating server!"

"I thought you said that was useless, that the server was some giant googolplex server or something."

Kumar sighed, "Yes, the Google Gmail server. Yes, that is completely anonymous, very secure. But you see, she used a different service for the second email—Hotmail—and you see Hotmail includes the entire path in the header, all the way to the first server in the chain."

"And you say that is somewhere in Franklin County, in northern New York."

"That is correct. In fact, very precisely, it is in Chateaugay, New York."

"So the girl is in Chateaugay, New York."

"No, she is in Franklin County, New York."

Babineau felt a flush starting to rise to his face. "But you just said Chateaugay!"

"Yes! That is where the *originating server* is, however, the server covers subscribers all over Franklin County. She could be anywhere in Franklin County."

Babineau really wanted to relight his cigar, if for no other reason than to annoy Kumar as much as Kumar was annoying him. But now that he finally understood what Kumar was saying, he kept his temper under control.

"Okay. So there is no more information that could give us a tiny bit more precision than a needle in a 1000 square mile haystack?"

"Well, we do know from her email that she has a job, and there is a limit to the number of jobs available for a young woman, especially in such a remote area. I don't know about your country but in India, those jobs are often menial and in farms or factories."

Kumar wasn't wrong, there was a severe limit to the options for a girl of fifteen in an area like that, at least jobs that wouldn't ask questions. And thanks to the fact that there wasn't a lot to do in the Adirondacks in the winter, he had several suppliers up there doing a brisk business and they would know all the street girls.

"All right, Kumar. Keep working to see if you can come up with any other info. Maybe there are some hints in this 'Macbeth' person's emails."

"Oh no, not 'Macbeth,' it is 'MA' . . . 'BETH'," said Kumar, but he was speaking to Babineau's back as he had already stepped out of the little windowless cubby office and started walking purposefully toward his own spacious office, taking the time to re-light his cigar on the way.

24

JEREMY

One week later, Tuesday, March 6th
Malone, New York

Jeremy Hector Baker lay on his back staring into the nothingness that was his ceiling. It had slowly changed from nearly black to a light gray in a period of time that could have been ten minutes, could have been hours. He took a deep breath and let it out slowly. He might as well get up, he thought. Jesus Christ, he'd been awake since 3 am. Same thing every morning since he'd turned—what, sixty? seventy? Sleeping through the night? Hah! That was a fond memory—waking up at 8 am, thoroughly rested. Those were the days. If he'd known what it would be like now, he would have spent a little more time each morning back in the day, enjoying the sensation.

Back in the day. Back in the day. What day was it today anyway, he wondered? He forced himself to slide his legs out from under the covers and push himself upright. He looked at the clock again. 6:24 am. Well, that was a bit of good news, at least. He'd managed to hang in there for a few extra hours. He wagged his head back and forth trying to wake up his brain. C'mon, Jeremy, he thought, get the blood moving. You're only seventy-four for God's sake, it's not like you're on your death bed.

He took a couple more deep breaths and then stood up and shuffled toward the bathroom. He looked at the calendar tacked to the door and remembered. Today is Tuesday. Thank-God Tuesday. He felt a little better. Tuesdays were always good days. Tuesday was really the start of the week for him. It was the one day that gave him the energy to drag himself through the rest of the monotonous week. He stepped into the bathroom, turned on the light, and looked in the mirror at the haggard old man that stared back at him. His face looked a little better than it did most days because it had a smile on it today.

He brushed his teeth and put on deodorant twice, just to make sure. Didn't want to smell like old man today, he thought. He pulled on some clean pants. He sniffed the armpits of his best shirt before putting it on and then took a final look in the mirror. Put a brush through that hair, old man, he said to himself. Don't want to look like street trash.

When he finally was satisfied, he put on his coat and stepped outside into the crisp morning air. The walk to Flo's was brisk but it wasn't brisk enough to flush all the morning fuzziness out of his head. There was only one thing that could do that: He needed coffee.

He pushed through the familiar diner door and walked into the warmth and aroma of Tuesday morning at Flo's. The tinkle of silverware, the murmur of small talk, the sizzle of food on the grill, and the luscious smell of the diner combined to create a delightful symphony that almost made him do a little dance step. He slid into his usual spot, right under the neon sign, and as he took off his coat, a cup of coffee magically appeared in front of him. He stopped moving, his coat half off, and closed his eyes as the luxurious aroma wafted over him. He breathed deep and sighed. This was not the swill from the big coffee station that Flo served the drive-throughs. This was the special pot from the kitchen. The green pot.

The Sumatran dark. Flo may have put on the guise of a diner queen, but she knew good coffee and she knew her regular customers.

"God bless you, dear. This is a breath of fresh air from heaven." He didn't even need to open his eyes to know that it was Sam that had put the cup before him. He looked anyway just to watch as her bleach blond hair, highlighted by a dark swath of grown-out hair at the part line, swayed and bobbed as she wove through the tables on her way back to the kitchen.

He finished taking off his coat and closed his eyes again as he lifted the steaming cup to his nose. It was the simple things in life that gave him pleasure now. The aroma of really good coffee in the morning. The simple comfort of walking into a diner where the people knew him. The joy of eating a really well-prepared breakfast. Didn't matter that he could only afford it once a week. It was enough. It made all the other days that weren't Tuesday bearable.

He tipped the last drops of coffee out of the mug and as he lowered it, there was Sam, standing right in front of him, pot in hand. He put his mug down. She filled it to the brim and sat the pot on the table while she pulled a pad and pen out of her apron. She studied him carefully.

"What do I look like this morning, Sam?" he asked.

Sam tapped her pencil pensively on her pad. "You look like you want a stack of blueberry pancakes with big slabs of butter and a half-gallon of maple syrup, but you know deep down that what you really need is some scrambled eggs and sausage. No hash browns. Look at that belly!"

His laugh came straight from his belly, and he said loudly over her shoulder, "Flo, you aren't paying this girl enough!"

A husky voice from the kitchen replied, "I'm paying her too much already! Pretty soon she'll be driving around in a Porsche, and I'll still be driving my rusty POS Chevy!" A head with brown hair and a strong-featured face appeared in the kitchen doorway and continued, "And you should stop tipping her so much. You're going to spoil the girl."

He winked at Sam and said, "You're worth it. So what am I actually going to have this morning?"

Sam scribbled something down on her pad and then stuffed it and the pencil into her apron pocket. "You're having two scrambled eggs, *no* cheese, a *single* patty of maple sausage, some orange juice and..." She picked up the coffee pot and topped off his cup, "One *small* blueberry pancake."

"Well, bless you, mother Sam. I don't know how you do it, but you nail it every time." He looked up at her and gave her the warmest smile he could muster. It wasn't hard because it was sincere. This child was a wonder. He had no doubt that if he were fifty years younger, he would have fallen for her. As an old man, though, all he felt was affection and admiration. This was no coddled airhead, this was a solid young woman with her head screwed on straight. And she had a kind of feminine perception that you just didn't run across very often. Those kinds of girls didn't grow on trees. Especially nowadays. But she was young, oh so young.

She gave him a half-smile in return.

"You have to work on that smile, though, Sam. Only half your face seems to know how it works. Does the other half ever give it a go?" He immediately regretted his words as her look grew suddenly distant. The half-smile seemed to lose its energy, though it didn't go away.

"Sometimes," she said. "Just not recently."

"I'm sorry. That wasn't very polite of me." Her smile looked like it might collapse completely, and she abruptly turned away and headed for the kitchen. "Hey, you okay?" he called after her.

She stopped and turned, and as she turned, her eyes caught the light just so. It was like she had a ring of fire inside her eyes. It was just a flash, but nothing like he'd ever seen in his life. The expression on her face was clearly struggling to suppress something.

Happiness? Sadness? Both? After a moment of hesitation, she said, "Don't worry about me, I'm fine." Then she turned and disappeared into the kitchen.

Nice job, Jeremy, he thought. Way to screw up Thank-God Tuesday. He pulled his wallet out and looked inside. Looked like he could at least leave a bit extra in the tip today. A good extra bit. It might make up a little for him being such an ass.

25

REALITY REDUX

The following weekend, March 11th

Blue surveyed her miniature kingdom as she munched on a bite of steak. Even though it was a day old, it was still delicious. Chet was always giving her bits of leftovers at the end of her shift. She turned the leftovers into her dinners and managed to stretch them into at least one or two more meals.

Her kingdom, the little one-room flat she had called home for the past few months, was in a giant, ancient wood-frame house. At first, she didn't think much about the building other than it was old and run down but bit by bit she noticed some details that weren't typical of the average run-down building. In fact, it must have been quite eloquent in its time—she could see the remnants of ornate trim under its faded peeling paint—but its heyday was long past. Its once spacious living space was now chopped into small cubby-like apartments inhabited by the people living hand-to-mouth— the people who served coffee, cleaned houses, dug ditches, washed dishes, bagged groceries. People like her who couldn't afford anyplace better.

Flo's beau, Alan, at Flo's insistence had forgone the usual first and last month's rent and deposit and let Blue stay there month-to-month, as long as she paid cash at the end of the month. Another blessing as her ready cash had been in very short supply when she stepped off the silver Greyhound weeks ago. More than weeks ago, months ago, she realized.

The room was tiny, but it suited her. In one corner was a kitchenette with a small sink, a small under-counter fridge, and a two-burner stove. In the corner across from the kitchenette, there was just enough room next to the hall door to tuck in a dresser and a mirror. A single ladder-back chair sat next to the dresser and was piled high with her dirty clothes. Then came the door to the bathroom which had a sink, toilet, and shower all crammed into a space that could be generously described as a large closet. When she sat on the toilet, her knees rested partially under the corner of the sink, where her right knee would lean against the cold and sweating drainpipe. There was something about that sensation that freaked her out. She had finally gotten fed up and wrapped a towel around it, securing the towel with a broken shoelace.

The door to the bathroom barely cleared the foot of her bed, which dominated the wall under the only window. This was where she really lived. Her bed was her couch, her desk, her easy chair, her art studio, her dining room table, and, of course, her bed. It was more of her world than anything else right now, except when she was at work. She spent a lot of time on that bed. Alone. No one to bother her. Just what she always wanted. It was remarkable how quickly it had become a new normal for her. She wasn't sure how she felt about that—it seemed wrong for her previous life to have faded into the past so quickly.

She ate the last bite of steak, picked up the plate, and got off the bed, needing only one step to get to the little sink. She rinsed off the plate and fork with soapy water, dried them, and sat them on the counter. It was Sunday evening, the end of the first day of her weekend. Nothing to do until 6 am Tuesday.

Winter was starting to blow itself out, but it still got dark early.

She climbed back onto her rumpled bed and pulled out her laptop. It was almost time for one of the bright spots in her life. She wasn't sure what inspired her to download a copy of *Realms of Zokar* and join back in January. Maybe it was because she was starting to tire of Netflix. It was Sam's favorite RPG[1], of course, but she had never really been that interested in the game, even though Sam never stopped talking about it.

And she really didn't know why she said "Sam" when Flo asked her for her name that morning back in November. She guessed that it was because she had just left all her friends—Sam, Wu, Nate, Ma Beth, Pa Bill, Rose, Mrs. Woods, Will. Those names were all rattling around in her head at the time and "Sam" is what came out. So now her nom de guerre was Samantha Keller. Sam for short. And she was playing a game with the real Sam, Sam Roth, foster son of Beth and Bill O'Day. Of course, the real Sam didn't know it was her.

She had practiced with the RPG version of the game for a week before she decided to download *Worlds of Zokar,* the MMO[2] version. She had found Sam's avatar with the hope of joining him in a few quests, and had crafted her WOZ avatar, Snow Princess, in a way she knew would be intriguing to him. When she introduced herself, he had immediately invited her to join in a quest.

That was a month ago. It hadn't taken long for her to become really good at it. In fact, she was so good now, she had become one of the most powerful members of her virtual tribe. It had gotten to the point where she had almost forgotten that Sam was part of her normal world life a few months ago. He was now Agathar, the Gaul, with the ability to fly short distances and cast fireballs. When they came across a Stark Crystal, he could use it to detonate his super-fireball that wiped out all enemies in a twenty-meter circle. She was a Winter Demon that could freeze her enemies and cast water that froze into walls. She could make and throw spears of ice and when she got a Stark Crystal, she could create a giant sword of blue ice that cut through anything. They each had a spirit animal that they acquired after reaching level five. She had a white fox, and he had a grey goat with curved horns.

Tonight they were meeting at 8:30 pm with the rest of their tribe to try to kill a Heng Skullion Prince that was guarding the Bridge of Krespar that was the key to level six. They had tried the week before and failed. Tonight they had only a couple of hours to accomplish this before Agathar, that is Sam, had to sign off. He had a computer curfew. Blue, of course, did not.

It took them only an hour. Blue had learned online how the Heng Skullion had a vulnerable spot just under his left chest plate and she was able to jam an ice spear on that spot at exactly the right moment just before she was about to die herself. The Heng Skullion disintegrated in the most spectacular and satisfying fashion, uttering a final ghostly wail as her character danced triumphantly on top of him, with the rest of her tribe saluting her. A screen with her character and profile background picture appeared, a list of her trophies and victories underneath. It was the first time she had scored the crucial winning blow, and everyone was congratulating her in the chat window. She felt very fond of them all just then. She let the moment glow, even though she knew it was all virtual. Nothing real.

Eventually, everyone signed off early with the excuse of the late hour or school the next morning. All except Agathar. He kept typing.

Agathar: That's a really cool
background picture. Did you draw that?

Snow Princess: Yeah, I did

Agathar: Wow, you're really good

Snow Princess: Thanks

Agathar: Did you ever see mine?

                       Snow Princess: Yeah, that's a really good one, too! Did you draw that?

Agathar: No, a friend did

                       Snow Princess: Nice! Is he on WOZ?

Agathar: He's a she.
No, she wasn't really into it

                       Snow Princess: Oops! Well, tell her I liked it!

Agathar: I can't. She's gone

                       Snow Princess: You mean she moved away?

Agathar: No. not exactly.
She ran away

                       Snow Princess: Ran away? I'm sorry. Why did she run away?

Agathar: We found out
she was in some sort of trouble
and the state was going to
take her back into custody

Snow Princess: We? Custody?

Agathar: Yeah, me and
my foster family.
I mean my real family now

Snow Princess: I'm confused

Agathar: Sorry. I was a foster
kid and she was my foster
sister but after she ran away,
our foster parents decided to
adopt us. Me and my brother.
If she came back she could
be my sister

Snow Princess: She'd be
your sister?

Agathar: Yeah. A real sister

Snow Princess: But if she
came back, wouldn't the state
still take her into custody?

Agathar: No! That's the thing.
That's all fixed with adoption

Blue sat with her hands hovering over her keyboard. Her fingers were paralyzed and speechless. Adoption. Sister. These words slapped her around so suddenly that she couldn't think straight, but she had to say something. She didn't want Sam to sign off. She managed to get enough control of herself to hammer out a response.

Snow Princess: Does she
know this?

Agathar: Probably not.
Maybe. I don't know.
We have no way of
contacting her. Maybe
she just doesn't want to
live with us

Snow Princess: I doubt that

Agathar: I don't want
to talk about it anymore

Snow Princess: Hey. I'm sorry

Snow Princess: Agathar?

Snow Princess: You there?

<**Agathar** has left the chat>

Adopted! The room suddenly felt very hot. The walls seemed to press in on her. She slapped the laptop shut and jumped out of bed, grabbing her jacket as she went. She yanked her door open and slammed it behind her as her feet flew down the hall, down the stairs, out the front door, and down the steps onto the wet, cracked sidewalk. The dirty melting late winter night surrounded her almost like the walls of her room. The damp cold air was suffocating, but she gasped it into her lungs anyway. She looked back at the building and stared at the dim glow of light coming from her one window on the second floor. The window looked lonely and forlorn, surrounded by the massive architecture of the ancient building. She imagined her face there, peering out, day after day. She couldn't help feeling like she should run, that someone would be coming after her any moment to pull her back inside and lock her back up in that room. But she knew that she was the only one that would make her go back inside.

She turned and walked. She walked and walked through the vaguely familiar streets of the town. She got lost more than once and didn't care. She trusted her feet would find the way.

She didn't know how long she walked. Her mind was not functioning fully—it was like it decided to power down for a while. Her body just moved on auto-pilot, and she watched from inside her head. At one point, she noticed she had stopped. She was standing at a street corner, waiting to see which way she would step next when she heard a familiar voice coming out of the shadows down the sidewalk.

"Sam? Is that you, Sam?"

She looked toward the sound and saw the silhouette of a man walking slowly toward her. The silhouette resolved into the countenance of Jeremy, one of her favorite diner customers.

His voice simmered into a gentle greeting, "Well it's nice to see someone familiar out and about on this brisk evening. I find this weather refreshing but it seems everyone else wants to stay buttoned up inside. How about you?"

Blue thought it was a little too brisk. In fact, she realized she was shivering, but she still wasn't ready to go back to her hole.

"I had to get out for a while," she replied.

"I feel that way sometimes, too," said Jeremy. "And then when I go back inside, I can appreciate the warmth and comfort of my room and forget about how small it is. I was just about ready to step back inside and have a cup of tea. My apartment's right here in this building. Would you like to come in and warm up? Looks like you could use a little warmth."

Blue looked up at Jeremy. There it was again. That same smile that Ma Beth had, Mrs. Woods had, even Mrs. Jamison had.

Sincere, not condescending. The thoughts behind his eyes were entirely caring. A good soul. She could sense that even though his thoughts didn't coalesce into any words or memes. She could use the company of someone like that right now.

"Sure," she said, "I mean, I'd like that." It was only then that she realized her teeth were chattering, ever so slightly.

They stepped into a hallway of a contemporary brick apartment building just a few yards away from where they met. He ushered her up the stairs to a second-story landing with doors to three apartments. It was clean and tidy and there were decorations on the other doors.

"Just a bunch of sentimental old seniors in this building," Jeremy said. "I'm not sentimental, of course." He winked at her.

They stepped into a small apartment crammed with antique furniture. "You should sit here in this Stickley chair. It's one of my favorites and there is an interesting story behind it. I'll just pop a pot of water on. Do you drink tea? What would you like?"

"Do you have anything with ginger?"

A few minutes later she was breathing in the hot mist swirling off the top of her mug of ginger spice tea. The heat was prickling her cold fingers in an oddly comforting way. It was like demons were being driven out through her fingers.

"You probably know most of the people in this building," said Jeremy after about a half cup of tea. "We all come in on Senior Tuesday, you know. We're all fixed income types. Mrs. Jackson lives right across from me."

Blue smiled and looked down at her cup. She liked Mrs. Jackson. She was a short, stout woman who used a cane because of a weak leg. The cane never seemed like a handicap, though, it just seemed like it was an extra limb and it allowed her to roll along in a most intriguing rhythmic gait. She was always smiling and giving Blue advice about men. "Don't you settle for anything less than true love! Don't let anyone talk you into marrying them! If you need to be talked into it, you don't need them! You listen to your heart! You hear?"

"She looks forward to Tuesday breakfast," said Jeremy.

So did she, she thought. She looked up at Jeremy.

He chuckled. "She looks forward to it because of you."

Because of her? "Yeah, I doubt that," she said. She glanced up at Jeremy. He was looking at her thoughtfully.

"You live over in the old Cady mansion, don't you? Do you know the story behind that mansion?"

That was what they called the aging building her apartment was in. The Cady mansion. It wasn't much of a mansion now. That was all she knew about it though. She shook her head.

"Eli Cady made all his money in the lumber trade back in the 1920s. He was a millionaire back then when there weren't many millionaires and he became rich when he was young. Naturally, he attracted quite a lot of attention from the women back then, being young and rich. But none of the women got *his* attention. They tried —he was a prize catch. They invited him to parties and teas and outings, and he went along with it but always managed to get away without any of these women getting their claws in him. Except for one. There was a pretty girl who was the daughter of the minister. I know you must think I'm making this story up, but it was true. It was the daughter of the minister that caught his eye. It was because she wasn't even trying. She had no interest in the game the other women were playing, she seemed to be very content being on her own. She was very active in the community and doted on her father and it looked like she was going to spend her life happily as a spinster."

Jeremy paused and took a sip of his tea. "I'm probably boring you with this story. I'm an old man and I tend to ramble on a bit too much."

"No, please go on." Blue realized that he was teasing her with the story, and she was happy to play along. It sounded like a good story.

"Well, I'll go on then, but I'll try not to get too long-winded. You just let me know when you're bored by making a heavy sigh or check your phone or something. I won't be offended." He winked.

Blue laughed. It felt like ages since she had laughed spontaneously like that.

Jeremy continued. "Well, young Eli wooed that young woman and after a while, it looked like she would give in. After all, her father wasn't going to live forever, and women back then didn't have a lot of options. It wasn't that she didn't like him, it was more that she was independent and didn't want to give that up for a marital commitment. Eli didn't wait. He decided that building, a beautiful home, would seal the deal. He didn't spare any expense. Being a lumber businessman, he had access to all the finest supplies and craftsmen in the area. I don't know if you've noticed, but that building is still straight and strong even if it is worn around the edges. Two-inch thick ash flooring and heavy timber construction throughout. You should go in the basement. You'll see lovely arched stonework in the foundation. It really is quite something."

Blue could imagine that building in its heyday. It was just an apartment building now. But she had noticed that the floors were level, and the stairs were solid as a rock. And the place was huge.

"Well, as I said, the minister's daughter was very nearly caving in, and the house was hard to resist, but then her father passed away. She was distraught, as you can imagine. As it turned out, she was so forlorn, she couldn't bear the thought of living in Malone anymore with reminders of her father everywhere. She wound up moving in with relatives in Syracuse and she never came back."

Jeremy sat back thoughtfully and took another long sip of tea.

"But what happened to Eli?" Blue asked.

"Eli? He was so forlorn for having lost the only woman he loved that he closed up the entire house except for one bedroom and the kitchen. He lived there the rest of his life, all alone. The rest of the house sat there, unused, just gathering dust. He had no heirs, so when he died, the house went up for public auction. By that time it needed a lot of repairs, having been neglected for so long, and no one wanted to take it. It sold for a song and now Flo's beau owns it, and you are living in one of the divided-up rooms."

Blue sat thoughtfully as she finished the last drops of tea. Why would anyone give up their whole future to live in misery, alone, just because of a lost love?

"That chair you are sitting in came from the mansion," said Jeremy.

Blue twisted herself around on the chair to look at it in closer detail. It looked elegant, but not old.

"After Flo's beau, Alan, bought the mansion, he auctioned off the furniture that was in it. As you can see, the wood parts in that chair are hardly worn. The cushions are new because the old ones were rotted with age. And if you look on this shelf over here . . ." He pointed to a picture on a bookshelf, "That is Eli himself sitting in that very chair."

The picture was a yellowing black and white photograph mounted in an ornate frame. The seated figure was elegantly dressed and holding a top hat in his lap. From his bearded face, his eyes cast a faraway look at nothing in particular.

"Alan found that picture, along with a trove of other memorabilia, in a chest that was in a locked room in the mansion. There were pictures of Eli as a boy with his family and letters from his family and his beloved. It was rather sad looking at it all. Alan let me have that picture and I display it there to remind myself to never let the past hold me down. I don't want to become that man. And now that I have that chair, I let visitors enjoy it, like Eli should have done. I have this crazy notion that I have a duty to undo his legacy." Jeremy sat back and sipped his tea, a faraway look on his face.

Blue, on the other hand, sat straight up, rocked by a picture from her own locked room. It was another flash, another memory from her life before. A box—a big metal box where her father kept important things. She had forgotten completely about it, like so many other memories she had forgotten but had been trickling back. This one was special, though. That box—her father had called it "the rocket box"—had been a source of fascination for her because her father never allowed her to see what was inside and its location was supposed to be secret. He kept it somewhere in the maple sugaring shed . . .

She looked up at a sound.

"I said, are you okay? You look a little rattled," said Jeremy.

"I'm sorry," she said. "I'm fine. I just remembered something. I probably need to get back."

Jeremy didn't look convinced, but he didn't press it either.

"Of course," he said. "You know, you would do me the greatest favor if you allowed me to walk you home. I am sure you are most able and independent, but it would make me feel more comfortable to see you home safe. Would that be all right?"

It was impossible to say no to such a respectful offer and to tell the truth, she thought it would be nice to have company walking the few blocks back to her small room in the corner of the big mansion.

It was a short walk and not so chilling as before now that she was warmed up inside and out. Without the cold to distract her, she even sensed there was a tinge of spring in the evening air. When they reached the mansion, Jeremy held out his hand.

"You know, you should come to dinner. We do a little potluck from time to time. Would you like that?"

Blue shook his hand and replied, "Yes, very much so. Thank you."

"Well then," he said. "We happen to be having one tomorrow at 6 pm. Just drop by the old dodgers apartment house. No need to bring anything, just yourself. Everyone will be glad to see you."

"Thank you so much. I'm really glad I ran into you tonight."

"I am, too," he said, and his eyes spoke, too, in a quiet *chiss*, "You LOOK LIKE THE WEIGHT OF THE WORLD IS ON YOUR SHOULDERS."

She looked down and voxed, knowing he couldn't hear, "IT IS."

Jeremy continued, "And if you ever need anything, don't hesitate to ask. Old people are full of good advice. Sometimes they even wait to be asked before they give it out."

Her laugh rang out again. Twice in one night, she thought. She turned to face the mansion and the forlorn light that was her window and it reminded her of why she had run out in the first place. She turned back to Jeremy and gave him a forced smile. "Thanks, Jeremy. Guess I should go in. G'night."

"Good night, Sam." And once again his eyes whispered without his knowing, "*A ROSE BY ANY OTHER NAME. BUT THAT'S NONE OF MY BUSINESS.*"

His *chiss* didn't shock her. She was pretty sure Flo knew she was a runaway, and Jeremy appeared to have the same shrewd intuition as Flo. She turned back to the house, took a breath, and stepped through the door.

As she stepped in, it was as if she was stepping into a different building. Jeremy's stories had given the mansion a new aura. This house had been a house where she thought she would be safe and isolated from her old life. Instead, it had unlocked a memory from her history, a memory that seemed to glow with importance, like a Stark Crystal that might unlock a weapon to slay a Heng Skullion Prince.

26

THE CATCH

Later that evening

"Where's Nora?" Becky threw this question at Chainy at the same time that she peeled her jacket off along with her purse and threw them both on the couch in obvious irritation.

"Out working, same as you," Chainy said as casually as he could. He counted the bills Becky had handed him and peeled off three twenties and threw them on top of Becky's pile on the couch. She had already stormed off into the bathroom and slammed the door. He could hear the squeaking of the tub faucet followed by the hiss of the shower. Her agitated mood puzzled him. It wasn't like her to be this bitchy. She'd been pretty reliable and never seemed perturbed coming home after turning a trick so he had assumed she was pretty well settled into the work. She should be—it was paying her pretty well. Paying him pretty well, too.

Just one of those days, I guess, he said to himself as he wrapped the fresh cash into his roll and stuffed it back in his pocket. He pulled a cigarette out of the pack in his breast pocket, lit it, and took a long, thoughtful, drag. Maybe I should cut her in a little more if this works out, he thought. Nah, you idiot. She'll think she just won the lottery with the $500 you're going to entice her with. No need to give her more.

He pulled the news clipping out of his pocket and looked at it again, peering closely at the face of the girl that was mid-stride flying around the corner of a school building. If you just ignore the hair, he thought, you can tell it's her. Even from across the street and through the window of the diner, the closest he'd ever been to her, he could see the resemblance in the intensity of her look—a look not of astonishment but of resignation and determination.

Now he just had to talk Becky into confirming that it was the same girl. She used to work at that diner so it would be natural for her to go in there and chat with her, this Samantha Keller, and see how she responded to the news clipping picture and the name of the girl in the picture: Blue DuBois. All they needed was the right reaction and he could call this in for an easy ten grand.

He heard Becky getting out of the shower and moments later she stomped out of the bathroom wrapped in a towel, her hair tousled and dripping.

"This place is a pig sty. You could try doing some cleaning around here instead of leaving it all to me and Nora." She plopped down on the couch and picked up the remote, flicking the TV on, instinctively glancing to her left and snatching the three twenties, stuffing them into her purse.

"Yes, honey, anything you say," he said with a grunt. She rolled her eyes and turned up the volume on the TV.

"Hey, mute that for a second, I've got to talk to you," he said

She rolled her eyes again but muted the TV and gave him a make-it-quick look.

"How would you like to earn $500 for doing nothing but having breakfast at Flo's. I'll even pay for the breakfast."

He watched as her look of annoyance turned into a look of skepticism. But it was skepticism mixed with interest. He smiled. It's all about marketing, he thought to himself.

"What's the catch?" she asked, now paying full attention.

"There is a catch, but it's not what you might think." He tossed the picture of the girl onto the couch.

She picked it up and studied it closely. "I remember this. This was from the news, like around last Thanksgiving, right? There was some school shooting in Vermont."

"Bingo." Chainy paused for a moment, wondering if she would make the connection on her own. If she did, it would be a pretty powerful indication that he was on the right track. He watched as she studied the picture.

"Does she look familiar to you at all?"

Her eyebrows creased in intense scrutiny for several moments until they suddenly melted into perfect arcs of astonishment.

"Shiiiiit! No way!" Her eyes turned toward him. "You think . . . ?"

"There's a reward for information on her whereabouts. Apparently, she ran away from home." Chainy hoped she would take the bait without asking questions. It wasn't the girl's parents that were offering a reward, of course, but she didn't need to know that. "Now I don't think she would spill to a scary guy like me . . ."

"You're not scary. At all. To anyone, Chainy."

". . . but she would talk to you. The people at the diner—they know you there, right? You do this and I'm willing to split the reward money with you."

Becky's eyes went into an instant squint, "Split, huh. What's your idea of a split, I get 5 percent?"

Chainy actually got caught flat-footed at the accuracy of her accusation and hesitated for a moment too long.

"You bastard! What is the reward, $2000? $5000? Fuck you, if you can't do it without me, I'll take the whole reward myself."

"Yeah, right. Good luck with that. Go to the cops, show them your ID. Oh, you don't want to show them? Afraid of what will happen when they find out who you are? You forget about that?"

"Fuck you, you greedy bastard, I still won't do it for a measly $500. Good luck getting Nora to do it, too." Becky stomped out of the room into the girls' shared bedroom.

Chainy twisted his wrist back and forth thoughtfully, letting the rattle of the chains steady his mind. "Okay okay," he said through the bedroom door, "I'll give you $1000 but that's it." He could hear muttering and swearing and the sound of clothes being zipped up. "C'mon, Becky. Look, we'll be doing a good deed, getting her back to people who care enough to offer a reward."

"Yeah, they care so much about her she ran away! What was she running from?" More muttering and cursing.

He played his trump card. "She's fifteen," he said softly, but just loud enough.

The muttering stopped. Becky's face appeared in a narrow gap as she cracked the door open. "She's fucking fifteen?" she said, a sudden softness to her voice. Chainy nodded.

"Fucking A."

27

POTLUCK

The next evening, March 12th

Blue hesitated at the door to the senior's apartment building. Jeremy said she didn't have to bring anything, but she still felt guilty standing there with nothing in her hands. She was looking forward to this, though, and the thought of that pushed her through the door and into the hallway of the ground floor. She could hear the sounds of familiar voices from the end of the hall where there appeared to be an entrance to a large room. She stepped down the hall and shyly peeked through the doorway to see a large, brightly lit common room full of a dozen or so lively, animated gray-haired folks chatting away. It suddenly became silent as everyone turned to look in her direction. She was overwhelmed by the intensity of the joy that emanated from the smiles and it took a moment for her to realize that it was directed toward her.

Jeremy appeared out of the crowd, to her relief, and stepped up to her, grasped her hand, and said, "Well there you are! How wonderful!" He took her in tow and led her around the room for introductions. Most of the faces were familiar, but she noticed one woman she didn't recognize in the corner of the room. She seemed to be the only one that wasn't smiling. Instead, she wore an odd, neutral expression on her face and her head bobbed ever so slightly. Before she had time to wonder at this, Blue was swept up by the attention she was getting from everyone else.

"You look so wonderfully healthy. You must take good care of yourself," said a woman in a bright red dress, a regular at Flo's. Gayle was her name.

"I do my best."

"Well, you're doing well. You just keep doing what you're doing," said Gayle with a pat on Blue's shoulder.

"Thank you, I will."

"I love your hair, it is almost as silver as mine! Except at the roots, of course," said another regular named Harriet. "What I wouldn't do to have dark hair like that again. Can you believe it? Mine was once as dark as yours!"

"My goodness, you look so young! I hope you don't mind me asking what age you are?" This from a gentleman who was so bent by age that his face was nearly level with hers. She recognized him but couldn't recall his name.

"Not at all. I'm seventeen."

"Oh my, I remember seventeen. Such a wonderful age. And you're hard at work already and on your own. Good for you!"

It went on like this non-stop for so long, she lost track of time until someone finally spoke up and said, "It's time to eat. Let's give that girl a rest and have some dinner while it's still hot!"

It felt like she was finally able to take a breath as she stepped back and let people gather around the food table. Jeremy came up to her and said, "Aren't you the popular girl? You have to forgive them, they crave a younger audience. Me, too." He winked. "Now, after you get a plate of food, I'd like to introduce you to someone special. She has a wonderful sense of perception, like you, and I think you two will get along famously. He gestured toward a corner where the woman with the bobbing head still sat. Now that she had time to get a good look at her she realized that although her mouth was not smiling, her eyes were. Blue smiled back and then turned to Jeremy.

"Is there something wrong with her? Her face is smiling but her mouth isn't."

"See what I mean?" replied Jeremy, "You are very perceptive, like her." "*THEIR EYES ARE THE SAME, TOO,*" he noted with a *chiss.* "She has had many challenges. A stroke has left her with AOS—apraxia of speech, another way of saying she has a very difficult time trying to speak—but she is still sharp as a pin inside. And if that wasn't challenging enough, she has Parkinson's Disease which makes it difficult for her to show facial expressions and causes the little bit of head waggle. But she is quite amazing. She can communicate by writing and using a keyboard, and she can whisper some words very quietly. Before this all happened she was a firecracker, and her crackle is still all there, you can see it inside."

They moved together to the food table and as she filled her plate, she noticed Jeremy was making an extra plate. She guessed it was for the woman. Jeremy waited for Blue to finish getting her food and then led her over to sit with the firecracker lady.

"Stella," Jeremy said, "I'd like you to meet my young friend, Samantha Keller. Sam, this is Stella Winslow, also known affection-ately as 'Bird Whisperer'."

Blue looked at Jeremy somewhat astonished, and then turned to Stella and said, "Nice to meet you. That's an interesting nickname."

Jeremy, watching Stella, said, "It is, and if Stella doesn't mind, I can tell you why we call her Bird Whisperer."

Stella nodded, her eyes still sparkling. Now that she was closer to her, Blue caught just a glimpse of the color and detail of Stella's irises, and the little she saw nearly made her gasp. She tried to look again, but Stella had turned away from her to look at Jeremy.

"We call her Bird Whisperer because she has a remarkable rapport with a wild bird. A raven, I think, right, Stella?"

Stella nodded and then started pointing at a plastic card that was on the table next to her. Her hand moved rapidly, and Blue realized the card was a picture of a keyboard and her finger was spelling out something. Jeremy was apparently accustomed to this and was following her finger intently.

"Blackbeard! That's right. She has named this raven Blackbeard ... and ..." He was watching her finger again, "... he is very intelligent! Absolutely!" Jeremy turned to Blue and said, "You really must see him sometime, Blackbeard that is. He will actually come at her signal. I don't know how she does it, but he comes. She always makes sure she has a treat for him, right Stella?"

Stella nodded. Blue noticed that while they were sitting there, she heard the low murmur of *chiss* all around her from the people in the room, but Stella was notably silent. Not unusual, but along with the eyes ...

Jeremy stood up and said, "I need something to drink. Can I get you two something? Water? Juice?"

Stella typed something again, and Blue followed her finger this time. "W-A-T-E-R—P-L-S." Blue looked up at Jeremy and said, "Water for me, too, please."

Jeremy chuckled and said, "Quick learner! I told you she's a sharp one, Stella." As he stepped across the room to where the drinks were, Stella started gesturing to Blue and tapping on her keyboard card. Blue turned her attention to it as Stella typed, "S-A-M—S-T-A-Y—C-A-L-M—A-N-D—L-O-O-K—A-T— M-E."

Blue mouthed the words to herself as she followed Stella's finger and felt her brow crease and at the same time she felt a flutter of excitement rise in her breast. She turned her eyes slowly to look at the placid face and bright eyes of a woman who had the sculpted beauty of an aged and sage shaman, the deep texture of her rumpled features framed by a cloud of silver hair softly reflecting the colors of her brightly patterned scarf. And the texture of her irises was so rare and so familiar that when words formed clearly and deliberately in Blue's head, the only truly shocking thing about them was what they said:

"HELLO, BLUE DUBOIS."

28

RAVEN LADY

The next morning, March 13th

B lue drifted through the period of time after the potluck in a fog. It was as if Stella's words had pulled the final Jenga block from the seemingly stable tower of denial and subterfuge that she had created here in Malone. Of course, the tower had been rocked already by Jeremy's story of the Cady Mansion with its hidden chest of secrets and that singular heart-piercing word from her WOZ chat with Sam: "adopted." And yet it had taken the completely unexpected discovery of one of her own people, Stella, to finally wash away any notion that the life she had built here was going to isolate her from her past.

But what should she do? It wasn't like running away again was going to help—it seemed her past was determined to dog her wherever she went. It was as if her past was demanding that she deal with it and get back to her people and her family and it was Stella who might hold the key. It was Stella's final words at the potluck that rang in her head from that moment until now. *"I KNOW THINGS ABOUT YOU THAT YOU NEED TO HEAR. BUT NOT HERE, NOT NOW. COME TO MY APARTMENT TOMORROW WHEN YOU CAN."*

So now, after a night of fitful sleep followed by a torpid morning shift at Flo's she was standing in front of Stella's door. As she reached out to knock she felt a flutter in her chest. It was as if the page of a book turned inside her and she sensed that no matter what Stella had to say, it was going to decide what was on the first page of her next chapter.

The door opened to an apartment bathed in green-tinged sunlight. She could see plants lining a big south-facing double window and she thought how fortunate Stella was to have such exposure, so bright compared to the single, cold north-facing window of her little apartment. Stella herself was clothed in a colorful flowing robe and her radiant face beamed delight in its own unique way, her Parkinson's causing her face to bob like a flower in the breeze. It was hard to regard her as disabled as she seemed so comfortable in her body even with its many limitations.

"BLUE! I AM SO GLAD YOU CAME. AND I AM SO SORRY TO SHOCK YOU AT THE PARTY. IT WAS RUDE OF ME, BUT TO TELL YOU THE TRUTH, I WAS IN SHOCK AT DISCOVERING THAT THIS GIRL JEREMY HAD SO MUCH TO SAY ABOUT WAS ACTUALLY YOU. I HOPE YOU WILL FORGIVE ME."

It made a deep impression on Blue how eloquent the voice was that was hidden inside this woman, only able to be appreciated by a fellow vox and not her friends.

"OF COURSE I FORGIVE YOU!" voxed Blue. "BUT WHO ARE YOU? HOW IS IT POSSIBLE THAT YOU KNOW ME?"

"THAT IS A LONG STORY, SO I THINK WE NEED TO SIT AND GET COMFORTABLE. HERE, I HAVE SOME TEA ALREADY MADE. I HOPE YOU LIKE LEMON GINGER."

Stella ushered Blue into the cozy apartment and took her coat while gesturing to an easy chair by the window. A china pot and two cups sat on a large windowsill. Next to it sat what looked like a bowl of crumbled scones. It seemed like an odd treat to be offering a guest.

Blue sat in the sun-warmed chair and gazed out the window.

She was amazed to see a large yard adjacent to the building. "THIS IS A REALLY NICE APARTMENT."

Stella sat down opposite her. "YES, I HAVE NO COMPLAINTS. AND I HAVE A FRIEND TO KEEP ME COMPANY, WOULD YOU LIKE TO MEET HIM?"

"BLACKBEARD?" Blue asked. Stella nodded. She reached over to the bowl of crumbled scone and picked out a large piece. A deep vein of curiosity welled up in Blue as she watched Stella turn to the window and vox very powerfully, "BLACKBEARD, BLACKBEARD, WHERE ARE YOU? TIME TO SNACK IT'S A QUARTER TO TWO!"

Stella turned back to Blue. "IT'S NOT REALLY QUARTER TO TWO, BUT I LIKE TO MAKE A RHYME." And then, from outside the window, there came a distinct "Kwa-koo!" and Blue turned just in time to see a large black raven alight on the branch of a tree not far from Stella's window.

"It's just like my raven!" Blue blurted out.

Stella's crooked smile expressed a sentiment of camaraderie rather than surprise at Blue's statement. "DO YOU FEED YOUR RAVEN?" she asked, and as she did, she slid the window open a crack and tossed a big chunk of scone out the window. Blackbeard instantly swooped down and pounced on it, hopping triumphantly, carrying it in his beak and cocking his head and croaking his contentment.

"HE LOVES THE CRANBERRY. THE SPINACH-CHEESE—NOT SO MUCH! THEY'RE ATTRACTED TO OUR EYES, YOU KNOW. THEY CAN SEE THE SPARKLE. AND THEY ARE REMARKABLY INTELLIGENT, ESPECIALLY WHEN IT COMES TO GETTING FREE FOOD!"

Blue watched Blackbeard's antics. He made a couple of sounds she'd never heard from a raven. One of them sounded distinctly like "scone."

"IT'S NOT LIKE I REALLY HAVE A RAVEN, I MEAN THERE IS A RAVEN THAT HANGS OUT IN A TREE IN OUR YARD. I MEAN THE YARD WHERE I USED TO LIVE."

"YOUR FATHER HAD ONE, YOU KNOW."

Blue nearly passed out with the completely unexpected

mention of her father. She felt herself holding the arms of the chair to steady herself.

"Yes I did!" voxed Stella.

"What?"

"To answer your question, yes I did. You just asked me if I knew your father."

Blue realized that she must have voxed that question without realizing it in her shock. "How?" she asked.

"Have a sip of tea, dear. I'm afraid I've upset you again."

"No, not upset, I'm just totally . . . I don't know. Lost."

Stella reached out a finger and tapped Blue's steaming teacup. Blue picked it up and took a sip and closed her eyes. The warm liquid and spicy aroma transported her back to the living room in Westbury, putting ground under her feet and steadying the world that had just spun out of control. After she took a slow, deep breath and let it out, she opened her eyes again. And when she did, Stella began her story:

"I first met you . . ." Stella began.

Blue gasped.

". . . yes, you! When you were only a toddler. Of course you won't remember me. You see, at that time my husband was a U.S. Marshal, a Senior Special Agent in the Federal Witness Protection Division. He was in charge of protecting you and your family. He was the one that gave you the new surname of Stanton! That's why I know your original surname, too! Of course, my husband was not supposed to share that information with anyone, but this was a special case—your family were vox, like me! And no one knew except myself and my husband—who was not a vox, but he was so adorable I married him anyway—so we came up with a ruse: they needed someone to take care of you from time to time while your mom and dad were busy with the marshals in setting

UP YOUR NEW LIFE, AND I VOLUNTEERED AND TOOK AN OATH OF SECRECY.
WHAT IS IT, DEAR?"

Stella's question was in response to Blue shaking her head in confusion. *"I'M SORRY, I CAN'T BELIEVE THAT I RAN INTO YOU! HERE! IN MALONE!*
I ALMOST DIDN'T BELIEVE YOU UNTIL YOU SAID 'STANTON.' I'VE NEVER TOLD
ANYONE THAT. HOW IS THIS POSSIBLE? I MEAN, WHAT ARE THE ODDS?"

Again, Stella's face was impassive, but her eyes were smiling and Blue could sense the warmth and compassion coming from her. *"YES, IT IS QUITE AMAZING, ISN'T IT? I WAS QUITE SURPRISED*
MYSELF, OF COURSE, BUT I KNEW THE INSTANT I SAW YOU LAST NIGHT
THAT IT WAS YOU. EVER SINCE YOUR PICTURE WAS IN THE NEWS, I'VE BEEN
FOLLOWING WHAT HAPPENED, SO I KNEW THAT YOU HAD RUN AWAY. FOR
YOU TO SHOW UP HERE, WELL . . ." A chuckle came from Stella that was both vocal and from her eyes, *". . . IT WAS A DELIGHTFUL*
SURPRISE, AND NOT SO SHOCKING TO AN OLD LADY LIKE ME. I THINK YOU
WILL BE AMAZED AS YOU GET OLDER HOW SMALL THE WORLD IS AND HOW
OFTEN SEEMINGLY IMPOSSIBLE COINCIDENCES OCCUR."

Blue took another sip of tea as she took in Stella's response.

"IT WASN'T UNTIL YEARS LATER THAT I LEARNED MORE ABOUT YOUR
FAMILY. BY THAT TIME, MY HUSBAND WAS THE HEAD OF THE SPECIAL
AGENTS. ONE DAY HE CAME HOME VERY UPSET. THERE WAS A BIG TO-DO AT
WORK, AND FROM WHAT HE HINTED, I SUSPECTED IT HAD TO DO WITH
YOUR FAMILY, BUT WHAT IT WAS EXACTLY, I DON'T KNOW. WHAT
HAPPENED NEXT WAS VERY UNUSUAL. WE TOOK AN IMPROMPTU VACATION,
JUST THE TWO OF US! AND GUESS WHERE HE TOOK US ON VACATION?"

Blue was silent for a moment, her brain slogging through all this new information.

"UM, WELL, MAYBE HERE? MALONE?"

"THAT'S A GOOD GUESS, AND NOT FAR OFF. HE TOOK US TO BURLING-
TON, WITH THE RUSE THAT WE WERE GOING TO VISIT SOME RETIREMENT
PROPERTIES. YOU SEE, HE WAS WITHIN A YEAR OF RETIRING AND WE
WANTED TO GET OUT OF WASHINGTON D.C. WE'D OFTEN GONE SKIING IN
VERMONT, SO IT WAS ALL VERY ABOVE BOARD, BUT THE MINUTE WE

LANDED, HE RENTED A CAR AND WE DROVE TO A LITTLE TOWN CALLED BLUE RIDGE[1] IN NEW YORK AND VISITED A VERY SPECIAL FAMILY THERE!"

Stella's eyes were shining extra bright as she said this, and Blue wondered if Stella was aware of what arrows would be loosed by speaking the name of the town where her family had lived. But she was so rapt with the story that it almost seemed as if it wasn't about her and her family. She wanted Stella to go on. *"YOU VISITED US IN BLUE RIDGE?"*

"YES! YOU MAY NOT REMEMBER, THOUGH, YOU SEEMED VERY WRAPPED UP IN A GAME YOU WERE PLAYING WITH YOUR SISTER. AND THAT WAS WHEN I WAS INTRODUCED TO YOUR FATHER'S RAVEN. HIS NAME WAS . . . HMM . . . LET ME THINK, IT WILL COME TO ME . . ."

"ARDETH!" Blue spit the name out reflexively. It had come out of nowhere. And as if that name along with "Blue Ridge" and "sister" were a secret code, another little door in a dusty back corner of her brain unlocked. At the same time, all her external senses slowed down and instinctively went into a kind of automatic maintenance mode, allowing her to turn all of her focus inward to prepare for what was about to explode through that door. Her reflexes told her to bar the door as she had so many times in the past, but whether it was that she lost the will or that she was overcome with desire or just that she sensed that the time had come, she let the door open.

And then they came. The scenes, the images. Of course she remembered. Of course she could remember. The memory that was front and center was of a warm, sunny early fall afternoon. There were visitors. They didn't get many visitors, so any visitor was a memorable event. These visitors came in a big black SUV and her father always referred to people like that as "paper-folk"—people who seemed to have a great deal of paperwork that needed to be read and discussed and signed. She sensed that neither her father nor mother liked it when these people came, but the visitors on this day were different. It was an old couple, old enough to be her grandparents. Her father greeted them warmly and that caught Blue's attention. Heather kept bugging her to keep playing in the orchard, but Blue's curiosity overcame her, and she shushed Heather and voxed to her, "FOLLOW ME AND STAY QUIET!" Quiet in their family meant undetectable and even little Heather could move as silent as a shadow. As soon as she sensed her sister's mood, Heather promptly fell in behind her and the two of them spooked through the orchard following the steps of her father and the old couple as they made their way down the path alongside the orchard until they reached the sugarhouse[2].

The sugarhouse is where her dad kept all "the papers." He didn't like them in the house, explaining that they might contaminate it with "paper mites." She remembered worrying about paper mites and wondering what they looked like. For a long time, she checked her bed every night in case she might see one, but all she ever found was the occasional granddaddy long-legs.

He stored their "papers" in a heavy aluminum box that he called "the rocket box" because it had once been used in a war to carry rockets. "If it kept rockets safe, it should keep our papers safe," he would say. She had gotten a peek once and could tell there was a lot more than just papers in the box. There were pictures, something that looked like a war medal, an old watch, and more. But she never got a clear look at all that was there. One time, when he caught her sneaking a look over his shoulder, he quickly covered the box and told her, gravely, "MAYBE FOR WHEN YOU'RE OLDER."

This day, however, something was very different. By the time Heather and Blue reached the sugarhouse, their dad had pulled out the rocket box and the older man was studying some papers. He then turned toward their dad and the discussion between them became very hushed and very serious. Blue couldn't pick up any of their voices and there wasn't a speck of *chiss* from the old man but after a last intense exchange she did pick up on the final words of the old man, "I just hope you know what risk you're taking, André. And God be with you."

She had nearly squeaked with surprise. Everyone knew her father as Samuel. Heather grabbed Blue's face and held it close, both her hands surrounding their faces so their dad wouldn't over-hear her vox, "WHO IS ANDRÉ?" Blue had hesitated but realized there was no hiding it from her sister, "THAT'S DAD'S SECRET NAME! WE CAN'T TELL ANYONE!"

Her sister had always been the serious one, mature beyond her years in that regard, and she could tell that the secret was secure and that a bond of trust passed between them at that moment. A loud "Kwa-koo" distracted them both.

"IT'S ARDETH," voxed Blue.

The big black raven landed in a tree close to the sugarhouse, not far from where the girls were hidden. Ardeth looked straight at them and squawked before turning away and flying down to peck at a tidbit that their father had thrown out to him. The woman was watching in fascination and turned to her father and this time it was Heather who made an audible squeak when they both heard the woman vox to their dad, "WHAT A BEAUTIFUL BIRD, IS HE A PET?"

"NOT AT ALL. HE'S A FRIEND. RAVENS CAN SEE OUR EYES WHEN WE VOX, YOU KNOW." Their dad turned toward the orchard as he said this and looked straight toward the two girls. Blue was sure he had heard Heather's squeak, but he never said anything afterwards.

Heather turned to Blue, "SHE'S A VOX!" Neither of them had met another vox in their entire life outside of their mother and father.

AND NOW BLUE was sitting in that woman's living room and feeding her raven.

"WE HID IN THE ORCHARD AND WATCHED YOU." She turned to Stella, not sure how much time had passed or even if Stella had remained there with her the whole time. "I REMEMBER NOW. WHY IS IT I ONLY REMEMBER NOW?"

Stella's expression was the same, but her eyes expressed sadness. "IT WASN'T LONG AFTER THAT YOU LOST YOUR ENTIRE FAMILY. THAT MUST HAVE BEEN A HORRIBLE TRAUMA TO YOU. IT'S NATURAL TO BLOCK OFF THOSE MEMORIES. I'M SURE THAT SEEING ME AND BLACKBEARD

HELPED BRING THOSE MEMORIES BACK. YOU KNOW, I WAS SO ENTHRALLED BY ARDETH'S INTERACTION WITH YOUR FATHER, I STARTED CALLING RAVENS, TOO, AFTER THAT. AND CROWS, BUT RAVENS ARE SO MUCH MORE INTELLIGENT. CANTANKEROUS SOMETIMES, BUT THEY CAN ALSO BE VERY AFFECTIONATE AND SENTIMENTAL. ONCE I SETTLED HERE AFTER EDWARD PASSED AWAY, I BECAME FRIENDS WITH BLACKBEARD."

"EDWARD, YOUR HUSBAND? I'M SO SORRY."

"YES, I DO MISS HIM, BUT HE WOULDN'T WANT ME TO WALLOW IN SORROW. IN MANY WAYS, BLACKBEARD IS EASIER TO MAINTAIN THAN A HUSBAND!" She chuckled to herself.

Blue was astonished at such a statement. She felt like she should be aghast, but it was said in such a loving way that she wound up smiling along with Stella's version of a smile.

Stella sat staring out the window with a wistful look for a moment after that. Then she turned to Blue and voxed very softly, "I NEVER LEARNED WHAT IT WAS THAT EDWARD DISCUSSED WITH YOUR FATHER. I FEEL IT HAD SOMETHING TO DO WITH YOUR TRAGEDY BECAUSE WHEN WE HEARD ABOUT IT, EDWARD TOOK IT VERY HARD, AND I AM AFRAID HE NEVER FULLY RECOVERED FROM THE SHOCK. HE RETIRED SHORTLY AFTER THAT. AT ONE POINT I EXPRESSED MY SORROW AT THE TRAGEDY. I REMEMBER, I SAID, 'IT'S ALMOST UNBEARABLE TO THINK OF A YOUNG FAMILY LIKE THAT, GONE.' HE PUT HIS HAND ON MY SHOULDER AND SAID, 'THEN IT WILL WARM YOUR HEART TO KNOW THAT THEY DIDN'T ALL PERISH.' THAT'S WHEN I KNEW THAT HE MUST HAVE PULLED SOME WITSEC MAGIC BEFORE HE RETIRED. AND HERE YOU ARE!"

There was a long silence after Stella finished. Blue didn't know what to say and Stella appeared content with the silence. They both turned at the sound of Blackbeard's "Krrraawk . . . scone" and Stella slid the window open and tossed him another chunk of scone. Blue watched him hopping up to it, taking two tries to pluck it off the ground, and then launching himself back up onto a tree branch.

"YOU'RE THE FIRST PERSON I HAVE EVER MET FROM THE TIME BEFORE," Blue voxed, breaking the silence, "AND THIS IS THE FIRST TIME I'VE RECALLED THIS MUCH ABOUT IT. IT FEELS WRONG. I FEEL GUILTY."

"*It would be wrong of me to tell you not to feel wrong or guilty about it. We each have to find our own path to come to terms with tragedy. I had to say goodbye to my lovely husband and goodbye to part of my brain and goodbye to some of my mobility. It can be quite difficult, but with the help of my friends, I am quite content.*"

Stella's words injected a new kind of guilt into Blue. Stella had survived a stroke, lost her husband, has Parkinson's, and yet she talked about it as if it were no more than a few passing clouds. And there she sat as radiant as any healthy person she knew.

Stella continued, "*You have a lot of melancholy built-up inside you, Blue. I hate to see that in such a beautiful, strong, young person with so much life ahead of her. I wonder what it is that is keeping you from moving on.*"

She sounded so much like Dr. Woods, talking about keeping things bottled up inside.

"*Dr. Woods, she's . . . she was my psychiatrist . . . she said that sharing my story with someone I trusted would help. And I have, and it helps. Just meeting you has . . . well, I don't know yet. I mean, this is the first time I've had a real live person from that part of my life to talk with. Before you, I had nobody. No keepsake. No pictures, no mom, no dad, no sister, no friend, no toys, not even my clothes! They even threw the clothes I was wearing out because they were ruined in the fire. And not a single vox to talk to. Everything was unfamiliar. It was like I was reborn half-grown on a different planet. Nobody talked about my family, and I never saw my home again, even just to say goodbye.*" Tears were streaming down her face now, but they felt like healthy tears. She wasn't sobbing. She was just feeling . . . melancholy.

"*I think,*" Stella began, and then paused. "*I think—and I am no psychiatrist—but I think that the opportunity to say goodbye is a very powerful thing. I can't imagine not being able to see Edward after he passed away. Looking at his peaceful face and saying 'goodbye' made it so much easier to let go. You say you never saw*

YOUR HOME AGAIN. PERHAPS VISITING IT WOULD BE A WAY TO PAY RESPECTS TO YOUR FAMILY AND A CHANCE FOR YOU TO SAY GOODBYE."

Blue took the tissue Stella offered with her wobbling hand and once again marveled at how Stella took everything in stride. She dried her face and looked up to see Stella's mouth curved ever so slightly upward in a smile. A wave of admiration and gratitude swept over Blue.

"I THINK YOU'RE RIGHT."

Blue Ridge wasn't far. She'd always known that in the back of her mind, but the actual possibility of going there was never entertained by her brain. Now it seemed as though that door was open. In fact, maybe that knowledge is what had guided her to Malone in the first place.

29

PIECES FALL INTO PLACE

The next morning, March 14th

"Y ou are one distracted girl this morning. Everything all right?"

Flo wasn't usually this nice when Blue spaced out an order.

"Sorry," she replied. "Maybe just a little fuzzy-headed."

"You want to take the day off? It's okay. You haven't taken a single one off since you started."

Blue glanced at Flo. She had her 'real-concern' face on which meant Blue was not hiding her internal tumult very well. She slapped on her own 'don't-worry' face and said, "No, that would leave you short. I'm fine. I'll just have another cup of coffee." She grabbed her order from the pass window and went out into the dining room acting as un-fuzzy as she could, but her mind was a confused mess, and she couldn't seem to sort everything out.

Stella's suggestion to visit her family homestead and say goodbye was intoxicating. It seemed like the closest thing to a magic bullet she had ever found for quelling the ghosts in the dark closet of her past. But the thought of actually doing it terrified her. Was she ready? How would she react? Would she find the rocket box? Would the memories massacre her? For once she longed for a therapist's advice—Doctor Woods' advice. She could do it if she was with her. That would be a reasonable excuse for risking going back to Westbury. And if it were true that she could be adopted, that would take one barrier away, but there was still the Babineau problem. How much of a risk would there be? Maybe she was overblowing it, she thought. No, you're just letting your desire to go back jeopardize everyone else. Jeremy's comment at the potluck hadn't helped: "You should be with folks your own age, not us old farts." Yeah, Jeremy, but not if I am putting them in danger.

She was spacing again. She found herself standing next to the booth under the front window. It was still half full of the dirty dishes she had started to clear. She was wondering how long she had been staring at it when a tapping sound made her look up. Becky was standing outside the window. She must have been tapping on it for some time because she had a 'finally!' look on her face. She pulled something out of her pocket and slapped it up against the window. Blue recognized it instantly and it sent such a shock through her that she had to grab the table to steady herself. It was the news clipping with the photo that had changed her life. Becky nodded with a smug grin and pointed at the picture, and then pointed at Blue. Becky mouthed, "You. I knew it," and at the same time her *chiss*, barely detectable to Blue through the heavy glass, whispered, "YOUR LITTLE SECRET IS OUT NOW."

Becky turned and walked off quickly, and Blue jumped away from the table and sprinted to the diner entrance, but it was blocked by a family crowding their way through the small entry-way. She paused, trying to be polite, but quickly lost her patience and plowed through them, ignoring their protests. She burst out onto the street just in time to see Becky hop into a waiting car. She ran toward it but was too late as the car pulled quickly away.

She was still standing in shock and panting great clouds of dismay into the cold air when she felt Flo's hand on her shoulder.

"Sam, what the hell just happened?"

Blue turned and looked into Flo's eyes and what she felt pouring out of those eyes convinced her that Flo was just the person she needed right now.

"Flo, can we talk?"

Later that day
Westbury, VT

CHIEF HANNAH's pencil skated too quickly across her notepad creating a barely legible scrawl, in other words, she was writing using her normal handwriting. "Franklin County, NY" is what the words said.

"Are you sure?" she asked into the phone as she scooted herself into a better writing position, certain that there was going to be more to write down.

Rodney's voice belied speculation rather than total confidence, *"As sure as I can be considering the source. It's a CI[1] I've had for a while. Haven't heard from him in a long time because apparently, he's staying out of trouble. When he does contact me, he's usually looking for a lighter sentence in exchange for information. This time he had a different motivation. A reward."*

"A reward?"

"Yes. There's a reward for information on Blue's whereabouts."

"A reward? I think I'd know about a reward. Nobody's offered one that I know of. Certainly not the O'Days. Was he just playing you?"

"Um, no. In fact, I followed up on it. He had a phone number and a case number. I called it and they sounded very professional and polite, though it was clearly an overseas call center, and they said that indeed there was a reward and to submit a location and a photo through their website and they would follow up on it and get in touch with me if it was verified."

"But wait, how does he know this reward is for Blue?"

"Well that's the thing. This information is being passed around with the photo of Blue at the shooting—the front-page photo—and it's not being passed around widely, it is only going to very specific drug dealers in northern New York. You're not going to see it on any milk cartons anytime soon. And it's for $10,000 so no one is going to give this information away unless they can get something out of it."

"Ten thousand? Jesus Christ. Can't you shut this down? I mean it sounds illegal as hell."

"What is illegal about it? People pay for information about someone's whereabouts all the time. And it's a phone number that anyone can call. I called it and there is nothing criminal in anything they told me."

"It sounds like you're defending them!"

There was a heavy sigh on the other end of the line. "Summer, you know the law. We can't do anything to anyone who isn't showing criminal intent. Just because you and I see circumstantial evidence and that we think it is Babineau behind it—it's just not enough."

"I know, I know. It's just that I've been sitting here for months feeling totally helpless and then this comes along, and we can't do anything about it."

"Well, that's where you're wrong. If it is Babineau, he is focusing on Franklin County which means we can focus on Franklin County, too, and we have a lot of resources—namely local police, state police, and county sheriff, as well as the FBI. If Babineau is behind this, he may have made a tactical error in letting out the Franklin County location, but he may have been betting that he could act on it far quicker than us if he passed that information out to the street. My gut feel is that he is onto something and that things could unravel quickly. I've already got someone working on getting the word out to all the law agencies in Franklin County."

Chief Hannah paused. She had let her frustration get hold of her and Rodney was right to call her out on it. "Well, that makes me feel a lot better. Sorry if I got frustrated. So much of it is out of my jurisdiction, which makes me feel powerless, but I don't give you enough credit for being on top of it. If this information leads us to Blue, give that CI my gratitude."

"Hey, no worries. We've all been there," replied Rodney. *"And that being said, I hate to bring up more worries, but there is another consequence of this information."*

Now that her brain was settled down and she was thinking like a cop again, the words were barely out of his mouth before Chief Hannah blurted out, "Bronco! He will be tapped into the street info if he is still active. He will be doubly motivated if there is a reward involved."

"Or he may be working directly for Babineau already based on past association," said Rodney. *"Regardless, I have included his profile in the package of info going out to Franklin county law enforcement. Like it or not, this is turning Blue into Bronco-bait. We just need to be the better fishermen."*

Again, she was relieved by Rodney's acuity and professionalism. And though she should have been mollified, a completely different and unprofessional urge was overtaking her: the urge to take action herself.

"Rodney, I know this is a little obsessive, but I'm going crazy sitting on the sidelines. What if I went to Franklin County and just acted as an extra set of eyes. I could take vacation time and coordinate with the sheriff in Franklin county. As a citizen, of course."

"Summer, I don't think it is obsessive or crazy. You know, there is a point where getting personally involved is warranted. I'll vouch for you with the county sheriff and state police. Just don't get yourself in trouble."

"Thanks for that," she said and finally relaxed. She had something she could do, and it would get her out of town. She sighed and realized that it was probably audible over the phone. She didn't care.

"You know, Rodney, you have been the best law officer I've ever worked with outside Vermont. That means a lot. Thank you."

There was a pause on the other end of the line and then Rodney replied, *"Likewise. And I mean that."* Another pause and then, *"But before we pat ourselves on the back too much—"*

Chief Hannah interrupted, "Let's find our girl, grab Bronco, and then take down the big bad Babineau!"

A laugh came out of the phone and for the first time in months, a feeling of optimism came over her. She couldn't wait for tomorrow and the promise of actually getting off her ass so she could stop some really bad people and, with luck, save a life.

That Afternoon
Malone, NY

HER PENCIL SLID across the paper's finely textured surface. The pressure on the tip was carefully modulated by her fingers to create a nuance in the stroke that skillfully rendered the illusion of fur. Stroke by stroke, the form of the creature she was creating was gradually revealed, given depth, and glued to the earth with her smudging stump.

Blue sat back, her body receding into shadow while her brightly illuminated sketchpad rested on her crossed legs. A snag of pencils, erasers, and smudging stumps were gathered about her in the little valleys created by the weight of her thighs pressing into the soft comforter.

Once again, drawing was helping her put order back into her universe, a universe blown apart by Becky's discovery of Blue's true identity. She was reassembling it in a way that was beginning to make sense, and what was making sense was that it was time for her to move on. However, there was one thing she had to do first. She needed to do a proper farewell to her past.

"YOU NEVER HAD A CHANCE TO SAY GOODBYE. IT IS VERY HEALING, THE ACT OF EMBRACING THE PAST, HUGGING IT TIGHTLY, AND THEN BIDDING IT FAREWELL. MAKE A TIME TO HONOR YOUR FAMILY AND SAY GOODBYE." These had been Stella's parting words after a long afternoon of revelations. Stella was the missing narrator in her life story, a surprise character who was a treasure trove of missing details from her past.

Part of that past was something she didn't want to face. Her father was a marijuana grower. That was a realization that was tough to swallow. The redeeming factor provided by Stella was that his marijuana was legendary as the finest healing strain ever developed, a strain that had brought great relief to Stella and others with ailments like hers. But her father's horticultural skill and reputation attracted more than just pain relief seekers. It attracted Babineau. He entrapped her father and mother in his illicit business and forced them to grow marijuana exclusively for him. And then when her mother became pregnant with Heather, her dad decided to escape Babineau's control and became an informer for the police. The ensuing law enforcement operation ruined Babineau and killed his brother and nephew. And that's when she, her father, her sister, and pregnant mother went into witness protection and changed their name from DuBois to Stanton. Blue was two at the time and had no memory of this, but she had picked up on fragments of it from overheard furtive conversations of her parents. And now it was all confirmed by Stella.

Stella had related these memories so vividly that Blue got wrapped up in it as if it were someone else's story. She was anxious to know how the story ended, but, of course, the story wasn't at an end. It was still her story, and it was still very much alive, and she was still very much in it.

She looked at the nearly completed drawing. She knew what she was about to do would give her location away, but by the time it did, it wouldn't matter. She would be gone.

She picked up a tattered scrap of paper that sat on the bed next to her and studied it for the umpteenth time as if doing so would reassure her that this was the right decision. The paper had been wadded up and re-flattened so many times, the creases had created spider webs of white running through it. It was still readable, though for her, readability wasn't necessary. The words had been burned into her brain long ago and then buried, just like this paper had been buried in the beat-up portfolio she had carried her important papers around in for the last five years. All that was written on it was a simple address:

Stanton
5296 Bear Mountain Road,
Blue Ridge, NY

That was where she needed to go. That was where she could remember, embrace, and then say goodbye. Sylvie agreed to take her there tomorrow morning and, surprisingly, when they checked the map, it was only a two-and-a-half-hour trip to get there.

Her heart started beating hard in her chest as she thought about it. She wasn't sure what she would encounter in Blue Ridge, but she was ready. It was time. All the pieces had come together. And then what afterward? Well, she was sure of two things: she was moving on even though the path she was to take had yet to reveal itself, and, after her goodbye, and maybe because of her goodbye, her heart would show her the way.

That evening
Westbury, VT

WILL DIDN'T KNOW how long they stood there staring at the screen on Sam's computer. They had all been stunned into silence when Sam brought up the image. Will studied every detail of the drawing again. In the center was a white fox staring straight out of the screen. Behind her was a huge bear, arms stretched wide, his claws spread menacingly. On either side of the fox there was a mink and husky, and beside them were a grey goat and a meerkat. They were the animals Blue had assigned to each of them the summer before —Sam, the goat, Wu, the mink, Nate, the bear, Will, the husky, and

Rose, the meerkat. And of course, Blue, the little fox. The whole picture was framed in the ornate decoration from *Worlds of Zokar*. There was absolutely no doubt that this was Blue's work, but it was one he had never seen before. And what was it doing in *Worlds of Zokar*?

"This isn't a drawing Blue gave you?" he asked.

"No! I've never seen it before! And I *told* you, this isn't my profile!"

"Whose is it?" asked Wu.

"She calls herself Snow Princess," said Sam.

"It's Blue's," said Rose.

"Exactly! It's *got* to be!" said Sam, "And I've been playing with her for a month and didn't even know!"

"What! How could you not suspect? It's obvious with this picture" said Wu.

"I *told* you! I've never seen this picture before! It just showed up today! She had a different one there before. I just knew her as Snow Princess. She joined our tribe about a month ago. And she's amazing. She killed the Heng Skullion Prince!" He paused waiting for them to react. "I just said she killed the *Heng Skullion Prince*! He's just, like, the toughest Skullion in the game. Hardly anyone gets past him. He's the key to level six!" Sam looked at their blank faces like they were all idiots. "Haven't you ever heard of the Heng Skullion Prince?"

Nate said, "Hey Sam, we don't know that much about this game. What you're saying is that Blue is really good at it?"

"Duh! She was good when she joined, but she got better real fast. We were really stuck in level five until she finally killed him. That was last Sunday. But then get this. I talked to her online for a little while after..."

"You actually talked to her?" said Wu.

"Not *really* talked to her. You know, just the chat window on the side. She asked about my profile background picture, you know, the one she did for me last summer. I said the girl that did it ran away, and I told her about us getting adopted. Then I signed off, but when I signed back in today, I went over to her profile and found this new picture!"

"She went on *Worlds of Zokar* 'cuz she knew she'd find you there," said Rose. "And she drew that picture because she misses us."

"But why would she do that?"

"Because it's a way of talking with us without being traced," said Will. "Did she ever ask about anyone? Did she ask about where you lived?"

"Well, yeah, a little, we all do a little bit. We all have profiles and stuff, and we can put down where we're from and what we like to do but I'm not supposed to put down anything real private, like my real name and stuff."

"What does it say about where she's from?" asked Wu.

"She never filled that in. It's just blank," said Sam.

"Show us," said Will.

Sam clicked on an icon on the screen and an information page came up. He gasped.

Where I live: Malone, NY

"Whaa . . . !" he cried. "I'm not kidding!" "It really was blank before!"

"She wants us to find her," said Will.

30

IDUS MARTII

The next morning, March 15th

9:00 am, Bronco's Camp

"Stanton." The voice in the phone paused and Bronco could hear someone taking a draw on a cigarette and then blowing it out impatiently. "*I said, Stanton. Now you're supposed to say . . .*" The voice paused again. Bronco intentionally waited long enough for the person on the other end to get impatient and then he calmly said, "Bluebell." Another pause, another draw, a calmer exhale, "*Right. Now here's the deal,*" said the voice. "*Stanton is going by the name Sam Keller. I'll text a picture to you. The address is 18 Oak Street in Malone. Keller works in a diner, Flo's diner, morning shift, Tuesday thru Saturday. That's it.*"

"How do you know this is really Stanton?"

"*I verified it with your boss. It was your boss that gave me your number.*" Another quick draw-exhale. There was another strange sound, a kind of jangling, like a bunch of chains being swung around. Bronco could imagine the guy swinging his keys or something in exasperation. The guy continued, "*Look. If I'm lying, you*

*don't get Stanton and I don't get paid. I wanna get paid. That's how you
know it's really Stanton. Trust me. I've been watching this one a long
time."*

Bronco grunted and hung up without any other reply. He could
imagine the guy on the other end staring at his phone, the line
suddenly dead, a totally pissed-off expression on his face. That gave
him an odd sense of satisfaction. But the meaning of this call was
even more satisfying. What it meant was that the end game had
started. The waiting was over, and he could get this done, retrieve
his gold, and get the hell out of this place forever.

He stared at the hot pan, all ready to receive a fresh filet of
breaded trout. It was tempting—it wouldn't take more than twenty
minutes to follow through with his thoroughly delectable breakfast
plan. Unfortunately, the lure of the opportunity to get this over and
done overruled his stomach. He was not going to waste another
second now that the finish line was in sight. He turned off the
burner and reached in the cupboard to grab a couple of granola
bars—a poor substitute for pan-fried trout—and then went over to
his laptop, peeling and crunching the granola bar like a banana as
he went. He quickly got directions for Flo's diner in Malone. Only a
little over two hours away. It would take him less than ten minutes
to pack up what he needed—he'd had everything prepped for
months waiting for this moment. He could be there before noon—
before Sam Keller/Stanton was even off his morning shift. Perfect.
He would follow him until the right opportunity came up,
shouldn't take long, nab him and then get in contact with Babineau
to decide on a rendezvous.

The notion that he might be able to get this done today intoxi-
cated him. He hummed to himself as he texted Babineau to inform
him of his plan. He hit send just as a new text came in. It was from
the jangling-smoker-loser informer. It contained a picture of Stanton. As he watched the picture slowly display, the phone nearly
slipped from his hand as chunk-by-chunk the screen revealed a
picture not of a guy, but of a bleach-blonde girl in a waitress outfit,

her hair clearly brunette at the roots. Sam Keller was a "her." Not only that—the eyes, the cheekbones, the nose, even the mysterious look on her face, there was no doubt about it—Sam Keller was *her!* The demon. The mind reader. The flying witch. Sam Keller/Stanton was Blue DuBois.

"JESUS FUCKING CHRIST!" He shouted to the cavernous living room, slamming his fist on the table. Babineau surely knew all along and didn't tell him. And right now, without a doubt, Babineau was laughing his ass off. That fucking son-of-a-bitch bastard.

Bronco sat down hard and ran his hand through his hair. He was trembling. He had known this job wasn't going to be as simple as Babineau had made it out to be. He knew Babineau would throw some curve ball. But he wasn't expecting a knuckleball like this. Shit. Babineau must be after her because of her mind-reading powers. That's why he wanted her alive. But does he know that I know, he wondered? How could he? It was probable that Babineau knew this was the girl he had kidnapped, but it wasn't like she had a tattoo on her forehead that said "I can read minds" so there would be no reason for him to suspect that he knew. And why was he using the code name "Stanton" for this girl? Was it just to throw him off—or some sort of mind game reminding him of his father's last job years ago?

Shit. Well, it didn't change anything except that now he had to be extra careful in nabbing her. It was a good thing he had been practicing with some of this new gear. All he had to do was get close and be quick. Her mind-reading had limited range—he had tested it when he had her tied to a chair during their last encounter —so either the tasers or pepper ball gun should do it.

As he gathered his long prepared kit for the job, his mind was working. This is the girl that knew his father killed his brother. This is the girl that might know that he killed his father, and she was being delivered right to his lap. But Babineau wanted her alive.

What for? Well, fucker, maybe I'll just delay bringing her to you until I have my own little chat with her.

He shook his head. Don't lose focus, man. Right now, it's time to get moving. He polished off the granola bar, washed it down with coffee, and tossed the wrapper in the fireplace. He would have at least two hours in the car to figure out exactly how this new wrinkle factored into his reality and what he was going to do about it.

11:00 am, Malone

"CAN YOU BELIEVE THIS WEATHER?" said Sylvie as she walked to the driver's door of the rusty little Nissan sedan.

Blue, standing by the passenger door, looked up at the clear sky and took a breath of crisp, unseasonably warm March air. As she let it out, she turned to Sylvie.

"Hey, I really really appreciate this. I know it was a big favor to ask."

"Pish," said Sylvie, "I needed an excuse to take a break and get out of town." She ducked into the car, leaned over, and unlocked the passenger door. Blue slid into the passenger seat and had to tug hard on the door before it made a ka-klunk sound and closed suddenly with a slam.

"Welcome to the life of a poor student. At least she runs and has a good heater. She's been good to me, for the most part."

Sylvie turned the key, and the car eagerly came to life. "See what I mean? Never let me down." She paused before putting it into gear and looked at Blue with a serious expression. "You sure you want to do this? You going to be okay?" "*VISITING WHERE HER FAMILY DIED? GOD, I CAN'T IMAGINE. SHE SHOULD HAVE SOMEONE WHO KNOWS WHAT THEY'RE DOING. I SURE AS HELL DON'T KNOW WHAT I'M DOING.*"

It was at times like this that Blue was glad she could hear people's *chiss* and even feel a little *veraque*. Sylvie was a good person through and through and really that's all she needed for this—having a good person by her side.

"With you along, yeah. I'm going to be fine. Really."

Sylvie considered this for a moment. "*OKAY, SYLVIE, YOU FOOL, HERE YOU ARE GOING ALONG WITH IT.*" "Okay then. We'll do this thing, whatever it is, together." She reached over and grabbed Blue's hand and gave it a firm squeeze that sent an odd sensation through her. It was as if the touch of Sylvie's hand had pulled the trigger that was launching her into the next phase of her life and there was no going back.

"Okay," she said, and as Sylvie smiled and put the car in gear, Blue's mood turned from doubt to a sudden hunger to see if this was really going to work, really going to release her from her past and let her move on. And if she found the rocket box still intact, this might be more than a goodbye to her family: what was contained in that box might change everything for her forever. She just didn't know what the hell that change might be.

11:05 am, Westbury

"WHY WOULDN'T she just come home? Why wait until now to drop a clue and then leave us hanging? Could she be in trouble?" Wu was asking this as he piled into the back seat of Jack's old Buick.

"Well, there is just this little thing about being stalked by a creepy mobster," said Will.

"But the police know all about that. It's not like she wouldn't have protection here. Chief Hannah would make sure she was safe. I mean, what protection could she have in Malone?" said Wu.

"Well, she has anonymity. Plus, she still doesn't trust anyone with any authority," said Will. "She only trusts us. And there is the whole DFC thing. I bet she wants to get the full story about adoption before she commits. Look, she went to a lot of trouble to hide herself and she isn't about to give that up until she is absolutely sure she's not going to get dragged off by the DFC and is safe from Bronco and Babineau."

"And *I* think she is absolutely brilliant," said Anna as she slid in next to Wu in the back seat. "I bet she is doing just fine on her own but really misses us. Why would she want to give that up? For the crazy high school scene? No way, uh-uh. I'm with her. In fact, you might have trouble getting me to come back. I think she and I would do fabulously well in Malone, New York."

"God, Anna, don't say that in front of Blue, please? Don't you want her to come back with us? We've been completely off balance since she left," said Will.

"Honestly, Will, you take me too seriously sometimes. Of *course* I want her back. More than anything. Together we can take on the worst WWHS, Babineau, and the DFC can throw at us. *Especially* if the adoption goes through."

"It will, absolutely," said Wu. "*I STILL THINK SHE COULD BE IN TROUBLE.*" Wu was looking at Will.

Will just held up his cell phone and pointed.

"*OK, I GET IT, WE CAN ALWAYS CALL FOR HELP,*" Wu conceded.

"OK what *are* you guys signaling here?" asked Anna. "No secrets in this group, right?"

"I was just pointing out that we've got cell phones. We can always call somebody if we need to."

"Don't worry, we won't need to. C'mon, we're going to get to see Blue! Let's cheer up everyone!" said Anna.

"If we find her," said Wu.

"If she's even still in Malone," said Will. "She might have left that clue because she was moving on."

"Are you guys done overanalyzing this yet?" Jack had been patiently sitting at the wheel. "We could've been there and back by now you know."

Anna laughed. It was amazing how her laugh always seemed to neutralize any high emotions, thought Will. It was like a smile bomb. Everyone relaxed.

Wu said, "Yeah, sorry, Jack. And thanks for doing this. We're ready."

"Glad to do it. I owe it."

"You don't owe anything, Jack," said Anna.

"OK, then let's just say I need to do it," said Jack.

"Jack, you are just the biggest faker. You love Blue just like us, you sweetie." Anna leaned over the driver's seat and gave him a big kiss on his cheek. "Now let's go get 'er!"

Sweetie? Was something going on between Anna and Jack? That was such a foreign notion to Will that he instantly brushed it off. There was way too much other stuff to think about.

1:30 pm, Stanton Homestead

"You okay?" asked Sylvie. She had just shut off the engine and was looking at Blue as she spoke.

"Yeah, I think so. It's just so . . . so . . ." She stopped for lack of words. She was also stopped because of the lack of emotion, the emotion she had been anticipating she would feel as soon as she started seeing familiar things, an anticipation that had been building ever since they left Malone. But the anticipation evaporated as they pulled into a broad well-groomed driveway, hardly the grassy track she remembered. The drive continued down its carefully graded path and through the ravine that had once been clogged with trees and brush but was now thinned and well-groomed. And as the drive rose into the clearing where the cozy farmhouse, immense barn, and greenhouse had stood, she saw that in their place was a palatial log mansion. It was utterly and completely foreign to her.

"Wow," said Sylvie as she got out of the car, gaping at the wooden monstrosity. "You lived in this place?"

"No," replied Blue standing next to her open car door. "This is all completely different." In fact, she started to wonder if they had pulled into the wrong driveway.

"Are you sure this is the right place?" asked Sylvie. "Maybe we should knock and ask."

"Yeah, maybe."

As Sylvie went up on the porch and knocked, Blue's eyes scanned around the property, and a flicker of recognition caused her to catch her breath. She squinted and started to walk away from the car and the building, focusing on a tree that caught her attention. As familiar details began to emerge, she started running and shouted, "Wait, this is my tree! This is our orchard!" She ran up to the apple tree that had caught her eye and reached out her hand to touch it. There was no doubt that this had been at one time her favorite climbing tree as her fingers instinctively moved to familiar knots and handholds. But it wasn't the same. It felt so much smaller than she remembered, and it had gone wild, no longer neatly trimmed by caring hands. She scanned the other trees, still in their neat rows. All of them were overgrown with suckers that should have been pruned long ago.

She heard Sylvie come up behind her and say, "Well, no one is home, but it looks like you've found something." She felt a gentle hand on her shoulder, and she turned to Sylvie. "This was my family's orchard. My orchard. My sister and I would run from tree to tree and climb them and pick apple blossoms in the spring." And just like that, she realized she was saying these things out loud. There was no panic, no volcano, only the feeling that, like the trees and the log mansion, the world had moved on.

"Her name was Heather, she was two years younger than me. She would be thirteen by now." Speaking this did bring on tears, but they were different now. These were tears of acknowledgement and reverence rather than tears of anguish and despair. They were comfortable, like a hug.

She felt a squeeze on her shoulder, then a warm embrace. She wrapped her arms around Sylvie, and she felt as if she was holding

Heather, holding her mother, holding them both. They stayed like that for a while.

"Thanks for being here with me. It really helps," she whispered to Sylvie. She gave her a hard squeeze and then released her. Sylvie held Blue by the shoulders and looked her in the eye and said nothing, but her *chiss* whispered *"Oh, honey."* Then she leaned in and kissed Blue on the forehead.

"I want to see if there is anything left of the sugarhouse." Blue turned and stepped along the first row of trees to the edge of the orchard and was surprised to see the path to the sugarhouse almost like she remembered. The only reason for it to still be there would be to maintain the sugarhouse and her heart leapt at this thought.

"Maybe they still use it for storage or something," she said as she started to trot down the path. Sylvie followed, calling after her, "What? Hey slow down, girl, wait for me! But Blue accelerated as she became more and more certain it was still there. She reached the end of the orchard and there it was exactly as it had been five years ago as if out of a photograph album. She had a brief sensation of deja vu and half expected to see her father step through the door of the sugarhouse, but that sensation rapidly dissipated as she noted how the area around the sugarhouse had become overgrown with weeds giving it an abandoned, forlorn look, much as the orchard had.

"Looks like they don't use it at all," said Sylvie as she caught up to Blue.

Like the orchard, the shed should have been well-tended and humming with activity about now. It was sugaring season and a day like today would have seen the sap running fifty gallons a day and steam would be pouring from the cupola. Instead, it was silent and cold with unused sap pails stacked along the back of the shed and the wood rack empty.

"No, it's like it was frozen in time."

Blue opened the unlocked door and it swung open with a creak. Inside, the slanting light from the cupola illuminated sugaring equipment that sat silent and dusty and waiting. In one corner, an ornate cast iron wood stove crouched like a lonely little watchman. She stepped in almost expecting to feel the hot humid breath of the steaming evaporator and the sweet green aroma of fresh sap. Instead, she was greeted with old cobwebs and dust.

"So this thing you're looking for—it would be in here?" asked Sylvie, who had cautiously stepped inside behind Blue.

"I think so. My dad kept it out here somewhere, but I never knew exactly where he hid it."

"How big is it?" asked Sylvie as she lifted some old burlap sacks off the floor, looking underneath. The dust that arose from moving the old bags started them both coughing.

After the dust settled and she stopped coughing, Blue replied, "It was quite big, but I was small, so everything was big. I'd guess about like this." She gestured dimensions with her hands for a box about 24" x 18" x 12" in size.

Sylvie gazed around the room and said, "Well, unless it's in that big pan there or underneath it, there isn't much place for it to hide."

Blue looked in the evaporator and then inside the firebox underneath. Sylvie was right. There wasn't anywhere it could be hiding inside the sugarhouse. Her shoulders slumped as she started to accept that it might be gone for good. It's just the sort of thing someone might pilfer. Most everything else was too big or heavy to carry off. She was disappointed but not really surprised. Like the house and the driveway and the orchard, the missing rocket box was another indication that the world had moved on and it was just waiting for her to move on, too.

She didn't want to leave empty-handed, though. She took another poke around inside to see if there was something else she could take with her as a memento. She rummaged in a box of wooden spiles and found one that looked new and unused, one that may well have been the last one her father carved. It was elegant and simple and felt solid and perfect in her hand. It was something.

She stepped back outside and sat on the ground, leaning back against the sugarhouse with a sigh. Sylvie came out and sat beside her.

"What is that thing you took?" she asked.

Blue held it up. "It's a maple tree tap. It's called a spile. You drill a hole in the tree, stick that in, and hang a bucket underneath. The sap comes down the groove and drips into the bucket."

"Wow. It sounds so primitive."

"Simple. Like life was here. Simple and sweet and peaceful."

"And lonely, I would think."

"Lonely now."

"Oh gosh, I'm so sorry. I didn't mean it that way."

"It's okay. It doesn't feel right here now anyway. Now that someone else owns it, everything feels wrong. I thought it would feel like home, but it feels like—I don't know—like walking through an empty school and all the stuff is there, the lockers and walls and doors, but none of your friends are there. They've left, just like you and now the school is nothing but an empty shell. There's no more life to it."

Sylvie reached over and grabbed her hand. It felt good because it had life to it.

"Well, there is still some life around here. Look at all those deer tracks and all those crows over in that tree. They're bitching about something."

Blue followed Sylvie's gaze to where a bunch of black specs were whirling and cawing around a tree. An involuntarily vox blurted from her eyes, "*ARDETH?*"

Almost immediately there came a "Kwa-koo" from the midst of the murder of crows and a large black silhouette emerged from the tree, scattering the crows. The silhouette flapped its wings powerfully and headed straight toward them. Blue's heart skipped a beat in disbelief as she slowly stood up, swaying a little bit.

"IT COULDN'T BE YOU! COULD IT? ARDETH?"

"Shit! That bird is coming right at us." Sylvie stood up in a panic and grabbed Blue's arm. "Is it dangerous?"

"No, no, don't worry. It's a raven, but I can't believe . . ." She trailed off as she watched, mesmerized by the approach of the huge bird, and then a realization came to her and she turned to Sylvie, speaking urgently, "Do you have any food on you? Crackers? Granola bar? Anything?"

Sylvie balked in surprise but rummaged in her vest pockets and managed to come up with a bag of nuts.

"Perfect!" Blue opened the bag of nuts and took a few out. There was a tree stump about ten feet from them and she stepped over to it and as she watched the approaching raven she made a grand gesture of placing the nuts on the log. She then stepped back while staring hard at the raven, voxing, ""ARDETH, ARDETH, WHERE ARE YOU? TIME TO SNACK IT'S A QUARTER TO TWO!"

"Kwa-koo!" replied the raven.

"Jesus, I don't know what the hell you're doing but it sure looks like devil worship to me," said Sylvie nervously, putting Blue between her and the approaching raven.

The raven landed cautiously near the stump but after a moment of croaking and eyeing the two of them, he hopped over to the stump and pecked the nuts expertly, swallowing them with the bird-beak equivalent of smacking lips. He looked at Blue expectantly and she held up the bag and voxed, "YOU WANT SOME MORE?"

Then the raven did the most curious thing. After tilting his head a couple of times he croaked something in raven that sounded remarkably like "Box!" and hopped over to the shed. The base of the shed was covered with a board skirt that reached from the ground up to the bottom of the wall. There were ventilation gaps in the boards and the raven started pecking with purpose into one of the gaps, and as Blue and Sylvie watched in astonishment, on about the third peck, the raven pulled out a string with a ring on the end and he hopped back and gave it a yank. Blue and Sylvie stood speechless as a two-foot portion of the skirt flopped to the ground and there behind it squatted an olive green metal box.

The three of them stood motionless for exactly the space of a sheep's baa and then exploded simultaneously,

"Jesus Christ!"

"Ardeth it *is* you!"

"Krrra-kree!"

Ardeth hopped backwards in alarm, but Blue had enough composure to shake out some more nuts and toss them his way. Then she jumped over to the shed, dropped to her knees and dragged the box out of its hiding place.

Sylvie came up behind her saying, "Jesus, what did I just witness? This is some spooky shit, Sam. How . . . how did that bird know . . ."

"His name is Ardeth. My dad trained him. Words, tricks, all for food as a reward. I had no idea he would be here. And I definitely did not know he could do this." She grabbed one handle of the box. "Please help me to get this inside the shed."

Sylvie grabbed the other handle and together they carried the box into the shed. It wasn't terrifically heavy but it was hefty enough to tell Blue it was full. She just didn't know with what.

1:40 pm, New York City

"Jim, get down to Kumar's office right now." Babineau put his phone back in his pocket without taking his eyes off Kumar's monitor. "When exactly was this?"

Kumar pointed to the screen, "You can see right here, the video clock in the lower . . ."

"God dammit, Kumar, just tell me when!"

"As I said, it is right here, 1:32, about nine minutes ago." Babineau glared at Kumar not knowing whether to be annoyed or impressed at how impervious to frustration he was.

"Just send me that video clip and then update me if anything changes." He turned as Jim Purcell stepped through the office doorway. "Jim, change of plans. Get the Escalade now. We need to meet with Farrell today as soon as possible."

1:45 pm, Malone

THE RATTLING chains were starting to drive Bronco nuts. He reached across the car and seized the guy's wrist in a crushing grip.

The guy—he called himself "Chainy"—gave Bronco a fierce but properly nervous look.

"Sorry!" said Chainy.

Bronco released him but didn't say anything. He returned to studying the windows of the diner across the street while Chainy caressed his bruised wrist and mumbled under his breath, "Jesus fuck, it's just a habit."

"It's been an hour," said Bronco. "You said she worked until two."

"I don't know what's going on," muttered Chainy. "She should have been here."

Bronco didn't doubt him. Chainy had shown him pictures of the girl that had been taken on his phone from this exact spot: a gas station across from the diner. Even from that distance, the pictures were high enough resolution that once zoomed in, there was no doubt it was the girl.

It was irritating that she wasn't here, but he wasn't that surprised. He'd worked service jobs and knew that service people tended to have irregular schedules. For Chainy's benefit, however, he preferred to put on the act of extreme disappointment.

"No girl, no reward." He leaned forward to turn the key to start the car.

"Wait!" said Chainy. "Look, I'll call somebody—one of my girls that used to work at that diner. I'll have her go in and see what's going on."

Bronco grunted but leaned back in his seat without starting the car. He stared at Chainy who had pulled out his phone. "Five minutes," he said sternly. "After that, I track her down my way and no reward."

Chainy waved his left hand, palm down, in an 'okay, okay' gesture while he barked into the phone, "Becky, I need you right now . . . At the Sunoco . . . What?! God dammit . . . all right, all right, $1500, but only if you get over here in less than five minutes . . ."

BECKY SPOTTED the car and gave it a once over before she walked up to the passenger-side door and tapped on the window. A late-model Mustang with New York plates didn't seem to go along with the whole Vermont-state-agency-looking-for-a-runaway story. She wouldn't put it past Chainy to be working a deal with someone else, but she'd be damned if she was going to let it cut into her share. Chainy rolled the window down and she knew instantly that his hey-there-how-you-doing smile was covering up one nervous individual. A glance at the driver confirmed that this was not the promised "caring guardian" looking for his lost sheep.

"Hey there, Becky, how you doing?" said Chainy.

"What's the fucking deal, Chainy? And who's this guy?" She heard a grunt and glanced at the driver and thought she almost caught a smirk on his face.

"This is, uh, George. He's helping Sam's family, that is *Blue's* family, get her back. We were waiting for her to get off her shift, but it looks like she's not there today. I figured since you know Flo that you could go in and find out where she is."

"What the hell? Why don't you just go knock on her apartment door instead of hauling me out here?"

Chainy looked like he was thinking hard to come up with a

plausible story so when he said, "Umm, well we did, but she wasn't home," she knew he was full of shit. She went along with it, but with all her shields up.

"So why don't I just call her? I've got her number . . ." She pulled out her phone. She didn't have Blue's number, but Chainy didn't know that.

Chainy rubbed his chin nervously. "No! No, don't do that. Look, if we call, she might run away again. No Blue, no reward. For either of us. Just go in and find out where she is!" He was starting to get impatient, but then "George" leaned over and spoke. Whether he was legit or not, he certainly was a lot more composed than Chainy.

"Hi, Becky. Nice to meet you and I apologize for bringing you out here. I don't have time to stay here much longer today and was hoping to bring good news to the family. I would very much appreciate your help if you wouldn't mind asking about her for me."

She examined "George's" face and though his words were silky and polite, she didn't like what she saw. Most of the men's faces she saw were simpletons—puppy dogs looking for pleasure, and most were harmless and somewhat pathetic, but every now and then she saw one like this: pleasant smile, a little too pleasant, polite, a little too polite, and eyes that seemed to have nothing pleasant or polite behind them. They were cold and calculating and scary. Something was definitely going on here and she did not like it.

She turned away from them both without saying a word and made her way across the street. Fuck them, she thought. I'll ask Flo, give them her answer and then leave. If Chainy got their money, fine. If not, well, maybe she didn't want to be involved in this anyway now that "George" was eroding the whole reunite-the-happy-family fable.

The cheery little "bing-bing" that rang out as she entered the diner sounded as sarcastic as she felt. She marched straight back to the kitchen and barged through the door, spotting Flo holding a tray loaded with food and she stopped directly in front of her.

"I need to talk to Sam. Where is she?"

Flo looked back at her without flinching, as if this was the most normal occurrence in the world, which, of course, it had been during Becky's time there as a waitress.

"Hello to you, too, Becky," said Flo.

"Well?"

"Well, a) you look terrible and b) I'll answer your question after I get these plates out to customers and not before."

Flo pushed past her with a linebacker's poise leaving her standing there in the familiar kitchen, steam coming from the dishwasher and fog filling her head. The smell of Chet's cooking and the sizzling sounds and the clanking dishes just added to the babbling in her brain that was telling her to get this over with and get out of there at the same time it was telling her to stay. God, what am I doing, she asked herself. Chainy was only an asshole, but that other guy was a bona fide horror show.

"You doin' okay, Becky?" asked Chet, peeking over his shoulder as he flipped a couple of his signature grilled ham-and-cheese. Her growling stomach nearly drowned out the background noise and she swayed a little bit, causing Chet to pause with a concerned look on his face. God, she needed a hit badly, but she needed money badly for that.

"Imfinethanksforasking," she said in a flat tone.

Chet turned away looking as unconvinced as she was.

BRONCO WATCHED with a practiced eye as the girl walked back across the street from the diner, noticing the worn-around-the-edges look of every part of her—her jacket, her pants, her shoes, her hair, her skin, even the way she walked. She looked like she was in her thirties, but he was sure she was a burnt-out early twenty-something, just as he was sure that at one time she was a beautiful girl. Addicts looked that way—he had seen enough of them to know. They had been his customers, after all. He shrugged. That's free choice for you, he thought. She was free to ruin her life in whatever way she wanted.

The girl came around to Chainy's window and as he rolled it down she was literally spitting as she shouted at him, "She's gone, asshole! She quit this morning! And good for her!" She turned and stomped off while Chainy leaned out and yelled, "Wait, where did she go?"

Becky turned around and walked backwards yelling, "Fuck if I know! I wouldn't tell you if I did!" She flipped him a double bird and added, "I'm gone too, asshole! Find yourself another girl!"

Chainy turned to Bronco and said, "Wait just a sec, I gotta go talk some sense into her." He got out of the car just as Bronco felt a buzzing in his pocket. He pulled out his phone and swore when he saw who it was. He answered the call anyway. He didn't really have a choice.

"*I bet you didn't find her in Malone,*" came Babineau's voice.

Bronco scowled at the phone as if it had just bit him, "Just what the hell are you up to, Theo. I'm getting tired of being fucked around with."

A chuckle came out of the phone. "*I think you mistake me. I fully expected you to find her there, but I just received some unexpected information.*"

"What kind of information?"

"*Our little friend apparently found someone to take her for a drive in the mountains and wouldn't you know it, right at this moment they are parked in the driveway of your camp and taking a walking tour of the property.*"

Bronco was stunned into silence. His mind was racing to make sense of what Babineau had said and it was only just now dawning on him how masterfully he was being manipulated. He was accustomed to anger but not accustomed to what he was experiencing now which was honest-to-god fury with this man. He didn't dare let it show or he would appear to have capitulated completely. Instead, he calmed down and in his most languid tone of voice he replied, "I assume you mean the camp I am caretaking."

Laughter on the other end of the line. Just more manipulation, Bronco told himself. Keep your cool. Babineau finally stopped laughing and said, *"Yes, that camp."*

"And you would know this how?"

"The camp has surveillance cameras, right?"

Bronco knew the surveillance cameras were online and being monitored, and not just by him, but how could Babineau have accessed them? "You hacked them."

That irritating laugh from Babineau again, and then, *"No, I didn't hack them. Why would I need to hack them when I have the monitors in my office? Didn't you ever wonder who owns that camp?"*

2:00 pm, Malone

"Omigod, it's the Wilder Farm Museum!" Anna leaned over from the back seat, "Guys, we have to go there sometime. I can't believe it's right near Malone!"

Will stared at her with a mix of consternation and amusement. Anna's light-hearted observation was just what he needed right now. Still, he couldn't resist a little admonishment. "Anna, we're here to find Blue, remember? Our friend who's in danger and that we've been searching for the past four months?"

"I know, I know, but I just think it's cool that she decided to come here of all the places she could have gone. I just loved the 'Little House on the Prairie' books when I was growing up, didn't you?"

"Um, sorry, but I kind of never read them." He looked over at Jack expecting him to return his 'not-a-guy-thing' grin but instead Jack was glancing at Anna in the rearview mirror.

"Laura Ingalls Wilder," said Jack. "Yeah. I liked those books. Pa

Ingalls was my hero. He could take anything and turn it into something."

Anna laughed. "Don't look so shocked, Will. Jack has more to him than you think."

Will realized his mouth was hanging open in surprise and quickly shut it. Fortunately, everyone's attention was drawn back to the highway as they drove around a long bend and it became clear they had started getting into the town of Malone proper.

"Well, we're here," said Wu, "but where do we start?"

"There's a diner right there on the left," said Anna. "We could start by getting something to . . ."

There was a sudden screech of tires and Will was thrown against his seatbelt and Anna's upper body was jammed into the gap between the front seats.

"Shit!" shouted Jack. The car was at a standstill and in front of them, in the middle of the road, was a girl with wild black hair and a gleaming silver nose stud. For a very weird moment, Will thought, "Blue?" But a glance at her face confirmed with relief that it wasn't. The not-Blue girl was glaring at Jack and banging on the front hood with her hands while shouting choice obscenities at him. A shout from their right turned his attention to a creepy looking guy yelling at the girl and walking toward her. The girl was now yelling at the creepy guy, and she kept yelling at him while she continued to cross the street, not even watching for traffic. The creepy guy came to a sudden halt and turned quickly around. He saw something to make him curse and run back the way he came. Will turned around to see what he was chasing and saw a silver sports car pull out of a gas station and accelerate away.

"Jesus, what was that all about?" said Wu, helping Anna to extract herself from between the front seats. "Are you okay?"

"I'm okay," she said. "But that was a little too exciting for me. Is that girl okay?"

Jack let out a long "woo" and shook his head. "Yeah, I don't think I hit her. She was sure pissed at us, though. I didn't even see her—she stepped out of nowhere." He took a couple of deep breaths and then carefully navigated the Buick into the diner parking lot which was right across the street from them. "I think I need a minute to recuperate. Maybe we should go in and get some coffee, at least."

"Is that weird guy gone? I'm not sure I want to get out of the car with him around," said Wu.

"Yeah, he's down the block trying to catch up to that girl," said Will. He took in a deep breath himself and let it out slowly. His first impression of Malone had sure been submarined. The wholesomeness of Laura Ingalls Wilder had been blasted into fable-land.

"Drug deal gone bad, I think," said Jack. "That girl definitely had the look of a junky." Jack looked a little shaky getting out of the car. Will felt a little shaky himself.

"Well at least this place smells great," said Wu as he opened the door to the diner and a warm, homey aroma wafted over them. Will was the last of them to go through the door and his impulsive glance at the front window of the diner caught a middle-aged waitress staring out the window down the road where angry girl and creepy guy had gone.

As he stepped through the entryway and into the dining room, the same waitress from the window came over to greet them, "Welcome to Flo's. I'm Flo, go ahead and take any table that's open. Coffee?"

The four of them found a table and sat down and Flo came over with a pot of coffee. Will looked around and saw that the place was almost empty, but a lot of the tables hadn't been cleared yet. He glanced at his phone and saw that it was 2:15. It was well after the lunch rush. He looked up at Flo who was hovering with the pot and reaching for his inverted coffee cup.

"Ah, no thanks, I don't drink it, but I'll take a coke." He noticed Jack was already sipping coffee and his hand was shaking a bit.

Flo hesitated and then looked at each of them in turn. "Were you kids in that car that just about hit Becky?"

"Um, yeah," said Wu. "It scared the crap out of us. You know her?"

Flo looked at Jack. "Nice reflexes to stop that quick. That could have been bad. You kids from Vermont, then? I saw your license plate." This last she said in response to Wu's look of surprise. She suddenly reached out and took Jack's cup and without explanation turned on her heel and headed for the kitchen. Will looked across at Jack who had a confused look on his face and then to Wu who was thinking "DOES SHE HATE VERMONTERS OR SOMETHING?" But before any of them had time to react further, Flo was back, only this time with a different pot.

"That was the swill we serve the drive-throughs. This is the good stuff we reserve for our regulars. This round's on me, you look like you could use a break. What are you kids doing in New York anyway? It's a school day. You all playing hooky?"

Will looked nervously around at the rest of them who looked as surprised as he was at this unexpected question.

"We, ummm . . ." Wu started.

Anna interrupted Wu and with her usual frankness, which made Will cringe just a little, said, "Yeah, we kinda bent the rules and ditched early, but it was for a legitimate reason. There are times when it's legitimate to bend the rules, don't you think?"

Flo crossed her arms in a motherly posture, but her mouth was bent up in a half-suppressed smile, "Perhaps you'd like to elaborate for me?"

Anna reached into her purse and pulled out the infamous photo and slapped it on the table. "This is our really good friend and she's been missing for four months. We just learned last night she's in Malone somewhere."

They all looked to see what Flo's reaction would be but what they saw, none of them anticipated, not even Will, who only caught two words of *chiss* from Flo: "*JESUS CHRIST.*" She slowly lowered the pot and set it on the table as if it had become too heavy. She closed her eyes and stood stock still for so long that Will started to feel awkward and as he looked at each of the others, he could tell they felt that way, too. But then Flo turned and dragged a chair over from another table, sat down, and said, "Her name wouldn't happen to be Blue DuBois, would it?"

4:00 pm, Stanton Homestead

"HEY." The whispered word startled Blue and she turned to see Sylvie's face close to hers. There was a gentleness to her look and Blue realized she had been totally engrossed in the contents of the rocket box and completely forgotten about Sylvie. "I'm sorry. God, how long have I been sitting here?"

"Doesn't matter. You take as much time as you need. I just wanted to tell you I'm going back to the car to get our jackets."

The cloud of vapor that accompanied Sylvie's words puzzled Blue until she felt her own goosebumps. The temperature had dropped dramatically. She glanced out the window and saw snowflakes. A lot of snowflakes.

"Snow," she said, stating the obvious. She wasn't exactly sure what it meant for them. Was this going to end the visit?

"Yeah. Snow," said Sylvie. "We can stay a little while longer, but if it starts to get worse, we should go. My little car can handle a little snow okay, but I don't like the idea of going down this crazy-ass steep road if it starts getting deep."

"Okay, thanks," said Blue. She was barely engaged in the conversation—just enough to respond to what was being said. Her brain was still wallowing in deep nostalgia. She was just going to have to trust Sylvie's judgment on when to leave. She turned back to the items she had pulled out of the rocket box barely registering that Sylvie had taken off her own fleece vest and put it over Blue's shoulders and then slipped out the door of the sugarhouse.

She looked again at the framed picture she had pulled from the box. It had been over five years since she had last seen that picture, or any picture at all of her family. It was the four of them standing in front of the flower bed by their front door. It was just as she remembered it—Heather was a beautiful six-year-old with a peaceful smile, buttercups stuck in her hair, Blue, eight years old, with her long dark hair festooned with bluebells, her dad standing behind them, his brown hair almost to his shoulders, a tightly trimmed dark brown beard completing the frame around a deeply tanned face with deep smile creases in his cheeks, and her mother, glowing with benevolence, beauty, and love, her arms surrounding her two children.

After a long look, she put the picture down feeling like she had absorbed all there was to absorb. The image was now indelible in her mind, unchangeable, frozen in time. She took a deep breath and turned to an envelope that she had noticed earlier, one that had a return address for a testing lab. That had spooked her but also intrigued her, and now she felt compelled to open it.

She pulled out about ten pages of documents and laid them out in her lap. The top page contained a spreadsheet with an array of rows labeled "Genetic Markers." When she read the heading of the table, her whole body tensed up: "Paternity Inclusion Report: André Paul DuBois." It took a couple of seconds to digest that. She had to read it again. Paternity Report. What the hell? She studied the table and as she did she experienced a little flutter of panic:

Personal Information of Subjects

Name	Relationship	Date of Birth
Heather XXXXX	Daughter	1999-4-14
Amélie E. DuBois	Mother	1974-4-2
André P. DuBois	Alleged Father	1972-12-18

Alleged father? She froze for a moment, unable to take her eyes off those two words: Alleged Father! Her father wasn't Heather's father, just an "alleged" father? She scanned down the second table and then gave out a partial sigh of relief when she found the crux of the report:

Probability of Paternity: 99.87%

She read that line over again. Probability of paternity 99.87%.

Why in hell would her father have needed a report to know? She quickly thumbed through the other pages from the packet until she came to a page that contained a name that nearly stopped her heart. Under the letterhead for the testing company was the addressee: Mr. Theodore Babineau:

September 17, 2006
Dear Mr. Babineau,

At the request of an anonymous client we are sending you a Paternity Report disclosing the probability for paternity of Heather [surname redacted], born 1999-4-14 to Amélie E. DuBois, being 99.87% for alleged father André P. DuBois. Most courts use a value of 99.5% or higher for legal determination of paternity. Although this report is not a legal document, it is generally accepted evidence in a court of law when it comes to custody disputes.

Best regards,
Charles R. Cottle
Customer Relations Coordinator

Her hand dropped to her lap still holding the letter as her gaze drifted aimlessly. What was the purpose of this? What was the meaning? The letter was sent in September 2006, just weeks before the fire. Why would her father feel compelled to send this letter to Babineau? It would have been a huge risk contacting him even in this anonymous way just to prove to Babineau that her father was the real father of Heather?

And then it hit her.

"NO! No no no no no," she covered her eyes and repeated

over and over again while shaking her head. "It can't be, it can't be, it can't be . . ." Her heart felt like it couldn't take any more of the whiplash of emotions. She pushed the box away from her. Her legs wanted to get up and run—anywhere—and they didn't wait for her to make the decision. They started on their own to launch her up and out the door but just as they did there was a "pop" and her body locked up as if every muscle had cramped at the same time. She wanted to scream but nothing would come out. Her body, paralyzed and caught off balance, rolled on its back like a toppled beetle and as it did, her head was pivoted in such a way that she was staring directly at the sugarhouse doorway. And when she saw the upside-down beardless features of a face she had drawn likeness of for the police, her lungs found the reserve to push out a single strangled scream.

THAT WAS ALMOST TOO EASY, thought Bronco as he pulled a couple of heavy zip ties out of his jacket and set the clicking taser gun on the wood stove just inside the sugarhouse door. The girl lay paralyzed on the floor staring at him with a frozen grimace on her face. "ARE YOU HEARING WHAT I'M THINKING NOW, DEVIL GIRL? YOU CERTAINLY WEREN'T WHEN I SNUCK UP ON YOU." He crouched down and zipped her feet together. He deliberately did the feet first, remembering how fast she was and how she was probably even faster now that she'd grown up a bit—at least two inches since last summer, he thought as he looked the girl up and down. Focus, Bronco boy, you've probably got another ten seconds in the taser discharge and then another thirty seconds before she's fully recovered enough to put up a struggle. He zipped her hands next and hesitated just a moment before pulling out a small roll of duct tape and peeling a piece off.

"Goddammit!" gasped the girl when the taser finally timed out. She was panting for breath but wasn't able to move much yet. He let her breathe for a moment and then put the tape over her mouth before she recovered enough to spout more profanity.

He turned to look at what had been distracting her so much, wondering what could have been so engrossing for him to catch her unaware. It looked like an old ammo box filled with memorabilia, almost like a time capsule. Photos, papers, trinkets. He grabbed a picture that was lying on top. A family photo.

A squeal came from behind the duct tape, but he ignored it. He recognized the girl in the picture right away. "Hmm. So this is you when you were . . . what . . . eight? nine? And that's your mom and dad and sister?"

He turned to look at her glaring face. She didn't nod or shake her head, she just glared, but the glare was tempered with a sense of profound sadness. Tears were pooling up in her eyes. He thought about bumping her to see if they would spill over and trickle down her face, but an odd stirring inside his chest reached out to restrain him.

He turned back to the box and rummaged through a few more of the items. There were more photos, a couple of war medals, random correspondence, and scattered throughout were the same names repeated again and again: DuBois, Amelie, André, Heather, Blue. It must have been her family's time capsule, the girl's, Blue's. But what was it doing out here in the middle of nowhere in an old dusty sugarhouse? And in particular, what was it doing at what he now knew was Babineau's Adirondack hideout?

"Hmm," he repeated and turned back to the chest. There were some papers on the floor next to it, scattered when she dropped them the instant she was tazed. He picked up the one closest to him —a DNA paternity report.

"André and Amélie DuBois. Your parents?" He looked at her and watched her eyes squeeze shut. The pools spilled over. "And this must be your sister, Heather. Last name redacted. Hmm."

He picked up the next sheet and a flush of anger rose to his face the instant he saw Babineau's name. "What the hell?" He read the letter and then put it down in disgust. "Jesus fucking Christ." He turned to look at the girl. As he did he noticed a sign leaning against the wall behind her. It read "Stanton's Genuine New York Maple Syrup."

Stanton?

And then the realization of what Babineau had done revealed itself like an enemy map being rolled out in front of him. This was the Stanton place. Babineau bought it and put up this mansion of a camp. This was the site of the last job of El Segador and son. And he had been caretaking it for him all this time without a clue while Babineau had known all along. His loathing and fury with Babineau had already been burning at its highest level and so the effect of this new revelation was new and strange to him. It was loathing and fury now joined with certainty—certainty that he was no longer going to let Babineau manipulate him.

An icy puff accompanied by a cloud of snowflakes blew through the still open sugarhouse door and sent a chill through Bronco. He looked again at the girl, who by this time was curled up in a fetal position, eyes squeezed closed but with tears dripping to the floor. She appeared oblivious to the snow or cold or Bronco, trapped in her own little hell. He looked at his watch. Almost 4:30. Babineau would arrive in a couple of hours.

"Christ. Let's get out of this icebox before we freeze. After we're warmed up, we're going to have a little talk." He didn't know if she heard or not, and maybe he was just talking to himself, but either way, it was time for him to get one step ahead of Babineau instead of the other way around.

4:15 pm, Westbury

"WHAT DOES THIS MEAN?" asked Chief Hannah, holding her phone to her ear as she stepped over to the coat rack to collect her off-duty heavy down jacket. Rodney had just jolted her with ominous news:

Babineau and Purcell had left the city and been spotted on traffic cams heading north. She knew what that meant for her—she was going to start her vacation early, like right now, but she was wondering what it meant for Rodney.

"It means that we have to move. I already have people alerting law enforcement in Franklin County and I am going to leave right away. Unfortunately, I am guessing that I am about three hours behind Babineau. Our estimate is that they will be in Franklin County around 6 or 7 pm. I can't get there sooner than 9 or 10."

Chief Hannah checked her watch and calculated quickly in her head, "I can be there sooner—like 7 pm or better. I can post myself somewhere further south on I-87 even sooner, maybe by 6 pm, and watch for them. I can't see them taking anything but I-87."

"Okay, that will work as I don't exactly know how well the State Police will be able to monitor I-87. Babineau and Purcell should be easy to spot; they're in a black Escalade. You and I can meet in Saranac Lake when I get there. The biggest towns in Franklin County are Saranac Lake, Chateaugay, and Malone, so we want to focus on those."

"Got it." Chief Hannah grabbed more winter gear as she continued, "You do know there is a winter storm warning in the Adirondacks. Don't forget to put on your long johns and bring your snowshoes."

Rodney laughed and said, *"Yeah, well I don't own either. Did you know it got up to 60° today down here?"*

She smiled grimly and said, "Yeah, and it was 48° up here—what we consider tropical and now it's dropped to 34° and that doesn't bode well. I'm really not kidding about the long johns and maybe not the snowshoes either. A March snowstorm in the Adirondacks is no joke."

A much more sober voice said, *"Okay, noted. I'll see what I can beg or borrow, but my gut feel is that speed is more important at this point, so I may have to come as I am."*

"Okay. Keep me posted and see you soon."

She hung up and looked at Ed who was fully aware of her original plan and was now looking at her with raised eyebrows. "News?"

"Perps on the move in New York. I'm leaving earlier than expected. Think you can handle this town by yourself?"

"Go get 'em, boss," he said as he reached over to the coat rack. "But please put one of these on." He handed her a Kevlar vest. "I'd make a lousy Chief of Police."

4:30 pm, Stanton Homestead
Snow 1.5"

BLUE TUGGED AGAIN at the bindings that had her immobilized in the hoop-back dining chair. It was pointless but it was an outlet for the rage that was burning inside her—rage at the injustice, rage that she had put Sylvie in danger, rage that some cynical twist of fate had placed this miserable excuse for humanity inside this obscenity of a lodge that had been built over *her* home, over *her* families ashes, and now he was calmly pouring himself a drink and acting as if he owned the place.

As Bronco walked toward her and pulled a chair out to sit opposite her, she seethed, willing her bindings to release themselves so she could scratch his eyes out, but they held fast. Bronco took a sip of his caramel-colored drink, and an aroma of alcohol wafted her way.

"Well, here we are again," he said after a pause.

She snorted in derision and swore at him in her mind and as best she could from behind the tape that was covering her mouth.

"Okay. I get it. I know you'd like to kill me, and I wouldn't blame you, but right now, you and I have a shared problem and that problem is coming here in about an hour. Now . . ." Bronco looked up at her and she was shocked to find that he seemed nervous, almost like he was truly afraid.

"CAN YOU REALLY READ MY MIND?"

The unexpected *chiss* and Bronco's obvious discomfort momentarily quelled her rage. Of course, the answer should have been an instant "no," but something about his demeanor, the situation, and the sincerity of his statement about a threat coming their way gave her pause and against her better judgment, she found her head nodding.

"Okay," he said and took a deep breath. "We need to talk. Let's get that tape off."

The tape came off fairly easily and as soon as it was gone she screamed, "You fucker! What did you do to Sylvie? Where is she? If you hurt her . . ."

"Calm down. Fair question. I didn't hurt her but I did tie her up, of course. She is in the laundry room next to the garage."

"How the hell did you find us here? And why is your slimy ass desecrating my family's land?"

He sighed and sat back in his chair as his thoughts leaked, "GOOD FUCKING QUESTION." "I think we can both thank Babineau for this," he said after a moment. "That's who will be here in about an hour or less."

"Babineau!" she shouted. "You *know* him? *He's* coming here? What the hell!" She thought the situation had been as bad as it could get, but now it was evolving into an endless sick joke. And what Bronco said next pushed it right off the charts.

"Who do you think built this place?"

Blue didn't really remember what she said in her cross-eyed rage after that, but it caused Bronco to lean back in awe. When she was finally spent, he spoke, but in a voice that seemed tinged with empathy, and that might have been the biggest shock so far.

"Look. I didn't know until a few hours ago that the owner of this place that I've been caretaking for the past five months was Babineau. I've been his fucking houseboy. And I never knew this was your place until about thirty minutes ago." He paused, staring at the drink in his hand. "YOUR PLACE AND THE SITE OF THE LAST JOB OF EL SEGADOR AND SON."

"Shit," he said after a moment and then he lifted his glass and took a big swallow.

"What do you mean 'last job'? Who the *hell* is El Segador? Is *he* the one that killed my family?"

Bronco raised his eyebrows, "Damn, you are one spooky kid." But he answered her question. *"IF YOU DIDN'T LIKE THE LAST THING I TOLD YOU, YOU'RE REALLY NOT GOING TO LIKE THIS. EL SEGADOR WAS MY FATHER. AND YEAH, HE'S THE ONE. HE AND MY BROTHER."*

"What! Your father? Your brother?" Blue didn't have any words left to scream. Instead, she threw herself against her bindings with such fury the joints of the chair felt they just might give way.

Bronco sat across from her watching, once again with something that seemed like empathy, and as she started to slow down out of sheer exhaustion and frustration he quietly said, "He let you go."

"What?!"

"My brother. Now calm down before you hurt yourself. We haven't got much time so just listen. Babineau hired my father to kill your family. He was the one that killed your parents and burned down your house. My brother was with him, and he was supposed to kill you and your sister, but he let you go." As he said this Blue saw a replay in her head of what she saw so long ago when she was last sitting opposite Bronco. His father pushing his brother down the stairs, Bronco suffocating his father. But this time, the missing pieces were filled in.

"And your father killed your brother because he let us go ..."

"Yes. But as far as I'm concerned, Babineau killed my brother."

"Because if he hadn't hired your father ..."

"... my brother would be alive."

"... and my family would be alive."

Blue slumped back in her chair, completely spent. There it all was, laid out in front of her. The last gaps in the story of her past had been filled in. The story was so improbable she wondered if she was just experiencing her most cruel nightmare ever. She tilted her head back, closed her eyes, and opened them again. No, this was real life, and she wasn't sure she wanted it anymore.

"Just kill me now," she said quietly staring at the ceiling. There were probably tears trickling down her face, but she was numb to them. "Do you have any heroin? Finish what you started before? I think I want to be with my family now. I want to die here, where they died. And I don't want it to be him."

It was quiet. That was fine. It seemed like the quiet was agreeing with what she said. But then the quiet was broken.

"It's not going to be you that dies today."

5:00 pm, Malone

WITH A CLANKING OF KEYS AND A "SNICK" the door to Blue's apartment opened and Flo's boyfriend, Alan, stood back and gestured them in. "Be respectful, I could get in a lot of trouble for this."

Will and Anna stepped in first with Wu and Jack behind them. There wasn't a lot of room for the four of them, but there wasn't a lot of stuff for them to look through, either. The apartment was tiny, almost not classifiable as an apartment—more like a dorm room— but there was no doubt it was Blue's. Her drawings were tacked up all over the walls. One of the drawings was the background for her WOZ profile.

Will spotted a pile of books and drawing pads on her bed. He picked up the top book and started to open it and then he realized it was a journal. He closed it again. A journal was sacred unless— unless someone was in danger and there might be a clue in it, right? He reached to open the cover but was stopped by a voice.

"Hey, look at this." It was Wu. He was looking closely at the WOZ drawing and pointing to a ragged piece of paper clipped to the bottom right corner of the picture. Of course. That's where she would leave a clue, thought Will.

"It's an address!" said Wu.

"Where?" asked Anna.

Wu read off the address, "Stanton, 5296 Bear Mountain Road, Blue Ridge, NY."

"Stanton," said Will. "That's her WITSEC name. That must be her old address."

Wu and Anna and Will looked at each other. They were all thinking the same thing.

"Seven fifteen," said Jack. He was staring at his phone.

"What?" said Wu.

Jack looked up at them. "That's when we can get there from here if we leave right now if the snow doesn't get too bad. So why are we standing around?"

6:15 pm, Stanton Homestead
Snow 4"

BABINEAU STOOD on the porch and brushed the snow off his shoes as he surveyed the scene inside the house through the big picture window. It looked like a family scene with Bronco standing in the kitchen at the stove cooking something while the girl sat in a chair next to the dining table. It would have been a benign scene if it wasn't for the tiny detail of the girl being securely tied to her chair.

He turned to Purcell who nodded, signaling that it was clear to enter. He opened the door and the two of them stepped inside. Bronco turned to look at them but didn't act surprised in any way. An aroma of freshly fried trout wafted through the door to greet them. All in all, it was a very pleasant background, something Babineau wasn't expecting. He shrugged his shoulders. Maybe this wouldn't go so badly after all. Didn't mean they weren't prepared for the worst.

Babineau pulled off his coat, hat, and gloves and draped them on the couch while Purcell stepped over to Bronco who raised his arms compliantly without missing a beat in the well-practiced drill of being frisked. Purcell then proceeded to check the room and adjacent hallways. Only after he was satisfied did Purcell nod at Babineau and then take his own coat off, exposing a firearm that carried its own unspoken message.

The girl watched this routine silently and intently from her chair. She was obviously very alert, and very, very angry.

"Well, I finally get to meet this girl I have read and heard so much about. I have to tell you, I am very impressed with your resourcefulness. It reminds me very much of your father."

"Fuck you, you bastard! I hope you rot in hell!"

Babineau chuckled. "And spirited as well!"

Bronco turned casually and said, "You want me to tape her mouth? She can curse a blue streak if she has a mind to. You want some fish? I was just about to eat."

Babineau chuckled again. This was going much better than he expected, not that he had been that worried. After all, he had Purcell. He had anticipated that Bronco might be difficult after having been pretty much out-maneuvered these past months.

"No, no need, and I'm not hungry. We don't intend to stay long. I don't know if you noticed, but it's snowing pretty heavily outside, and we don't want to get stuck here tonight."

"You're not staying here tonight?" Bronco grunted. "Suits me." He put on a pot of water and then sat down at the table with his pan of fish. He stuck a bite in his mouth and said, "Well? What now?"

Babineau turned to the girl. After all, the girl was all he was interested in. Her eyes were flashing bright, and he could imagine what she was saying to him in her head. *"YOU CAN SAY IT OUT LOUD TO ME, YOU KNOW, YOU DON'T HAVE TO VOX IT. I'M SURE YOU ARE BEING QUITE COLORFUL."*

He could see she was surprised at what he said with his *chiss*.

"YOU DON'T KNOW WHAT I AM, DO YOU? IT IS PRETTY CENTRAL TO

THE REASON I WENT TO SO MUCH TROUBLE TO BRING YOU HERE. I AM A
NOCTE VENATORI."

He saw a flash of recognition in Blue's eyes.

"AND IN CASE YOU'RE NOT FAMILIAR WITH THAT, IT MEANS I CAN SEE
THE LIGHT FROM YOUR EYES—YOUR VOX OCULIS. I CAN SEE THE LIGHT
FROM MOST PEOPLE'S EYES, IN FACT, ALTHOUGH THEY ARE VERY DIM
COMPARED TO A VOX. BUT IT MAKES IT VERY DIFFICULT FOR PEOPLE TO
SNEAK UP ON ME AT NIGHT. AND AS FOR VOX, I CAN SPOT YOU A MILE
AWAY, EVEN IN THE DAYTIME."

"Fuck your nocte venatori," hissed the girl. "You're a monster is
what you are. You killed my family and then you built this log
mansion on their graves. So fuck you all the way to hell."

He smiled but it wasn't his pleasant smile. "I could say the same
to you since your father was responsible for the death of my
brother and his son."

She was clearly taken aback by this statement. "He didn't kill
them, the police did."

"Well I didn't kill your family," he nodded toward Bronco. "His
father and brother did. So you see, righteousness is a point of
view."

"So your righteousness says it's okay to rape my mother?"

This caught him a little by surprise. She knew more than he
expected.

"Rape is a strong word and I do not consider what I did with
your mother rape. I am not that kind of man. But you see, you and I
are the last of our respective kind. I wanted my own heir. So I gave
your parents a good life—a job, protection, money, security, and
your father turned out to be very good at what he did, and your
mother provided an opportunity for me to have an heir that was
either vox or nocte venatori. Your father was not exactly fond of my
desires and so he chose to betray me. Do you think betrayal is okay?"

"To put a criminal like you in jail, of course!"

"You and I look at the law a little differently. The law says we should be allowed the inalienable right of life, liberty, and the pursuit of happiness. Cigars make me happy and they happen to be legal. Your father's marijuana made a lot of sick people feel better. It made them happier. So why are cigars legal while marijuana is not? Look. You're young. Life seems simple to you, but it's not so simple."

Something he said must have gotten her thinking because she didn't respond instantly. He took that opportunity to pull a cigar from his leather case and carefully cut the end, tap it clean, and take a cold draw. It was a well-practiced routine that calmed him down. The girl had gotten his dander up a bit.

"Now, let's stop talking about the past. As far as I'm concerned, it's water under the bridge. Let's talk about your future."

"My future? You mean how you're going to kill me?"

He laughed. "You are being a little over-dramatic, I think. If I had wanted to kill you, you would be dead already. You think I'd go to all this trouble to capture you alive and personally come up from the city, just to kill you? No, you should consider it a good sign that I am actually talking to you."

"So you always taze and tie up people you just want to talk to?"

"Well, sometimes. Would you have come willingly?"

Her response was a glare accentuated by two blazing red dots where her eyes were. She had a very effective glare. "No then," he said. "Let's get back to the subject: your future. I have a proposal. I can offer you a nice nest egg that would give you a good start in life —enough that you could even go to college and live quite comfortably until you found the right place to land. In return, I am looking for only one thing from you."

The girl displayed a very generous dose of sour skepticism on her face and from the dead silence in the room, he realized that she was not the only one waiting for him to finish his proposal. He glanced at Bronco who was very alert, and then Jim, who was stone-faced since he already knew what the proposal was going to be. Babineau turned back to the girl and leaned in slightly for effect and finished his proposal.

"An heir, of course."

7:00 pm, Sunset, New York

"ARE YOU SURE?" said Rodney into his phone. "Is this junk dealer reliable?"

The voice that came out sounded confident. It was the Essex County Sheriff.

"I've known this guy since high school. He's a bit rough around the edges but as reliable as the day is long."

Rodney paused for a moment, partly to consider what he had just been told and partly because he was having difficulty concentrating on the road. His headlights were reflecting off the blowing snow and cutting his visibility. He had to slow down and focus on the lane markers as they only became discernible a hundred yards out. "A silver late model Mustang, you said."

"That's right. I'll text you the license number," said the sheriff.

"Thanks," said Rodney. He put his phone back on the dash and considered this new information. It had come from the junkyard man, the gruff character that had shown him Bronco's Camaro. He had been returning from Plattsburgh and stopped in Keeseville for gas. While he was there, a guy pulled up in a silver Mustang to fill up and he recognized the guy as Bronco. He became certain when he probed the guy by casually mentioning, "I see you got a replacement for the Camaro." He said the guy didn't say anything but reacted in a way that made him sure it was the same guy. The curious thing was, the junkyard man said the Mustang was headed south on I-87 *toward* New York City. He would have expected him to be heading northwest towards Franklin County.

He did some rough math in his head. The junkman had spotted the Camaro around 3:15 which meant if Bronco had been headed for

New York City, he'd be nearly there by now. But wherever he was headed, the big takeaway was that Bronco was in New York State and they now had a car make and model and a plate number. That was huge. Second was that if Bronco was headed away from Franklin County, either he didn't know about the reward for Blue and it was coincidence that he should be traveling from Franklin County that afternoon, or it could mean that he did know about the reward and had captured Blue already and was delivering her to Babineau. If that was the case, it could mean that Babineau wasn't headed for Franklin County but instead had headed north from New York City to meet Bronco somewhere between the city and Franklin County. He looked at his watch. 7:10. Babineau should be in Franklin County by now but no one had reported spotting him yet.

He let his brain ruminate on the possibilities for a minute and then he dialed Chief Hannah.

"*Hey, Rodney. Where are you?*" came Chief Hannah's voice.

"I'm in a snowstorm somewhere just north of Albany. What about you?"

"*I've been parked on an I-87 on ramp near Keeseville for about an hour and a half.*"

"Any sign of the Escalade?"

"*Nothing.*"

He paused for a moment making sure his gut was feeling right about this.

"Okay, look. I just learned something. Bronco's car has been identified and was spotted driving south from Keeseville around 3:15 pm."

"*Bronco? South? Shit!*" she replied.

"I know. Here's what I am going to do. I have a hunch. I'm going to call the Essex County sheriff back and have him check the old Stanton homestead. You watch for another half hour in Keeseville and if you don't spot anything and we don't hear anything from Franklin County, I want you to head there, too. If my math is right and the snow doesn't get any worse, I should meet you there about the same time you arrive, around 8:30. If it turns out to be nothing we can continue north."

"*Wow. Okay. I get it. I think you might be onto something.*" There was a pause and then she said, "*Rodney . . .*"

"Yes?"

"*Trust me. The snow is not going to get better.*"

7:05 pm. Stanton Homestead
Snow 7"

BABINEAU TOOK another puff on his cigar as he peeked back through the picture window to see if things had calmed down. "Let's go back in and see if the girl's ready to listen."

He was speaking to Purcell who had stepped out on the porch with him to escape the violent and ear piercing display of outrage and frustration that erupted from the girl after he delivered his proposal. He was expecting a reaction but not to the extreme they had just witnessed. Bronco offered to tape her mouth again, but Babineau said, "No, no, let her get it out of her system. She'll be easier to talk to after she tires out."

Purcell grunted and brushed off the snow that had blown in under the porch roof and onto his shoulders. "This snow concerns me," was all he said.

Babineau nodded. "I'll keep this as brief as possible, but I want to get started tonight."

As they stepped through the door, Babineau could see the girl was panting and exhausted. Her cheeks were still wet, but her crying had stopped. Bronco sat unperturbed at the table.

"Well now, Blue," he began, "I fully understand your frustration and you have a truly impressive vocabulary to express it, but that's about all you're in a position to do right now. We can keep going like this or you can listen to what I have to say and then we'll be out of here."

The girl let out a loud steamy huff but didn't say anything.

"I think you're going to find that what I've proposed isn't as bad as you might think. You have shown that you are a very smart and resourceful girl and I think that when you hear what I have to say, you will see that there is a huge benefit to you in the long run if you just look at the big picture, so listen carefully."

"You will carry my child and will be well cared for by a very nice couple who are very experienced at helping out young pregnant teenagers. After you deliver the child, he or she will be adopted by my widowed sister-in-law. And that is that. I will not interfere with your life anymore, you will be sixteen and have the rest of your life ahead of you, and you will have a trust fund that I will create with $200,000 in it that you will come into when you turn eighteen. In short, you will be able to pick up your life where you left off and join the company of thousands of other pregnant young teens that gave their kids up for adoption, the main difference being that you will be substantially richer than they are."

The girl bristled. "What the hell makes you think I would go along with any of this? You. Killed. My. Family. I'd rather kill myself than carry your child!" Her voice was hoarse but controlled.

Babineau took a thoughtful puff on his cigar. "You might find this hard to believe, but I am sympathetic. I have lost a lot of family, too. Violently. But you are young, and you will learn as you get older that everyone suffers tragedies in their lives and there is a point in your life where you have to make a choice. You choose to either wallow in bitterness and dream of vengeance and live the rest of your life an angry unhappy person or . . . you accept that there are things you cannot control and cannot change and you move forward and live a happy and productive life."

He could tell he hit a nerve. She's thinking things through, he thought to himself. She knows she's cornered. And she's smart enough to understand the alternative. He didn't have to tell her. No one wants to die, especially so young. Not when there is a way out.

"It is your only way out of this," he said, taking a puff. "It's not such a terrible way out."

"You have to guarantee Sylvie's safety," she said after a surprisingly short pause, "and give her $50,000. And leave my friends in Westbury and Malone alone."

He felt his eyebrows rise in sincere pleasant surprise. "I can do that," he said. "I won't give you a guarantee, only my word. You may think I am a criminal, but I am true to my word. You can ask Bronco or Jim or anyone, even the police. It doesn't matter what your business is, you can't be successful if you're not holding up your end of the deal, and I am very successful."

"Okay," she said, her eyes on the floor. Her body had sagged in defeat, a good sign, he thought. The first stage of acceptance.

"Good," he said, stepping over to the liquor cabinet and pulling out a bottle of Scotch. "Bronco, I sent a kit to you. Can you go fetch it? Jim, please check the guest bedroom for anything that . . . shouldn't be there."

"Now?" she screamed in panic.

He sighed. She thought she could buy time by agreeing, find another way out. He tried to remain upbeat without being condescending. "It's best to yank the Band-Aid off quick—avoid the anxiety of anticipation. Don't worry, you won't know what's happening and you won't remember a thing. We're going to use ketamine. Very common and very safe."

"Ketamine! That's a date rape drug!" she shouted. "God damn you!"

He sighed again. "It's also an anesthetic. Remember, this is consensual."

"With a minor!"

"Who posed as someone much older."

She didn't reply with anything but a bright flash from her eyes. He ignored it and gestured to Bronco, who had returned with the kit. "Ketamine," he said. Bronco raised an eyebrow but nodded and crouched down in front of the girl and opened up the kit, picking through the bottles of drugs and selecting one. "You know the drill," said Bronco to the girl, and then she actually spat on him. Babineau had to admire her spirit, but he hoped she mellowed out once she was pregnant, otherwise, it was going to be a long nine months.

Bronco brushed off the spit nonchalantly but he fixed her with a glare. Babineau could only imagine what the girl read from Bronco's faintly glowing eyes, but he imagined it was choice. She returned Bronco's glare and then she turned toward Babineau and he could see the full intensity of her high beams. She kept them fixed on him as Bronco went about the business of expertly preparing a shot and then administering it intravenously with a slow push on the hypodermic. The intensity of her stare made him uneasy for the first time that evening, but it passed within seconds as the ketamine went to work, causing her eyes to dim and her entire body to slump. She tried to utter something, but it came out slurred, "I ai oing da gilll eeooo." Her message was clear though.

He watched as Bronco placed the spent syringe on the table and immediately set about removing the bindings holding the girl's arms to the chair. Babineau was surprised at how quickly things were progressing. "Shouldn't you at least wait a few minutes?"

Bronco replied by lifting the girl's arm and dropping it. It fell limply to her side, swinging like a pendulum briefly before it came to a stop. "IV ketamine works fast."

Babineau shrugged and took a pull on his cigar, which he had almost forgotten about. It was out. Just as well, he thought. "Fine. Just get her down to the bedroom." He put his cigar down, poured a shot of Scotch, and downed it.

Bronco had finished releasing the girl and was propping her up in the chair so she wouldn't slump to the floor. He turned his head and faced Babineau. "And what about our deal?"

"Right. So, like I promised, once this is done, I consider your father's oversight accounted for. However . . ."

His words were cut short because he was witnessing something other-worldly unfolding in the girl's chair. What he saw appeared to be the crumpled body of a comatose girl suddenly reanimating —unfolding and swelling as if inflated by an invisible force. As he watched, this revitalized body transformed into something more than just a human, more than just a girl. She had transformed into a terrifying banshee, her dark hair framing her screaming face, her flaming eyes burning his retinas, her piercing shriek rattling his eardrums. And this nightmare apparition was now hurtling toward him with impossible speed. He tried to move his arm to a defensive position, but it was as if his arm was moving through mud. A sudden, raw fear gripped his chest and squeezed hard just as the banshee's body slammed into his, knocking him off his feet. A sharp blow to the back of his head sent him into almost instant blackness but his consciousness lingered just long enough to register an image that seared his brain as he sank into the folds of oblivion: two eyes sputtering with rage like a pair of fiery crucibles ready to smother his rotten soul with their molten vengeance.

JIM PURCELL WAS WATCHING the scene of Babineau bartering with the girl, but his mind was distracted. He knew what Babineau had planned and he was there just to make sure nothing went amiss and so far there were no warning flags that he could see—Bronco was unarmed and there were no weapons in plain sight, even though he had no doubt Bronco had hidden something some-where. The guy wasn't stupid. But everything was going as planned so far and that let him free up a little of his mind to observe the architectural features of the interior of the Adirondack log camp and register that they were pleasing. He made a mental note to look at it more closely when all this was over.

Bronco stood up and propped the girl's limp body in the chair and turned toward Babineau. The girl was obviously no longer in control of her body and maybe even unconscious. He had watched carefully as Bronco administered the ketamine to the oddly passive and unresisting girl. He had expected her to put up more of a struggle.

Bronco turned to face Babineau, who was standing in the kitchen sipping a glass of Scotch, remarkably relaxed and unconcerned, as if this was a daily occurrence in his life.

And then Babineau spoke to Bronco and got to the part that Jim didn't like.

"Just get her down to the bedroom," Babineau told Bronco.

To Bronco's credit, he didn't seem at all keen on that plan, but Jim was ready to enforce it, even though he wasn't too keen on it, either. This was the dark dark side of Babineau. This was the dark dark part of this job.

What happened next took Jim so much by surprise that he actually froze in shock and confusion. The once comatose girl literally exploded out of the chair with an ear piercing scream and with such power that it seemed she flew across the floor without touching the ground, slamming directly into Babineau, knocking him backwards and causing him to strike his head on the stainless steel stove behind him.

Jim's mind went blank. The situation before him was not in his playbook. He had no response. He found himself stupidly staring at a yellow can of cooking spray that had been set wobbling by Babineau's impact. It continued to wobble for a ridiculously long time without falling over and he felt like he couldn't move until he saw if it would fall over or not.

It was a chair that distracted him back to reality, a hoop back chair that struck legs first into his side with enough force to knock him off balance and tangle his right arm in the rungs. As he untangled himself and threw the chair to the side, he turned to see Bronco heading down the hallway toward the bedrooms and out of sight. At the same time, he saw the girl disappear down the hallway in the opposite direction toward the garage. He instinctively put a series of rounds from his Smith and Wesson into the hallway wall along the path that Bronco would be running. If this was an ordinary house, the drywall would be no match for the full metal jacket rounds, but without seeing the results, he had to assume that Bronco was coming back fully armed.

He took a quick look at Babineau, who was completely inert on the floor. On the stovetop above Babineau, the can of cooking spray had fallen over directly onto a burner that was glowing with a blue flame. He realized Babineau must have hit the controls as he fell, igniting the burner.

What happened next added a whole new dimension to the scene as Babineau was suddenly engulfed in an impossibly huge fireball. At the same time two shots rang out and Jim turned to where he could see Bronco crouched with his smoking gun pointing toward the kitchen. Jim took advantage of the distraction and put his red-dot site on Bronco's forehead but as he squeezed the trigger, Bronco's head disappeared behind the wall. Once again he put several rounds in a projected path where Bronco might have gone, realizing that he now had the upper hand and Bronco was trapped unless he found a different route out of the house.

Jim remembered his prime mission, to protect Babineau and he knew he had a moment while Bronco prepared for his next move, so he scooted toward the kitchen, gun sited on the hallway, and reached out to grab Babineau's foot to pull him clear of the mess, but one glance was enough to see that it was too late. Whatever had caused the fireball had ignited nearly every inch of the clothes on Babineau's inert body. His head was cocked at an odd angle and one bloody patch on his shirt indicated where one of Bronco's rounds had hit home.

A gunshot rang out and as a bullet grazed Jim's scalp he dropped and rolled across the floor toward the shelter of the couch, additional bullets stitching the floor as he rolled. One of the bullets found his foot and he nearly screamed in agony. But he had been returning fire as he rolled and that ended Bronco's fusillade. Bronco's momentary pullback allowed Jim time enough to crawl to the front door and tumble out into the now howling storm.

THE AGING Buick crawled its way over the white unbroken carpet, the headlights almost a liability rather than an asset as the brightly illuminated windblown snowfall acted like a blinding blanket, almost completely obscuring what they could discern of the roadway. The road would have been treacherous enough even without the snow, with its steep grades, writhing path, and menacing trees hovering close to the shoulder.

"Are you sure we shouldn't turn around? We could try tomorrow after the roads are cleared." The nervous whisper came from Anna who was leaning forward from the backseat, her worried face close to Jack's ear.

"I don't think we have a choice," said Jack. "There's no place to turn around."

"We could back down," came Wu's voice from the back seat.

Jack looked at Wu in the rearview mirror and made a face that clearly said, "Really?"

Will, sitting in the front passenger seat, had been watching the road intently. He glanced over at the speedometer and said, "It doesn't matter, we're almost there. I think I see a mailbox up ahead."

"I thought your map application stopped working when we lost cell reception," said Jack.

"It did, but I've been watching the odometer. Look, that's gotta be the driveway."

Jack saw the mailbox through the blowing snow and he cautiously brought the Buick the final few yards, but he kept it moving—he didn't dare lose momentum or he might not be able to get traction to get started again. He strained to spot the track that would mark the start of the driveway. If he missed, they would be ditched. He felt the tension of the three other people in the car as he gunned it for the near side of the mailbox and swung onto what he hoped was solid ground. The inertia of the heavy Buick showed its worth as it drove its way up the remaining piece of roadway and onto a surprisingly smooth, solid, level driveway entrance. Jack brought the beast to a stop and breathed out a sigh of relief.

"Nice work," said Wu.

"There's the house," said Will. He was pointing to a steady glow coming through the trees. The glow was from a lighted window and diffused by the heavy snowfall.

"Are you sure this is the right house?" Jack asked.

Will glanced at his phone again. "It's gotta be. It's the only other house other than the one we passed a mile back."

Jack looked at the glow and then looked at the path of the driveway. About fifty feet ahead it appeared to slope down steeply. It must have to go through a small ravine to get to the house, he thought. "I don't know," he said "This doesn't look good. We may need to get out and walk."

"Can't we just try going further?" asked Anna. There was some apprehension in her voice.

"Um, yeah," said Wu. "It's not like we were expecting this weather. I mean I've only got tennis shoes and a windbreaker. It was almost fifty degrees when we left Westbury."

Jack looked down at his jeans and fleece sweater. He wasn't much better off. He studied the driveway ahead. He could at least go a little further safely. He eased the Buick forward slowly, studying the driveway carefully as the headlights illuminated each new feature. The road felt solid and smooth. It must have been well-kept, and he could tell there was good gravel underneath. He tapped the brakes and felt the tires slip a little and then grip. Much better than the pavement.

"Driveway looks pretty solid," said Will. Jack glanced at him and saw the determined look on his face. It had been like that the whole trip. He turned his gaze back to the driveway. The car had reached the start of the downslope and now that they were closer, he could see that it didn't look as bad as he thought. If it was the same on the uphill side, they should make it with no problem.

"Well, what's the worst that could happen," said Jack. "If we get stuck at the bottom, it will just be a shorter walk." He heard a nervous laugh from the back. "Don't worry, we'll make it fine."

He inched the car forward and then let gravity gradually accelerate them down the hill until they reached the bottom, crossed a culvert, and rolled back up a gentler slope on the other side. He gunned it carefully up the last stretch with only a little bit of waggle as the back tires spun and then caught again at the very top and pulled into the spacious level parking area in front of a garage. It was lucky that it was spacious because there were three cars there already. As he pulled to a stop, he took note of the layout of the house. The bulk of the house must have been on the far side of the garage, which had its doors facing toward them. To the right, he could see a glow in the snow, probably from the lights shining out the front windows of the house. There was a steep upward slope to the left that faced the back of the house. The drive was blocked from view from the house except for a dark second story window that peeked out above the garage roof. Whoever was in the house couldn't see them now, but they might have noticed the beams of his headlights in the snow as they drove up.

"Holy crap," said Wu. "Look at all the cars. Weren't we just expecting to find Blue and her friend?"

Jack studied the three cars. One was a rust-bucket Nissan—a Japanese analog to his creaky Buick. The other two were higher-end: a silver late-model Mustang and a black Escalade with blacked-out windows. The Nissan and the Mustang didn't bother him but the sinister-looking Escalade looked like trouble.

Will was already getting out of the car and the minute he

opened his door, a blast of snow and cold air slapped Jack in the face like an icy glove.

"Jesus Christ! How did it get cold so fast?" said Wu.

"Hold up, Will," said Jack, "I don't like the look of things. I think we should rethink this."

"What's to rethink?" said Will. "I've got a . . . well a gut feeling about this. I feel certain Blue is here."

Jack hesitated. "I don't know. This isn't what I was expecting for Blue's old home. This looks more like we've stumbled on a mob meeting at a private camp."

Now it was Will that was hesitating. He was standing outside the car door, blinking and squinting at the house through the blowing snow when suddenly he jumped.

And then he vanished.

WILL HAD HESITATED at Jack's words. Jack wasn't wrong, he thought as he stood next to the open car door. This place wasn't what he expected either. But he had sensed something that only could have come from a vox. He couldn't quite put his finger on what it was. He tried to pierce the blowing snow with his eyes as if he could find an answer by staring at the glow of lights emanating from the front of the house. I can at least go around and peek through the windows and check it out, he thought. And simultaneous to this thought entering his mind came something else: a piercing vox scream followed by "YOU BASTARD! YOU KILLED MY FAMILY!"

Will shot toward the house. He moved so fast, he lost control halfway down the path and careened into a bush as his feet went out from under him. He scrambled back to his feet and reached the stairs to a porch that ran all along the front of the house. He jumped up the steps and then came to a frozen halt in front of a large picture window.

It was as if he had come across a big-screen monitor displaying

an image from an Agatha Christie whodunit. On the left he saw a
girl, a bleach-blonde with short hair, standing in an aggressive
stance that made him think of a manga samurai. She was in a
kitchen area off of a massive living room. As he scanned across the
scene, he saw someone standing behind a chair. He had no trouble
identifying that one. It was Bronco. The shock of seeing him almost
prevented Will from noticing another dark figure who was facing
away from the window and standing to the right of Bronco. That
figure was holding a gun. The whole scene seemed like it had been
put on pause just for him so that he could take it all in before the
action started. And then the play button was hit and suddenly all
hell broke loose. It started with the dark figure raising his gun but
before he could fire, Bronco flung the chair toward the figure. Will
flinched as a gunshot rang out. He turned his gaze toward the girl
to see if she had been hit. Apparently unharmed, she had twisted
away and was running off toward the back left corner of the room.
In the brief instant that she was turned toward him, Will recognized the facial features that left no doubt in his mind: It was Blue.

His attention turned back to the dark figure who had disentan-
gled himself from the chair and had turned his gun toward Bronco,
but Bronco was disappearing behind a wall in the back of the room.
Will instinctively ducked and jumped off the porch as a series of
gunshots rattled off.

As he landed, without missing a stride, he hurtled toward the
garage. That's where it looked like Blue was heading. Halfway down
the path he nearly slammed into Jack.

"Will, what the hell is going on?"

"Bronco, guns, no time to explain." He grabbed Jack's jacket and
pulled him along behind him. "Get back to the car, I think Blue is
going to come out through the garage!"

"Fuck!"

Jack said this in response to a new barrage of gunfire. It was still
coming from inside the house. As Will rounded the corner of the
garage, he saw Wu and Anna standing next to the Buick.

"Will, what the hell!" said Anna.

"No time, get back in the car!"

Will ran to the garage door and tried pulling it open, but it wouldn't budge. He headed for the far side of the garage, looking for a side door. As he rounded the corner, he slammed into someone coming the other way, knocking them off their feet and into the snow. He reached down to help them up, expecting to find Blue but instead found a strange young woman. She was gagged with duct tape, and her hands appeared to be bound behind her back. She struggled to get up off the ground, but he stood frozen in momentary confusion until somebody grabbed his arms and shook him. He turned to look right into the face of Blue.

"*Jesus Christ! Will! How . . . where . . . what the hell are you doing here! How did you get here? Never mind, it doesn't matter, you're in terrible danger! We have to get out of here! Sylvie has a car! Help me with her.*"

She reached down and tried to help the young woman up but it was more than she could handle. Blue looked up at him and voxed fiercely, "*Will! Jesus Christ, help me!*"

Her plea pulled Will out of his shock and he reached down and helped Blue pull the young woman off the ground, and together they stumbled toward the rusty Nissan.

"*Forget this car. Get in Jack's car,*" voxed Will. He looked toward the Buick and saw with relief that everyone was inside and waiting except for Wu, who stood by the back door waving them inside.

This time it was Blue's turn to stop in shock. "Wu? What the hell, and Jack and Anna?"

Will dragged Blue toward the car, and together they stuffed the poor bound woman, the woman Blue called Sylvie, into the back-seat. He jammed himself in beside Sylvie and pulled Blue in after him.

He yelled at Wu, "Get in the car, move move move!"

Jack leaned over and pushed the passenger door open, and as

he did, there was a *thwack!* followed by a *pow!* and Will saw a round starburst hole in the windshield right where Jack's head had been a moment before. Jack gunned the car in reverse, and Wu dove head-first into the passenger seat. Jack shouted, "Stay down!" He had turned around and was staring intently through the back window while working the steering wheel with one hand. They accelerated backwards down the driveway and Will heard another *thwack* from somewhere in the front of the car. Instantly a whining noise came from the Buick's engine. Jack kept the car moving down into the ravine where the woods started to give them protection from the line of sight of the house. "C'mon, baby, just keep running," pleaded Jack to the whining Buick as they started out of the ravine and back up toward the road. But midway up the incline, Will could feel the rear of the car break loose as it lost traction. The car lost momentum quickly and gravity started to steer the car the wrong way. Jack was trying to compensate but Will was familiar enough with winter driving to know that the battle was lost. Jack took his foot off the gas and hit the brakes, but it did no good as the heavily-laden car slid sideways and tilted into the ditch where it finally came to a stop.

Jack popped open his door and in a quiet but insistent voice said, "Get out of the car! We'll have to hoof it from here."

Will popped his door latch and he and Blue and Sylvie spilled out into the ditch where they found themselves tangled together in the astonishingly deep snow. Blue managed to find her footing first and got herself upright. Will scrambled to his feet and once again found himself helping Blue lift Sylvie, still bound and gagged, off the ground.

Will looked around to get his bearings but Jack must have killed the headlights and all he could see in the darkness was the pale white of snow everywhere with only the dim silhouettes of trees visible behind swirling clouds of endless snowflakes. The only solid reference point was the Buick. He looked away from it toward where the road should be and could just make out the dark forms of the others who had already started up the drive.

Blue tugged at him. *"COME ON!"*

As they left the solid bulk of the Buick to catch up to the others, he felt very exposed with only a few trees between them and the house to stop a stray bullet. But the gunshots had paused for the moment and there didn't seem to be any pursuit. At least none that he could see. It was impossible to know because the wind had turned the heavy squall into a nearly total white-out. Someone could be following them, and they wouldn't know it until they were right on top of them. The only thing that penetrated the blowing snow was the glow of light coming from the house. There was something odd about the light—it had an other-worldly throbbing orange tint to it. He paused, staring at it, wondering what that meant. A tug on his arm interrupted his thought and he willingly resumed following Blue and Sylvie.

As he strained to see the others ahead, he realized that they could quickly lose sight of each other if they didn't stay close together. Right now that seemed as terrifying as what they were leaving behind. The others had reached the road and stopped. When Blue and Will and Sylvie caught up to them, everyone was strangely silent. Blue immediately knelt down and started working to get the bonds off of Sylvie's wrists. As soon as they were free, Sylvie reached up to her mouth and yanked off the duct tape.

"Jesus Christ, Sam, this is some crazy fucked-up shit you got me into!" said Sylvie.

"Sam?" said Will.

"Long story," said Blue, "for later."

The sound of their voices in the hushed atmosphere seemed to break a spell that had been cast by the shock of the moment.

"What the hell happened back there?" said Wu, "And what do we do now?"

"We keep moving is what we do," said Jack, "we can't go back."

"And where exactly do we go? I'm f-freezing!" Anna was standing with arms wrapped tightly around herself. It was then that Will realized she only had a sweater on and when he saw her feet he was aghast. Birkenstocks. He looked at the rest of the group and was shocked at the state of their clothing. Only he and Jack and Wu had anything more than a sweatshirt on. And no one had boots—just running shoes except for Anna who had stubbornly worn her Birkenstocks. They'd all been lulled into the warm weather of the past couple of days and now they had to walk through the dark, through the cold and snow, down a road they could barely see, and bad guys with guns behind them. Suddenly the threat of being shot by a pursuer was joined by the possibility that they could freeze to death.

"So, no car, and I suppose none of your phones work up here in this godforsaken Siberian backwoods?" asked Sylvie.

"I lost coverage about a mile down the road," said Will. "Right near the last house we passed. There were lights on there. I think that is our best bet."

"A m-mile!" Anna looked down where the road was supposed to be, "in this?"

"Let's get moving," said Jack. "It will warm us up." He turned immediately and started leading the way, pulling Anna behind him. Wu trudged doggedly behind. Will turned to Blue and was glad to see her and Sylvie with arms around each other following the others. It looked like they could hold it together for a mile, maybe, but after only a few steps through the dense unbroken snow, he wasn't sure anymore.

He slogged over to Blue and Sylvie. "BLUE, IS THERE ANOTHER OPTION?"

She turned and looked at him. Her face was barely discernible in the dark, but the snow dispersed what light was available in such a way that it provided a soft illumination to her familiar features. He was still a little startled at the change in her hair, and in this light, it gave her a bit of a ghostly look. But that didn't deter from the fact that even here, under the most ridiculous of circumstances, he was feeling a rekindled fire inside him, a fire that he only just now realized had nearly been extinguished by the months of endless searching. The search was over now, and even though the situation was deteriorating, a spark of hope and optimism surged through him.

"MAYBE," she voxed. "THERE'S THE SUGARHOUSE. IT HAS A WOOD STOVE IN IT."

"A SUGARHOUSE? BUT WE'D HAVE TO GO BACK. THAT'S SUICIDE."

"NO, WE CAN BUSHWHACK ACROSS THE RAVINE TO THE ORCHARD. THE SUGARHOUSE IS IN THE BACK OF THE ORCHARD SO IT'S NOT VISIBLE FROM THE HOUSE."

"BUT WHAT ABOUT BRONCO? AND THOSE OTHER GUYS? WHAT'S GOING ON BACK THERE?"

Will wasn't the only one wondering as Sylvie spoke up. "Blue, what happened back there? How did you get away? I thought we were both dead meat. And you, where in hell did you come from? And who are all these people?"

This last question was directed at Will but Blue answered first. "Bronco helped me escape."

"What!?" This was uttered by three voices simultaneously but before Blue could explain, Anna stumbled and nearly fell saying, "Um, my toes are numb."

And then everything fell apart.

BRONCO TOOK a moment to recover and consider his next move. He was pretty sure he hit Purcell in that last volley. And he heard the front door open, too. If that was the case, Purcell was probably outside considering his next move. With the log wall, Purcell was in a damned fine fortified position. Bronco glanced down the hall toward the kitchen and living room and saw a lively orange glow dancing on the wall. Christ, where the hell had that fireball come from. If Babineau wasn't already dead from the combination of the shocking move from Blue or the round that he had let fly at Babineau's chest, it looked like the flames of Satan were going to consume him.

He took a moment to put a fresh clip in the Glock and did a quick count of the remaining rounds in the ejected clip. He needed a full clip to keep Purcell pinned down. Blue had probably slipped out through the garage and freed the other girl by now. If so, they would be easy prey for Purcell. About the only way to keep Purcell off of them was to go outside and flank him.

That settled, he got on his hands and knees and crawled to the bedroom at the end of the hall. He would go out the bedroom window and run to the woods and snipe Purcell from there. He took a moment to put on the down jacket he'd left in the bedroom. His father's words echoed annoyingly in his head, "Always be ready for the weather because if the other guy isn't, you're one up on him." Fucking asshole. He was right, though.

He winced as he eased his bloody left arm into the jacket. The wound wasn't terrible, through-and-through, but damn it hurt. He gritted his teeth and pushed through the pain, he didn't have time to waste on being gentle to himself. He had already decided his best move was to dive through the window and run like hell for the woods with the presumption that Purcell had a bead on him.

He inched to the window and pushed it open. Then he positioned himself in a crouch on the floor and before he could talk himself out of it he sprang through it in a diving motion and into a tuck and roll with his gun hand pointed safely away. He was dimly aware of the discharge of a gun and noted its relative location as he rolled a second time through the surprisingly deep snow. He rolled up directly into a running stance and booked it for the woods. He knew he had reached a good position when he heard the whacks of rounds hitting trees behind him.

He stopped behind a tree, counted to three, crouched, and fired five rounds, spreading them across the position he reasoned the firing was coming from. It worked. The shooting had stopped for a moment, and he took a glance around him to assess his new position. He had a full view of the front of the house though it was obscured by the windblown snow. The light from the flames inside was starting to overwhelm the electric lights and it made for a spooky landscape. The flickering shadows were hard to interpret but he saw a muzzle flash and ducked behind the tree. The bullet was way off the mark, so Purcell was fishing. Bronco decided to take a chance and swept three rounds across where the muzzle flash came from. He heard two whacks. That means one might have hit home.

Two rounds smacked into his tree to let him know that nothing was fatal and that now Purcell knew where he was and had him zeroed in. It was going to be cat and mouse from here on out.

WILL FOUND himself groveling in the snow after a flurry of gunshots, accompanied by whizzing sounds and thwacks all around them, sent him dropping flat to the ground.

"Jesus, they're shooting at us!" came Wu's panicked voice.

"No!" said Jack's voice, "They're shooting at each other. Those were two different guns. Those were stray bullets."

Another volley of shots, more thwacks—too close—and once again Will flattened himself in the snow. He turned to see that Blue and the others were all down, too. They were also illuminated in an orange glow. He turned to look back toward the house and in place of the winking light of windows in the woods he saw the intense wavering light of flames.

"Jesus, the house is burning," said Sylvie.

"C'mon, we've got to get away from this crossfire," hissed Jack and he pulled Anna up out of the snow, hoisted her on his back, and started hustling down the road.

Will grabbed Blue by the arm and tugged, "Let's go! Up up up!"

Blue stood unsteadily and looked down at her jacket. She put her hand on her pelvis and she looked up at him and said, "I . . . I think I've been shot." Then her legs wobbled and she sank to her knees. She pulled her hand away from her side and stared at it. He reached down to where she had been holding her side and felt a distressingly familiar warm and slippery substance. He looked her in the eyes, and he could feel the throbbing and numbness in her gut and sensed her starting to get woozy. She started to keel over but he scooped her up before she could fall. He stood up, holding her in his arms not quite sure what to do next.

Sylvie, however, seemed to know exactly what to do and said, "Hold still for a minute." She started peeling Blue's sweater up. "Shit. It's a gut shot."

Will looked down and could see blood streaming slowly out of a hole that looked sickeningly familiar to him. "Is there an exit wound?"

Sylvie probed Blue's back and shook her head.

Will realized everyone had gathered around him. Blue was starting to groan. Anna and Wu were in speechless shock, and Jack said, "I'll have to go back for the car. That's the only chance."

"No way," said Wu. "Someone's coming already." They all turned at the sound of a revving engine up toward the house. The beams from a pair of headlights swung like a spotlight through the woods revealing that a vehicle was leaving the burning house. As they watched, the car started to negotiate the long driveway across the ravine. The end of the driveway wasn't even two hundred yards away from where they stood.

"Shit, if that's the Escalade he can make it past the Buick," said Jack.

"*It might be Babineau's goon,*" came Blue's vox, "*Purcell. He'll kill us. We have to get off the road.*" She was moaning and breathing in gasps, but she seemed lucid and her vox was loud and clear.

Will spoke sternly to the others "Everybody, off the road! It might be Purcell. He . . . he might try to kill us."

"What? Who's Purcell?" asked Sylvie, but Will was already negotiating his way off the shoulder, across the ditch, through the brush, and into the protection of the woods. He looked behind to see that everyone was following.

Will glanced up the road and could see that the headlights had reached the top of the drive. He said a little prayer to make the headlights turn away from them and then watched in horror as they swung down the road right toward them. In sixty seconds, the car would reach the spot where all of them had just been standing in the road.

He moved as fast as he could without dropping Blue, but a sense of inevitability was growing; Purcell would see their tracks in the snow and would easily be able to find them. He racked his brain for some plan for defense. He could put Blue down and find a big stick, or a rock. He started looking for something when he heard a voice from behind him. It was Jack.

"Everyone keep going. I've got this guy."

Will turned and wasn't sure he could believe what he was seeing. Jack had positioned himself behind a large tree and was holding something out for them all to see. It was a handgun. Will didn't have time to digest what this meant, the headlights were approaching and he had just enough time to duck behind a fallen tree before they got there. As he crouched with Blue in his arms, he cringed, waiting for a gunfight to erupt, but all he heard was the sound of a car passing by without slowing, the muffled crunch of the tires receding quietly and then disappearing altogether. He ventured a peek over the log and saw Jack standing in a stance of disbelief and relief. Jack turned away from the road, head shaking, and joined the rest of them.

"I don't know what that was all about, but I am damn glad he kept going. I think I should go back for the Buick now."

"Y-yes, p-p-please!" said Anna.

She and Wu had hunkered down behind a rock. Wu was

looking at Will and his *chiss* was urgent, "*ANNA'S IN A REALLY BAD WAY.*"

Will wasn't sure what to do. There was still Bronco. Jack had a gun, but he'd be a sitting duck if it took him too many tries to get the Buick out. And then there was the chance he couldn't get the Buick out. Then what? He felt a little shiver in his arms and looked at Blue. She was getting cold, and with her wound, it could be deadly.

"Blue! How far to the sugarhouse?"

Blue opened her eyes, "*NOT FAR. SYLVIE'S BEEN TO IT.*"

Will turned to Sylvie who had crouched down next to them. "Blue said there is a sugarhouse with a wood stove in it. She said you know where it is."

Sylvie stared at him, head tilted in puzzlement, "What? How?"

"Do you or don't you? Just tell me, can you get us there?"

Sylvie shook her head, looking at Blue. "Oh honey, you put a lot of faith in me, but I don't think a hound dog could guide us through this blizzard. I know I'd get us lost."

Then, as if the situation couldn't get more surreal, Will heard Blue's clear voice in his head saying, "*CALL MY FATHER'S RAVEN.*"

He stared at her, confused, but a vivid picture appeared in his mind: He was staring at a raven in a tree and voxing to it, saying "*HELLO, ARDETH, WANT SOME FOOD?*"

"*CALL HIM.*" voxed Blue. "*HIS NAME IS ARDETH. HE'LL GO TO THE SUGARHOUSE AND CALL BACK. FOLLOW HIS CALL.*"

Will turned to Jack. "Do you really think you could get the Buick out? And what about Bronco?"

"Well, I have to try. What else can we do?" said Jack. Then he leaned in close and whispered in Will's ear, "Do you think Blue is going survive being carried a mile in this? And what about the time it takes for an ambulance to reach us?"

"Look, Jack," replied Will. "You should go down the road until you get reception. It shouldn't be more than a mile. The rest of us can make it to the sugarhouse. Blue said it has a wood stove and it's hidden from the house. We can get out of the snow and get warm there. It's our best chance."

Jack mulled this over for a moment and then said, "You're right. Good plan." Jack turned to Wu. "Give me your phone, so I have a backup phone. You won't need it here. And Will," Jack held out the gun, "do you know how to handle this?"

Will contemplated it for a moment. What if they did encounter Bronco? Blue said he let her go. And Will had never fired a handgun in his life. It might be worse than useless in his hands. He shook his head, "Keep it. In case you encounter Purcell down the road."

Jack nodded. He took Wu's phone and said, "Don't get too comfortable in that sugarhouse, I'll have help here in no time." And then he vanished into the silent wall of snow.

Will turned and looked away from the road and into the woods. He voxed with as much effort as he could, *"HEY, ARDETH! THIS IS WILL! WANT SOME FOOD?"* He waited.

Nothing.

He was skeptical that the light from his eyes could penetrate this snow, but then he became aware of how bright the glow from the fire was and he remembered his and Blue's experiments with their vox and the infrared camera. He took a deep breath and tried again, *"HELLOOO ARDETH! WANT SOME FOO . . ."* and before he finished he heard a distant "Krrraw" followed by a distinct "Kwa-koo!" He couldn't believe it. It was like a fairy tale. He voxed again, and again there was a "Kwa-koo!" in reply.

"C'mon, that raven is our guide," he told the others, who were staring at him with astonished looks. "Don't make me explain, just trust me." He looked down at Blue as he stood and voxed, *"MAN, WE HAVE A LOT TO DISCUSS LATER."*

"YES, BUT LATER! PLEASE!"

Her anguish penetrated him, and he called again, urgently. The raven's reply seemed to be coming from the same place, so he started trudging through the woods in that direction. He kept calling and the replies got louder and louder until, miraculously, a rectangular shadow emerged from the blowing snow as if out of a book of mythology. The shadow quickly consolidated into the classic form of a backwoods maple sugaring house and hopping on the ridge, like a weathervane come to life, was the silhouette of a huge raven.

"HELLO, ARDETH," voxed Blue.

"Kwa-koo!"

THE DOOR to the sugarhouse was ajar and Sylvie started filling in her story as they pushed inside.

"Blue and I came down here earlier. That's when she started that thing with this crazy raven. You won't believe this, but that damned raven showed her where this box was." She pointed to an open aluminum ammo box. It was full of pictures and odds and ends. "It's all stuff from her family. All that's left."

Will looked at the box and then at Blue. She was shaking and her breath was coming in gasps, but even so, she managed to vox, "DON'T LET ANYTHING HAPPEN TO IT! PROMISE ME!"

Will replied, "I PROMISE. DON'T WORRY." But he was exactly the opposite of not worried. They had to get a fire going fast. He looked for the promised wood stove and saw that Wu had already found it along with some kindling. Anna was crouched on the floor and still shivering but in better shape than Blue. Sylvie had started pulling some burlap sacks from a corner and stacking them on the floor.

"Will, put her down here," said Sylvie. She started pulling her sweater off, and as she did, she turned to Will and said, "And get your jacket off and put it on her." Will kicked himself for not thinking of that sooner, but he wanted to get a closer look at Blue's wound first. He set her gently on the pile of sacks and pulled out his phone. After Sylvie covered Blue with her sweater, they both leaned over to examine the wound in the phone's light.

Will gingerly pulled up the hem of Blue's blood-soaked sweater and they saw the mess. It looked like the bullet had entered through her side just above her hip leaving an oozing hole.

"It's not bleeding bad now, so we should just leave it alone or we'll make it worse. The best we can do is keep her still and keep her warm," said Sylvie.

Will covered the wound back up and peeled his jacket off and laid it over Blue's shivering form. Her eyes were still closed so he leaned in and whispered in her ear, "We'll get you warm, just hang in there."

He turned to Wu who had been rummaging frantically through the sugarhouse. "What's the problem?"

Wu replied, "Matches. I can't find any. Give me your phone so I can use the light."

"Dammit," Will said under his breath. "We get all this way and wind up with no matches? Sylvie, matches? Lighter?"

Sylvie slowly shook her head.

"J-j-jack h-h-has a l-l-lighter," said Anna.

"Not much good now," said Will. Could they hold out until Jack got back, he wondered? They'd have to if they couldn't find a way to get that stove going. Will looked at the window that faced the orchard, and beyond it, the house. The fog from their combined breathing had started to create a solid frost on the window and it was glowing an ominous orange from the light of the flames that were consuming the house. He might be able to pull out a burning piece of wood and bring it back to start the stove. The problem was Bronco. Where was he? He might be dead. He might be turned to ashes by now. He might have left in his car, like Purcell. He might be wounded and lying in the snow somewhere, but still dangerous.

Which was it? There was the last barrage of gunfire that got Blue, but nothing after. That would make it likely that Purcell killed Bronco and then made his getaway. That would mean it was safe for him to go to the house. Did he want to risk it? He looked at Blue and Anna shivering and realized the cold was starting to get to him, too, now that he had relinquished his jacket. If he didn't go soon, he would be in as much trouble as Blue and Anna. He had just about made up his mind to try when Wu shouted out.

"Found some!"

"T-thank G-god!" This was from Sylvie. Even she had started shivering by now.

Wu pulled open the small dusty box of wooden matches and took out a match. He struck the match on the side of the box and sparks flew, but there was no burst of flame. He struck again. More sparks, no flame. He kept striking until no more sparks came and he was left holding a bare wood stick.

"Shit! These must have gotten wet."

"Hold the next one close to the kindling. Maybe the sparks will ignite it," said Will.

Wu struck the next match and the results were even worse. He only got a few sparks and still no flame.

"God damn it! There's only one match left." Wu held out the last match in frustration and said, "You do it. Maybe I'm doing it wrong."

Will took the match and the box and said a little prayer as he scrubbed the last match across the rough striking surface on the side of the box. A small shower of sparks leapt into the kindling in the stove, but there was no burst of flame. Will went through the motions again and again and each time he got the encouraging shower of sparks, but the kindling just wouldn't take. When no more sparks came, he threw down the useless box and stood up, now convinced of what he had to do.

"I'm going to the house and bringing back something to start this fucking stove."

"W-w-what about B-b-b-bronco?" said Anna.

"He's got to be dead. There was no shooting when Purcell drove off. Purcell must have . . ."

A sudden blast of snow and cold cut him short as the door to the sugarhouse burst open and a body fell through it onto the floor.

From the light of the phone in Wu's hand, Will could see that the body's head was matted with blood and its face half covered in it. But the body wasn't dead. Amazingly, it was alive. Its head lifted and a hoarse voice cracked through its lips.

"Huh. I guess this room is taken. Mind if I come in?"

The man didn't wait for an answer. Instead, he started dragging himself in by his elbows. The four of them were frozen in shock as they watched the man haul himself inside the door and prop himself against a wall of the sugarhouse. "Someone get the door," he croaked, "it's a fucking blizzard out there."

The light from the phone suddenly went dark and Will felt a commotion to his right. He turned to see a figure silhouetted in the window. It was wielding a crooked piece of firewood. The frosty orange glow illuminated a face that was twisted with fear and confusion.

"Bronco!" Wu said, "You son-of-a-bitch!"

As Will's eyes adjusted to the light he could see that Bronco had held up his hand in a protective gesture. His hand was empty. His other hand dangled by his side, bloody and apparently useless.

"*TELL WU NOT TO HURT HIM!*"

Blue's vox came out of the dark along with a groan and an ache Will could feel in his side. He seized Wu's arm and said, "It's okay. Blue says it's okay." He could tell Wu had already held back even without Will's words. Will felt held back himself. He had fantasized about killing Bronco a dozen different ways the past few months but now that he was face-to-face with a brutalized human being, the urge to do him harm had evaporated. As he looked at the dark form of Bronco, he saw more evidence of the gritty confrontation with Purcell, and when his eyes finally met Bronco's, a burst of insight calmed him as he realized that Bronco had no intention of harming them and wasn't capable of it. In fact, Will could tell that he was going to die.

"Christ," said Bronco, "you're one of them, too. Aren't you?"

"*YOU CAN READ MY MIND, LIKE BLUE?*"

Will hesitated, but then nodded. Bronco's head lolled to the side where his gaze fell on Blue and Sylvie. Sylvie was cradling Blue's curled-up body. "I see you two made it out," he said.

"And I s-see you got what you deserved, y-you bastard, I hope you die," said Sylvie, "Look what y-you've done to her!" Sylvie stroked Blue's head tenderly even as her own body was seized by spastic shivers.

"Damn," he grunted. "Stray bullet, eh?" He closed his eyes and was silent for a moment and Will wondered if he had died, but then he heard a groan and then a pause and then, astonishingly, a chuckle. "Well, at least we got that fucker, Blue. Boy did you surprise him. And Purcell . . ." Bronco started chuckling harder, but it ended abruptly with a long groan followed by, "God dammit that hurts!"

Bronco was silent again for a long moment, his eyes remained squeezed shut as he dealt with whatever physical hell he was enduring. The rest of them were silent as well. Whether it was the shock of Bronco's appearance or the cold or the dark, it seemed as if time had stopped for all of them. The only movements were the shadows that pulsated with the wavering orange light from the glowing frosted-over window. Wu was still standing and holding the log but he was not moving. The only evidence that there were living beings in the room were the little clouds of fog puffing rhythmically out of their faces.

Bronco finally opened his eyes and appeared to be cogent again, but Will could sense that there was not enough energy or will remaining for Bronco to ever rise again under his own power.

"YOU CAN HEAR ME?" came the *chiss* from Bronco.

Will nodded.

"LOOK, I'M ALMOST DONE. DIDN'T PLAN IT THAT WAY, BUT AT LEAST THAT FUCKER BABINEAU IS DEAD. GUESS THAT'S ALL I WANTED ANYWAY. IT WAS HIS FAULT MY BROTHER IS DEAD. HIS FAULT HER FAMILY'S DEAD," He tilted his head toward Blue and managed a smile. "LISTEN, KID, THAT GIRL IS A PIECE OF WORK. IF YOU COULD'VE SEEN . . ."

And then Will did see. It was just like with Jordy. Bronco's mind replayed a scene where Blue catapulted out of her chair and slammed into Babineau and then there were shots followed by a fireball explosion.

Will could sense a feeling of relief over the waves of pain from Bronco. "IF THERE IS A HELL, BABINEAU'S FRYING IN IT RIGHT NOW." His eyes turned toward Blue. "WELL, I HOPE SHE SURVIVES." He looked back at Will. "YOU PROBABLY FIND THAT SURPRISING COMING FROM ME, RIGHT? WELL, NOBODY EVER REALLY FIGURED ME OUT. NOT EVEN ME."

"Will, what are you doing?" hissed Wu. "You're just staring at him! We've got to do something! Anna's shaking like mad and not talking. It's scaring me!" Wu had squatted down next to him, still holding the log.

Wu's words broke the mesmerizing slew of thoughts that Bronco had dumped on him and he stood up, looking around the sugarhouse. Wu's fears were more than justified. Blue and Anna were in a bad way, and Sylvie, huddling with Blue, wasn't far behind. Only he and Wu seemed to still be functioning, but Will could feel his own capacity slipping away. If they didn't do something, this was going to end very badly.

"I've got to go to the house. Bronco's not a threat anymore so there's no reason I shouldn't go. You should stay and try and help them get warm." He started for the door, but a hand grabbed his leg.

"You won't get . . . close . . . to that place."

Will looked at Bronco.

"JESUS CHRIST, KID. THE HEAT OF THAT PLACE WILL FRY YOU LIKE A FISH BEFORE YOU CAN GET WITHIN FIFTY FEET. IT'S A FUCKING INFERNO RIGHT NOW. EVEN THE CARS ARE FRIED. WHY DO YOU THINK I'M STILL HERE?"

Will yanked his leg away.

"Well what else am I supposed to do?" he hissed. "My friends could die if I don't try."

"Hold on . . ." Bronco's good hand drifted to his jacket pocket and fumbled around for a moment. "It's not . . . a gun . . . moron." He said this last bit to Wu, who had lifted the log again, ready to strike. Bronco found what he was looking for and held his closed hand out to Will.

Will stared at it.

"Put . . . your hand out . . . you idiot," said Bronco.

Will reluctantly held his hand out and Bronco dropped something hefty into it.

"DON'T LOSE IT." His eyes closed again.

Will looked down at his open palm. There, reflecting the pulsing orange glow from the frosted sugarhouse window, was the highly polished and intricately engraved silver jacket of a well-worn vintage cigarette lighter.

8:30 pm. Stanton Homestead
Snow 12"

IT COULD HAVE BEEN AN HOUR, or it could have been only minutes, but either way, it seemed to Jack that he had been walking forever through an endless surreal paradox of blinding whiteness billowing through a void of darkness. Purcell's tire tracks, shadowless and barely discernible, had soon been erased by the unbelievably quick accumulation of snow, leaving nothing to guide him except for his own dead-reckoning and the sudden appearance of tree trunks looming through the cloud of snow, nudging him back toward the center of the road. At times, he didn't even know if he was still on the road and at one point found himself stepping straight into the ditch. It was like walking through a cold, dark dream.

He came to a spot where the road leveled out and he stopped. He peered out into the nothingness. Had he passed the house? It was entirely possible that he missed a driveway or mailbox. He checked the phones. Still no signal. He looked behind him and swept his eyes across the blank landscape, looking for any tiny glow that might indicate a lighted window. When he was facing forward again he realized that there was a brightness, not of a window or porch light, but a broader light.

Headlights. There must have been a car somewhere down the road in front of him. He moved cautiously forward until the road reached a crest and headed down again. Then he saw it. There was a car off the road ahead of him and the headlight beams shone in an awkward angle into the snow-filled sky.

Shit. Purcell. He'd forgotten about him. The notion that he might have spun off the road in this mess had entirely escaped him. He pulled out his gun, an old Smith & Wesson single-action .32 his dad had given him when he was thirteen. Bringing it had been an afterthought. He had used it for plinking back when he was a kid, but it had sat in a drawer since then. He had no idea if it was still a weapon or just a hunk of useless metal, but it made him feel a little more confident as he slowly moved forward toward the helpless vehicle.

As he got closer and closer an inkling of hope welled up in him as he saw the dark silhouette of an emergency vehicle flasher bar on the roof. The hope was confirmed when he could discern the black bumper crossbars of a police cruiser. He almost wanted to sit down in the snow in relief but then he noticed a trail of footprints in the snow leading from the cruiser up the road he had just come down. Did he miss someone walking past?

"POLICE! DON'T MOVE!"

Jack nearly jumped out of his skin from the sudden shout from behind him. He tried not to move but whether it was fright or cold or both, his entire body was shaking.

"I SAID DON'T MOVE! DROP YOUR WEAPON!"

Jack realized the gun had already fallen from his hand when he jumped. He splayed the fingers of both hands and held them out, praying the cop could see them. A bright flashlight beamed out

behind him throwing his shadow like a dark ghost onto the undu-
lating snowfall in front of him.

"T-Turn around!" came a more reasonable voice.

Jack was sure he detected a note of fear. He slowly turned
around and said, "Sir! I need help. My friends are in trouble."

"S-shut up and kneel on the ground. Put your hands behind
your back." The cop was fumbling to get the cuffs off his belt while
juggling his flashlight and gun.

"Officer, I'm serious, my friend is shot. My car's in a ditch."

"Just shut it," said the sheriff, finally getting the cuffs off and
giving Jack a wide berth as he approached him from behind, "and
d-don't move."

Jack could feel the cuffs being put on and he did his best to help
the fumbling officer because he was clearly having a hard time
with it.

"Now stand up and walk in front of me to the car."

"Please, sir! I'm telling the truth. My friend could die."

"Why were you approaching me with a weapon then? Huh? Tell
me that!"

"I thought you might be the guy who shot her. A guy in a black
Escalade."

"Okay, hold up there." Jack stopped and the cop came around in
front of him, shining the flashlight directly in his face. "Who are
you?"

"My name is Jack Menhoff. I came with three of my friends in
my car to a place up the road. The old Stanton place. Look, it's a
long story, but we barely got there when there was all this gunfire. I
tried to drive away but got ditched and a stray bullet hit my friend. I
left them up there to come for help. There's no cell phone coverage
up here. Please, you gotta believe me!"

The light stayed stationary for a moment and then it dropped
and Jack could see the sheriff in the half-light. "I hope you have a
license for that gun, son." He paused and then went on, "That
Escalade is why I'm in the ditch. He came piling down that hill and

barely stayed on the road himself. Scared the shit out of me. Hell, you scared the shit out of me. About your friend—if what you say is true, I'm not sure what we can do about it until some help comes."

"Can we at least please call an ambulance or rescue squad or something?"

"I can do that. I already have a wrecker coming. And a cop from Vermont and a cop from New York, and God knows who else. Jesus, as far as I know, you're as guilty as anyone else in this clusterfuck. Hey, settle down!"

Jack was jumping up and down, he couldn't help himself. "Chief Hannah is coming?" He laughed with relief and at the look of shock and puzzlement on the sheriff's face and then he plopped down in the snow and said, "Thank God," just as a pair of headlights rounded a corner 100 yards down the road.

"My feet hurt," said Anna. She was sitting on a stack of burlap sacks and snuggled against Wu. Her legs were scrunched up with her stockinged feet resting on a small box close to the wood stove, which was now filled with the comforting muffled crackle of burning wood. Will reached out and touched one of her feet. "Ow!" she cried.

"That means they're warming up."

"How's Blue?" she asked.

Will looked down at his lap where Blue's head was resting, her face illuminated by a dancing glow leaking from the grate of the wood stove. What he saw in that face was an expression that was created by layers of emotion so deep he was afraid to find what was underneath. He longed to, though. "*How is Blue?*" he voxed.

"*Blue is scared,*" said Blue. "*I don't want to die.*"

Will stroked her forehead tenderly and wondered what expression she could see in him because he was piled deep with emotions right now, too. "Don't be scared. We're here. Jack will be back with help." "*AND DON'T BE RIDICULOUS. YOU ARE NOT GOING TO DIE!*" He forced himself to be positive, but he knew that she would sense the worm of fear that was squirming in his chest right now. God dammit, Jack, you better get back soon he thought to himself. He closed his eyes with this last thought to cut off any chance that it might leak to Blue.

"The bleeding has slowed down a lot," said Sylvie. She was huddled next to Will. The two of them had been by Blue's side comforting her as best they could ever since they had gotten the fire going. It was the only thing they could do for her until help came. "How does it feel?"

"It burns, like a hot poker in my side. And I have, like, gas pains. It's not terrible but it's no fun," said Blue. She reached out her hand and touched Sylvie's arm, "I am so sorry I got you into this."

"Oh, sweetie, just forget about that. You don't worry now, okay?" Sylvie's words were tender, but her quick concerned glance at Will told another story. Will winced because he knew Blue could hear Sylvie's *chiss*, "*GODDAMMIT WHERE IS HELP!*"

It reflected the same worry that had been growing in him exponentially. It felt like they had been sitting there too long without doing anything except waiting. He looked back down at Blue and voxed, "*JACK WILL COME THROUGH.*"

"*WILL, I WANT TO TELL YOU WHAT HAPPENED.*"

"*WE'LL HAVE TIME FOR THAT LATER.*"

"*I NEED TO TELL YOU NOW. IN CASE SOMETHING HAPPENS.*"

Her urgency penetrated his objections, but he was not going to entertain any thoughts of doom or gloom. "*OKAY, BUT NOTHING IS GOING TO HAPPEN, GOT THAT?*"

"*BRONCO DIDN'T KILL MY FAMILY.*"

"*WHAT?*"

"*BRONCO DIDN'T KILL MY FAMILY. HE WASN'T THERE. IT WAS HIS DAD AND BROTHER. HIS BROTHER COULDN'T BRING HIMSELF TO KILL ME AND HEATHER SO HE FAKED IT. HIS FATHER FOUND OUT LATER AND THAT'S WHY HE KILLED HIS BROTHER BY PUSHING HIM DOWN THE STAIRS. BRONCO*

SMOTHERED HIS DAD IN HIS SLEEP FOR THAT. BUT HE BLAMES BABINEAU
FOR HIS BROTHER'S DEATH."

"HE TOLD YOU THIS?"

"YEAH. HE TALKED A LOT WHEN I WAS TIED UP."

Will couldn't think of anything to say. Everything he'd felt about
Bronco was getting turned on its head. "BUT HE TAZED YOU AND
SYLVIE. HE TIED YOU UP AND DELIVERED YOU TO BABINEAU."

"JUST LISTEN. LET ME GET IT ALL OUT. BABINEAU'S A NOCTE VENA-
TORI, NIGHT HUNTER. THEY CAN SEE OUR EYES WHEN WE VOX, WILL, LIKE
YOUR DAD'S IR CAMERA. I REMEMBER HEARING ABOUT THEM WHEN I WAS
A KID. BABINEAU WANTED MY MOM TO BEAR HIS CHILD BECAUSE HE
COULDN'T FIND ANOTHER NOCTE AND HE WANTED AN HEIR THAT WAS VOX
OR NOCTE. THAT'S WHY MY DAD TURNED ON HIM. AND THEN WHEN
HEATHER WAS BORN, MY DAD SENT AN ANONYMOUS DNA TEST TO
BABINEAU THAT PROVED HE WASN'T THE FATHER. THE LETTER AND DNA
TEST ARE IN THE ROCKET BOX. THEN WHEN BABINEAU FOUND OUT I WAS
STILL ALIVE, HE WANTED ME AS A BREEDER, WILL. YEAH, I KNOW. HARD
TO BELIEVE, RIGHT? AND HE WAS GOING TO GIVE ME KETAMINE AND DO IT
RIGHT THERE, TONIGHT! BUT BRONCO CHISSED ME TO ACT OUT BEING
DRUGGED AND GAVE ME A CAFFEINE INJECTION INSTEAD OF KETAMINE.
YEAH, HE KNEW ABOUT CHISS, I DECIDED TO EXPLAIN SO WE HAD AN
ADVANTAGE OVER BABINEAU. HE WANTED BABINEAU DEAD AS BADLY AS I
DID."

She paused as she winced and groaned but then kept going. "AS
SOON AS BRONCO UNTIED ME, I WAS SUPPOSED TO RUN AND CAUSE A
DISTRACTION WHILE BRONCO TOOK DOWN PURCELL WITH A TASER HE HAD
HIDDEN. BUT INSTEAD, I TOTALLY LOST IT AND JUMPED UP AND SLAMMED
THAT SHORT, FAT, SLIMY, SORRY EXCUSE FOR HUMANITY RIGHT INTO THE
STOVE. I DON'T KNOW WHAT HAPPENED AFTER THAT BECAUSE I RAN. I
WENT STRAIGHT TO SYLVIE IN THE LAUNDRY ROOM NEXT TO THE GARAGE
AND PULLED THE ZIP TIE OFF HER FEET. AND . . . WELL, YOU KNOW THE
REST. GOD WILL, I WAS SO HAPPY AND TERRIFIED AT THE SAME TIME TO
SEE YOU . . ."

"*I SAW YOU AFTER YOU TACKLED BABINEAU. WE'D JUST GOTTEN THERE AND I WAS ON THE PORCH AND SAW YOU RUN TOWARD THE GARAGE . . .*"

Will felt a nudge and turned toward Sylvie.

"Will, Jesus. We've got to do something. You can't just stare at her and make her better." Then she mouthed something, "She-needs-to-get-to-a-hospital! We-can't-just-sit-here!"

Wu spoke up, "She's right. And you know, if Jack doesn't know Bronco is dead, they might be waiting for SWAT or backup or something. Maybe they're out there now. And do they know the way to the sugarhouse?"

Will turned to look at Bronco's battered body sitting in the shadows. By the time they got the fire going with his lighter, he was gone. He turned back to the three faces of Wu, Anna, and Sylvie looking expectantly at him in the dim firelight. He looked back down at Blue. "I'm going to go and meet Jack at the road and tell them the coast is clear. I'm all warmed up now."

Blue grabbed his hand and squeezed, "No, I don't want you to go!" He could sense how much weaker she had become. It seemed her story had drained her energy. The ache in her gut was starting to intensify, too, now that her adrenaline was wearing thin. Will turned and looked at the rest of them. Wu was dressed lighter than him and Anna's Birkenstocks were just not going to cut it. Sylvie seemed to know first aid better than him, so he was the one.

"It's got to be me. Sylvie will take care of you." He leaned down and kissed her cheek. And then he didn't want to go either. He was afraid that when his lips left her soft cheek, it might be for the last time.

Sylvie was elbowing him hard. He sat up, still looking at Blue. "*THERE ARE STILL A LOT OF QUESTIONS YOU NEED TO ANSWER, SO YOU HAVE NO CHOICE BUT TO HANG IN THERE. OKAY?*"

She smiled, weakly, but with both sides of her mouth. "*OKAY.*" She squeezed his hand and let it go.

9:00 pm. Stanton Homestead

"GOD DAMMIT, Jack. You—all of you—are going to be the death of me. What in God's name were you kids thinking coming here? Don't answer that. We don't have time. Just get your snowshoes on and let's get going." She said this as she finished fastening her own snowshoes. She had managed to plow through the snow with her very able SUV and get to the point where Jack had parted from the others.

God dammit, what was *she* doing, she asked herself? She should never have let Jack come along. With Bronco still at large, she would be putting him in immense danger. She couldn't even believe she let him bring his gun which he'd retrieved from the snow once he'd been released by the Sheriff. But Jack was eighteen and could make his own decisions and the Sheriff had to stay back and direct the emergency vehicles when they got there. She had no time to wait for other backup. Rodney was still a half-hour away and who knows when the State Troopers would get there.

Still, she was having huge regrets. The memory of Bronco's marksmanship in her previous encounter—two shots, two head-lights—deliberate super-accurate shots from fifteen yards—it came back to her a little too vividly.

Dammit, she'd screwed up. She just prayed nothing bad would happen to Jack.

"Keep low and let me take the lead. If ANYTHING goes wrong take my car and get help. And don't show that goddamn gun to anyone else or you are going to wind up in jail." It was the Sheriff who volunteered to forget about Jack's unlicensed gun, God bless him.

They set out into the woods where the deep gouge caused by five kids plowing through the woods was still visible even with the fresh snow on top. She was praying that she wouldn't find five mounds in the snow. It was unearthly quiet and peaceful now that the storm had relented, and the forest had reappeared with the stark black tree trunks thrust up like sentinels from the deep snow.

The snowshoes allowed them to move quickly and quietly, even through the ravine that separated them from what appeared to be an orchard on the other side. As they cautiously emerged from the ravine and moved across the edge of the orchard, the acrid smoke and ash from the still roaring fire wafted over them, but they saw no movement other than the intricate shadow dance performed by the apple branches in the firelight.

And then there it was—a real movement. A figure moving through the trees. She raised her gun and crouched down and signaled with her free hand for Jack to stay down, but instead of staying down she watched in disbelief as Jack leapt up and loped past her with a shout.

"Will!"

The figure stopped for a moment and then plowed headlong through the snow and waved shouting back "Jack? Is that you?" In seconds Will closed the distance. Chief Hannah stood up cautiously, her gun only partially lowered. "And Chief Hannah! Jesus! What the hell?"

"Where's Bronco?" she asked.

"Bronco is dead and we need . . ." He stopped, his gaze suddenly pulled toward something behind her and then he let out a whoop and charged past her, prancing through the deep snow like a deer. She turned to see what had excited Will. Across the ravine came the lights and roar of a giant plow truck followed immediately by the very welcome swirling lights of an ambulance.

As she watched Will step through the door and out into the snowy darkness, Blue was overwhelmed with the sensation that he took time continuity with him. Her awareness of what was happening started to come and go, like subway stations flashing past the windows of a rapidly moving train that refused to stop. The first flash came with a blast of cold when Will returned with a pair of EMTs. Then there was the comforting warmth and pressure of blankets as she was bundled onto a stretcher, wrapped like a mummy. Then another flash and there was a lot of bumping and the sounds of heavy breathing and low talking as she was carried over the open ground under the crisp, dark night sky with its frowning crescent moon. *"DON'T BE SAD, MR. MOON,"* she voxed wondering if he could hear her. In another flash, she saw a black-winged silhouette hover above her. "Hello, Ardeth" she thought or voxed or said or dreamed. Next, the rumbling undulations of a vehicle traveling fast. She opened her eyes to the familiar interior features of an ambulance. It made her wonder: was this a dream from her past or was this now? She'd been in an ambulance so many times it was hard to know. Another flash and the feeling of a warm hand in hers. She squeezed and the hand squeezed back. Next, the bright lights of a hospital ceiling rolling by. There was something unmistakable about a hospital ceiling. She tried to put her finger on what it was but then she winked out and when she came to again, masked nurses and doctors were hovering above her. A mask for her. A voice saying, "Just breathe naturally." What does that mean, "breathe naturally," she wondered? . . .

RODNEY'S HEADLIGHTS swept around a corner to a familiar scene—emergency vehicles arranged semi-randomly along a wide bend in the road with their light show of flashing reds and whites and blues. There was a wrecker pulling a county Sheriff's car out of a ditch, a fire truck idling with full-clad firemen huddled together in an intense discussion. There was an ambulance with a couple of EMTs that looked like they were waiting for something, and then down the road came a rugged-looking SUV. It pulled to a stop next to the ambulance at the same time that Rodney pulled over and got out of his car. He walked over to the SUV and was unsurprised to see Chief Hannah get out, but was shocked to see who else got out. It was a bunch of kids. He recognized the Asian boy, Wu, but there was another boy and a girl. The girl looked like she was hobbling and the not-Wu boy was helping her. The EMTs quickly met the two and helped the girl into the ambulance. His detective instincts sensed that whatever had happened here tonight was already over. Everyone was moving at a post-crisis pace. Chief Hannah caught sight of him and waved him over.

"Glad you could make it," she called, "but you're late for the party."

He walked over to her SUV. "Um, yeah, it looks like it." He gestured at the two kids who were now both standing next to the ambulance. "What is the boy, Wu, doing here? And who are these other kids? Can you fill me in?"

She smiled. "Well that could take a while, but I will give you the short version. First and most importantly, everyone we care about is accounted for—that includes those kids, Wu and Jack and Anna."

He looked over at the ambulance. The EMTs handed blankets to the two boys. "Is the girl okay? She was hobbling."

"She will be. She got some frostbite in her feet and probably some mild hypothermia, but she'll be okay. There were also two other kids we care about and your hunch about one of them was right: Blue DuBois was here, but also Will Woods. They both left earlier by ambulance."

"Blue *and* Will?" He felt a little bit of relief that his hunch was correct and that they hadn't gone on a wild goose chase by coming here, but it was clear that a lot more went on than he'd ever guessed. "Are they okay?"

"Well, no. That's the grim news. Blue was shot. Once in the abdomen. We don't know how serious it is, but she was more or less conscious and the bleeding was never heavy, so we're optimistic. There was a gun fight, and she was hit by a stray bullet. The gunfight was between Bronco and Purcell. . ."

"So they *were* rendezvousing here."

"Wait, it gets better. Babineau is allegedly dead, but we can't confirm because the fire at his camp is still burning and he was inside."

"*His* camp? It was here? The same road that the Stanton's lived on?"

"Hang on to your hat, Rodney. His camp *is* the old Stanton homestead."

Rodney had seen and heard a lot in his career so he normally wasn't shocked by revelations like this, but this one was a true stunner. Babineau had bought the land of a family he had murdered. That was a sick act even for Babineau. And now he was dead. That is a game-changer right there, he thought. His detective brain overcame his momentary shock and went into overdrive working on how this was going to change everything he did from this point on, but he also stayed in the moment well enough to pay attention to Chief Hannah as she went on.

"Purcell we don't know about. He escaped. I have an APB out for his car and we believe that he was seriously injured in the gunfight. He's the one that ran the Sheriff off the road."

"And Bronco?"

"He's dead."

"Dead," he repeated. He scratched his head. All this time and energy and suddenly both perps were gone. "Babineau and Bronco in one night. Well that makes life simple, I suppose, but it also means we can't take the investigation any deeper unless we can get Purcell. Babineau's organization is still intact."

"I know, I know," said Chief Hannah, "but I've got some good news for you." She stepped to the back of the SUV and opened the hatch. Lurking inside like a drab sarcophagus was a large olive-green ammo box. "I think you're going to find more than you'd hoped for inside this. This was found in a sugarhouse where the kids sheltered. The sugarhouse was the only building left from the Stanton homestead and was apparently untouched. I think this is what Blue had come looking for. It looks like André DuBois held back a whole lot of stuff about Babineau's operation in here. I just took a quick peek, but I think you're going to be happy. I do have to insist on something, though. There is a lot of stuff in there that is family stuff."

"You mean memorabilia? Blue's family stuff?"

"Yeah. Like original birth certificates, letters. And it looks like some valuable bonds. And most importantly, family pictures. Possibly the only ones that still exist. You've got to promise me that it will get back to Blue as soon as possible."

"My God. Yes, of course, I will make sure she gets it all back." He stood in a slight daze, reeling from the combined impact of the chaotic winter scene, this windfall of possibly incriminating documents, the unexpected presence of all these kids, the news that Blue was shot, the still unknown circumstances of the gunfight, and the burning house.

"Hey, Rodney," said Chief Hannah.

He looked at her. She was looking at him in a strange way.

"It was your hunch that brought us here. If it hadn't been for that . . ." She stepped toward him, and he suddenly found himself in a tight embrace. He returned it and didn't worry about professionalism. After all, it was personal for her and, he had to admit, getting to be pretty damned personal for him, too.

9:30 pm, Near Elizabethtown, NY

"SHE YOUR SISTER?"

The question came from the EMT sitting across from Will. They were both rocking with the motion of the ambulance and the EMT was adjusting the oxygen mask over Blue's quiet face. Her eyes were closed and she lay strapped and bundled securely on the gurney that was anchored between them. There was a silent monitor above her head tracing out a neon-green zig-zag marking for each beat of her heart. Will's gaze had been fixated on that trace because its strong and steady rhythm was giving him a good dose of very welcome reassurance.

"No, just a friend. A very good friend," he replied.

"Well, look. I haven't seen a lot of gunshot wounds, but this doesn't look too bad. Some bleeding, but not life-threatening. She is suffering some shock, but her vitals are strong." He looked up at Will. "*This kid looks like he's in a little shock himself.*" "Just wanted to give you some good news. It looks like you need some."

"Thanks. Yeah, I do. It's been a rough day." He reached out and wrapped his hand around Blue's. It felt cool, but not cold. His heart skipped a beat as he felt her hand squeeze his. Just that small squeeze gave him more reassurance than any words or monitor. He squeezed back.

"When are we going to get there?" he asked, peering anxiously out the windshield of the ambulance. There was no sign of civilization just darkness and highway.

The EMT smiled. "Not long. Elizabethtown is just a few miles ahead. My name is Simon, by the way."

"I'm Will."

"Good to meet you, Will," he said. "I have to ask you. Do you know how old your friend is? Blue?"

For some reason the question irritated him. He really didn't want to chit-chat right now, he just wanted to get to that hospital. "She's fifteen. Is that important?"

"Medically? Yeah, it's important to know. But there's another reason I was asking."

The cautious way he said it caught Will's attention. He looked at Simon's eyes to see if he could catch any of his thinking and what he heard made him pay even more attention: "*That girl would have been about fifteen by now, but it couldn't be.*"

"You rescued another girl from the Stanton place, didn't you?"

Simon's eyes grew wide. Will pressed on, "About five years ago.

A fire. There were two girls. One was airlifted to a burn center, the other girl was taken to Lake Placid."

"Um, yeah, that was us . . . but how . . ."

"This is that girl."

10 pm, Saratoga Springs, NY

THE ESCALADE BUMPED over the curb and came to a final rest in front of an elegant Georgian architecture home with a large front yard. The huge car was probably half on their lawn, but he didn't care. He'd made it to Saratoga Springs and the closest safe harbor available. He picked up his phone with his good arm and tried it again, but it was fried, the victim of a rock he had fallen on as he tried to dodge the final volley from Bronco. He dropped the phone and looked to the front door of the house, judging the distance. He was just going to have to drag himself out of the car, limp up there, and knock on the front door the old-fashioned way. A complete violation of protocol when seeking this mob doctor's services but he was out of options.

He groaned as he eased his right foot off the brake pedal which was slick with blood. He had no feeling below his right calf and his left arm hung useless at his side. He looked glumly at the thirty feet or so of snow-covered lawn he would have to navigate to get to the front door and took a deep breath which was a mistake. He was seized by a wracking cough that nearly shook his ravaged body to pieces. When he caught his breath again he spit a bloody gob out of his mouth and shivered. That episode had nearly done him in and the cold seemed to be penetrating every layer of his clothes. He reached for the heater controls but they were already turned full blast. Shivering, he leaned back into his seat and looked out his window at the front of the house. The front door was right there. He was running out of time. He reached for the door handle and hooked his fingers on it and pulled, but his fingers slipped off. He tried again but he just couldn't get his fingers to pull. It was like his hand had fallen asleep. He attempted a couple more times and then gave up, completely spent from the effort. He finally just let his head rest against the door post and he stared at the front door, willing someone to come out and spot him.

As he waited, he noted the Doric columns supporting the roof over the door stoop. It was nice architecture, he thought, and he admired how it fit into the rest of the house. He tried to see more but it seemed that it had started snowing again. It was a strange snowfall, one that only obscured his peripheral vision at first and then it slowly closed in around the center of his vision until he could see almost nothing. At the same time he got colder and colder until he was so cold that he stopped shivering and he realized in a final flash of lucidity that in a moment, he was never going to feel the cold again . . .

31

OUT OF LIMBO

The next day, March 16th
Elizabethtown, New York

"Do you want to finish your yogurt?" The nurse held up the half-eaten yogurt cup.

"No thanks," said Blue as she eased herself carefully back onto the hospital bed. The yogurt had triggered her first adventure to the bathroom and she didn't want to experience that again for a while. Between the cramping in her gut, the dizziness of the meds, and the indignity of the hospital gown, she was quite content to lie quiet for a while.

The nurse helped her get settled and said, "We're going to get you up and walking around in an hour or so. It's important to get you active so your bowels can sort themselves out."

Blue groaned. She just wanted to lie there and not move. "Can I at least get some coffee?" she asked hopefully.

The nurse smiled wryly and said, "Afraid not. No caffeine for a couple of weeks." She took the yogurt cup and left Blue alone to contemplate this last piece of bad news. She closed her eyes and took a deep breath. At least I'm still alive, she told herself. And as if to verify that a little machine next to her bed woke up and purred reassuringly as it took her blood pressure. She turned to look at the monitor where a little blue line hopped its way across the screen to the rhythm of her heart. She lifted her arm and examined all the paraphernalia attached to it: a blood pressure collar; an IV needle with its tube trailing over to the drip bag hanging on a stand next to her bed; a little sensor attached to her ring finger. She rested her arm back on the bed and looked down at her abdomen where a tube came out from under the dressing and ran to a bottle attached to a strap around her waist. That had freaked her out until a nurse reassured her that it was just a temporary drain. That was such a lovely word, 'drain' she thought sarcastically. She sighed again and looked around the empty room. Yep, alive and alone.

She wondered where everyone was. She remembered talking to people after she woke up from surgery in post-op but it was all a weird mish-mosh of images in her post-anesthesia fog—a nurse talking to her, and Wu and Will were there, and Chief Hannah. And then she must have been rolled to her room, and she remembered someone being there when she woke up in pain during the night—it was Wu or Will, she couldn't be sure. Whoever it was called the nurse and she came in and adjusted something, the pain went away, and she went right back to sleep.

Well, wherever they were now, she hoped they were getting some sleep. It wasn't like she was desperate to see them right now, anyway. She was in a weird space. The stark furnishings and light blue color of the walls and the fluorescent lighting all contributed to this feeling. It was as if she was at an intersection where all her past lives had come together in a colossal collision leaving just this space, this blue room, for her to pause and contemplate, once again, exactly how these lives had crafted this battered person that she had become and to wonder who she was going to be in the future. She closed her eyes. There were too many pieces to her puzzle and right now she was sick of trying to figure it out. All she wanted to do was zone out and wait for someone else to tell her what was next. It was like this was the waiting room for her next life.

"I guess this is what Limbo is like," she said to the walls.

And as if that was what the walls were waiting to hear to unlock the next level in her life, the nurse popped back in and asked, "Are you ready for a visitor?"

Was she? She had a weird notion that whoever the visitor was, they were going to indicate the direction her next life was going to go. Well, better than hanging out in Limbo, she thought.

"Why not," she said.

The nurse stepped over to her bed and raised the back to more of a sitting position. Blue gingerly arranged herself for minimal discomfort and tweaked her gown and blankets to make sure they were doing their job at keeping her decent.

The nurse left and moments later her visitor stepped in and when he did, a churning, confused wave of apprehension, guilt, relief, and elation enveloped her. It was Will, exactly who she had been hoping for and yet dreading at the same time. She had put him through so much. She looked him up and down as he stood hesitantly just inside the door. A scent of woodsmoke emanated from him and she saw streaks of ash on his pants and shirt along with a bloodstain. Her blood. His face was smudged with dirt and ash and his hair was a mess, but his eyes shined brightly, even more so because of the wordless emotion that passed through them and into her. Two strides and he was at her bedside wrapping his arms gently around her. The touch and warmth of his body against hers, the smell of woodsmoke, and the hot tears running down her cheeks combined to create a soul-soothing balm and she knew at that moment that her next life was going to be okay.

As soon as he held her in his arms, a fatigue washed over Will as if his body had been holding out just long enough for this moment of affirmation and now it was saying 'all is well, time to rest.' He sank into the upholstered chair next to her bed, a chair he had occupied for half the night in a tag team with Wu. He allowed his exhausted body to nestle into the generous padding, resting his head against the back, all the while keeping his eyes on Blue's face. He reached over and took her free hand in his. It felt warm and alive.

"*THAT HAIR IS GOING TO TAKE SOME GETTING USED TO,*" he voxed. He smiled happily when he heard a "ka-huh" in reply, her signature sound of amusement, a sound that had been missing from his life for months.

"*YOU'RE A MESS. YOU SHOULD GO TAKE A SHOWER,*" she replied.

"*TOO TIRED.*" His eyes fluttered shut for a moment.

"You can't fall asleep, you have to tell me how everyone is. Is Anna okay?"

He let his eyes stay closed but stayed conscious enough to reply, knowing how anxious Blue probably felt. "She's okay. She had some frostbite but they took care of that overnight. Her feet will be tender for a while. Her mom came and picked her up early this morning. Pa Bill came at the same time to fetch Wu and me."

"Pa Bill," she said nervously. "Is he still here?"

"No, he left with just Wu. You were still asleep, and he didn't want to wake you. He had to drag Wu out of your room, you know. He tried to drag me out but I'm afraid I was a bit stubborn."

He felt her squeeze his hand. He squeezed back.

"And Sylvie?"

"Jack gave her a ride back to Malone. He got his car pulled out and believe it or not, he managed to fix whatever the bullet hit. They didn't leave until you were out of post-op, though. Chief Hannah is still here in the waiting room. I'm under arrest, you know."

"What!?"

"Yeah, my mom insisted that Chief Hannah arrest me and accompany me home where I am grounded for the next ninety-two years." He cracked one eye open and gave her a tired grin.

"Very funny, you jerk," she said, but she was smiling. It was a tired smile and her eyes looked like they were barely staying open themselves.

"Yeah, I'm a jerk." He let his own eyes close again and he felt her hand squeeze tight. He squeezed back. He took in a deep breath and let it out slowly and every part of his body relaxed except for the hand that was holding Blue's. That hand seemed like the only part of him that wasn't tired and he was glad because he didn't want to let go.

THE NURSE STEPPED into the room, stopped, and stepped right back out again with a satisfied nod. The two kids were dead asleep and their hands were locked tightly together. She was wise enough to know that there was nothing she could offer that could eclipse the healing power of that.

Later that day

"MRS. JAMISON?" This startled remark came from a startling-looking girl who was sitting up in her hospital bed. She was startling not only because of her dramatic two-toned hair but from her alertness and the mere fact that she was able to sit the way she was so soon after surgery for a gunshot wound. For a moment, Detective Rodney James wondered if he and Blue's DFC caseworker, Mrs. Jamison, had stepped into the right room.

Slumped in a chair next to the bed was a dozing teenager who looked almost worse off than the girl in the hospital bed. The boy, Will Woods, looked like he was in danger of falling off his chair.

The girl rescued Will from falling with a just-in-time nudge that brought him to a groggy state of alertness. He blinked a couple of times then sat up and with a smile of recognition, held out his hand. "Hey, Detective James," he said as they shook hands.

The woman who had accompanied Rodney held out her hand to Will and introduced herself.

"Hello, Will. I am so glad to meet you. I have heard quite a bit about you. My name is Mrs. Jamison. I am Blue's caseworker from the DFC."

"Caseworker?"

"Yes. We are still Blue's legal guardians even though her foster parents, Mr. and Mrs. O'Day, are the day-to-day guardians." She turned to Blue and said, "And don't worry Blue, I am not here to take you away from Ma Beth and Pa Bill. I am only here because Detective James would like to ask you a few questions that would help him with his investigation and he is not permitted to do that without a guardian's approval and your approval. Would that be all right with you?"

Rodney watched as Blue and Will turned toward each other. He was struck by the impression that they were conferring with each other, only without words. Blue then turned toward Mrs. Jamison and then toward him. He felt like he was being put under a magnifying glass. "Yes, that would be okay," she said at last. "If Will can stay."

"Yes, of course," said Rodney. "Are you sure you're up for it? We can leave if you are at all uncomfortable."

"I'm okay, I mean I'm a little spacey and my gut hurts, but I actually would like to hear your questions."

"That's great. I only need to ask a few and Will already knows what they are, but first I wanted to tell you that your box, the ammo box, is safe . . ."

"But you need to keep it," she said.

". . . Yes. I am afraid it is evidence, and it can't be returned to you until we have fully documented it." He paused, knocked a little off balance by her quick and keen perceptiveness. "But I want you to know that I will personally see to it that it is processed and returned as quickly as possible." He reached into his briefcase and pulled out a sheet of photo paper with an image on it. "I took the liberty of making a copy of this. I thought you might like to have it in the meantime." It was a copy of a picture of her family he had found sitting at the top of the ammo box. As he handed it to her, she glanced at it and then immediately hugged it to her chest looking happy and sad at the same time.

"Um, thank you," was all she could get out.

Her reaction sobered him a bit. He paused before he continued. "There are some papers from that box that are going to be instrumental in disrupting organized crime in the New York area. Your father was a good man, and he collected information on a lot more people than just Babineau." And, he thought to himself, there were papers that were heartbreaking in their implication, but he was not going to mention those now.

"I already know about the paternity report. And I know what it means," said Blue.

Again, he was startled by her perception. All he could say was, "I'm sorry."

"What do you want to ask me?" asked Blue.

Surprisingly, Will jumped in with the first question. "Are you Blue Stanton?"

She turned to Will with a surprised look on her face. There was a pause as they stared at each other and then she blurted out, "Because I didn't want to remember!" She then quickly turned back to Rodney, "I mean, yes. That was my name. I . . . " she stopped and glanced at Will again before turning back, " . . . I worked hard to leave that all behind. After the fire, any reminder of my family, including the name Stanton, sent me into panic attacks and depression. It happened a lot. I just learned to push those memories away. It really has only been the last couple of months that I have been able to think about it and not freak out. If you asked me that question a year ago, I probably would have just clammed up."

Rodney stared at his hands. He was used to taking statements and interviewing people, but this was very different. He looked back up at Blue and said, "Thank you for that, Blue. That really helps. I'm sorry for all you have gone through."

She nodded and said, "I'm learning to deal with it thanks to Will's mom and Jeremy and Stella." She turned to Will, reached out, and squeezed his shoulder. Again they seemed to be conferring with each other silently.

She turned back to Rodney and said, "You need to meet Stella. Her husband used to be the head of WITSEC in Washington. I think he was the one that gave me my new I.D. His name was Edward Winslow."

Rodney sat back in honest astonishment. "Edward Winslow!" He knew exactly who that was. It seemed his name came up in every interview and meeting that he had with WITSEC during his investigation. But not once did anyone indicate that he might be involved in any part of this case. "I am very familiar with who he was. But I never suspected he would be directly involved in this . . . did you learn anything else about him?"

For the next ten minutes, Blue told them her story about her friend, Jeremy, who introduced her to Stella. And then she related her long talk with Stella. When she finished, Rodney ran his fingers through his hair and took a deep breath. He had spent months trying to track down this information and here in the space of ten minutes he'd learned more than he had in all that time.

"Wow. This really fills in a lot of gaps. Thank you. I can't believe you just ran into Edward's widow by happenstance. I really look forward to interviewing her." He felt lighter. He finally had solid leads to work with.

He smiled at Blue and could see that she was exhausted, as if she had held up just long enough to pass on her story and was now ready to collapse. "Look, I don't want to put you out anymore. This is more than enough to keep me busy for a long time. You take care of yourself. I would love to talk to you more after you are better . . . with the proper permission." He looked at Mrs. Jamison who had been sitting patiently to the side.

Mrs. Jamison smiled and said, "I don't think that will be a problem with the DFC. I will leave that up to Blue and the O'Days."

"If the O'Days will take me back," said Blue, looking down.

"Oh, I think you'll find that they will more than take you back," said Mrs. Jamison. "Their application to adopt you has already been submitted. It's really going to be up to you now."

Blue seized Will's hand, holding it to her chest with both hands and then Rodney watched as the purest expression of joyful relief that he had ever witnessed blossomed across her face. He quickly looked down for fear that his heart was going to throw him head-long over his moat of professional indifference, but it was too late. There was no way to completely escape the electric emotional atmosphere in the room, even if he did look away.

He cleared his throat and said, "Well, that's none of my business, really, but please do keep me apprised of any change in Blue's guardianship." He was still face down, but he couldn't help looking back up and saying, "Um, but hey, congratulations, I'm really happy for you." She didn't reply but her eyes were fixed on his and he could swear they said, "Thank you." He quickly turned toward Mrs. Jamison. "We should go now, I think. We've more than used up our time."

As they left the room he could now understand the passion Chief Hannah had for protecting these two extraordinary kids. He could feel that passion growing in him in spite of his reflexive warning flag flashing, "Don't get emotionally involved!" But for the first time, he felt like ignoring that flag. After all, wasn't passion, *com*passion, what got him into this job in the first place? It wasn't just his love of solving puzzles, was it? He thought about Blue's show of emotion and how she had clutched that picture to her heart, and he considered the other items that he'd seen in her ammo box: a highly charged blend of heart-breaking family legacy mixed with potent legal retribution. How could he possibly examine those contents without compassion? He couldn't. There was a limit to professionalism and that limit was sacrosanct: his duty to always be a decent human being.

32

BACK HOME

A week later, March 24
Westbury, Vermont

The familiar warble echoed in her dream like a distant call to reality, which her sleepy brain eventually acknowledged was exactly what it was. Her brain responded by flopping her arm down to the floor where it knew her phone would be, chanting its morning reminder for her to get up and get ready for work. Her fingers instinctively found the side button to shut the thing up.

It kept going. Her brain yanked her more awake to figure out what was going on. She picked the phone up off the floor, brought it up to her face, and flipped it open. It took her a moment to figure out what she was looking at and meanwhile the warbling kept warbling away on the floor like a chick that had fallen out of its nest.

Of course, she thought, wrong phone. She reached down again and silenced the other phone that was still on the floor. The Malone phone. She wasn't in Malone anymore. She closed her eyes and let out a long sigh. She didn't have to get up. She didn't have to get dressed and make the long walk through the cold and dark to

Flo's Diner. She could sleep in as long as she wanted in her warm, cozy, familiar bed in the old Victorian house in Westbury that surrounded her with familiar sounds and scents almost as if she were in the presence of a doting grandmother.

She pulled her hands back under the covers and slid her left hand down until it touched the dressing covering the puckered, scabby holes that had been made in her abdomen. Yeah, that really did happen, she thought. She didn't dream it.

Her other hand still held the first phone—the one she had taken with her when she left this house, this room, in the dark of a fall morning just before Thanksgiving. She clutched the phone to her chest like the electronic rosary it was, filled with prayers imploring her to: stay safe; contact us; have a happy Thanksgiving —Christmas—New Year; we love you; we miss you; please come home. The messages had poured into the phone the minute she had dug it out of her duffle and found the courage to turn it back on for the first time since she left. There were hundreds of texts and dozens of voicemails, bottled up for months, unheard and unread, futile anguished pleas from all the people who loved and cared for her more than she imagined or deserved.

She sighed again, this time letting the sigh relax her whole body all the way to her toes and fingertips. She felt lighter, as if she wasn't lying on the bed so much as hovering above it, released from the weight that had been pressing her down for so long—a weight she had grown so accustomed to, it was only its absence that made her realize just how oppressive it had been. Now it was gone. They were gone—really, truly gone. No more Babineau, no more Bronco, no more Purcell, no more running from her past, no more running away. Each one, a burden she no longer needed to carry. She was naked and unencumbered and just plain Blue DuBois. She was free to put that girl back together, piece by piece, reassembling her past, mending her present, and filling in the blank pages of her future, a future filled with friends, young and old, more than she ever imagined she could have or ever would have.

Was this what normal felt like?

HE HEARD the thumping just in time to open his eyes and see the shadow of a flying meerkat as it plunged toward his bed. He rolled in time to protect his most vulnerable spots just as his sister landed right on top of him.

"Wakeup Willy!"

"Ahhh! You animal!"

"Raaairr, raaaiirr, Hchchchch!" She pawed at him with her hands as he batted them away with his.

"Meerkats don't go 'raaaiirr'!"

"This one does! Raaaiirr!"

He rolled her over and flipped above her pinning her arms to the bed. "Gotcha!"

"Rraaaiir!" she raired as she struggled to get free. She kicked at him with her feet but he managed to pin those, too.

"Congratulations, annoying little sister, I'm awake now. And don't call me Willy," he said.

"Willy Willy Willy Willy Willy Willy Willy Willy, aaahhh!" she squeaked as he leaned down and blew farting noises on her belly, her arms still pinned to the bed.

"Stop stop stop!" she cried, laughing.

He stopped and flopped back on the bed, letting her go.

Rose stopped laughing, caught her breath, and said, "I can't wait to see Blue at breakfast, is she really okay?"

Will turned sideways and propped his head up with his hand and elbow. "Yeah, she's really okay. I mean she's going to be okay— she still has a long time to go before she's fully healed. Remember my shoulder?"

"You think she'll have a scar?"

"Oh most definitely, maybe even more gnarly than mine."

"Willy," she said, suddenly thoughtful, "how many kids like me have brothers that have been shot? And how many have friends that have been shot?"

Will shook his head slowly. "Not many. Trust me, this is not normal."

"Is it because we're not 'normal'?" She put the last word in air quotes.

He shrugged and then said, "We're normal. The rest of the world is crazy."

Rose looked even more thoughtful and said, "Will anything ever be normal again?"

He leaned over her and held her eyes with his. "*Yes, absolutely! Don't you worry, little meerkat. The wild tempest has passed, and we are going to have clear skies for a long time before the next storms are visited upon us.*"

They kept their eyes together for a long moment. "*You're so weird,*" she replied at last, smiling. He could sense her relaxing and knew that she believed him. He believed him, too.

It was a sunny, blue-sky morning and they only needed light jackets for the walk from their house to the O'Day's, but their words were still coming out in foggy puffs.

"Why is it only you and me invited over to breakfast? Why not Mom and Dad, too?" asked Rose as they stepped up onto the porch of the O'Day's house.

"Doctor's orders. Keep the visitors down to one or two at a time." He reached up and knocked on the front door. "And remember, she is still real tender around her middle, so don't . . ."

"Rosie!" Blue had opened the front door before Will could finish.

Rose squealed and jumped through the door into Blue's arms, stopping just short of tackling her.

"Rosie!" said Will, sharply.

"It's okay," said Blue looking over Rosie's shoulder. She closed her eyes and squeezed Rosie tightly to her, whispering, "I missed you so much!"

"I missed you more," said Rosie.

They stood hugging in the doorway for a long enough time that Will suspected something more than just a welcome was going on inside Blue. Her eyes were closed, so he couldn't really read her that way, but then he became sure as he watched tears from each eye crawl slowly down her cheeks.

Blue and Rose finally released each other, and Blue stepped back to let them in.

"Sorry," Blue said, wiping her cheeks, "it just felt extra good to hug you, and I owe you a lot of hugs." She turned to look at Will, smiling awkwardly.

"Hey."

"Hey."

He lifted his arms tentatively, not sure of the proper way to hug a girl that was recovering from a gunshot wound to the gut, but she stepped over and wrapped her arms around him, leaning her head on his shoulder. He pressed his cheek to her forehead and smelled her hair. It still smelled like Blue.

"Hey, you okay?" he whispered.

She whispered back, "Yeah, I'm okay."

And for the very first time, Will was convinced that she really was.

33

CATCHING UP

A week later
Friday, March 30

"So, amazingly, you didn't miss much at school."

Will and Blue sat cross-legged on the floor of his bedroom, each with a pile of schoolwork in front of them. "I mean with the holidays and the closure and all the assemblies for school safety training and drills, we probably didn't have more than a month's worth of assignments."

It had been a week since he and Rosie had breakfast with the O'Day's; a breakfast that resonated in his mind as the closest thing to a perfect get-together as he could remember. No one could wipe the smiles off their faces and the image of it in his mind was that of a joyful Norman Rockwell painting. They left when it looked like Blue started nodding off and Ma Beth hustled her upstairs for a nap. Blue claimed it was being denied coffee and Ma Beth claimed that it was her body demanding some healing time.

In the week since, Will, along with everyone except Blue, had to return to Westbury reality which meant a return to a normal school

week with the added privilege of being in mandatory detention for
an additional hour after school: the bureaucratic penalty for their
skipping school to rescue Blue.

Blue, meanwhile, had spent the days home alone with Ma Beth
hovering over her like an anxious hen. But her evenings were spent
catching up with Wu and Sam and Nate with occasional visits from
Anna and Jack (because they were now officially referred to as a
couple: "Anna-and-Jack") and, of course, Will and Rose, and a
couple of times all of them at once, at least until Ma Beth came in
and clucked them home. But today, Friday, Ma Beth had allowed
Blue to walk down the block to Will's house for the evening. It was
the first time he'd been alone with her since she was in the
hospital.

Blue rummaged through the papers in front of her. "Yeah, it
doesn't look too bad," she said. "Baxter is letting me off with just
some reading and a 1500 word essay on anything I want. I pretty
much kept up with Algebra on my own in Malone. Miss Kendrick
just asked me to do a couple of open-book tests and get them in
when I could." She looked at Will. "I'M NOT LOOKING FORWARD TO
SEEING HER. I KIND OF SCREWED HER OVER."

"WHAT DO YOU MEAN?"

"I DON'T THINK I HAD THE CHANCE TO TELL YOU BEFORE I LEFT.
THAT DAY . . ." she looked away for a moment before turning back,
". . . I'VE BEEN DOING A LOT OF THINKING ABOUT THAT DAY. I'VE GOT A
LOT OF GUILT ABOUT IT. YOU SEE, AS SOON AS WE HEARD SHOTS FROM THE
CAFETERIA, EVERYONE STARTED RUNNING AWAY EXCEPT ME. I STARTED
RUNNING TOWARD IT, TOWARD YOU. IT WAS MISS KENDRICK THAT
COLLARED ME AND DRAGGED ME INTO HER CLASSROOM AND BARRICADED
IT. AND THEN, EVEN THOUGH SHE TOLD ME NOT TO, I JUMPED OUT OF
THE WINDOW."

"AND THAT'S WHEN THAT PICTURE WAS TAKEN," voxed Will

"AND HOW MANY THINGS WOULD BE DIFFERENT IF IT HADN'T? AND
WHAT IF I HAD MADE IT TO THE CAFETERIA? WHAT WOULD HAVE
HAPPENED THEN?"

"As my mom says, be careful with 'what-ifs'. You can kill your-self with what-ifs."

"Easy to say," she replied.

And not so easy to avoid, he thought, but he didn't say anything. He'd already killed himself with his own what-ifs. He looked down at his hands and another hand came and joined them. He looked back up at Blue.

"Hey, I'm sorry," she voxed. She knew what he'd been through. He knew what she'd been through. They knew it to a depth that their friends couldn't. That was the curse of vox and yet, that was the blessing of vox, too. She put her hand up and pressed it into his chest where his scars were. It felt as warm as the affection that was radiating from her eyes.

"Um, I can't help it. I still feel guilty about this."

"I think you've been more than punished." He put his hand on her stomach where her wound was. She pushed his hand away.

"Sorry!" he said

"It's okay. Wait."

She pulled her shirt up and pulled her waistband down. She was no longer wearing a dressing so he could now clearly see the three scars—one from the bullet and two more for the laparoscopic surgery. She took his hand and placed it over the scars. Her skin felt soft and warm. He looked in her eyes and then it was just like the time she fell on top of him last fall. He could feel his body through her. He could feel his touch on her skin. He gasped as a hot wave started at the top of his head and draped down over him like a warm shower and suddenly his lips were on hers, and his arms were wrapped around her, and hers around him, and she wrapped her legs around him and pulled herself against him. Their eyes locked on each other exchanging a sensation that was impossible to describe. It was the same ecstasy from their encounter last fall that he had feared would never happen again, but here it was.

And like last fall, this encounter was interrupted far too soon, only this time it was a squeak and nervous giggle from Will's bedroom doorway that ended it. Both his and Blue's eyes were diverted to the doorway by the sound, and the spell was broken, the two of them jolted back from nirvana to reality and a red-faced ten-year-old who was in her own ecstasy of scandalous discovery. Rose was giggling so convulsively she could barely get out the message she was sent to deliver, which was, "Mom says . . . <giggle giggle gasp> Mom says . . . <giggle giggle giggle>"

"Spit it out, Rosie! What is it!" Will was seized with a confusing mix of exasperation and amusement with his sister.

She finally blurted out, "Dinner's ready!" and she ran laughing hysterically down the hall.

As she took the final bite of Mrs. Woods' amazing lasagna, Blue closed her eyes to concentrate on the flavor as well as give her eyes a moment of relief. Between the lively dinner conversation and the brief yet intensely sensual snogging session with Will, her eyes had started to ache. It was a small price to pay for what felt like the high point of her new life so far.

She thought about that. Her new life. It wasn't that anything was really that new or different, it was that she was experiencing everything the way she should have the first time around—free of the dark clouds that had hovered over her for so long. Everything was the same and yet fresh. All the people were their same interesting selves, but now rather than shying away from them, she embraced them. Even tonight, feeling self-conscious as she came from Will's bedroom to the dining room, afraid everyone could see the flush on her face or the throbbing of her lips, she knew that their rolling eyes and knowing smiles would all be from a place of love and acceptance. These were her people, after all, and maybe that was the most significant change for her: acceptance that her family was gone and that it was time to let them go and embrace others.

There was still one remaining shadow, however. Every time she glanced or smiled or talked or voxed with Rosie, a little twinge would pluck her heart. Her parents' deaths she could accept now, but she just couldn't shake the injustice of her sister losing her life so young. The twinges weren't enough to spoil the evening, unlike that dinner at the Woods last fall when they exploded into a full-blown meltdown, but she could tell they would always be there in the background for the rest of her life.

A nudge under the table from Will's knee caused her to open her eyes.

"*You okay?*" he asked. "*Getting tired?*"

"*I'm great. My eyes are just a little sore.*"

"Mine, too," he whispered, with an embarrassed grin. He handed her a plate that had been passed down from his dad, who was dishing out dessert.

"Chocolate mousse pie."

She glanced across the table at Rose and was not shocked but a little concerned at the look of apprehension that was on her face. Rose is anticipating another meltdown from me like what happened last fall, she thought to herself.

"*Don't worry, Rosie. I'm much better now.*"

She saw Rosie visibly relax and reply, "*I am sooo glad!*"

Rosie was sooo adorable, Blue thought.

Twinge.

Mrs. Woods smiled but said nothing even though she heard the whole exchange. Blue was certain Mrs. Woods was watching her for any warning signs. That kind of scrutiny used to make her angry but now, it was welcome comfort.

A buzzing caused Mrs. Woods to glance at her phone, and she apologized, "I'm sorry, I think I should get this." She stood up and stepped out of the dining room. While she was gone, the rest of them chatted and finished their amazing chocolate (I still can't believe it was made with tofu!) mousse pie and then together went about a ritual of meal cleanup that was so similar to the routine at the O'Days that Blue slipped in seamlessly to help. Mr. Woods washed while Rose rinsed and Blue dried and Will put away, placing Blue in between Rose and Will where she found that the urge to quell her heart twinges by hugging Rose was competing with the urge to drag Will back to his bedroom and shut the door. The close proximity and occasional body contact as they worked was not helping the situation.

She was so distracted by this that she didn't notice that even though they had finished the cleanup, Mrs. Woods had not reappeared and now Blue was at a point where she had to decide whether to appeal to Ma Beth to stay later than she had been instructed or to get her jacket and head home. It occurred to her that either way, Will would be walking her home, the two of them, in the dark . . .

Just as she had that thought, Mrs. Woods stepped into the kitchen where the rest of them were still gathered. Blue's attention was instantly drawn to Mrs. Woods' demeanor. She seemed flustered, which was remarkable as Blue had always known her as an exceedingly composed person.

"Um, I would like us all to come into the living room," said Mrs. Woods, hesitantly. "I have just had a very, um, interesting conversation with Detective James, and he had some very, um, important information."

The "ums" were what captivated every ounce of Blue's attention. She looked at Will and saw that he was just as captivated. Mrs. Woods led them into the living room where they all sat down. Blue sat between Will and Rose on the couch while Mr. and Mrs. Woods took the easy chairs opposite them. Mrs. Woods was looking down as if she didn't want them to see her face as she prepared for what she was going to say, but Blue could sense something very emotional coming from her even with her meager capability of *veraque*. Blue wasn't surprised to find her hand was reaching over to grab Will's, but she was a little surprised to feel Rosie's hand reach over to hers.

Mrs. Woods finally lifted her head and spoke directly to Blue.

"First of all, Detective James wanted me to tell you that he would like to return your rocket box tomorrow and that the information they have gotten from it has been invaluable."

"Invaluable?" asked Blue.

"Yes, he didn't give me details but said that instead of trying to do that over the phone, he would love to brief everyone in person when he comes up tomorrow. I've already checked with Ma Beth and Pa Bill and they said that would be fine, if it's okay with you."

The apprehension that had been building was eased a little bit with this news. Blue had been anxious to get the rocket box back and hadn't expected it so soon.

"Yeah, absolutely."

"Okay, great. I will let him know. Now there was, um . . ."

There was the "um" again. It started a little flutter in Blue's stomach, a flutter that had been absent for a long time and she was suddenly hyper-alert.

". . . a very exciting and positive discovery that he made . . ."

The flutter was morphing, and it was morphing into something uncontrollable, like a panic attack, but it was a panic from the fear that she wasn't going to be able to contain the frantic joy that was welling up . . .

". . . about one of your family . . ."

"Heather's alive!" she screamed. And then her eyes rolled back, and everything went black.

"OH MY GOD!" Anna gasped. "She actually passed out? What did you do?"

It was Saturday morning and Anna and Jack were with Will in his bedroom. It had been a chaotic twelve hours since the shocking news was delivered.

"Well, I was so surprised I didn't notice her passing out until she was keeling over and I barely kept her from rolling onto the floor. And then my mom . . . I've never seen her so totally freaked out. She was actually swearing at herself for having let Blue get such shocking news before she was fully healed from her gunshot wound. I was the one that wound up having to calm my mom down. Blue came to almost right away and was really fine. She wanted to get up and jump up and down, she was so excited, but my mom was holding her down, convinced that Blue would pass out again."

"My dad called the O'Days and every single one of them came over. And then it was a hug-and-tear-fest. Blue went from person to person hugging and crying. It was almost as if she would fall over if she wasn't hugging someone."

Will noticed Anna tearing up herself. "Omigod, I can't wait to see her!"

"Mom wants us to hold off a bit. It's kind of chaotic over there. Apparently Heather and her parents only learned all this yesterday, too."

"It's so weird to say 'and her parents.' Her sister is adopted?" asked Anna, wiping her eyes.

"Yeah, five years now."

"Wow. Did they send a recent picture of her?"

"Yeah, but beware: she has some pretty bad scarring from her burns." He pulled out his phone and brought the picture up.

"She looks so much like Blue!" said Anna. "And the scars . . . they really aren't terrible at all. And she looks so happy!"

The scars weren't terrible but they were there. And Anna was right, She did have Blue's nose and chin, and, of course, eyes. She looked like a younger, more impish version of Blue.

"Is Heather a . . . vox?" This came from Jack, who had been so quiet, Will almost forgot he was there. Will wasn't sure about having him part of their group now. He and Jack still had never broached the subject of his role the night of the kidnapping. It was an elephant in the room, and they both seemed content to just let it sit there for the moment. The surprising thing was that Anna and Jack had become a couple. "There's a lot more to Jack than you know," she had said more than once. Will had to concede that Jack had exhibited some uncanny instincts and been an incredible help both at the school shooting and at the Stanton homestead shootout.

"I think she's a vox," said Will. "At least her eyes look like vox eyes from the picture. It's hard to be sure, though, just from a picture."

Jack sat thoughtfully for a moment. "If she is, would her adoptive family even know? Or could they be vox, too?"

God, Will hadn't thought of that. What were the chances? "I don't think that's likely. There aren't many of us left."

"But you didn't know about Blue until she came to Westbury, and you didn't know about the woman Blue met in Malone."

Will suddenly felt uncomfortable and turned his 'how-much-did-you-tell-him' look on Anna. She gave him an apologetic look back.

"I'M SO SORRY! JACK IS REALLY REALLY SMART AND HE IS REALLY INTER-ESTED IN VOX."

That didn't comfort him that much. All his protective instincts were coming alive. Their carefully guarded secret was starting to seem not so carefully guarded anymore. And now there were more of his kind to consider and protect: Heather and Stella. He was starting to understand the wisdom of his parents keeping the secret close. Jack's knowledge felt like an invasion of privacy.

He turned his concerned look on Jack. He tried to read any *chiss* from him, but he was silent. Had Anna already given him some instruction on how to control it?

"Hey, Will, I'm sorry. I didn't mean to pry," said Jack.

A sudden wave of discomfort and unease enveloped Will.

"Look, Jack, I don't think you could possibly understand how important it is to keep this secret. The whole reason I nearly died and Blue ran away and nearly died *twice* is because the wrong people found out about us!"

"Will, I'm so sorry . . ." said Anna.

"What do you know about my family?" asked Jack.

"What?" This question from Jack caught him totally off balance.

"Did you know that my father was an alcoholic and beat my mother regularly? Did you know he beat me for getting home too late, not taking the trash out, for dressing wrong, for not picking up my room, for getting high, any reason at all. Did you know he couldn't keep a job and we were so broke I turned to selling dope just to keep the lights on? Did you know that he is in jail because he beat me so badly I wound up in the hospital? That was the night you got shot. Yeah, I was in the hospital the same time you and Blue were."

Will was so stunned his ears were ringing. Even Anna was shocked and staring open-mouthed at Jack.

"I didn't think so. I just wanted to let you know that yeah, I do have a clue on how to keep a family secret. And I promise that your secret is absolutely safe with me."

Jack stood up and said, "I should go now. It wouldn't be right for me to go with you guys to see Blue but tell her I'm really happy for her. And Will, I hope we can talk more sometime."

Will and Anna sat in silence after Jack left. Will felt as if his whole world was shifting, again. New characters, new insights on old characters, villainous characters vanquished, surprising relationships.

"I guess I see what you mean," said Will. "There is more to Jack than I thought."

"I know. In a lot of ways, he's like Blue. I think that's why he wants to help her."

"Yeah, I can see that now. But please, can you not tell him any more about vox just yet?"

"Of course! I promise. From now on I'll tell him he'll have to ask you."

Just then both their phones buzzed. It was a text from Blue.

Blue: I'm going to meet Heather tomorrow!

"Wow. Just wow," said Anna as she typed.

Anna: 🤍🤍🤍🤍🤍🤍🤍 We're coming over!

Will thought for a moment before replying:

Will: 🤍

34

REUNION

T he four of them walked the short walk to the O'Days: Will,
Rose, Anna, and Will's dad. His mom was already at the
O'Days coordinating with Heather's family for what Will could
only imagine was going to be an epic reunion on Sunday.

"DAD, HOW MANY MORE OF US DO YOU THINK THERE ARE? NOW WE
KNOW ABOUT STELLA IN MALONE AND HEATHER IN BOSTON. IS ANYONE
KEEPING TRACK? DO WE EVEN KNOW IF HEATHER'S ADOPTIVE PARENTS ARE
VOX?"

His dad hemmed and hawed and then said, "WELL, A WHILE AGO,
YES, SOMEONE KEPT A SECRET REGISTRY AND THERE WERE WAYS OF
CONTACTING OTHER VOX, BUT THAT WAS WAY BACK, THIRTY OR FORTY
YEARS AGO, AND FOR A WHOLE HOST OF REASONS THE REGISTRY WAS
DESTROYED. I HAVE SEEN BLIPS OF ATTEMPTS ON SOCIAL MEDIA TO PUT IT
TOGETHER AGAIN, BUT I THINK EVERYONE, INCLUDING ME, IS WARY OF
THESE ATTEMPTS BECAUSE THEY MIGHT BE PHISHING. THERE MIGHT BE
ANOTHER BABINEAU ON THE END OF ONE OF THOSE."

"ARE THERE NO COPIES OF THE REGISTRY FLOATING AROUND?"

"WELL PROBABLY, BUT WE CERTAINLY DO NOT HAVE ONE. THAT
DOESN'T MEAN SOME OF THE PEOPLE ON THE REGISTRY DIDN'T KEEP IN

TOUCH. I'M ACTUALLY ANXIOUS TO MEET STELLA AND SEE WHAT HER HISTORY IS AND WHAT CONNECTIONS MIGHT BE THERE. I'M AFRAID YOUR GRANDPARENTS ON BOTH SIDES WERE WARY OF EXPOSURE AND RETREATED INTO ISOLATION AS MUCH AS POSSIBLE. I COULD NEVER PRY ANY CONNECTIONS OUT OF MY DAD OR MOM AND IT'S ONLY COMPLETE CHANCE THAT I MET YOUR MOTHER, JUST LIKE IT WAS COMPLETE CHANCE THAT BLUE AND HEATHER AND STELLA STUMBLED INTO OUR LIVES."

"Rosie, are those two voxing to each other?" Anna and Rose were walking side-by-side a couple of steps behind Will and his dad.

"Yeah, it's rude."

Will and his dad spun around and said "Sorry!" simultaneously.

"It's okay." Anna turned to Rose and said, "You and I can keep our own secrets, right, Rosie?"

Rose nodded and said, "Right!" and then she squealed and ran up the porch stairs to the front door of the O'Days where Blue was standing with her arms wide open. Anna wasn't far behind.

"I'm so glad you guys are here!" said Blue as she was enveloped by Anna and Rosie.

"Blue, I am so excited for you I feel like popping," said Anna. "Your sister looks so much like you!"

Blue looked over Anna's shoulder at Will, "YOU SHOWED THEM THE PICTURE?"

"YEAH, THEY LOVE HER. SCARS AND ALL."

"THANK GOD."

"Is that Detective James's car in the driveway?" he asked.

"Yeah," replied Blue. "He needs to interview me in private this morning and then he is going to tell us how he found Heather and what he's found with the investigation of Babineau. You're going to stick around, right?"

"If you want us to."

"Please! I am so fu ... effing ... nervous!" said Blue, glancing at Rosie.

"About what he is going to say?" asked Anna.

"Yeah, but mostly about meeting Heather." She looked at Rosie. "I want her to be as sweet as you but I'm afraid she'll be as neurotic as me."

"I hope she's just like you!" said Rosie.

"Have you heard anything from them at all?" Will asked.

"Your mom has talked to her parents and her therapist—yeah she has a therapist, too. Seems to run in the family. They're talking about a meeting tomorrow somewhere in New Hampshire about halfway to Boston."

"Hey, don't worry, she's going to be just as nervous and excited as you!" said Anna. "And no matter what, it's going to be amazing."

Blue gave Anna a squeeze. "Thanks, Anna. I hope so."

"Blue, Detective James wants to talk to you now." Ma Beth had come to the door and waved them all in.

"See you on the other side," said Blue, and she walked off with Ma Beth toward the family room.

Will saw his mom across the living room near the bay window. She looked flustered. *"HEY, MOM. EVERYTHING OKAY?"*

She waved him over. When he stepped up to her she surprised him with a very strong hug. She held him an extra-long time and he held her tightly back.

"You okay, Mom?" he whispered.

She released him and grabbed him by the shoulders. *"I HAVE TWO CHILDREN THAT ARE ALIVE AND HEALTHY AND ONE OF THEM HAS SCARED THE LIFE OUT OF ME THREE TIMES THIS YEAR. BLUE IS GOING TO GET BACK SOMEONE SHE WAS SURE WAS LOST AND THANKS TO YOU I KNOW EXACTLY WHAT SHE'S GOING THROUGH. SO YES, I AM OKAY. I THANK GOD YOU'RE ALIVE AND I THANK GOD ROSE IS ALIVE AND I THANK GOD FOR RETURNING HEATHER TO BLUE."*

He was used to his mom being very controlled in her expressions of emotion but the affection pouring out of her eyes now was beyond anything he had an explanation for. For the first time, he realized that she could be fragile.

"Now I need your help with something," said his Mom

"Yeah, anything, Mom."

"I need your input. Heather and her parents want to come up today."

"Today!?"

"Yes, today. They say Heather is never going to sleep until she meets Blue face-to-face. I really don't think Blue will either, but she still isn't fully well, no matter how good she looks or acts. You and Blue are really tuned in to each other. Do you think it would be better for her to meet Heather today or to wait until she is more recovered?"

A bit of pride in his mother's confidence was mixed with surprise at the question, but his reply was swift and certain. "Today, no question. I think she'll be a wreck until she sees her in person."

"Thank you! I agree." She gave him a quick peck on the forehead. "I think I need to bounce ideas off of you more often." She turned toward Pa Bill and said, "Bill, can I speak with you and Beth for a moment?" leaving Will standing there feeling a warm glow.

"Dude!"

Will turned to see Wu emerging from the dining room. "Dude!" said Will. "It looks like a party around here."

"I know. So much going on. It's been the wild west since we got the call last night. Detective James showed up early with Blue's rocket box and even Chief Hannah stopped by and congratulated Blue. You know . . ." Wu looked both ways and then back at Will, "I don't think she slept much last night. I'm worried she's not going to sleep tonight and she has to go to New Hampshire tomorrow."

"Well, no worries about that. Apparently Heather and her family are coming up here today instead."

"Today?"

"Yeah. I think it's a good thing. She'll get it all over with today:

meeting her sister, getting the lowdown on how they got separated, getting her rocket box back. I bet she'll sleep tonight."

"Wow, all that today. Maybe I'll sleep tonight, too." Wu looked sidelong at Will. "Are you becoming your mother? You're starting to sound like a psychiatrist."

Will replied by giving Wu a shove.

"MOM, I'm nervous. Maybe this wasn't such a good idea."

Hattie and her parents had just passed a green sign: "Welcome to Westbury, Home of Westbury College." The reality of what was about to happen, after biding its time with their casual light-hearted speculation during the hours-long drive up, punched her in the chest like a hard-kicked soccer ball, releasing a wave of anxiety that went right to her armpits.

Her mom turned around in the front seat and looked her in the eye. "I'm nervous, too, but excited. Don't worry. You'll be fine."

"But you're always telling me I don't think things through before I dive into them!"

Her mom smiled and said, "There wasn't any thinking involved because this dove into us. We didn't really have a choice."

"But we could've waited!" She knew when she said it what her mom would say. Waiting wouldn't have done any good. "I know, I know. We talked about this. I'm still nervous."

"Just be your normal, charming self, Hattie."

Hattie slumped back in her seat and pulled out her phone for the fiftieth time. The photo of the girl that was looking back at her from the screen had a smile like Mona Lisa—mysterious, like she was holding back a million secrets—and her hair was the coolest looking platinum bleach blonde with dark roots at the top. Her mother would never in a jillion years let her do her hair like that. She looked at the girl's nose and then touched her own nose. Her

mom had said, "She has your nose, and your eyes." It was that statement that had awoken something in her, like an arm that had fallen
asleep and was only just getting its feeling back. She had heard
those words so many times, only from other people talking about
their own blood relatives. She could never say those things about
herself. She didn't have her adoptive mom's straight nose or her
adoptive father's green eyes, because they weren't her natural
parents. Her natural parents and sister had been dead for a long
time, leaving her no one to compare herself to. Until now. Now one
of them had come back to life. A sister. A sister with her eyes and
her nose.

She picked up the picture that was lying on the seat next to her.
This picture had woken other memories, memories of her past that
had never had a key to unlock them. This was the key. A picture of
herself and her real family when she was six years old and called
Heather. Heather Stanton. It reminded her of the first time she was
called Hattie, in the hospital by the nurses. They had nicknamed
her that and it stuck. She'd been Hattie ever since. There wasn't
much else she remembered from the hospital other than she was
there for a long long time. Long enough for her favorite nurse to
fall in love with her and become her adoptive mother. And since
then she's been Hattie McReynolds.

From the picture, she could see that she had her real father's
hair, and her real mother's face. And her sister, Blue, had her mother's long, dark hair. It was decorated with bluebells. Not for the first
time, she pressed the picture against her chest and closed her eyes
feeling her heart pounding. She was anxious because even though
the picture was oh-so-familiar, her memories of that time were oh-
so-faint. What would Blue think of her if she couldn't recall things
from that time? Her life had restarted when she arrived at their
little house in Boston and it had been filled with five years of
memories that were vibrant and fresh. The memories from the time
of this picture were distant and dusty. She looked back at the

picture of Blue on her phone. Blue had been filled with five years of fresh memories, too, but hers had been very different.

"Mom, you said Blue has had lots of difficulties. What were they?"

"All I know is what Dr. Woods told me in her email this morning. She said that she's been moved around a lot in the foster system and she is recovering from an injury from two weeks ago and that we should be mindful of that, and everything else is best to hear in person. She assured us, however, that Blue is a remarkable girl and very hard not to like."

"And she said she's still a 'reader' like me?"

"Yes, she is a reader, but it is secret. I don't need to remind you to keep it that way. They keep it very tight and only a few people know about it, just like us."

"She had a different name for it, too, right?"

"Yes, apparently there is a scientific name for it. She called it 'vox oculis' which is Latin for 'voice of the eyes'."

Vox. She remembered that now. When she was little they had just called it vox without the 'oculis' part. A pang of guilt stabbed her for having forgotten that. Of course Blue was a reader. A vox. Their whole family had been. That's practically the only way they communicated when she was little. It had just been so long ago. She did remember that no one in the hospital could vox and no one could understand her, but she had been so out of it then that she just stopped trying and took up talking ever since. It wasn't until she was home convalescing from her burns that her mom realized that her adopted daughter could read her mind. Her mom quickly took it in stride, accepting Hattie's trait as if it had been nothing more than a run-of-the-mill personality quirk, but she had come up with a set of rules that she administered rigidly, rules that Heather followed dutifully . . . except when it was just too tempting not to.

"It looks like we're almost there. The house is on this street," said her dad. His words brought her brain back into focus on what was about to happen and she was seized by a spasm of anxiety. But the hunger to find out what it really meant to have a sister again, a real sister with her nose and her eyes, a sister that she could share her thoughts with, and who could hear them the way she did—that hunger pushed down the anxiety and replaced it with breathless anticipation.

"There it is," said her dad.

As her dad slowed down and brought the car to a stop, Hattie looked out her window and saw that they were in front of a beautiful old house with a white picket fence. She waited for her mom and dad to get out of the car and then she slipped out to join them on the sidewalk. She leaned against her mom wondering who should take the first step, but almost immediately the front door of the house opened and a figure stepped out onto the porch, a figure with the face and hair of the girl in the photos that she had been studying obsessively since yesterday. But there was an infinite difference between the photos and the girl standing on the porch. The girl on the porch was a flesh-and-blood human being, and she was real and alive and animated, and she was her sister. And as that realization was washing over her, she heard a voice, and it nearly took her breath away.

"*HEY THERE, HEATHER FEATHER. ARE YOU AS NERVOUS AND SCARED AS I AM?*"

That sweet voice—so clear and sonorous in her head, after years of hearing nothing but whispers of unfiltered garbage from the people around her—rang like a church bell. Heather Feather. Her mom and dad had called her that. Blue never did, she always called her "Heather" but mocked her with "Feather Brain."

She replied hesitantly, but was so out of practice she had no idea if Blue would hear. "*BLUE? BLUEBELL?*"

"*THAT'S MY NAME, FEATHER BRAIN. DON'T WEAR IT OUT.*"

And the next thing she knew, hands were helping her up off the ground as her legs had collapsed underneath her, sinking her to her knees. And then she watched in a daze through a flood of tears as a blurry figure ran up and embraced her and whispered in her ear in a quivering voice, "I can't believe it's you, really you. I just can't believe it, I can't believe it." Hattie's arms felt strangely weak, but she wrapped them around her sister—her *sister!*—and as she did, they grew in strength and the two of them became so tightly wound it felt as if nothing could tear them apart.

35

ROCKET BOX

"You've got a glow about you."

Will had been sitting with Blue in her room for about an hour. She had invited him over after school to share with him some of her favorite items from the rocket box. The box itself was now a permanent fixture at the foot of her bed—a reservoir that Blue dipped into from time to time, retrieving another memento with its own story that she would share with him.

It had been five days since the reunion and every minute of those five days Blue had been hovering about five feet off the ground. She had also become an avid texter. In the time that he'd been there that afternoon, they had been interrupted at least half a dozen times by texts on her phone. She responded each time with a smile and a quick reply. He didn't ask, but she usually volunteered the content of the messages: "Heather says she's convinced her dad about getting her hair dyed, but not her mom yet. I said wait a day and let her dad convince her mom." "Heather said she's debating whether to change from Hattie to Heather with her friends. I told her I would call her whichever one she chooses." "Heather picked out a comforter for my bed. Here's a picture. I told her it was perfect." "Heather's mom framed the heather flower pressing we found in the rocket box. I think I should do that with my bluebell pressing."

Will usually just smiled and nodded appreciatively or gave encouraging answers like: "That's great!" or, "Really cool," etc., etc. What else could he say? Blue was in a bubble of happiness and contentment, a state he had never seen her in before. Who was he to pop that bubble? And he really meant it when he said, "You've got a glow about you."

She turned and smiled warmly at him which gave his heart a bit of a boost. It needed it badly. It had been in a funk ever since Heather and her parents had returned to Boston with a promise that she could come down and spend spring break with them—the implication being that it was a trial run. A trial run for adoption. For adoption into Hattie's family, not the O'Days. Hence, Hattie's fixing up a room for her. Hence, his heart funk.

He didn't know why it hadn't occurred to him before—that Blue might want to move in with her sister rather than stay in Westbury. He had taken it for granted that the adoption by the O'Days was a done deal but now that Blue had a living blood relative it was no longer a slam-dunk or even the preferred option.

He hid a sigh as he watched her browsing through the pictures that were part of the treasure trove from the rocket box. He was doing his best to bottle up his own bubble of angst so it wouldn't leak out and contaminate her glow. He did this by admonishing himself: he should be happy for her; he should be supportive of her being with her sister; he should feel guilty about his selfish desire to keep the first person he had ever felt such a strong bond with to himself; he should feel especially guilty about the waves of carnal desire that had been reanimated with Blue's return and then been frustrated by the sudden appearance of an emotional rival. It was disgusting that he should even consider Heather an emotional rival and it was this disgust with himself that steeled his determination to not spoil this for Blue. He was not going to be "that" guy. He was going to be the best friend ever.

He was suddenly aware that Blue was staring at him, smiling, but with slightly creased forehead.

"You're thoughtful. Are you okay?" she asked.

"Yeah, of course! I'm just still processing all this."

He looked away, afraid of what else she might read from his eyes but she reached out and turned his head back toward her. "*HEY. I'M REALLY GLAD YOU'RE HERE. IT REALLY HELPS HAVING SOMEONE TO SHARE THIS WITH.*" She pulled him toward her and kissed his lips gently, lingering there for a long delicious moment. He closed his eyes to pinch off any extra-sensory pleasure that he knew would stoke the contradictory fires that were burning inside him. As it was, the sensation of her lips and breath alone were enough to toss his feelings into chaos again.

She was making it damned hard for him to be just a friend.

———

BLUE PULLED AWAY from him enjoying the tingle on her lips in spite of being deprived the pleasure of his eyes. He was trying to keep something from her, she could tell, but that was okay. Things were different now. How could they not be? How often does someone witness an honest-to-god resurrection? How could your life not be altered by that? So yeah, she was sure it was as strange for him as it was for her.

It was a lot to take in, this utterly fundamental change in her life, and yet she was gobbling it up with the intensity of a starving cat. She turned back to the pictures and picked up one that had stood out from the rest. It was a picture of her father and Edward Winslow, Director of WITSEC. They were both smiling and standing next to each other in front of the sugarhouse. He had been the key to it all along. The full story had been revealed by Detective

James at the end of that day after she and Heather had finally managed to peel themselves apart and get acquainted more like teenage sisters would. As dusk came and dinnertime approached, the intense emotions had ebbed to a simmer and Detective James succeeded in corralling them all in the living room. And then he laid out the whole story, at least the sanitized version as far as he could understand it with his ignorance of vox oculis.

"So it was this guy, Edward, he was the key to the whole thing," said Will, pointing to the picture she was holding. "The reason you and Heather were separated."

"Yeah, and I should feel angry about it, but he was kind of a hero. He had to make some hard decisions. I was pretty out of control back then. Confused, scared, angry. And violent. For some reason I became obsessed with our real name, my real name: DuBois. It became my anchor, my focal point. I didn't want to hear Stanton or anything else. Only DuBois."

"It was probably the only thing you had left to cling to. You'd lost everything and everyone else," said Will.

"Yeah, and I thought I'd lost Heather. I guess I can't say whether knowing she was alive would have sent me off the edge back then or not—dealing with her for months in intensive care and multiple surgeries and skin grafts. God, I have a hard time thinking about it even now."

"And he wasn't planning on keeping you separated forever."

"No, and that's the hero part. He was a really compassionate guy. Stella speaks so sweetly about him. She said he was devastated when he heard about the fire. He worked hard to make sure Heather and I were safe and had new identities and he had to keep it all a secret. It must have been a terrible strain on him. It might have even been the reason he passed away so suddenly—from the stress. I feel so sad for her."

"It is sad. But on the other hand, Detective James said that Stella was ecstatic about discovering you and then again after he found Heather in Edward's private records."

"Yeah, I guess that's true." She paused, thoughtfully. "You know, we have to go visit sometime. You've got to meet her. Stella. Her and Blackbeard."

"Ravens. I'm still having a hard time believing I actually talked to a raven."

"Ardeth probably saved our lives, you know."

"He definitely saved *your* life. And found your rocket box."

It was you who saved my life, she thought, looking at him, but she kept that thought to herself. "Yeah, and the rocket box," she said.

"But still no sign of your raven here?"

She shook her head. She had been hopeful. She wanted to try and befriend the raven that had frequented the Smurf tree and squawked at her outside her window last fall. She felt she owed all ravens something. She'd like to befriend Ardeth again, but he was way off in the Adirondacks. She was going to go back and find him again someday, though. She owed him everything. He was as big a link to her past as anything—the messenger from her father that led her to all the memories spread out on her bed now.

Thinking of Ardeth, she turned and pulled over the big box that had come from Malone. Everyone from Jeremy's building had put something in it for her along with all her belongings from the apartment. She pulled out the book that Stella had sent along, *Mind of the Raven: Investigations and Adventures with Wolf-Birds.*

"Have you read any of it yet?" asked Will.

"I just started it," she replied. "It's pretty amazing how humans and ravens have evolved together. It makes me wonder how important they were to our kind since they have such an affinity for our eyes."

"My dad is pretty intrigued by that. He's not sure why ravens respond to vox because birds don't usually have vision in the infrared. He thinks they may have cone cells in their eyes like ours that decode vox."

"You mean they might hear us, like we do?"

Will shrugged. "Maybe. But he said it's not like nocte venatores, like Babineau, who could actually see vox but not hear it."

"Well, thank God for that. I'd hate to think that Ardeth or Blackbeard were in any way related to Babineau."

"No way. They are far more intelligent."

She smiled. "That's for sure. Maybe this book will tell me just how much more intelligent. Maybe I'll write my paper for Baxter on it." Ah yes, Baxter, she thought. She had to go back to reality next week. Her first week back in WWHS and she had no idea how it would go.

"It's going to be all right," said Will. She turned to look at him. "School, I mean. You're worried about it, aren't you?"

"You and your *veraque*," she said, "But yeah. A little. In a lot of ways it would be easier to make a fresh start somewhere else without all the baggage." Somewhere else. Like Boston maybe, she thought.

"You mean, move in with Heather."

Damn. She hadn't meant for that to come up right now. But there it was.

"Look, it's only an idea right now," she said. "Who knows how we are going to get along. And I might not even like Boston."

"Um, well, look . . . " started Will, staring at his hands, ". . . it's okay. I mean you should be with your sister. It wouldn't be fair not to. I've got Rosie and I couldn't imagine living apart from her."

God, Will, she thought. You and your mother with the 'ums.' Don't you know they're a dead giveaway? "Yeah, well, it's a lot different," she said. "You guys are six years apart and Heather and I are two. And thirteen-year-old girls? Unbearable sometimes. Just wait until Rosie's that age. You'll strangle her."

"You two are not going to have that problem. You didn't see what we saw when you two latched onto each other while we were watching from inside the house."

A warm glow swelled in her chest at the mention of it. No, she didn't see it, she just felt it. It was a feeling she'd never felt before. It wasn't a hug, it was something on an entirely higher level: an embrace where she and Heather held each other for the first time in forever. There was just no comparison to a hug and no word for it.

"It was magic," said Will. "That's exactly what it was. And everybody was bawling their eyes out."

"Yeah, well . . ."

"Except me, of course."

She gave Will a shove. He smiled but his usual playfulness wasn't there. It was a somber smile and it worried her.

Will reached down and picked up a picture from the pile on her bed. It was one of her and Heather. She was nine and Heather was seven. They were standing arm-in-arm in their apple orchard. Will held up his phone which was showing a photo almost identical to it only he had taken it at the reunion. It was her and Heather again, only now she was fifteen and Heather was thirteen. They were standing arm in arm just like in the older photo. In both pictures, Heather had the same impish grin and Blue had the same hesitant half-smile, the one Will always teased her about. There was much that was the same about them, and yet there was a five-year gap in their relationship. Would living together close that gap?

She turned to look at Will and now he couldn't hide that he was thinking the same thing. God she didn't want this to come down to a decision between a sister and a boy. Of course it was about more than just a sister. It was her history, her only living relative, her parents' legacy, everything. And yet it was also about more than just a boy. It was the O'Days, Dr. Woods, her friends, everything.

Ugh. She could feel the honeymoon period of her new life starting to lose its magic as hard decisions started to elbow their way in. She looked at Will and then leaned over and gave him a kiss. He returned it but only in an obligatory way. That was not good. Not good at all.

She scooted over to him and looked him in the eye. "*HEY. PLEASE DON'T GIVE UP ON ME. NO MATTER WHAT HAPPENS. PLEASE.*"

Will's shoulders slumped. "*IT WAS YOU WHO TOLD ME WHAT WOULD HAPPEN IF YOU MOVED AWAY. REMEMBER, THAT NIGHT BEFORE YOU RAN AWAY? YOU WERE WORRIED THE DFC WAS GOING TO TAKE YOU BACK TO BURLINGTON. YOU SAID WE'D DRIFT APART. YOU WERE READY TO GIVE UP ON ME THEN. WHAT MAKES THIS DIFFERENT?*"

Now it was her shoulders that slumped. He was right. But maybe she had been wrong. It didn't feel like drifting apart was inevitable now. She wasn't sure why she felt that way, and then it dawned on her. "*REMEMBER I SAID YOU WERE A GOOD ANCHOR FOR YOUR FRIENDS?*"

"*YEAH, WELL . . .*"

"*LOOK, I STARTED A JOURNAL WHILE I WAS AWAY. IT WAS THE ONLY THING THAT KEPT ME SANE. AND THE THING WAS, WHEN I WROTE, I WROTE TO YOU. YOU ARE EASY TO TALK TO. YOU ALWAYS LISTEN. DON'T YOU SEE? YOU ARE MY ANCHOR.*"

A look of surprise appeared on Will's face and when he replied it was not at all what she was expecting. "*YOU'RE FUCKING KIDDING ME!*"

She pushed away from him. "*JESUS, WILL! I JUST OPENED UP TO YOU AND YOU DON'T BELIEVE ME?*"

"*NO, NO, IT'S NOT THAT!*" His expression was one of astonishment and what he said next astonished her. "*BLUE, I KEPT A JOURNAL, TOO! I WROTE TO YOU!*"

They stared at each other open-mouthed for about three heart-beats and then found themselves wrapped in each other's arms.

"You kept me sane, too," he said softly. "I was in a total down spiral right after the shooting."

"God, what does this mean?" said Blue. She leaned back, looking him in the eye. "*I THOUGHT IT WAS INSANE TO WRITE TO YOU.*"

"*NO! NOT AT ALL. MOM SAID IT'S ACTUALLY GOOD THERAPY.*"

"*WHAT DID YOU WRITE?*"

He smiled and shook his head. "*I'll show you mine when you show me yours.*"

She snorted and then gave him a pinched smile, "*Yeah, right. Not in a million years, buddy.*" And then she leaned in and kissed him again. This time he kissed back, for real. Really real. God, she thought to herself, making this decision is going to really really suck.

36

SPRING BREAK. OR MAKE.

Two weeks later, April 14th

The ball arced through the air following a path that Will could tell was just a little off. Again. It hit just inside the rim but instead of bouncing off it rolled once, twice, three times around the hoop, each time coming very close to tipping off before deciding to take another spin and finally, rather than taking a fourth trip around the rim, it wobbled and fell outward into Wu's waiting hands.

"Now *that* is talent. Develop that shot and you can join the Globe Trotters." Wu snickered a little longer than necessary as he dribbled the ball back to the foul line where Will stood shaking his head.

"I give up. My head's just not in it today."

"Yeah, mine either, really," said Wu as he swished a shot from the foul line.

Will rolled his eyes. "Only Ben Wu can say his head isn't in it and still swish a shot from the foul line."

It had been a week since Blue had left for Boston to spend spring break with Heather and her family. Most of the week in

Westbury had been spent like this—trying to do normal spring break stuff but with a cloud of uncertainty and speculation hovering over it all. It didn't help that Blue's return from exile was only a few weeks old. To Will, it almost seemed as if she never returned.

Wu grabbed the rebound, dribbled the ball a couple of times, and then stuck the ball under his arm and walked over to the park bench and sat down. Will stuffed his hands in his sweatshirt pockets and stepped over to join him. It was too chilly, really, to be playing basketball in the park, but they had come anyway to distract themselves from the bombshell they'd gotten that morning: Heather's parents, the McReynolds, were checking into the possibility that Blue could finish out the school year down there, in Boston.

"What do you think?" asked Will.

"I don't know," said Wu. "I mean there's really no reason she has to finish the school year here. She's missed half of it anyway."

"Yeah, but the teachers know her here. She'd definitely graduate to sophomore here. What if they send her back a year in Boston?"

"Will, don't be stupid," said Wu. "She's smart enough to test out all the way to junior year if she wanted. Maybe even senior. In any school."

Will grabbed the ball from Wu and dribbled while still sitting down and then stopped. "What about you, are you okay with it?"

"Hell no! I want her here!" Wu snatched the ball back and threw it toward the basket. One bounce off the backboard and through the net.

"But we can't exactly tell her that," said Will.

"Why not? Everyone wants her to stay in Westbury," said Wu. "Shouldn't she know that before she makes her decision?"

Will picked up a pebble and threw it at the backboard. It hit with a clang. "She already knows we want her here. She already knows Rosie will freak out if she leaves. So why repeat what she already knows and make it harder for her? She wants to be with her sister. She should be with her sister."

Wu shook his head and looked at Will. "You are so full of shit. You want her back more than anyone else. You're just playing the stoic 'I can take it' hero garbage." He nudged Will. "Just tell her, for God's sake. She'll listen to you more than anyone else. Vox and voice and . . ." Wu made a kissy face.

Will punched Wu in the shoulder.

". . . Ow!"

"Sorry," said Will. "I'm just frustrated. You're right, I should write her."

"Well, do it soon," said Wu rubbing his shoulder. "Her bus back to Westbury leaves Boston this afternoon. She'll either be on it or she won't."

———

WILL SAT on his bed and scrolled through the texts from the past week looking for a clue as to what he should say to Blue. From what he could see it was just all light chit-chat about Heather's house, the suburb they were in, the visit to the Boston Science Museum ("Will, you and your dad would go bonkers here"), the day spent touring the historical parts of Boston, Heather's amusing teeny-bopper group of friends, etc., etc., etc. He did latch onto a couple of things: ". . . there are just too many people down here . . ." and ". . . the traffic is insane . . ." but not enough negative to offset the positive.

He dropped his phone on the bed next to his computer and sighed. Wu was right, this was his last opportunity to make his pitch, but what would it be? His phone and his computer stared at him from where they sat on the bedspread, silently nagging him to do something. He huffed at them and then grabbed his phone and typed out a text:

Will: Hey, just wanted to
double check what time
your bus would get here.

He stared at the screen waiting for a response from Blue. Five minutes. Ten minutes.

He typed again:

Will: You there?

Another ten minutes. He got off his bed and paced the room, running his fingers through his hair. He typed again:

Will: Hello?

An hour later he was flat on his back staring at the ceiling. This wasn't good. She would have replied by now. He'd texted Anna and Wu and they hadn't gotten any response either. Her bus had probably left by now and his thoughts were bouncing all over the place: Maybe she didn't want to reply because she had bad news. Maybe her battery is dead. Maybe she's at a movie. Maybe she just doesn't want to talk to him.

A buzzing put a stop to his crazy thought spiral, and he grabbed his phone, but it wasn't Blue. It was Wu.

"Hey," he said into the phone.

"*Hey. Blue's not coming today, maybe tomorrow.*"

"What!? Who told you this?"

"*Heather's parents called Ma Beth. They said that they were still talking about how it would all work and they needed more time.*"

Will's heart sank. This was not good news at all. "Why isn't Blue responding to texts?"

"*I don't know. Ma Beth didn't say.*"

"Shit."

"*I know.*"

"What are we supposed to do now?"

"*I guess all we can do is wait until she wants to talk to us.*"

"Just like before. Fuck."

After Wu hung up, Will flopped back on his bed and stared at the ceiling yet again and his thoughts started to go back into their crazy spiral. "Stop spinning," he told them. "Make us," they replied. "Okay, I will."

He reached over and grabbed his journal from his bedside table and turned it to a fresh page. He started by writing "Dear Blue," and then stopped. Why was he still writing to Blue in his journal? He closed his journal and reached for his laptop. He opened a new email, addressed it to Blue, and started writing . . .

Hey,

I'm writing like I did in my journal when you were gone, only this entry I'm sending to you. Mom said a journal is where you can store stuff that's on your mind so you can clear your head and let it rest for a while. I need to get this out of my head because it is driving me crazy keeping it inside and I need you to hear it. Here it is:

I will never give up on you. It doesn't matter where you are or who you're with, or what happens to you, I'm here. I don't know how or why I feel this way. Maybe it's because of what we've been through together, but I know right down to my toes that you and I have a bond that will last the rest of our lives. I don't know what that means exactly, only that you are a part of my life forever.

You have a sister that came back to life and you can't let that go, ever. I know how important family is. I've had one my entire life and I want you to have what I have as much as possible.

So what I'm trying to say is, no matter how much I want you to
come back to Westbury, I want more for you to be with your
family. And as for you and me, we can figure that out as we go
along.
Boston isn't that far away.
To be continued . . .

Love,
Will

He read it over. He read it over again. It said exactly what he
wanted to say. He hit 'send' and almost immediately a fatigue
washed over him. He let it close his eyes and push him down onto
his bed. He felt a little bit forlorn but a little bit relieved, too. He
had let go a little, but not completely. Just enough.

A familiar 'whump' made him open his eyes.

"HEY, LITTLE MEERKAT. YOU OKAY?"

She flopped down beside him. "NO! BLUE HASN'T WRITTEN BACK."

"I KNOW, ME EITHER. DON'T WORRY, SHE WILL. HER PHONE'S PROB-
ABLY DEAD."

"WILL, I JUST GOT HER BACK. SHE'S LIKE MY BIG SISTER."

"HEY, BIG SISTERS HAVE TO MOVE OUT SOMETIME, BUT THEY'RE STILL
BIG SISTERS FOREVER."

"BUT I WANT HER HERE."

"HER OTHER SISTER WANTS HER THERE."

"I KNOW, I KNOW. IT'S JUST . . ."

"YEAH, I GET IT. ME TOO."

HE WASN'T sure when he fell asleep but when his buzzing phone
woke him up he noticed it was 12:54 am. He looked at his phone to
see what had buzzed him awake and groaned. A text from an

unknown number. He started to delete it but stopped when he saw what it said:

Unknown: Hey

Will stared at it for a second, a little disoriented.

Will: Blue?

Unknown: Yeah, me

Will: WTF. I never heard from you.

Unknown: Yeah, sorry. I have a new phone

Will: What happened to your old phone?

Unknown: Long story

Will: So I guess that means you're still in Boston

Unknown: I'm in Limbo, actually

Will: ???

Unknown: It's a place you go when you are between two worlds. It's someplace but nowhere

Will: Oh I see.
You're dead then.
Not sure if you're
going to heaven
or hell?

Unknown: XD Oh I'm definitely
going to hell sometime. This is a
different limbo

Will: Ah! Between a
rock and a hard
place maybe?

Unknown: Not a bad metaphor

Unknown: . . .

Unknown: BTW, I got your email

Unknown: . . .

Unknown: Thanks. It
really means a lot to me

Unknown: . . .

Unknown:

Will waited a few more seconds but she seemed to be having trouble continuing. He didn't want her to stop.

Will: Tell me about
limbo

Unknown: . . .

Unknown: It's cold

                                           Will: Is there a
way out?

Unknown: I hope so,
but I'm waiting to see if it opens

                                           Will: A gate?

Unknown: Nope

                                           Will: A time portal?

Unknown: LOL, that
would be cool, but no.
One more guess

                                     Will: A swirling vortex?

Unknown: Of sorts

                                           Will: I give up

Unknown: It's a window

                                     Will: Ah, of course.
A window to what?

Unknown: Looks like a window
to a messy bedroom

Will: ????

Unknown: It's your window
dumbass XD

It took a moment for this to sink in and when it did, his heart nearly leapt out of his chest and he whipped his head around and there, behind his window hovered a ghostly smiling face lit by a phone from below and framed with luminous hair that started blue at the ends and then turned white in the middle and ended with a dark streak at the top of her head.

"ARE YOU GOING TO LET ME IN?" came a wry vox from the window. "OR ARE YOU JUST GOING TO SIT THERE WITH YOUR MOUTH OPEN?"

37

JOURNAL

April 20th
Dear Journal,

I think this is going to work out. When in my life have I ever been able to say that? I love my sister (my sister!) to bits and pieces and the week in Boston was amazing and yes I thought seriously about moving in with them but . . .

Heather has got her own life there and friends and parents and she's on a roll. I've got a life here and friends here and Ma Beth and Pa Bill are the best. And let's face it—I just don't like Boston. I mean it's great to visit, but there are Too! Many! People!

So I got to thinking about how fun it was when Heather and I texted every day after the reunion and I realized that's what would work. I actually think I can stay closer to her that way than I could being with her every day. I mean, staying in their house, I got the feeling that we would overdose on each other. I don't want that. And Mr. and Mrs. M were fantastic about it and Heather was on board, too. She's a smart girl and I think she sensed the same thing I did. And then, surprise! Mr. M bought me the latest smartphone so Heather and I can video chat anytime we want, and it is so much easier to type on the smartphone than that damn flip phone.

And guess what, there was a great sign that this was the right move—my raven came back! Yes! He (or she???) came back! I introduced him/her to Will and we gave him/her a name. André. Yeah, I know, my dad's name, Dr. Woods is going to have a field day with that one at our next therapy session.

Sooo . . . I'm supposed to be honest in my journal. What about Will? Yeah. What about Will? I hate to think that I came back because making out with him is, well, um, really really nice. Okay, it's, phenomenal, addictive, like the best chocolate you've ever had. God, did I even just say that? Yes, you did, you slut. Arrgghhh.

Okay I just re-read that. I'm not a slut. I'm normal. Yeah, making out with a vox is a big plus, but it's not the most important thing. What's most important is that I feel comfortable with Will and he has put up with me at my worst. I mean, what more can you ask for from a friend? A best friend?

But, you know, I think the biggest reason I came back was that it doesn't really matter where any of us live—Will and Rosie and Mr. and Mrs. Woods and Stella and Heather and I are all bonded beyond boundaries now. Wow, I just came up with that. That sounds very effing intellectual "bonded beyond boundaries." I should get an effing PhD for that.

The thing is, I am here, in my room, in Westbury, and I feel like

I'm back. Really back. It feels weird to say that. It's like the first time I've ever felt like I was away from someplace I really wanted to come back to. And now that I am here, it just feels right, like when you pick up a piece to a jigsaw puzzle and it's a weird shape and you know instantly where it goes and that it's going to fit. I guess that's what a home is, a place where a bunch of weird shaped pieces all fit together perfectly.

Yeah, that's it exactly. I finally fit somewhere.

I'm finally home.

EPILOGUE
AUGUST, 2031

"I've discussed the science of vox oculis and how this extra sense alters a vox's perception of reality. What I have not yet discussed is how vox are perceived in a social context, in particular how our unintentional biases apply to a vox. Most of our unintentional biases apply to visual differences: skin color, sexuality, dress, body decoration, etc. However, a vox looks like anyone else. It is not until they choose to demonstrate their ability that we can identify them as vox. Use of their ability is not threatening unless it is abused, but when that happens, the worst type of social bias is applied: relentless persecution. In other words, a witch hunt. We've made great progress in normalizing diversity in society— recognizing LGBTQ rights, women's rights, rights for people of color—yet people with vox oculis ability still feel fearful to emerge from the shadows. The big question for you, for society, is: Are we ready to accept them and bring them out of the shadows?"

— SOCIOLOGY PROFESSOR JACK MENHOFF,
PHD, FROM THE INTERNATIONAL SYMPOSIUM
ON GENETIC VARIANCE, CASTLETON
UNIVERSITY, AUGUST 14TH, 2031

ACKNOWLEDGMENTS

In writing *Forest*, the task of tying together all the plot twists and turns while weaving in the themes and character stories in a satisfying way was a challenge and would not have been possible without the support, encouragement, and feedback from family, colleagues, and readers. To those listed below and countless readers not listed, thank you for helping me tell the stories of Blue, Will, Bronco, and all the other fascinating characters that we picked up along the way:

Collin Parker
Esther Adele Martin
Elizabeth Cady Martin
Jessica Gang
Patty Brushett

POSTSCRIPT

Summer was checking herself in every reflection of every window she passed by. She was a bit stunned at what she saw and it helped distract her from the date anxiety that had plagued her all day. She had to beat her brain to remember the last time she had a date: twenty-seven months ago. And that wasn't much of a date. A first-last date. Not even a one-night stand, just a one-evening please-make-this-dinner-end-as-soon-as-possible date.

This date had much more promise. She paused for just a moment in front of the glass door of the restaurant and acknowledged what a miracle her friend April Woods had done on her face and hair. This wasn't Chief Hannah in the reflection, it was Summer Louise Hannah and she was a bit anxious to find out what that person was like.

Detective James had come to Westbury to take statements from the witnesses of the "Babineau Massacre," as they were referring to it off-the-record. In other words, he had spent the day interviewing Jack, Wu, Anna, Will, and Blue. He had said that since this was his final task on this case, as it was being transferred to the organized crime division of the NYPD, he felt, "Since there is no longer any potential for perceived inappropriate fraternization, I am free to follow-up on Mona's suggestion from November and treat you to dinner for your generosity to the homeless." As oblique a way of asking her out on a date as she could imagine, and whether he regarded it as a date or not, she was not going to waste an opportunity to put on something as different from a police uniform as possible and spruce herself up a little for a nice dinner out in public.

She took a last look at her reflection and then pulled the door open in a police-like fashion, taking a mental note to try and act more feminine. She strode through the doorway with a little more grace and spotted Rodney right away. As she approached the table he turned toward her and a look of recognition reached his face and then his features turned from those of recognition to those of astonishment. His gaze sent a tingling wave over her as it moved from head to toe and back. She had never in her life had that sensation and her cheeks had never felt so flush.

"I'm sorry," he said after a long awkward pause. "This table is reserved for myself and a very distinguished and stoic officer of the law. You must have the wrong table."

She hesitated for a moment, unsure of whether he was making fun of her or not, but that feeling was quickly dispelled when his mouth stretched into a big smile. He stepped over with arms outstretched and gave her a hug and she nearly melted when he said, "Goddamn you look amazing."

"You say that to all the female police chiefs in Vermont," she said blushing even more, thankful that he had stepped behind her to get her chair and couldn't see it.

"Every single one," he said as he sat himself down. "I'm not sure I can talk to you about police business tonight, it would seem wrong without having you in uniform."

"Please! Let's talk business. It's the only way I can make conversation these days. Anything else is way out of my depth." She grabbed her wine glass and took a big gulp.

"Well, maybe I can start with a segue question that isn't quite police business, but is."

Not a bad opener, she thought. "Okay, fire away."

"Okay, here it goes." The serious look on his face got her attention. "I've interviewed Will and Blue a couple of times and it blows me away what they've been through. I can't stop thinking about it and I'm afraid I got a little emotionally wrapped up. I really care about those kids. But there is also something really special about them. They seem to have this crazy perceptiveness, like nothing I've ever seen. Do you see that, too, or am I crazy?"

"Well," she said, "you're not crazy." She stopped and stared at her wine as she swirled it around in her glass wondering if she should tell him more. "And they are special . . ."

Rodney leaned forward slightly, his right eyebrow raised. "Aaand?"

He really was a damn good-looking guy, to go along with his damn good police work, she thought. Don't be a sucker, Summer.

"Aaaand, that's all you get."

The rest, she thought, all depends. It might be good to have an ally in the NYPD who knew about vox. She was going to have to know this guy way better, though, before she was comfortable going there. She smiled at him and looked into his rich dark eyes and realized that getting to know him better might not be such a bad idea.

GLOSSARY

chiss *noun* Thoughts that are expressed via infrared luminescence from vestigial tapetum clara.

nocte venatori *noun* Latin: "night hunter."

tapetum clara *noun* An active infrared luminescent lining behind the cornea.

vox *verb* Communicating using vox oculis ability.

vox *noun* A person who has vox oculis ability.

vox oculis *noun* The ability to communicate via specialized infrared sensitive receptor cones in the cornea, and tapetum clara, an active infrared luminescent lining behind the cornea.

ENDNOTES

1. Breakfast

1. **WITSEC** (Federal Witness Security program. Also known as WPP: Witness Protection Program): A witness protection program administered by the United States Department of Justice and operated by the United States Marshals Service.
2. **CODIS** (Combined DNA Index System): United States national DNA database created and maintained by the Federal Bureau of Investigation (FBI).
3. **NCIC** (National Crime Information Center): United States' central database for tracking crime-related information.
4. **NCMEC** (National Center for Missing and Exploited Children): A private, nonprofit organization established in 1984 by the United States Congress.

3. Will's Battle

1. **Veraque:** The ability of a person with vox oculis to sense emotions. This concept was introduced in book two: *The Innocence of Westbury.*

25. Reality Redux

1. **RPG:** Role Playing Game.
2. **MMO:** Massively Multiplayer Online game.

28. Raven Lady

1. **Blue Ridge, NY:** A fictional town located near the Blue Ridge Wilderness area in Adirondack Park, NY.
2. **Sugarhouse:** A large shed equipped for making maple syrup. Features such as a long, tall ridge vent, large adjacent firewood rack, and sap storage containers distinguish a sugarhouse from a general purpose shed.

29. Pieces Fall Into Place

1. CI: Confidential Informant.

ABOUT THE AUTHOR

Photo Credit: Dorothy Schnure

Frederic Martin lives and writes in and about Vermont. He was awarded the 2018 Vermont Writer's Prize for his short story *Maybe Lake Carmi*. His first novel, *Not Alone*, was published in February, 2020. *Not Alone* is the first book in the *Vox Oculis* YA science fiction thriller trilogy. *The Innocence of Westbury* is the second book, and *Forest* is the final book of the trilogy.